S0-BFC-006

Between the Empty *Other* Days . . .

Their picnic had been all right, Will thought, moving his hands up to Letty's outer thighs, but he knew it was not what Letty had envisioned. And as Letty lay there, she, too, was thinking about the lunch. Not one of my most successful endeavors, she thought ruefully, feeling Will's strong hands massaging her thighs, slowly, surely. Will I ever, ever cook a meal for this man, she mused? Will I ever, like every other woman in this world, who takes it for granted, just be there at six o'clock with the roast in the oven and the mousse in the frige. Sounds so simple, cooking for a man. What's the big deal? I will not think about it, she thought as he worked his hands up her back, kneading. I will be a member of the "Now" generation, the "me" generation, I will think of nothing but now.

Tuesdays
and Thursdays
Abby Mann

PUBLISHED BY POCKET BOOKS NEW YORK

Cover photo by Alex Gotfryd

POCKET BOOKS, a Simon & Schuster division of
GULF & WESTERN CORPORATION
1230 Avenue of the Americas, New York, N.Y. 10020

Copyright © 1978 by Abby Mann

Published by arrangement with Doubleday & Company, Inc.
Library of Congress Catalog Card Number: 76-2809

All rights reserved, including the right to reproduce
this book or portions thereof in any form whatsoever.
For information address Doubleday & Company, Inc.,
245 Park Avenue, New York, N.Y. 10017

ISBN: 0-671-82506-2

First Pocket Books printing June, 1979

10 9 8 7 6 5 4 3 2 1

Trademarks registered in the United States and other countries.

Printed in the U.S.A.

Tuesdays and Thursdays

Christmas was exactly three weeks away. Every year the streets of New York proclaimed the fact a little earlier. It used to be right after Thanksgiving that the helium-stuffed Santa bringing up the rear of the parade would prophesy the onslaught of decoration and display. Suddenly, New Yorkers would be bombarded by announcements of its arrival with chestnuts roasting by an open fire in the middle of FAO Schwartz's window, baubles and bulbs lighting their monochromatic way up and down Park Avenue as far as the eye could see. For the past few years, merchants exhibited their flashing lights and colored balls even before everyone sat down for stuffing and turkey and gave thanks. Christmas comes but once a year, but with longer notice each time.

It made everyone go double time. People walked faster, as rushing, a gross national product of the city normally, became accelerated; the step quickened, the breath shortened. People began a frantic race with time as the days before the big day became shorter and shorter. It punctuated the air, Christmas did, adding an excitement to a city already breathing with tension and stimuli. New York didn't have Christmas-card snow-covered cottages with chimney smoke and evergreens to remind itself what time of year it was; instead there was a raucous, raunchy beauty everywhere. Stores boasted their wares like sixteenth-century hawkers in a Breughel painting, and the utter crassness, the commercialism that burned within the heart of the city, was so blatant in its exhibitionism that it gave the streets a carnival air.

But no one was fooling anyone. The religious origins of the holiday were accommodated by organ and choir concerts here and there in churches and concert halls. But there was no question about it, the primary odor was one of money, its exchange, the avalanche of buying, the excuse to spend too much, to wrap, to trim, to tinselize. A paroxysm of buying and selling, aggravated by simulated or possibly bona fide good will infected the city.

It almost didn't matter whether the spirit was real. It was continuity that mattered. It meant that everyone had, after all, survived another year, hopefully intact.

Sighing, Letty Gold walked across the street, deciding she couldn't face the subway this morning, deciding to take a bus to work. Her image in the window at the pharmacy revealed a trim, very attractive woman, who, she thought ruefully, close up, was beginning to look a little worn. Hands deep in her pockets, she looked straight ahead, catching the eye of the men who passed. So many men. Their glances were fleeting. Why did it seem now, now that she was thirty-seven, why did it seem now that their glances never lighted, never stayed on her face.

It used to be, she mused, deciding to walk to the next bus stop, bearing the cold, bracing herself against the wind, it used to be that walking into a room at a party, a moment, that's all it would take, in a moment she would know who wanted to be with her, whom she had charmed, who wanted to see what was under her dress and what was inside her head.

It didn't work that way anymore. It was the up-turned breast and the clear eyes of the young girl that

2

men riveted, nailed their attention to, she thought, whether an idea clung to the waves of the brain or not. They looked, like the briskly tailored executive perusing her face at the moment, but they looked on, walked on by, as the song goes.

Letty was a tall girl with thick, black hair, and a generous body. Regardless of what she thought, she was still a beautiful woman, perhaps more beautiful than when she had been young, when there were hundreds of these Mediterranean types padding the streets of New York in their sandals and long, flowing hair, their smooth olive complexions bronzed by days at Riis Park or an occasional weekend at Fire Island, their bosoms full and high, bouncing unencumbered onto buses, into museums and zoos, restaurants and parks.

"Light changed, lady." A young man with just a jacket and scarf around his neck to protect him from the cold jostled her gently. She had been standing too long. In New York you had to move fast.

"Got a quarter?"

A distracted-looking woman with a felt hat and a feather pointing to a skyscraper jostled Letty. She was carrying a shopping bag in each hand and was wearing Murray space shoes out of which a bunion pushed on both feet.

"Yes. Yes, of course," Letty mumbled, unzipping the bag resting on her shoulder.

"Who the fuck do they think they are," the woman shouted as she picked up her shopping bags and wrapped them on her arms. "Cocksuckers. That's what they are. They wouldn't care if I froze in hell, that's what they wouldn't care."

3

2

There was a Friday sound in the office. Letty could always tell what day it was, Monday or Friday, with her eyes shut. Monday there was a passivity, a hush hovering; whereas Friday, voices were a few decibels higher, people talked faster. The tensions, the anticipation of the weekend, the relief that the week was over; all this Letty could sense in the voices.

Flo, the receptionist and switchboard operator, resplendent in a bright red turtleneck sweater that highlighted her coco-colored skin, smiled broadly at Letty as she got off the elevator. Flo always wore four rings on each finger, and Letty always wondered how she could push buttons and twirl numbers on phones with those encumbrances.

Letty looked out into the maze of offices that made up Robertson Stellar. The company, after a fifteen-year stint in one office, had moved to these more spacious and less expensive quarters on Broadway. The home office of the company was in Hartford, and, in order to compete with the mammoth Prudential and Metropolitan Life insurance companies, had reorganized and restructured itself seven years ago. Letty's floor included salesmen, agents, underwriters, associate and division managers, and the traditional office staff. The big brass remained uptown, and the bigger brass, of course, was housed in a copper-colored glass house

4

in downtown Hartford, where the windows had a bronzed tint and the floors were carpeted in a matching coffee shade.

Priscilla was in the middle of a snort when Letty walked into the ladies room. Some of the white grains fell to the floor after she jumped when the door opened abruptly.

"Caught in the act," she said with a big smile, and continued to finish the first cocaine of the morning. She walked toward a toilet and threw the packet into the bowl.

Priscilla Cochran's skin, at twenty-five, was translucent, unmarked, her eyes as clear as a Bahamian day. She wore very little make-up, knowing intuitively that the fresh glow to her skin, offsetting the perfect straightness of her nose, was enough. Under her very tight sweater her breasts were not overly large but were round and firm, the nipples always extended whether she wore a bra or not. There was one in every crowd, in every office, and Priscilla was it. The one girl every man would like to have, the girl whose overt sexuality was the secret envy of the women.

Wilma Scott came in. Wilma had worked at Robertson Stellar for ten years, ever since she was forty-one years old. She had started as a secretary and was now office manager. At fifty-one she was thirty pounds overweight with the plumped-out, unlined skin heavy people are blessed with.

As office manager, Wilma's duties ranged from making sure there were enough supplies in the supply closet to running cocktail parties when the bigwigs were in town. The latter involved, more often than not, calling local model agencies and hiring the most luscious and uninhibited girls she could find for the decorative and carnal pleasures of hungry and restless vice-presidents. She deplored the fact that this was expected of her but acknowledged that it had to do with being the most important woman on the floor.

After spraying Tabu on her blouse, Priscilla pulled a twenty out of her bag and handed it to Letty with a wink. "For Becky's wedding gift. Make up for some of the deadheads around here." With a blow of a kiss and a flounce of ass, Priscilla was gone.

"God, I can't stand her," said Wilma.

"Why?" asked Letty, amused.

"How can you ask that?" Wilma went over to the window and raised it to air out the perfume and coke.

"She's a little loud," said Letty, "but she's not offensive. Sometimes I think we'd all be better off if we didn't make such an effort to do and say the right thing all the time. And look at this," said Letty, holding up the twenty-dollar bill.

"Maybe I'm jealous. These girls are able to say anything they want to, screw anyone they want to, do anything they want to. Maybe I'm jealous that we weren't. Maybe I'm jealous that it's too late to do that now, and that everything we were brought up with was a lie. A goddamn lie."

Letty didn't like to think of Wilma envying the other girls. Wilma was Letty's defense against the future, the way she would like to be when she was fifty if she didn't marry. She felt Wilma could cope, was the best coper she knew, and she had just gotten a glimpse into something that frightened her, and she didn't want to hear anymore.

"I made a reservation at Armando's on Twentieth Street and ordered a bottle of domestic champagne to be brought as a surprise to the table."

"You're too much. Are you going to do the same for me when I get married?"

"I'll make a deal with you. I'll do it for you if you do it for me. How's that?"

"Who's kidding who? I'm not going to get married."

Wilma had ceased looking for a man. Finished, no more. To make that the concern, to make that the beginning and end of things was death, she had decided. Not in a world where there weren't enough men to go around, not in a world where there were no men her age, or older or younger, who were worth building her life around.

As they emerged from the ladies room, Agnes Friedman, lugging an enormous box, almost knocked them over.

"What on earth have you got there?" asked Wilma.

"Oh, just some stuff."

Agnes was one of the typists whom several salesmen shared. Agnes was in her middle thirties, Letty surmised. However, she gave the impression of being even more matronly, settled—or rather wanting to be settled—before her time.

Agnes lived for clothes. Letty knew the box was filled with newly acquired outfits scrimped and saved for, borrowed and begged for, for Agnes' upcoming week at the Lord Windsor. Agnes wanted so badly to get married, to have a man for herself.

Yet she never looked a man in the eye on the street. No matter what street. East Side, West Side, all around the town. She always walked close to the buildings, gravitating toward doormen, standing protectively in front of their territory. Once, when she was walking down a very good street, Eighty-third Street between Madison and Park, a man weaving in front of her wheeled around and demanded her money. For a split second, there was no one in sight. No one. It was one o'clock in the afternoon. Under his thin topcoat, she could see the man's fly was open, and his black penis stared out at her. She could barely move that time and had given him twelve dollars, which was all she had. His hands were shaking, and he obviously needed a fix very badly, and in a moment he and his bare penis and his threadbare coat and his red eyes were gone. As quickly as he had arrived. She hadn't gone to work for three days after that.

"What about chipping in for Becky's wedding present," Letty asked. "You haven't given me anything yet."

"Letty, I can't, I just can't give you anything for Becky's wedding present," Agnes said. "I must say it's something that indeed I don't think should be allowed in offices. Getting presents for people, I mean. I've never worked anywhere where it was allowed."

Agnes left quickly.

"I can't believe her."

"Did you know that Agnes walks to and from work every day to save carfare?"

"You're kidding."

"No," Letty continued. "She brings her lunch every day. Never goes out with the girls, never buys as much as a soda. And you know why?"

"Why?"

"Clothes. Walks about thirty blocks to and from, every day. On these dreary cold, biting days she saves every cent so that she can wear them for one week at some resort where she'll meet someone. Isn't that sad?"

Priscilla desk hopped, strutting along, wending her way to her own desk.

"How ya doin', Priscilla?" Fred Santini, Rookie of the Month last month, sidled up to her. "Did I ever tell you I can't concentrate on my work all day long with the hard on I get looking at you? When are you going to give me a little relief? I can assure it'll be a trip you won't soon forget."

"Fine, Fred," Priscilla said, taking him up on it. "It's a date. Will you reserve the room, or shall I? I think it's about time you and I stopped fooling around anyway, and you put your money where your mouth is, if you'll pardon the expression. What do you say we meet under the clock at the Biltmore at five? And listen, by the way, we can call your wife in the hospital from room 417 or whatever it is. Okay? When did you say she was coming home with the baby?"

"Cunt," Fred muttered under his breath as he walked by, smiling at the others who had been watching the interchange.

"Who does he think he's kidding?" Priscilla said to the women seated at the desks around her. "I always knew if I took him up on some of his dirty offers he'd start shaking. Isn't that just the pits, a man making a pass when his wife just had his baby? What a creep. I'd sure have to be horny as hell before I'd go off with a guy like that."

Janet Stevens nodded her head in agreement.

Janet was a small brunette who lived with her five-year-old son. By 9 o'clock she had already lived a full day. It was a hassle for her, dropping Terry off at kindergarten before work, leaving it to the sitter to pick him up, and then rushing home after work to relieve her. She had been living this way since Terry was two. It wasn't easy, and sometimes she thought the schedule would kill her, especially in winter when traveling could be dangerous and she worried about him so. Terry's father, Carl, had left her. She could get along without him or anybody, she thought. She made her own way. She and Terry would do fine.

For Janet, the tart reply was the way to ward off the blow, protect against the hurt. It was her way of acknowledging the simmering anger that lived under her skin. There was no trust in her. It had been burned out years ago by a mother who could not love her father. She had never seen them embrace, never seen them in an unrehearsed sweet moment together. Her father never made enough money, her mother

9

would say. He didn't get mad enough at the plumber, he had no balls. She would shout it about his not having any balls so loud that one Saturday night, one beautiful brisk fall night, John Henderson put his fingers around Janet's mother's neck. Janet heard the gurgling sound from the kitchen, and her brother had run in and pulled the old man off.

Her mother made her father move into the bedroom with her son and never spoke to him. Ever again. He didn't even have the balls to leave after that, Janet thought, feeling warm behind her neck and about her ears. He stayed there and took it until one day, selling lockets in his Bronx territory, he got trapped in a downpour, came home sneezing and wheezing, and caught pneumonia. He died months later. And he had never fought back, Janet remembered. Not once.

Somehow, without realizing it, Janet endowed every man she knew with her father's meekness and her mother's power over him. Yet, at the same time, she was determined, with all the strength she could muster, to make her son, Terry, a strong and decisive person. He brought tears to her eyes, her child did, and they would come, the tears, at the oddest moments, dropping onto a page she was correcting, smudging the signature of a letter she was placing in an envelope. There was no stopping them then, those salty reminders of her own vulnerability.

"Hi, Janet. I wanted to get to you before we all go off on Christmas vacation." Letty put a large envelope on Janet's desk. "I'm just finishing the final odds and ends on contributions to Becky's wedding present, and . . ."

"Letty, count me out," Janet said, sitting straight up in her chair. "Absolutely no sale. I think the whole thing is shit, if you ask me. I don't even know the girl, for God's sake, and Christ, every penny counts these

10

days. Anyway, I hear the guy she's marrying is loaded, so why does she need something gorgeous from us?"

"Janet, that's your privilege," Letty said. "There's no rule about this. You know that. I just thought it would be nice, since we all know her fairly well. Some of us, admittedly, are closer to her than others, but still after all, she's so young, and she's so excited, and we usually get something for most people who are celebrating something."

"I'm against it on principle, Letty. I can't. I've got to cut down somewhere, and this is one place. You forget, I have a kid to support. If I give to Becky, I'll have to end up giving to Herbie the mail boy, who I barely nod to in the morning. Sorry." Letty watched Janet's lips tighten over her teeth. Janet turned her back and put some paper into the typewriter.

"No problem, Janet," Letty said. "None at all."

This was not a job she enjoyed, Letty thought, this asking for money. What on earth is the matter with people, she thought, walking away after Priscilla signed the card with a flourish, drawing a picture of a sun with a smiling face under her name. All Janet had to do was give her fifty cents, a quarter even, for Christ's sake, just a thought, just a gesture. Why couldn't she see it that way? Why couldn't Janet just wish her well, give her a card, buy her a rose, throw her a kiss? Why couldn't people just care about each other, just one goddamn time?

3

"I'm telling you, Jack, come to Acapulco. How can you miss the sales meeting, for Christ's sake?"

Frank Fairchild was starting in on Jack Gaynor early. Frank was wearing a new mustache, a thick bushy black thing that, without realizing it, was designed to hide a moon sliver of an upper lip. Frank had started as an underwriter five years ago and within two years was earning triple the salary as a salesman.

"I don't think I'll go this year."

"Losing your nerve. Is that it?"

"Get the fuck off Jack's back," Will Robbins said curtly.

Will hadn't had his third cup of coffee yet and was still feeling residual irritability from this morning at breakfast.

In his early forties, Will Robbins was not a handsome man, and he gave the impression of being shorter than he actually was because he was so sturdily built. He had unruly brown hair, small eyes hidden under heavy lids, and a thick, sensual mouth. He had been an underwriter twenty years, and it was a tedious, exacting role he played; doing the same thing every day, examining policies, looking for loopholes, passing on potential clients, making medical reports.

Will liked Jack, who at thirty-five was beginning to

get a paunch and tried to cover the bald spots on his head by combing the hair forward.

"I'm telling you as a friend. His sales are down," Frank said.

"What the hell business is it of yours?"

"Listen, Robbins, Jack's a friend of mine. We came to the agency the same year. I'm doing just fine. I want the same for him."

"Crap."

"Look, Will, I'll come back later. I see you're busy." Bob McKern, a soft-spoken man whose hands shook when he lifted his cup of coffee to his lips, approached the desk as though he were going to say something and then stopped. Bob was Will's oldest friend in the office.

"Is Eleanor all right?" Will asked, looking at Bob with concern.

"I'll come back later; maybe we can have a bite at lunch. You look pretty occupied here."

"Okay, Bob. Pick me up about 12:15. We'll go to the deli. I'll treat you to a beer."

Not looking, Bob bumped into the corner of the door as he backed out.

"What's the matter?" Jack asked Will.

"His wife had heart surgery and may have to go again. They're close. Goddamn close. Anyway, Frank, why don't you just go on back to work. I've got a job to do and so does Jack."

Frank continued relentlessly. "He's got to get his ass out there. Listen, did I tell you Forsythe and French was courting me? Jack, the guy took me to dinner downtown yesterday. You should see the executive suite where we had drinks. They took me to this place, and I'm telling you, you should have seen the way those dudes were dressed. Five-hundred-dollar suits. Unlimited expense account. Just for starters."

"What they don't tell you, sonny," Will said, turning to face Frank, "is that you would be on call for twenty-four hours, you would have no personal life, you'd be in their pocket, even more than you fucking well are now." A vein was pulsing in his right temple.

Will's earliest dream ever since he could remember was to have a place of his own, a place of his own making. His father had died when he was four, and his mother, making no effort to keep him, farmed him out with relatives. When he was seventeen, he took off.

He had his own place, perhaps too early for a man so unseasoned by life, a man so unformed. He married at nineteen, before having seen the world, before having known women, before finding out who he was.

He had been going to law school at night for the ten years he had been at the agency. Slowly, painstakingly, he took courses, one each semester. It was grueling, finishing work, then traveling uptown to Fordham, keeping up with his studies, and trying to spend time with his three sons. It was one of the reasons he resisted his superior's and his wife's urging that he become a salesman, but he felt he couldn't take a chance on a commission job; the seventeen-five he was making at least was steady and secure. He had convinced himself that since he had gotten his Bachelor's degree at night, in only three years he could do his thing.

But he was in his early forties now, and what used to be baby fat on his face was turning into jowls. And he tired more easily running the track in Central Park with his boys.

"You didn't go to the last seminar," said Frank, continuing.

Jack pointed his finger at Frank. "You sound like Elise. I swear you do. I think you and she go over it word for word every night."

"Look, Frank, fuck off. Get out of my office. I

14

didn't invite you in here to begin with, for Christ's sake." The vein was throbbing, bulging out of his forehead.

Will hadn't raised his voice, but Frank knew he meant business. He knew you could only go so far with Will. No further.

"I'll speak to you later," said Frank, as he turned to leave.

But Jack wasn't as sanguine as he tried to appear before Frank. "I really haven't been making my sales for the past few months. I don't know what happened. Last year I could take the rejection, you know, but it chips away at you."

"Take it easy, Jack. Slow down." Will looked with concern at Gaynor. The pallor was the usual Christmas yellow of New York, but he looked green; he had dark circles under his eyes, and he had gained weight in the last few months.

"I'm telling you, Jack, don't let him get you down."

"I know he's going to somehow get it to MacKail, the shape I'm in."

"So what? So fucking what? Listen, Jack, a guy like Frank will never be satisfied. He wants to gobble up the world. He'll never be satisfied. There will never be enough suits or enough pussy, ever. You're not like that, Jack. You aren't. Maybe this race isn't for you."

"Elise wants . . ."

"For Christ's sake, what does Elise want?" Will exploded.

"Will, you've got to help me. I've got a pension case. Two partners. Two business partners. It's a good case, the commission would be great. I don't think one of them is going to pass his physical. Will, is that going to screw up the whole deal? It will be coming across your desk soon. Will . . ."

"I'll help you. Right now go to the coffee machine then go smoke a cigarette in the lounge."

"You know what, Will, you know when it all started? Remember when I went to that sales meeting in Miami? Remember I came back and I stayed home a few days?"

"Sure, I remember, and when you finally came in, you were pissing green."

"It was the pig contest." Jack sat in the chair, looking at his hands. He picked at the colorless nailpolish Frank's manicurist had painted on his nails.

"Bad enough we had to play softball and compete against each other. I thought some of those guys were going for each other's blood, with the V.P.s sitting on the sidelines sipping their rum punches. Bad enough they gave away trophies like we were in high school and were competing for who jumped the goddamn highest or who gave the best speech."

"Jack, calm down."

Jack drove on. "Bad enough we had to sit at a banquet and listen to speeches that would make you vomit about bigger and better years. Bad enough you had to suck up to the bigwigs and be afraid they were going to get mad at you if you looked at them sideways, and then be afraid they weren't going to give you a good recommendation if by chance some day you wanted to assert yourself and go somewhere else. But the pig contest got to me."

"What was it?"

"They told us all to go downtown and go to some bar and pick up the ugliest girls we could find, and the guy who brought back the ugliest girl would win. I didn't do it. I went to bed and threw up."

"Don't let it get to you. Move on, man. You're young. Move on. Don't let them get to you, Jack."

Jack got up abruptly and shook Will's hand with a palm that was moist and loose. It was also as though he was now sorry he had unburdened himself to Will making himself vulnerable.

16

"I'll be all right. Just a little nervous about this pension business. I'll be fine. See you around."

In a moment he was gone.

Who the fuck was I talking to, Will thought. He doesn't know where he's going.

Will lived on the Upper West Side in one of those formerly exquisite brownstones whose elegant moldings and high ceilings were the major testimony to vestigial grace between Columbus and Amsterdam. Saturdays he took whatever son would accompany him, sometimes all of them, for a walk on Broadway. They would go to Zabar's and explore the salami and copper fairyland together. They would squeeze through the multitudes together, between the shelves upon shelves of culinary artifacts, the wooden spoons and copper pots, the myriads of chrome and silver designed to make the kitchen a well-stocked place. He loved to go with the boys, especially Sean, the youngest, who loved the bulges of cheese, the rounded and oblong hanging, the breads twisted and kneaded into exotic shapes.

But early in his marriage Will had found that other women's bodies were more satisfying than Kathy's since she had been dulled by the admonishing of the nuns, since they had convinced her that even to look at her own naked image in the glass was a sin. His touch never liberated her. It conjured scenes too fearful to explain. She loved him, but it wasn't enough.

Beginning to work, adjusting his glasses, Will sighed, wishing it were next week. Wishing for, dreaming about the sun, wishing at this moment that the heat of it was burning a hole in his back. The sun and the heat and getting away. God. He was counting the days.

17

4

"I don't know, I think I may have to put her in a home."

Wilma looked up from her martini.

"Those furrows are going to be permanent if you keep frowning like that, Letty," she said.

"Those little crow's feet do seem to be getting deeper, it seems to me," Letty said. "Wilma, you should see her, she's got a black eye that covers half her face. When I came home from work the other day, she was lying on the floor of the bathroom all crumpled up. I thought I was going to die. I was so upset. Wilma, I thought I would die. She had tripped getting out of the shower. She just couldn't make climbing over the tub, and, Wilma, she just crumpled into a heap on the tile. And she lay like that for three hours until I came home from work, can you imagine? The next day her eye was a hundred colors. And she was crying, Wilma. Whimpering like a baby. She was so scared. I felt so terrible, I didn't know what to do. And I felt so sorry for her. She's always been so wildly self-sufficient, but now she's weak, she just doesn't seem to have the strength she used to. I feel so sorry for her, but I'm not home all the time and I can't watch her all the time. She'll go for weeks and be fine, and then all of a sudden her age catches up with her. It just makes me so sad to see her fall apart like that.

All of a sudden. I don't know. Sometimes I think she'd be better in a place where she had constant supervision. I didn't tell her but I went and looked at some of those places on the West Side and just turned around and ran out. I couldn't stand it, Wilma, all those old sad eyes staring out in those linoleum lobbies. They just stare out, holding on canes, all hollow-eyed. Sitting there waiting for the next meal to be announced, waiting to die. That's Fran, Wilma, that's my mother. She's getting crotchety, and sometimes she repeats herself so much I could scream. And I feel hemmed in by her, positively claustrophobic. She surrounds the apartment lately. She's everywhere, her voice, her solitude, her whining . . ."

Tears came to Letty's eyes.

"I don't know. Lately I feel restless, itchy. Waiting for something. Waiting for something, Wilma, that I know isn't going to come unless I do something about it. Unless I make it happen. Do you know what I mean?" Letty twirled her ring around her finger nervously. In her mind's eye she saw Fran's face, the black eye covering most of it, the rainbows in her pores. She had been so afraid.

"I'm starving, talking about food. Becky's late and I shouldn't be having these crackers and this cheese. I wish you'd stop me, but I can't just sit here watching them staring me in the face."

Letty saw the slight figure of Becky Kraus coming toward them from the front of the restaurant. Becky brought out the protective in Letty. She weighed under ninety-five pounds and had a waiflike charm that was affecting. Becky's mother was obese, and Becky was obsessive about keeping her weight down. Watching her walk toward them, Letty thought that she was indeed the only person in that whole office who could look beautiful under those glaring Robertson Stellar

19

lights, guaranteed to highlight every wrinkle, every puff and pore.

Once Becky had slept at Letty's apartment, after a terrible row with her parents, and long after Fran had gone to sleep, the two had stayed up.

She had confided everything to Letty that night and it had created a bond between them. She confessed to being into heroin at thirteen, becoming a groupie, following rock stars around the city, boozing and brawling at fourteen in hotel rooms swelling with buckets of ice and gallons of liquor. There the thick odor of hashish filled the room, and frazzled-haired girls calling themselves friends boasted of casting their guitar-strumming lovers' penises in plaster of Paris.

Her parents had had her too late in life, too late to understand the fine line between discipline and love. But she was almost nineteen now, and had lived a lifetime. She was burned out, almost. But now, with Arnie Berkowitz, she thought perhaps she had a chance for some kind of normalcy. A marriage, a house, dogs, things that were rooted. Security. Becky longed for security.

She was wearing a long black shirt, black turtleneck, and black boots. It accentuated her thinness, her vulnerability. She looks like a young Italian widow, Letty thought, a war widow, exquisite in her dignity. But beyond the softness there was sex. Letty could see the shadows of sensuality in her face.

"Oh, Letty, Wilma, I'm so sorry I was late. I had to rush uptown to leave my name at Tiffany's and Steuben's. That's how it's done," she said, excitedly, "and then when all the wedding guests come in to get a present for Becky's wedding, it's all on file, what pattern goes with what tablecloth, or whatever. I'm sorry. I hope you ordered."

"We waited and I've had one martini too many, but

since you're now here, I guess I'll have another. Hi, hon," Wilma offered her cheek.

Becky's cheeks, usually sallow, were pink.

"I couldn't get a cab, the city is starting to go crazy early, so I ran about four blocks. I'll have . . . look, let's get a bottle of wine. My treat."

"You've got to be nuts," Letty said, "this is our treat, the equivalent of the stag dinner."

"Do they still have those things?" Becky said. "I haven't heard Arnie say anything about anybody giving him one. I'm going to have the quiche, it's fabulous here, what about you girls?"

"I started a new diet today, you know," Wilma wailed, "and I've broken it before the day is half over. Might as well go all out." She avoided Letty's eye. "I'll have the quiche, too."

"My hips have a whole new layer on them," Letty said, touching the swells below her waist. "Screw it, it's Becky's day. Quiche it will be." Letty ordered the quiche and the restaurant's famous salad. It was cozy and warm, and the soft hum of voices hovered over the pink lighting in the room.

"O.K. So tell us. How are the plans going?" Letty leaned forward.

"I'm frazzled, I've been so busy. My mother's been great, helping me do everything, but it's hard for her since she works every day. Christ, the wedding's only a few weeks away and there's still so much to do. I haven't even had a final fitting on the dress." Becky ran her fingers through her long dark hair and the five-carat diamond on her finger flashed in the light.

"That is what I call a rock," Wilma said, putting her full fingers into the glass, trying to retrieve the olive.

"Do you know that I just got it. Just now, and we've been engaged for months. Arnie's mother wouldn't part with it or something. Maybe she thought we wouldn't last, and we wouldn't make it to the altar and

21

that I'd abscond with the damn thing. It is gorgeous, isn't it? It's a little overwhelming, isn't it? Oh, Letty, I forgot to tell you, they said O.K."

"O.K. to what?"

"No Rabbi. My folks would have a fit if there was a religious service. I tried to explain that to Arnie, but there's something I don't know. He is really afraid of his father, I think, and he never got around to telling him. I just know my parents would die if there was a religious ceremony."

"Why?" Wilma was beginning to feel the grateful whir of the gin.

"They're atheists," Letty explained. "I met them once and they're charming, a bit outdated, is that fair to say? You'd admit that, wouldn't you, Becky? They're the kind of thirties' left-wingers my dad used to know. You don't see much of them anymore."

"Wait, here's the champagne," Wilma said as the waiter brought the chilled wine to the table. "Well, in for a penny, in for a pound, the office just isn't going to get much work out of me today. God, sometimes I think I'm running a regular whore house. About twenty of the bigwigs are coming in from Hartford and Chicago this weekend and they've rented a whole suite at the Waldorf. I've ordered everything. Taken care of everything except the girls. Sometimes I wonder if the model agency knows what it's getting into. Who am I kidding? Of course they do. They send over portfolios with these girls, and believe me it's the ones who are wearing the skimpiest bathing suits who seem to get the jobs as hostesses."

"What happens at those meetings?" Becky said. "I know that the Waldorf can turn into a swinging place in some of those suites. I've been there."

"God only knows. I'm only there at the beginning before they've had their tenth drink. The girls wear these clinging sexy gowns and smile these big smiles,

22

and sometimes they all just wander off into bedrooms. Usually, my job is done by then."

"You're becoming a procurer in your old age," Letty bit her lip the minute she said it as she saw the cloud in Wilma's eye.

"Anyway, Becky, what's happening this weekend?" Letty asked changing the subject.

"Tomorrow Arnie and I are going out to lunch at the Berkowitzes'. It's wild out there, just wild. I've never seen so much food in my whole life. They put a spread on the table like you've never seen. They even have watermelons in the winter, can you imagine? I mean they've got two refrigerators just for fruit. Just for fruit! There's a couple of maids. But you know, there's something about it that gives me a good feeling. Like silly things, like in Arnie's room there are college pennants on the walls, you know, and trophies on the shelves for tennis and squash. I can't explain it. It's like solid. It all looks so stable."

Wilma and Letty sat quietly and sipped their wine, watching Becky. Letty's own feeling about Arnie was that he was too much. Too much teeth, too much lip, too much eyebrow. A silly thing to hold against someone, but Letty intuitively mistrusted him. He reminded her of a Jewish Elvis Presley . . . he looked like Michaelangelo's "David." She never let on to Becky how she felt, and just secretly hoped for the best.

"It means a lot to me, it just does. I don't know, I was talking to my mother yesterday telling her about Selma. She was my best friend when I was thirteen. And her parents were alcoholic and she was an alcoholic. At thirteen I swear. And my mother knew. And she kept on being my best friend. They knew it, and sometimes at two in the morning we would walk down to the East Side and meet these crazy people. Once I remember this guy was on acid at a party, it was just at the beginning of acid, you know, and this guy threw

23

a knife at me, and I ran down the stairs and Selma broke her tooth, I remember. And I took her home to my house and cleaned her up and took her home, and my folks let me. I told my mother that the other day. She couldn't explain it. We had a long talk, Letty, you know, somehow we've always been close with it all. Are you close to your mother?"

"Oh, God, who knows, now the roles are all topsy-turvy. She's like my child, and I worry about her so."

"And me," Wilma said. "I'll tell you, Becky, I envy you, even what you had, even though they were too permissive and let you go too much. At least you had a mother. Mine died so early. I missed her."

"I love my mother," Becky said. "I understand her, but they did—they did let me go too soon." She blushed and put her hand over her eyes. "They let me quit school. Can you imagine, did I ever tell you that, Lett? In ninth grade, they let me decide. They're hard to get mad at, you know, and I've called them on it since. But how can people let a kid . . . I was thirteen or fourteen or something . . . do that? Anyway," she said, taking a deep breath, "anyway, Arnie's family seems to like me. The house looks so strong, as though nothing could ever tear it down. I need that, I'm telling you."

Letty looked at Becky's slim fingers picking at the crust of her quiche. She remembered that night when she slept over when Becky told her, through her tears, that when she was fifteen, in a burst of self-preservation, she'd begged her parents—oblivious as they were on Christopher Street, permissive to a fault, Bohemian to a point of no return—she had begged them to send her to summer camp. The irony of it had floored Letty; this after having marked up her arms with needles, slept in East Village crash pads with hirsute drugged characters. She had wanted to go to summer camp, after a Mafioso lover sent his limou-

24

sine around to take her to Le Club for dinner. She had begged to go to summer camp with volleyball nets and the green team fighting the white team and swimming meets and learning how to tip a canoe.

"You know," Becky said, looking from one friend to the other. "The reason I want to get married is that I want to start a new life. I mean it. Listen, Arnie's father gets me very nervous sometimes. I know that it's all not perfect. I know that. But it's overwhelming. I want a solid place."

"But what about Arnold, Becky?" Wilma said, "how do you feel about him? Do you love him?"

"I think so. Look, he's really good looking, you know that, and he's really good to me. Really. He bought me twelve outfits in the last few months. He likes me to wear the same things he does. You know. He found this neat shop in the Village where he gets these twin outfits. One has a kind of twenties' hat that's adorable."

"But what is it about his father?" Wilma said, leaning over to take a piece of Becky's uneaten quiche.

"I don't know. He says *schwartze* all the time in front of the black chauffeur." Wilma looked at her blankly.

"*Schwartze,* it's Yiddish for black. Right in front of him. I think it's such an ugly thing to say. Sometimes I feel like calling him a kike. And, I don't know, he looks so elegant, but he's kind of coarse, you know. And Arnie never gets angry at him, he never stands up to him."

"Maybe he's being a dutiful son," Letty said, lamely.

"Arnie doesn't agree with him, I know it, but he never says a thing. You know. Like Mr. Berkowitz is only involved in the money interest. That's what interests him. It's a little weird."

"You know who was telling me in her begrudging

way this morning how much she wishes you well?"
Letty asked.

"No, who?"

"Priscilla."

"You're kidding. I don't believe it. She'd be the last person I'd think of who would wish a person getting married well."

"Why? Why do you say that?" Wilma asked.

"Because, I don't know, it's just that I get the feeling she's heading for a fall. I've been down, I know. I get the feeling she's heading in the wrong direction," Becky said.

"I can't stand her," Wilma said flatly.

"Oh, listen, I've known chicks like that." Becky sipped her wine.

"I think she's a nymphomaniac," Wilma said.

"Not at all. I think she's looking for something," Becky said. "And I also think she's going to get into a lot of trouble. She dresses like a whore and wants everybody to think she's one, the sexiest, most one-of-the-boys types there is, and yet to me that's not where she's at. There's something sad about her. Really sad."

"I agree," Letty said, motioning for the waiter. "I've always felt that way, that she's really good under all that. Really good. She has her own kind of integrity."

"She gives me a pain, and besides which she is absolutely awful to Agnes. Teases her mercilessly. And did you ever hear her and Janet go at each other? She is more foul-mouthed with Janet than anybody."

"Well, Christ," Becky said, "Janet asks for it. She is one pill. I think she's hard on Agnes and Janet because she's just tired of lies. It's as simple as that. I can understand that. Janet is so up-tight, so hung up, so defensive, so full of crap, and all Agnes cares about is how she looks. Priscilla cuts right through that."

"It's true, in a way, she has this strange vision, this

ability to cut through the garbage we all seem to put up with. Stuff we're supposed to forgive. But you know," Letty went on, flushed with a feeling of oneness with her friends, "there's something else, with Priscilla and me. And even you, Becky, if I'm being painfully excruciatingly honest about it. I'm afraid of her. Afraid of you. Afraid of your youth and your no bras and your options and your future. You know, you've got so much more time left. Sometimes I think that you are passing us by with your freedoms and your confidence."

"God, how the grass is always greener," Becky said.

"I think women in their forties and fifties have it easier," she said. "God. They at least live secure lives. They're secure."

"Not so. It may seem that way because the years have given us a certain ability to cope. But Christ, we wasted a lot of years. We only slept with men we loved, we were careful who we went out with, we had to scrounge for jobs and put up with a male supremacy, a male dominated . . . oh, God, I sound like *Ms.* magazine, and I barely read it anymore. But it's true, we were brought up with a certain standard that just doesn't fit anymore. It isn't appropriate, and still we have to go on. One man, one woman. There's only one man in the world we can be happy with, we are told. Bullshit. We all know that's not true. How come there's one out of every two people divorced, for God's sake. If that's true? They lied to us, our parents, our schools."

"I had something that suited me for a long time," Wilma said quietly. "A long, long time. Twelve years, to be exact. A man I loved, and couldn't have. Never could have had. But it was all right. That had nothing to do with society or what I was told. It had to do with that man, and him being what I wanted."

"So where is he now?" Becky said.

"Gone. No more. It doesn't exist anymore." Wilma

couldn't stop the rush of tears in her eyes. "I guess it doesn't much matter anymore."

Letty and Becky sat quietly as Wilma played with a matchbox.

"He was a Broadway producer. A great man at the time I knew him."

She looked away from them, seeing Julian Frank's face etched into the white coat on the back of a waiter hovering nearby.

"I worked for him. I went to every opening on Broadway. I arranged his lunches with the Lunts, organized parties for the Old Vic when they came to town. And I sent flowers to his wife."

Wilma brought her gaze back to her friends. "I never said anything before because there was no point. Maybe there's no point now. But he made me better than I was. I stretched and I learned. And I loved him. It's over and has been for years. But I'll never forget him. Never.

"So you see," she said, taking a deep breath, "I had it all. I'm spoiled for anybody. I had the best. How can anyone equal what I had? That's why it's so hard to make anyone mean anything. You know what I mean?"

"Well," Becky said, breaking the mood, "I wasted most of my life. Screwing around and drugs. I tried everything. I didn't get any answers. So what?"

"Yes, but you had more fun," Letty said wryly.

"Sure, for about two minutes," Becky said. "Look, let's change the subject. First, let's order dessert. And second, where have you all decided to go next week?"

"Big Sur," Wilma said, "I'm finally going to do it. I'm going to see the Seventh Wonder of the World."

"All by yourself?" Becky blurted it out.

"No other, just little old me and my shadow. Letty, have you finally decided what you're going to do? You keep waiting till the last minute. You'll never get reservations anywhere."

"Florida. Finally decided on Florida. The weather is always good there, and I'll get a tan."

"I thought you were . . ." Wilma was interrupted by the waiter with the dessert menu.

"Splurge, I'm going to splurge," Becky said.

"Big deal, it never shows on you anyway," Wilma said. "Listen, Letty, what happened with school?"

"What school?" Becky said. "Have you started school?"

"I don't know if I did the right thing. It was the scariest thing I've done in years. There I was in a room and was the oldest person there. I remember when I was always the youngest. I was always the youngest in any room, and here I was, the oldest. They're all these hot-shot kids who've read more than I have, and more recently. I walked in that room and if it wasn't for the teacher, I would have turned around and walked right out."

"Who? What? Who was the teacher and what was the course? You didn't even tell me," Becky said.

"Dr. Brandon. Miles Brandon, Ph.D. He's a practicing psychologist, and the smartest man I've ever met. The first assignment was Freud."

"When, when did you start this?" Wilma asked.

"Last week. Just last week. I'd had it. I'd had this sitting around. No goal. No future. Forty looming. It looms. Wilma, did it loom with you? I envy you," she blurted.

"What part of me is it that you envy?"

"First of all, that you can be alone. Live alone. You seem to be able to hack it."

"You're alone, too, Letty. Unless there's some guy on the horizon."

"No."

"Well, I've learned. That's true. I've learned how

29

not to be dependent on being with people. That's a kind of negative way of putting it, but it's self-protective. It's what I've come to. And you know what else? You know what else? I've learned how to reach out. I think that's the biggest lesson I've learned about loneliness, that it's not so terrible to call somebody up and say, 'I'm lonely, what are you doing?' You know? My life's all right. I came to the conclusion a long time ago that to base your whole happiness on whether you've got a man is dumb. Just plain stupid. Look at all the phenomenal ladies in history who did phenomenal things. Without a man. Why the hell do we center our lives on them? Why is it so terrible to be alone? All right. We need them. O.K. Granted. But to make that the be all and end all of life. Dumb. Unproductive. I've lived half my life. Remember that. I can't believe I'm fifty-one. My throat's still firm and I can have ten orgasms a night. Right? So what's the big deal about being past fifty? Except what I just said. Over half my life's over. Finished. Basta. So then really, instead of just folding up my tent and fading away, I say, shit, make each day count. Let's have a little joy around here in these fifties. Each fucking day. It's the only way to look at it. And if by chance there's no man, if by chance I have to eat alone at a restaurant or go to a matinee with a lady friend, an interesting lady friend, mind you, no duds, no deadheads for me of any sex. Those days are over. My life's O.K. Color. There's color in it. If you build your life around whether you have a man or not, you're dead. You might as well be dead."

Exhausted from her monologue, Wilma took a long drink of water.

"Wilma, I love you," Letty said.

"You, too, kid. You're O.K. You, too, Becky, old girl."

"But you see, it's why I started school," Letty said.

30

"It's not much. Just the New School. Just one course. But I thought maybe, just maybe I might do well and go for a degree. Maybe, just maybe, I could get out of insurance once and for all."

"I never heard you talk that way."

"Neither did I. Neither did I. Maybe it's Frank getting old all of a sudden . . ."

Maybe I'm terrified of being so dependent on two damn days in the week for my joy, she thought, my fulfillment. Maybe it's time to do something just for me.

"Maybe it's time to do something just for me."

"It sounds like it, babe, it sure sounds like it."

"It's not that I'm not scared."

"It's just a course, Letty, just one goddamn course. What is all the fuss about one course?"

"Symbolic. Symbolic. Finish my dessert, I can't. I've wanted to go back to school for years. Never could. Always talked myself out of it. It's the media. I swear. It's Betty Friedan and all those assertiveness training courses and articles. You cannot move without seeing them. Maybe finally it's beginning to sink in. I don't know. We're going to be late getting back."

"Thanks, Wilma."

The three women got up and gathered their belongings.

"For what?"

"Oh, I don't know. Just for being my friend."

"Always."

"You've got such sense."

"And you've got such love in you, Letty."

"How can you tell?"

"It's written all over you. It's how you tip a dollar to the lady in the bathroom instead of fifty cents. It's how you talk to Agnes in the office. It's how you are with your mother."

"I don't know."

"I'm telling you."

"Let's not go back to work. It's Friday. Let's go to the Philharmonic. Let's go to the '21.' Let's go to the moon."

They walked out of the restaurant, roaring, arms around each other.

5

Weekends were times of promise. Or fear. They loomed, like the shadow of some great bird, those two empty days and a night, stretching mercilessly against the skyline. Friday afternoons anthills of people streamed out of offices, crushing into elevators and running for subways and busses, filling the streets with a giant exodus into the haven or cage of home.

At five o'clock, Robertson Stellar was electric with chatter, the clatter of anticipation, then suddenly, the heavy after silence fell before the cleaning women began their chores.

For Letty it meant stopping off at the market, picking up some flowers for Fran who had been in all day. Unable to face the stridency of the subway, she rode all the way uptown on the bus, still feeling the afterglow of the wine, the sweet, yet vague uneasiness of her lunch.

It was the same. Everything would be the same. She could predict her mother's every word, the way the apartment would shine, the smell of disinfectant stinging her nose. Her mother was very clean. Compulsively clean. Hymie Gold had always kidded Fran about it, saying that his wife kept the house smelling like a hospital all the time. But she wouldn't change. "Hi, hon," she would say as Letty's key would turn in the lock. "What's new?" she would say before Letty put her packages down.

Letty was considerably taller than her mother. She had been ever since she was twelve years old. Whereas Fran was small and very round, Letty was tall and hard like her father. She was five-feet-nine-inches in her stocking feet. Unlike many tall girls, she never slumped, never tried to hide her height. Hymie had always convinced her to be proud of "the air up there." He always called her his *kindela*. Hymie was a gentle man, a family man, and Letty, being an only child and her daddy's darling, still had not been able to cry until years after he died. It was odd to look so far down on your mother, she always thought.

After Hymie died, they had moved from the Village uptown to Yorkville. Neither of them wanted to be reminded of the old neighborhood, the too sympathetic eyes of the butcher and the cleaner, bumping into all Hymie's friends, sitting on the stoop on hot Saturday nights. Fran and Letty had agreed that they would have to start over.

They had found a rent-controlled two-bedroom apartment on Eightieth and First in a clean building that was well kept by Mr. Gabor the super, an apple-cheeked Hungarian who insisted he was a distant cousin of "Jolie and the girls." In the ten years they had lived there, the neighborhood had run down a bit, but not too much. It was a family neighborhood, well lit, and on Sundays kids and their parents would ride their bicycles over to the river. Letty and Fran learned to like German food in the restaurants up and down Eighty-sixth Street, the bakeries with their heavy pastries. There were many Hungarians and Czechs too, and Indian and Chinese restaurants squeezed between the beer halls and supermarkets. Their street belonged to an association that gave gay block parties in the summer with flags rippling in the wind and rides for the kids and sauerkraut and knockwurst and strudels steaming on pushcarts.

The apartment was simple, with a small kitchen, dinette, a living room with a fireplace, and they each had their own bedroom. The fireplace was their solace, their luxury, their love. Except that wood was so expensive, so they only treated themselves to the crackling comfort on the most freezing and despairing winter nights.

Letty's room had green walls, which were lined with bookshelves. Her hi-fi nestled on the second shelf, with the speakers on the top. It was her oasis.

Fran had worked in the corset department of Lane Bryant's for the past ten years, retiring only three years ago when she found she couldn't climb the steps up onto the bus or down to the subway. She missed her job desperately, the interchange with the "girls," the destination to the day, and since she had retired had become crotchety, sharp.

"Hi, hon," Fran called from the kitchen as Letty walked in the door. "What's new?"

"Hello, Mother." There was a letdown, a moment of panic as the predictable happened. Is this it, is this it forever? "Hi, hon" every afternoon after five, forever and forever?

She was wearing dark glasses to cover her black eye. She had too much rouge on, Letty thought, trying to cover the discoloration in her face. She looked more like a clown than a mother. Fran.

"Coyne the goy, who Sarah Schwartz arranged. Tonight's the night he's taking you to dinner, Letty. Did you forget?"

"Ma, don't start in on me. I haven't even taken off my coat. I forgot, that's all. I just forgot."

"How can you forget?"

"I don't know, Mother. I just forgot. I've got a lot on my mind. Becky's getting married, you know, and we took her to lunch today, and Mr. MacKail thought up a whole lot of business for me to do at about four o'clock today. It's been a hard day. Is there any scotch?"

"You shouldn't drink before a blind date. Sarah says he's really attractive. Not a college man, but at this stage of the game, I'm not being so fussy." Fran was wearing black sensible shoes with black stockings with seams. Left over from another time, Letty thought. "You're not getting any younger, Letty."

Blunt. Fran was getting blunt, Letty thought. Her fall and incipient senility, whenever it would come full force, had not in any way softened her tart tongue. Instead of age mellowing her, it exaggerated her archness. It wasn't easy, this period, Letty thought, controlling her urge to lash out at her mother, put her in her place, tell her to mind her own business.

"I'll fix myself a scotch," she said.

"Rachel Ganz had a stroke."

"God, when did that happen?" Letty said, getting ice from the refrigerator.

"This morning. Her son Abel called me from the hospital. Rachel was calling for me. I wish I could have gone. But it was downtown, at Beth Israel. How could I? She's paralyzed on one side. Last year, remember, she had the breast removed."

"I remember, Mother."

"You're going to be late. What are you going to wear?"

"Oh, God, I haven't even thought about it. I want to relax. I'm going into my room, Mother. He's coming in an hour or so."

"I want to come in and talk. I've been so lonesome here by myself all day." Fran said it with as much dignity as she could muster. She didn't want anyone's sympathy, she didn't want anybody feeling sorry for her. And yet that is, indeed, exactly what she wanted. And the guilt-provoking response was there, if not in word, in intonation, in stance, in cadence. It was unmistakable. But Letty wasn't biting. It had been too long a day. She needed it, this hour to be herself.

"I won't be late, Ma. When I come home, we'll talk. James Garner is on tonight. Your favorite. He'll keep you company."

"A lot you care." It slipped out before she realized it. Letty was a good girl. She didn't mean it. It's just that time stretched on so long when she was gone all day and it was even too cold to go out and sit on a bench. And she kept forgetting things.

"Sorry," she mumbled.

Letty put her arms around her mother. "I know, Ma. Look, I'm going to bathe. We'll have a nice talk when I get home. I promise. I love you, Ma."

"Me, too. I love me, too. Go. Go run your water. Put some corn starch in it, it will take out the tired-ness."

Sighing, Letty shut the door to her room. It was dark already outside. It got so damn dark so damn early.

A blind date. She was too old for a blind date. She knew that, but Fran had talked her into it. In her own way, Fran was worried about Letty. This would have been the fourth Friday night in a row that she would have stayed home, reading, watching television, doing needlepoint. Fran didn't understand what Letty did with her time. She had told her that. Men never came to the house, Letty went out with the girls in the office every Tuesday and Thursday, but she never seemed to get involved or interested in anyone. Nothing was happening. She would go to the resorts or singles things occasionally, but she hated them with a passion, abhorring the flesh pots, as she called them, the marketplace. Sure, but now that she was almost forty, it wasn't so easy to meet men anymore, and Fran agreed that going to a singles bar was a humiliating experience and Letty was too good and too fine for that, but where in God's name was she going to meet men?

At seven-thirty sharp, Ed Coyne rang the bell. Letty was dressed and ready.

He must have been six-feet-four-inches tall, she thought. He filled up the doorway. He had a nice face with blue eyes and a fine red mustache.

"Letty?" He looked at her with relief. She was as attractive as Sarah had promised.

Ed was as uncomfortable as Letty with this teenage nonsense. For people in their thirties to "date" and pick each other up and say hello to the mother seemed barbaric. Ed felt like a kid, as though he should be carrying a corsage of carnations, as though he should pin it on her sweater with one of those pins with a large rounded head.

"Of course, Ed, come in. I'm glad to see you." Letty gave Ed a strong handshake. He liked that. He liked a woman who didn't give you one of those jellyfish dainty jobs that left your own palm moist and fishy feeling.

"Please come in, say hello to my mother."

Letty led the way into the living room, but not before she had noticed how uncomfortable he looked in a shirt and tie. She would bet that this man wore a shirt and tie once a month. He seemed to be the kind who was more at home in jeans and a shirt and sweater.

"Hello, Mrs. Gold, how are you?"

Fran had gotten herself up in a black dress from

her Lane Bryant days, with a string of pearls and high heels. She had on bright red lipstick and had toned down the rouge. She had taken the curlers out of her hair.

"How do you do, Mr. Coyne. Mrs. Schwartz has told me so much about you. You were a great friend of her son Roger's, weren't you?"

"The best. We were buddies in Korea and have been close ever since. Rog is the best. An all-around guy."

"I've known him since he's a little boy. Sarah is one of my oldest friends. I had a fall."

"Oh? What happened?"

"Yesterday, right in the bathroom. It was a miracle I wasn't killed. Right on the tile. I'd take off the glasses and show you, but I'm feeling better now. Much better."

"Well, that's good. I think we had better go, Letty. I made an eight o'clock dinner reservation and it's really a freezing night. We'll probably have trouble getting a cab."

"Oh, must you go so soon? Well, I suppose you better be on your way. What time did you say you'd be home, dear?"

"I didn't, Mother. It won't be late." Letty felt sorry for her mother.

"Why don't you get your coat, dear, it's in the hall closet."

Letty felt foolish. Sixteen. She wished the night were over.

"Let's go, Ed. Mother, I'll see you later."

"Are you dressed warmly enough, Letty? I think you'd better take a scarf."

Letty stiffened. "We're just going in and out of a cab, Mother. I'll be fine. Fix yourself some dinner, Mother."

"So nice to have met you, Mr. Coyne. I do hope we'll see you again."

Fran gave him her hand.

Ed didn't wear gloves. Riding up in the elevator of the Rockefeller Center building, Letty noticed how red and raw they looked. Oversized. There was dirt under his fingernails.

"Well, pretty soon I'm going to get my own garage. No question about it. There is good, and I mean good money in owning your own garage. I'm not kidding. Know anything about cars?" Ed let Letty go first as they arrived at the top of the building. Letty hadn't been in the Rainbow Room since high school when a whole bunch of them had gone to dance after the prom.

"Let's walk through the bar before we go into the restaurant," Letty said, "I haven't seen this view in years."

"Sure. This is really a swell place." Letty looked at Ed and saw the pride on his face. As though he were taking her to La Grenouille. Letty looked around the room that circled what seemed the millionth floor of the building. The view was still breathtaking, corny as it was. They had obviously redone the place since the last time she was there. She walked over to the window and looked straight down. They had designed the corner where she was standing so that mirrors on the ceiling above window boxes filled with fake flowers reflected the street thousands of feet below. It was dizzying, and Letty began to sway. She felt Ed's big hands around her waist.

"Whoa, there. You all right?"

"Fine. Sorry. This view is extraordinary, isn't it?"

"I always enjoy it," he said.

The bar was dark with electric candles on each table. There wasn't a New Yorker in the place, Letty could tell.

Inside the Rainbow Room, a circular dance floor was the focal point in the room. Piped-in music from records filled the room as the *maître d'* showed them to their table. The room was crowded and Letty noticed two middle-aged very round people definitely from Indiana twirling and doing their 1949 dip. They were having a wonderful time.

It was dark, and the tuxedoed *maître d'* pulled out a chair for Letty.

"So, what'll you drink?" Ed was settling into his role as date, taker-over, aggressive male.

"Scotch. Scotch, please, on the rocks."

"Sure thing. I prefer beer myself, but I'll join you in a scotch. So listen, Letty, tell me about yourself."

"Not much to tell." Letty noticed the orchestra members were wandering out one by one, taking their place on the round bandstand.

After his third scotch, Ed talked more and more about pistons. And carburetors. She could tell he liked her. Letty looked around the room at all those people out there from Iowa and Utah, Nevada and South Dakota. They were dressed in their Saturday best, like Ed. She felt out of place. She knew she looked totally right in her black silk dress, with the black stockings and high-heeled pumps. The small dangly pearl earrings and the Majorca pearl necklace made her look sleek, trim. Just right.

". . . it's true, ever since I was a kid I was good at fixing things. It's just a knack," Ed was saying proudly. "I'm good with my hands. My hands are golden," he said shyly, "not to brag or anything, but that's what my mother always used to tell me. I could have been an electrician, too, I guess, but cars, planes, anything mechanical interest me more. I can just look at a motor and tell what's the matter with it. Just a knack, I guess."

The orchestra leader announced the arrival of a

singer named Lanie Kazan whose décolletage and dramatic delivery was too loud and boisterous for Letty's taste. She seemed a very energetic girl. Ed couldn't take his eyes away from the girl's cleavage, which looked to Letty like the deep cleft separating the buttocks. For some reason that amused her and she started to laugh. Ed interpreted it as delight, and took her hand and squeezed it. He wasn't bad. He was beating the table with Lanie's rhythm with one hand and holding on to Letty with the other.

"Ed, why don't you eat," Letty said gently, "your lamb chops are going to get cold." Letty hadn't seen those little panties with frills on lamb chops in ages.

"Right, yeah, right. Is that girl great or is she great. Some chest, eh?"

"What's that got to do with anything?" she said irritably.

Lanie exited, and dessert was served.

"You're not one of those women's libbers, are you? You seem strong and certainly self-sufficient, but there's something nice and soft about you. If there's one thing I can't stand, it's those women's libbers. If they're out there working up a storm, you just tell me who's going to take care of the kids when a guy's there working hard all day."

Ed was ready for an argument, clenching his fists so that the knuckles turned white. Letty wasn't biting. She controlled her anger. The meal had been surprisingly good, the view heady. She had had enough. She wanted to go home. This all had nothing to do with her.

Ed sensed her withdrawal and asked if she wanted to dance. Letty looked at her watch. It was only eleven.

"Ed, would you mind terribly if we went home? I have to be somewhere at eight-thirty in the morning

41

tomorrow," she lied, "I'm awfully sorry, but I didn't realize it was so late."

"So late?" he said, disappointed. "It's really awfully early, Letty." He liked her. He liked her cool way. She was class. More educated than he was, but she didn't lord it over him. Nice. A nice broad. He'd like to see her again.

"I know, but by the time I get to bed, it will be midnight, and I have to get up early. I'm sorry, Ed. It's been lovely. Truly. I've really enjoyed it."

In the taxi, he took her hand again, and she let the gloved fingers be played with. She was bored, she was needful; all at the same time.

As Letty searched for her key, Ed took her bag and put it on the table in the hallway in front of her door. Within moments, he had swooped himself around her. In her high heels Letty was six feet tall, and she felt herself against his chest. He kissed her. Like a date does when he brings a girl home. Instinctively, she recoiled and slapped him hard in the face.

"What the hell was that for?" Ed said, surprised. What kind of crazy broad was this? "What's the matter? I thought we had fun."

"We did." Her heart was beating very fast. For a split second, his arms had felt warming. She could feel her heart beat through her coat. "Please forgive me. Excuse me, Ed. I'm just not myself tonight. Thanks for the dinner. The evening was fine. I had a good time. Thanks, Ed." Letty struggled to find her key and within seconds was gone.

Puzzled, Ed stood there for a moment, then pushed the button for the elevator.

"So?"

Fran was waiting in the living room.

"So what, Mother?" Letty was tired. She hung her coat up in the hall closet.

"So how did it go, Letty? What was he like?" Fran

was in her blue quilted housecoat with her hair in curlers. She had been sitting in the bedroom with the door closed expecting Letty to bring Ed into the apartment. But when she heard Letty come in alone, she came padding out in her slippers.

"Nice, Ma, he was nice. Thanks, thanks for arranging it."

"Now look, Letty, I didn't arrange it, he wanted to meet you. I just gave Sarah your number. Is it snowing, your shoes look all wet."

It had begun to snow and Letty had barely noticed. She kicked off her shoes, picked them up and bent down to kiss Fran good night. She suddenly felt overcome with fatigue. She wanted to creep under the covers and go to sleep.

"Let, how about a cup of tea?"

"No, Ma, not tonight. I'm beat." Letty started unzipping her dress. She couldn't reach it. "Mom . . . please?"

Letty leaned back and Fran reached up to unzip the dress. Fran touched the smoothness of Letty's back. Impulsively, she kissed it.

"Ma."

"Letty, you got a gorgeous back."

"Oh, Ma."

"Don't let its gorgeousness go to waste, girl."

"Mom, I'm going to bed, I'll see you in the A.M. O.K.?"

"Sit down, Letty, just for a moment."

Letty could fall asleep standing up. She did not want to talk. She could predict each word, every nuance.

Fran got up and gently pushed Letty onto the couch.

"Sit down, sweet. I'll go make us a hot cup of tea. I'll stick a bit of brandy in it to offset a cold."

"I'm not getting a cold," Letty was breaking down.

43

"Look, the fire has some nice hot embers for you. Warm up."

"Ma, Fran, for God's sake, I'm not cold."

Fran was in the kitchen already and Letty could hear the running water.

Letty sighed. She looked into the orange coals in the fireplace, and squeezed her wet toes. She reached up around her back and unhooked her brassiere and then took off her earrings. By the time Fran came in from the kitchen with a tray, she was almost asleep.

"I thought coffee would be better. Sip, honey."

"Ma, it was a nice evening. He's a nice good hard-working man and I had lamb chops with little panties on them and Lanie Kazan has enormous boobs and I had peach melba for dessert."

Fran was not impressed.

"Did he ask you out again?"

"He'll call, Ma. I promise you he'll call. This coffee tastes marvelous."

"You have a vacation coming up in a week or two, don't you?"

"Yes."

"You know I sent away for some brochures for you." Letty noticed that Fran had two hairs growing out of a mole on her chin. She remembered Fran's mother, who was tiny and trim and always wore her gray hair in a tight bun, tweezing the hairs out of a mole on her chin. She remembered as a child, watching, fascinated, as Selma held the little mirror close to her face and would tweeze in quick, short strokes, all the while chattering on in Yiddish.

"For where?"

"Well, there's still an opening or two on this cruise to the Bahamas, but you would have to call first thing Monday morning. It's a singles cruise, but I think it's supposed to attract a very high-type clientele.

"And, Letty, there is another singles charter flight

44

to London, six nights of theater and restaurants in-cluded. It seems to me the people on that would be very intelligent."

"Mother, I'm going to bed."

"Letty," Fran measured her words very carefully, determined not to avoid making her point, determined not to get Letty annoyed at her.

"Sweetheart, you know I'm not trying to push. That would be the last thing in my mind, to push. It's just that at the moment there seems to be a bit of a lull in your social life, and new places, new horizons, would be a perfect thing now. You've got a week, you've got the money saved up. I mean, after all, it's only a few weeks aways. I started talking about this to you way before Thanksgiving."

"I know, Mother," Letty was softening. She knew her mother was concerned about her singleness. So was she.

"But I've decided what I'm going to do, and you'll be thrilled," Letty said. "I'm going to go on a cruise. I was reading in the paper about this trip with just single people. I've never been, and you'll be delighted that every eligible man in New York is going to be on it that week, I have it on good authority!"

Fran smiled, and hugged Letty.

"Ma, you're spilling my coffee."

"Now you're talking sense. That's a marvelous idea."

"I'm going to go with some of the girls in the office. I saw them last Thursday night for dinner, and we confirmed it on the phone this morning. Wilma's com-ing. She'll make all the arrangements so I don't have to do a thing. She's been on a cruise before and knows the ropes. Now are you satisfied, Ma?"

Fran couldn't hide her excitement.

"Thank God. Just thank God, Letty. I know you're going to have a terrific time. Maybe Michelle's mother can make you a few new things. That woman is a whiz with a needle. It seems to me you need a few more long things; the new *Vogue* just came, maybe she could copy . . ."

"Mother, I'm exhausted. I'm going to bed. Leave those dishes, I'll do them in the morning."

"No problem. Sleep well, sweetheart. Forgive me for pushing. Really. Forgive me for . . ."

For getting old, Letty finished the sentence in her head. "Oh, Mom, I know. I know." Letty kissed her mother. The cheek felt almost too soft.

In her room with the door shut, Letty drew the curtain aside and watched the snow. It covered all the dirt, all the gray, she thought. The first blush of snow hid so much ugliness in New York, until the second or third day when boots and mud turned it all into slush and filth. The dirt somehow always came to the top. But at first, like some magic cleanser, it washed the city of its pain. She pressed her cheek against the window, letting the cold seep into her skin. She started sniffing and reached for a Kleenex on the night table. "No colds. Please, God, no colds," she said aloud. She wiped her nose, before the tears, stinging and hot, slid down her face.

6

Carefully, Agnes dressed. As though for a date, as though someone would soon be ringing the bell, throwing his fur-lined coat on the couch, making himself a drink while she put on her mascara, while she looked

46

into her oblong-shaped mirror in her bathroom surrounded by bulbs. But there wasn't anyone. No one was coming.

But Agnes was going out anyway. The Lord Windsor, and preparing for it had been taking a lot of her time, but still she had sent for a ticket to the theater months ago to see *Equus*. It was important to keep up. Everyone was talking about it; in the Sunday theater section of the *Times* there had been a whole controversy brewing. A psychiatrist had written about not agreeing with the playwright, and the critics were having a free-for-all about the boy who had blinded six horses and his psychiatrist. It sounded very intellectual, and Agnes thought she should go.

You really had to keep up with things; it had taken her a while, but she had finally finished *Ragtime*, forced herself, as a matter of fact, to finish *Ragtime* because it was in the windows of all the Fifth Avenue bookstores. At first she was going to wait until the paperback came out—since the man was getting almost two million dollars for paperback sales, he certainly didn't need her $8.95, or whatever it was, for the hardback. But she had felt compelled to read it; she had kept looking on the newsstands for the serialization, but it had never come, and she felt so out of things if she didn't at least read the flyleaf or a couple of reviews that would make her feel comfortable when referring to it. So she had skimped a little more than usual, borrowing from Peter to pay Paul, to pay E as a matter of fact, E as in E. L. Doctorow. Edward or Eliot or Emmet L. Doctorow was going to send his kids through college on her $8.95. He didn't need her money, nor did Mr. Shaffer whose play she had decided to see. But still, there were certain things you just had to do to keep up, Agnes reasoned.

She tried to read all the best sellers. She was, however, taken aback by some of the female writers like

Erica Jong and Judith Rossner who were too explicit for her. Judith Rossner's book about the girl who got murdered because she picked up a strange man and told him to go home after they had sex, upset her terribly. She couldn't sleep the whole night after she finished that one. It wasn't only the murder, but the way she described the sex that had made her feel uncomfortable.

Agnes did like to be neat. She took comfort, solace, in being neat. Her apartment, on the tenth floor of a neat elevator building on Lexington Avenue and Twenty-Second Street, was tiny but perfect. Like a doll's house. It made Agnes feel in control to be neat. She was that way about her appearance as well. She knew her faults, but being an avid reader of the women's magazines had learned how to circumvent them as much as possible. Her fantasy was to be made over by the *Ladies' Home Journal.* If there was anyone she envied, it was those women the magazine would pick up in Des Moines, Iowa, or Duluth for whom they would bring a carload of experts to do the skin, the eyebrows, trim down the excess areas. They would style the hair and hollow the cheeks and *voilà,* there would be a new Agnes.

People didn't dress much for the theater in New York anymore, and Agnes abhorred this lack of taste, the way they wore blue jeans and shaggy Afghanistan overblouses that made everyone look pregnant. It was as though there was no decorum anymore, no form or structure. Well, Agnes thought, I will be in style. She wore the green pants suit with a yellow turtleneck sweater, brown half boots, and carried the imitation Vuitton bag Alexander's had had on special this week. By seven, she had eaten, bathed, dressed, made up her face, and sprayed her hair so the teasing would stay in place.

It had turned very cold, and when Agnes got off

the bus at Forty-sixth Street and Broadway, the two-block walk to the theater brought tears to her eyes. The wind had wrapped itself around her.

Finally ensconced in her seat in one of the last rows of the balcony, Agnes took out the mother of pearl opera glasses her mother had given her when she left Boston to go to New York. She settled in her seat and found herself a bit confused by grown men playing the part of stomping horses with sculpted wire hooves that elevated them above the ground. Yet there was something absorbing about the play even though it seemed a bit talky.

Suddenly, they were both naked. The boy who had blinded the horses, and his friend, the pretty girl who worked at the stable. All of a sudden, she had taken off her jeans and her sweater and her breasts were bobbing on the stage; and then the boy, slim and muscular, his pubic hair the russet color of his head, was at the opposite end of the procenium. Agnes wasn't prepared for it. Nowhere had she read that there would be nudity on stage. Agnes felt herself get wet under the arms. The boy and the girl moved toward each other. Agnes could not pull the binoculars away from her eyes. They lay down on the floor together and the magnified glass made the flesh seem so close, the breasts pressed against the glass, the penis imposed itself onto her pupils.

Agnes felt the heat creep up from between her breasts across her neck to her ears. Her ears were red in the darkness. She felt as though she were on fire. She had seen art books, she had only seen two naked men in her whole life, she had seen her own body often, and Mrs. Friedman's breasts. That was all. On the stage. Pubic hair. Breasts. White bellies. White and round.

Agnes felt as though she were going to throw up.

"Excuse," she said, as she pulled her coat off the back of her chair, and picked up her bag from the floor. "Excuse."

She barely made it to the ladies room where she threw up. The cheese omelet she had made herself for dinner was on the tip of her tongue, and even after it was all over, she heaved and heaved. "You only sleep with men you love," she kept hearing in her head. "You only sleep with men you love," she heard herself saying over and over. Love is where you find it, love will find a way. Love me, somebody, love me.

Her pants were wrinkled in the lap. She would have to steam press them. As she walked into the lobby, she heard the applause. The first act was probably over, she thought. She began to run.

Several men were coming out of the bar and restaurant next to the theater. "Hi, babe," a fat man leered at her. She ran on down Forty-sixth Street. Several derelicts with a bottle in a paper bag were leaning on the building.

The streets were filled with people. Several boys on motorcycles flashed by. She felt pins come out of her hair. A black man had his arm around a pale-skinned girl with long blond hair. She had on no bra and Agnes could see her nipples through her open coat. There was water running in the streets into the drains. There were some banana peels and orange rinds floating down through the grate. She saw a Tampax cover and beer bottles and a copy of *TV Guide* in a pile on the corner.

She hailed a cab.

"So, what's a pretty girl like you roaming around Times Square on a Friday night?" the voice from the front said. "Listen, don't do it, these are troubled times. You can't roam around alone in these neighborhoods. A girl as pretty as you shouldn't go alone. Where to, honey?"

Emmanual Applebaum looked harmless enough. Agnes could still feel her stomach hurt. She was shaking. Emmanual Applebaum did not find her to be scintillating company.

7

Every weekend, Bob McKern got up an hour early to bring his wife breakfast in bed. He had been doing it for thirty years now, but since Eleanor's recent open-heart surgery, and the doctor's pessimism about her chances for recovery, he had prepared a tray for her before his shower, before shaving. He had bought a bouquet of roses from a man in the subway station Friday night, and Saturday morning took a single flower from the bunch and put it in a tin vase on her tray.

"Bob, you're too much. What a love. Bend down, sweet."

Eleanor, strong enough now to sit up in bed, kissed the top of her husband's bald head. A loud smacking sound.

"How do I look, sweetheart? I haven't been up yet and haven't had time to pinkin' the cheeks or at least slosh some Tabu or something on."

"You look divine, hon, good enough to eat. So eat what's on the tray before I take a bite out of you."

Bob touched his hand to her cheek and moved into the bathroom. The sound of her pouring coffee and clinking cup to saucer was a reassuring one. It relieved him. Eleanor had just returned after ten days in the hospital, and the isolation while she was away, the deadly quiet of the apartment, had been oppressive for him. They hadn't expected her to survive. He had never known such fear.

Maybe Will was right, that childless couples depend on each other more than most, that all the energy that usually went into the kids flowed back and forth to each other. Probably. If it hadn't been for Will's steadiness these past days, working at the office would have been unbearable. They would go out to eat on days when he couldn't make it to the hospital on his lunch hour and sometimes never say a word. Will would just sit there, sipping his coffee, staring into space after the office amenities were dispensed with. He never saw Will outside of the office, had never in all these years even met his wife, as a matter of fact. He'd met one of his sons one Saturday when they had to come in for extra work, and was enchanted by the mischievousness of the strawberry blond with freckles, his hands deep in the pockets of his overalls.

Bob was worried. As he stepped out of the shower, shivering in the draft of the bathroom, he turned on the electric heater. Even though his apartment was stifling most of the time, the radiators impossible to control, the bathroom was always cold. Probably didn't do Eleanor any good, either, that change of temperature from room to room. He pulled on his terrycloth bathrobe, tying it over a belly that was beginning to resemble a casawba melon. He just had to go on a diet. But sitting all day poring over figures didn't do much for combating the spreading of middle age. He felt his face. How he envied men who could at least cheat and go one day without shaving. By noon, his beard would begin to cast a gray shadow on his jawline; by five, the stubble would have to be shaved if he wanted to be at all presentable.

Shaking up the can of cream, watching it ooze like whipped cream onto his face, he couldn't remember the first time he had shaved. He had been very young, sixteen perhaps, about the same time he had met Eleanor.

They had been at Brighton Beach in Brooklyn for the summer. Both their families had rented summer cottages for the first time, and it was an anticipated treat for the McKerns and McNultys. They were three blocks from the water, and he would see her every day walking past his house, a book and blanket neatly tucked under her arm. She had had long red hair then, and sleek legs. He knew he wanted her, then and there. He'd already had neighborhood girls in the basement of his apartment house, had already been initiated into the sexual ritual of the streets, and he had been slim then, with a headful of hair. The girls liked him. Eleanor had ignored him for practically the whole summer, despite his manipulations of strutting himself in front of her blanket, trying to make conversation. She would not be picked up. Finally, the first week in August when he was about to leave for home from his job as soda jerk in one of the drug stores in town, she came in with a nosebleed. The blood was all over her white blouse, and the girl with her had lost her head and was flailing her arms about and trying to make Eleanor keep her head back at the same time.

Bob was overcome with stoicism and calm. He took charge. Took her in the back of the pharmacy where Mr. Epstein made her sit with her head back while he applied packing and ice. She had her eyes shut during these ministrations, but when the fear left her, she had peeked out from under long blond lashes and blinked her thanks.

They became engaged six months later. They waited until he finished high school till they got married. He never did go to accounting school as he had planned, and used his facility for figures to learn bookkeeping. He had been with Robertson and Stellar for thirty years now, doing the same thing, year after year. They had given him a gold watch, with a nice message written on the back when he was there twenty-five years, and last year, when it was thirty, he had been presented with a round sterling silver tray with "thirty years of loyal service" engraved on that. He'd seen them come and go, the bosses, the superiors, young and old, he saw them move up. He never did. He had gotten raises over the years, not particularly substantial ones, but at this point in his life new challenges were threatening. If he ever lost that job, he didn't know what he would do. He was meticulous about his work, but knew deep in his heart that there were younger, more astute men waiting to gobble up his duties and position. At this point, he was looking forward to his pension, the benefits he had been paying in for so long, the medical benefits without which he couldn't have paid for Eleanor's two heart operations. It was a job. That was all.

He took the towel and dabbed at his face. Damn, if he hadn't cut his chin. Someday he was going to get one of those Remington electric things. He was getting so absent-minded.

"What do you say, El, did you finish everything?"

Eleanor was dozing, her head had dropped to her shoulder, the tray precarious on her lap.

Bob took the tray gently from her and took it into the kitchen. She didn't look well, he thought, so pale and must have lost ten pounds which she couldn't afford in the hospital. There were dark circles under her eyes, and since her illness she had not been able to go to the beauty parlor to have the thick strands of gray at her temples dyed. Walking back into the bedroom, he stared at his wife. She was a continuation of him. He was not much for poetry, didn't even consider himself a romantic, but this much he knew. That woman over there in that bed was his best friend. She knew him inside and out, understood him. And he loved her. Sure she wasn't so sleek or supple anymore, neither, for God's sake, was he. He wouldn't trade her in for two young ones. Never. The woman completed him. If anything happened to her, he would die. Just crawl off in a corner and die.

Dressed now, he bent over to kiss his sleeping wife. He wore a thick béige sweater over his shirt since it was supposed to go below zero today. He put a note by her side on the night table. "Roses are red, violets are blue, the world is my oyster when I'm with you. Gone to do the shopping, be back in an hour."

Please, God, he thought, once out on the street. East Twenty-eighth Street was bustling so early with baby carriages and young mothers in jeans and parkas. The thermometer in the cleaners on the corner registered three below zero. Please, God, let her live. The Italian bakery was smelling homey and yeasty already, and two girls rushed by carrying silver-and-gold wrapping paper. Already a derelict was in the fetal position in a doorway. It's Christmas, God, let her live through Christmas, let her see the tree at Rockefeller Center, and let me be able to take her to Radio City, and let her trim the tree and have the whole McNulty clan in Christmas Eve for eggnog. Let her celebrate your birth by living.

Such a good woman, God. The tears had frozen on his cheeks.

8

Saturday night for Priscilla was an adventure. You never knew who you were going to end up with, she reasoned. She had a deal with Dolores, from the office, that if neither of them had a date, they would go to places where they would get one, one way or another. Dolores was a follower. Priscilla gave her courage, but more often than not, Dolores would have to go home alone since their deal was that if one of them found a man they liked at a bar, the other would have to shift for herself. Many was the night Dolores found herself alone in a cab on the way home, ruefully envying Priscilla's aggressive, irresistible ways. Sometimes the two of them would get lucky and end up with friends. Dolores had learned a lot from Priscilla, and unwittingly had become a predator. They were an attractive pair, they both knew that, and standing at a bar, be it Maxwell's Plum or Dionysus, they knew the men could take their pick. If they liked blondes with fair skin and tight sweaters, Priscilla was available, and if petite curly headed brunettes were their thing, there was Dolores ready and waiting.

  This Saturday, they had decided on Maxwell's Plum. Priscilla had it down to a science. When the best time to go was, which bars had the most attractive men, where the least amount of desirable men were. For some reason, many girls had forsaken Maxwell's once the word got out that it was a singles bar. The restaurant itself was primarily filled with out-of-towners these days, but the bar itself, situated smack in the middle of an extraordinary room, was a nub of singles activity. It was a drag to have to go and buy the first and sometimes the second drink for yourself, and stand around and look not too anxious and available all at the same time. It didn't bother Priscilla, though. Dolores marveled at the aplomb, the brazenness of the girl. She was phenomenal to watch. Part of it had to do with her horniness. Priscilla was horny all the time.

Sometimes it occurred to her that there might be something the matter with her. She seemed to wear men out. She didn't mean to, not really, it was just that her body was remarkably responsive. She hadn't always been that way. As a matter of fact, when all her friends were fooling around at fourteen and fifteen, she had barely known what was it you masturbated with. She did get a nice sensation by just rubbing up against the corner of the desk at school or feeling quite comfortable in the subway when some man would press himself up against her. But it wasn't until she was sixteen that she discovered it. The power. Because that's what her responsiveness was to her.

Evan Mahoney was eighteen and lived next door to the Cochrans outside of Mobile. Finally, one night he took Priscilla to the movies. She'd had a crush on him since fifth grade and he had always ignored her. But then, all of a sudden when she lost the baby fat and her skin cleared up, he took a second look. She was turning into a Southern belle. In the movies he had put his arm around her shoulder, just as they all did. But when Evan, who, the neighborhood gossip had it, was having an affair with a twenty-six-year-old married woman, moved his hand down to her breast and kept it there, she went crazy. Nobody had ever tried that before. She would never, to this day, remember what the movie was on the screen or what dress she wore, two things she always recalled. Nobody else had ever tried it, that's all. Evan was quietly relentless, he never let go of her breast, while he moved his other hand up her thigh. It was summer. She had no stockings on and just the briefest of bikinis. Her bottom was damp and her skirt stuck to the seat. He moved his hand into her panties, in the movie, sitting in the last row of that stuffy theater. She didn't know what to do with all those feelings. The funny thing was that Evan had never looked at her face, and she never looked at his, and she had her first orgasm, there in the back row at the end of the early show. She didn't understand how she got so wet down there, or why her body couldn't stop shaking. He had taken her hand and put it on his penis and showed her how to move it up and down the way he liked it.

For a year, she and Evan got together almost every day somehow. He taught her how to put it in her mouth and hold the staff tight just below the tip, and he taught her how to put vaseline on it and slowly stroke it up and down, and he taught her how to put it in her mouth with warm water at the same time. He loved that. And he would stroke the inside of her arm or the back of her ear and she would pull his face down onto her.

"You can never get enough, babe," Evan would say. Evan had a lot of pimples, was so thin that there was almost no flesh at all on his bottom, but he had what he called an "educated cock." She liked it. She was good at it. She took to it like a duck to water, Evan said. And he, his educated cock, or whatever it was that seemed to understand her body, taught her how to satisfy herself. He liked to watch her. And she found that she could have orgasm after orgasm. As a matter of fact, the more he would fondle and thrust at her, the more she wanted it and the more she would come. He would take her to porno movies and finger her there, and she was titillated by the big breasted undulations on screen, the threesomes and the orgies made her unbearably excited, and she and Evan would indulge each other by the hour at the inexhaustible antics on screen.

They would turn themselves on with *Playboy* and *Screw*. Priscilla dropped out of school. Her father threw her out finally, appalled at the tramp he thought she had become. She was disarming even to Charles Cochran, because she always looked so innocent. Once her white neck had a strawberry mark on it, where Evan had bored his teeth, and it seemed to the security guard, who was a Baptist preacher on the side, that his daughter was lost. It didn't matter that he had never been faithful to her mother, that Priscilla knew he went with whores. To him, that striking red mark on such a white neck was symbolic of her fall. He would cast her out of his garden. She could never forgive the hypocrisy of it, though. After all, he did it, everybody did it. What was the big deal?

So she moved in with two girl friends, learned how to type, and at seventeen was on her own. When she was eighteen, she and another girl saved their money and moved to New York. Evan had gone into the Army and wrote her from New Jersey that some hip chick had given him the clap and that he had a bad case that seemed to be rejecting the penicillin. Then he went to Vietnam and after his discharge decided to go back to the Orient. His last letter said he was living with a Chinese girl in Hong Kong and had a deal going to run a little club with a buddy who played piano.

It really didn't matter, because he had given her the

tool. He had launched her. But she had a difficult time finding another lover so finely attuned to her body. The search was on, and Priscilla, having discovered this power, exerted it.

It was almost like making love to herself, getting excited, watching men's eyes the first time they saw her nakedness, or the first time they discovered that if they just blew on her she would shiver. Her responsiveness always astounded men, but she found they could never keep up. They would thrust into her and come and finger her into relief, or go down on her and be proud as punch with the way she thrashed around and had her orgasm, shouting out to the skies. But she wanted more. When they were turning over ready to doze, she was ready to get started again. Only after long hours of love-making did she feel somehow complete.

She had gotten somehow cynical about the whole thing and didn't think too much of men, with their undependable erections and big-shot macho ways. She needed a lot of man, and didn't care how long it took to find one.

She felt important in bed. She felt in control. She knew how to make men hot. It was so easy. When she was in bed, she felt farthest away from being dead.

The bar was jumping at Maxwell's when the girls walked in. Priscilla was wearing a fake fur she had gotten at a crazy furrier she knew on Seventh Avenue. It had padded shoulders and long, gray skins that went down to the floor. She felt smashing in it. The *maître d'*, who knew them by now, smiled broadly and pointed up the few steps to the bar.

"I think you might find a tiny bit of space there, girls, not much though."

With a practiced eye, he looked their backs up and down as they turned away from him.

The girls squeezed into a spot at the far end of the circular bar.

The black bartender had on a flowered California shirt and an earring in one ear.

"Well, well, hi there, girls, haven't seen you in a while. Where you been? You been missed."

"Around, we've been around. How about two martinis." Priscilla made a production about taking off her coat. It was a thing she did that never failed. Dolores had watched her do it a hundred times. She wriggled out of both sleeves and somehow stood there helpless, unable to move either arm. Someone, someplace, somehow, would come to her rescue. This time it was a tall young man with tight brown pants and a white shirt open to his waist. A medallion hung from his neck, pressing into the hairs on his chest.

"Allow me."

Dolores watched. It never failed.

"Oh, thanks a million. It's a bulky thing."

"Well, you sure aren't. Hello there. What should I do with this?" The man looked at Priscilla's shirt.

"Just put it over there," she said, pointing to the edge of the platform on which the bar was stationed. "And thanks, thanks so much." She flashed teeth that caught the light from the overhead lights. They shone at him. He was dazzled.

Over the bar enormous goblets of colored cut glass stood on thick glass shelves. Long-stemmed wine glasses with bulbous globes stared out at the girls. Priscilla's brown satin blouse shone in the light. She felt beautiful. An enormous oversize Christmas wreath decorated the bar.

Turn-of-the-century gas lamps were nailed to the wall, shooting out a blue-yellow flame, and the stained-glass cherubs and wreaths lit with bulbs from behind flickered in the light. As Priscilla looked up, she saw the copper ceiling, the metal beaten into elaborate

61

design. Priscilla loved the statues that decorated the walls, Mercury and Diana deep in thought looked out on the proceedings, and china tigers and lions hung from the ceiling. The decor was extravagant, with copper molds and roosters, leaves, enormous cornucopias, and chandeliers of rubies and emeralds and giant yellow stones. There were hundreds of imitation flowers, all in red, lining the windows, planted in large green boxes. But if Priscilla were to explain really what the decor was about, why she loved that crazy place, it would have to do with tigers. Tigers, tigers burning bright. Somewhere along the line in high school, some teacher had read the poem and she had never forgotten it. She had never really understood what it was all about, but there was something compelling about it. In the forest of the night. And something about a fearful symmetry. Someplace in her, she understood that. A fearful symmetry, Blake had said and she, somewhere, understood.

The man with the open-necked shirt was after Priscilla. Dolores could see the empty long cab ride home alone, the handwriting was on the wall. Mr. Medallion was coming on strong. He hadn't even noticed Dolores, and Priscilla seemed to have forgotten about introducing her.

"How about another drink?"

"Love it. But look, doll, while you're waiting for the drink to come, do you think you could save our place while we go to the john?"

"Well, I'll certainly try, if you promise to come back."

"Girl Scout's honor."

Priscilla dragged Dolores away from the bar and led her through the restaurant up the stairs to the ladies room. After all the excessiveness downstairs, the john was a letdown. Three toilets, yellow tiles, a blue door. It was so tiny that the toothy black lady with a blue uniform standing in front of the mirror could hardly guard the saucer with the quarters in it, surrounded by a large bottle of Jergen's Direct Aid Lotion. Priscilla and Dolores had climbed three flights up to get there, following the arrow painted on the wall.

When Priscilla went in to pee, she noticed as she squatted that the toilet paper was not in the holder. She took some Kleenex from her purse. In the next cubicle, a pair of toeless shoes were doing something, and, from beyond, in the third, came a throaty laugh.

"So what's going to happen?" Dolores asked as she painted on a new mouth. Her skin looked very white in this mirror, her eyes wide.

"What do you think. He's cute, don't you think? Dolores, you've got to branch out a little. He sure looks like a good lay to me."

"How can you tell?"

"His balls were bulging."

"Honestly?"

"True, it's a sign. I love those tight pants they wear. His butt looked unbelievable in those pants, did you notice?"

"Not exactly. How did you like that plunging neckline though?"

"Not bad. His hands were small though, did you notice? Sometimes that means the cock is small and he's not such a good fuck."

"Stop it."

"No shit. You think about it sometimes."

"Would you fuck Johnny Carson?" The attendant was listening to them. The girls were oblivious of her.

"He's my idea of nothing," Dolores said, "but listen, I wouldn't turn it down. I wouldn't throw him out of my bed, that's for sure. I'd just put a sack over his head and fuck for glory!" The two roared.

"Priscilla, this is the last time I'm doing this bit."

"Shit, Dolores. I'll see if he has a friend."

"It's not that. I'm just . . ."

"Shut up. It has nothing to do with anything."

The black attendant wore brown shoes, and a black wig that didn't fit very well. "God bless you," she said as Priscilla gave her a dollar with a grand gesture. She handed the girls paper napkins for their hands. There were no towels in sight.

Priscilla gave an approving glance to her image in the mirror.

She wiggled a bit as she walked down the stairs, oblivious to Dolores' sullen air.

Mr. Medallion, let's just see, she thought, let's just go about finding out how the hell you measure up.

9

Saturday night dinner at the Robbins was always the same. Kathy had an unconscious ritual of serving the same thing every week. They still had fish on Friday despite the relaxation from the Vatican. Tuesday night was stew, and Saturday was linguine and meatballs. The meatballs were always bland, unseasoned, Kathy being timorous in terms of garlic and salt. Her mother was a more adventurous cook, but Kathy was cautious.

The boys didn't pay any attention, so used to the routine were they. Eating was to fill their stomachs and to get over with. There had been a craft fair at Columbia University during the day, and Will had taken the two youngest boys. It was a brisk Saturday, and they all wore matching red scarves that twirled around their necks with panache. They strained in the wind, and walking up Broadway before the cold got to them, and they yearned for a bus, the three window shopped, and for the moment, pretended they were on some Los Angeles side street jogging in the morning sunshine. Will loved these times. Good times.

The fair was held at Royce Hall, sponsored by WBAI, a public radio station Will enjoyed listening to. Will was always filled with a pang of regret every time he was in an academic setting. Time lost, experience missed. He felt it all in a single moment. The gray walls, the sense of belonging, the bearded young men, and intense young girls. He had never had any of it, never shared any of that excitement of discovery in learning. His schooling had been rushed. N.Y.U. at night seemed a factory to him.

Potters and weavers, silversmiths and leather crafters, every conceivable kind of artisan, displayed their wares. Sean had run from booth to booth wishing he could have made this, wishing he could have bought that. Joseph, a quiet child, fingered each item he saw carefully, finally deciding on a hand-tooled wallet to buy his father for Christmas.

The three had had a fine time. They had hot dogs and soda downstairs in a food booth and tacitly enjoyed the intimacy of the day. Robert was ice skating in the park with his friends, but the two younger boys were still unencumbered enough to unabashedly enjoy the attentions of their father. All their friends envied them Will's accessibility. He was always there for them. In the summer, he was in the park at Seventy-ninth Street by nine in the morning throwing the ball around. They had formed a neighborhood league and had a steady game going every week. Not many fathers would do that.

He was impatient with their mother a lot, but in some ways they were so used to it they barely paid attention to it anymore. Their dad was tops. He helped them with their homework, spent both Saturday and Sunday with them, took them to the movies a lot, sometimes without Kathy. He always seemed to have time to talk.

Joseph, the most introspective of the three, was the one who noticed the wandering look in his father's eye and was aware of some sadness somewhere. He figured it had to do with Will's mother, a story he made Will tell over and over, how she had just left him with relatives one day because she was too young and too poor to take care of him. Joseph, without knowing why or how, sensed some loneliness in his father's eyes.

"They had some batik shirts there, Ma, that you would love," Sean was saying. "You should go to the show tomorrow, they're going to keep it open for another day. All kinds of crazy stuff. Potters came down from Vermont to show their stuff. Some guy was explaining to me about how the kiln has to be fired or something for twenty-four hours, baked until they can take the dishes or bowls out."

"We should go see one of those places sometime," Will said. "It's really fascinating to see how they twirl the clay on the wheel, paint it, and then bake it. I'll find one for us to visit that's not too far," Will said, absent-mindedly mashing his meatball like a child. He looked at his wife. In the harsh overhead light of the dining room her face seemed a stranger's.

The nuns long ago had stamped upon her the sins of vanity, so she didn't do much to enhance her looks. Her face was still very pretty, but the emptiness of youth and innocence had evolved into an unlined vac-

66

uousness. Whatever intelligence and self-assertion had once lain hidden behind those eyes had now disappeared. Will long ago had convinced himself that those wide-set eyes, the broad almost Indian look of her face was enigmatic, mysterious. But in the nineteen years of their marriage, he had learned sadly that there were no secrets behind those eyes, no yearnings, no curiosities. Kathy did not participate in her own life, Will discovered; she existed only insofar as he and the boys affected her.

Will wondered how the boys really felt about her. He couldn't remember too much about his mother except that one day she had deposited him with the Robbins family. Just told him to be a good boy and that she would write. His father had long since gone, and Will and his brothers were too much for a twenty-two-year-old girl who hadn't yet lived and who could barely support herself.

She would visit once a year at first, times which would precipitate such diarrhea in the ten-year-old boy that his aunt had lost patience with him. Then she just stopped coming. Left him alone.

His father's sister on Staten Island had been the one to volunteer, and there he had to share a room with his cousin, Alfred. Alfred was spoiled and masturbated loudly all night long. Will, who had developed into a strong, strapping boy, did all the chores formerly done by Alfie.

One hot summer day when he was fifteen and while Alfie was swimming and his moony sister, Sarah, was sitting on the porch watching him with two of her sorority sisters, Will overheard her telling them that the only reason their poor cousin lived with them was to help out and to be a companion for Alfred.

Then and there he decided to be only where people wanted him. Will developed then and there the feeling that life was nothing if you weren't important to somebody. People kept leaving him, and he would be damned if he would leave anybody, ever.

He had wanted to go to college, to be a lawyer. Long ago, his teachers' words had brought spots of crimson to Mrs. Robbins' cheeks, so highly did they praise Will's logical mind, his quick study. He had been a voracious reader and, although he could never afford many books, had spent whatever spare time he had in the neighborhood library. But at fifteen, when he left Staten Island, daring the Robbins to find him, he took off for New York. He set his internal clock. He found he could make some kind of living easily, that employers liked him, whether he was a grocery clerk or a delivery boy. He waited on tables, washed dishes, saved every dime.

Kathy Cerutti had come along, a pretty, plump doe-eyed girl who thought he would swoop her away from the tyrannical ritual of her own family. His industry, his passionate sense of loyalty seemed the counterpart of her helplessness. They fell on each other like snow to earth. They were both nineteen when they married, the Ceruttis horrified that their daughter would marry someone with Irish blood. But as long as he was a Catholic, and the doctor examining her had attested to her virginity the week before the wedding, they yielded. There was no dowry, however, no large wedding, just a few family and friends. Kathy's hands shook when he slipped the ring on her finger. She loved him. He would save her.

She couldn't imagine him putting himself inside her. They had kissed, and after he had gotten her to relax, she could almost enjoy resting in his arms sitting on the bench at Seventy-ninth Street on Riverside Drive. They would watch the boats go by and Will was almost happy, welcoming the trap he was laying for himself. He embraced the responsibility of someone being totally dependent on him, he welcomed the opportunity to prove his reliability.

The first time they went to bed at a hotel in Atlantic Beach, Long Island, Kathy cried all night long. The nuns had told her that to look at her own image in the glass was a sin, and she had rarely seen herself naked, so when Will gently, but so desperately, wanted to caress her breasts, look at the beautiful mysterious mound between her legs, she cried out in fear. His touch did not liberate her. It conjured images too fearful to explain. She loved him but she couldn't let go. And she never did.

They had made love last night for the first time in a long while, and Will could have predicted every move, every association in his head as they went through the litany. Kathy tried so hard to please him, to move her mouth up and down his body but it was a cellophane act. Her lips were thin and cool, her body heavy in his embrace as though rooted to the mattress. She was almost embarrassing in her pseudo seductiveness, trying to move sensuously, coveting a familiarity and friendship with his penis. But it was an alien thing to Kathy, Will's penis, something to fear rather than fondle. But she would touch it. Do her duty. Give it its due. But she could not love it or become excited by it or let it sweeten her. She didn't ask for pleasure, her days were dedicated to denying herself. Like her mother before her, Kathy would endure the mysterious intimacies of bed because she loved her husband, but she would not enjoy it.

Last night, Will had cried out in frustration as Kathy had lain leaden, locked into the sheets. He had thrown off the covers and retreated into the boys' room, covering them, kissing them with a ferocity he had never felt before. He looked up and had seen her standing there in the doorway, her silhouette full and square in the light behind her. Tears were on her cheeks, staining her nightgown. The hem was ripped, Will noticed.

"I'll be back soon," he had managed. "Go back to bed, Kathy. I'll be back soon."

She had turned away. "I love you, Will," was all she could say, as she walked back into the bedroom.

Kathy was uncomfortable under his gaze.

" 'The Jeffersons' are on tonight," she said. "We can watch it before Dan and Joe come over."

"I told you, my brothers were coming over tonight," Kathy said, a whine creeping into her voice. "They haven't been here in ages. Joe's bringing his new girl."

"That sure is a dumb show, Ma, I don't know how you can watch it," Robert said, toying with his spaghetti. "I'm going out. I guess I'll have to miss them. Dad, me and Benjy are going to go down to Rockefeller Center and see the trees lit up."

"Oh, Will, I don't think they should go down alone on a Saturday night, it's too dangerous," Kathy looked with concern at Robert.

"It's all right, son, just leave early and be back by ten or ten-thirty. Kathy, you didn't tell me the gang was coming over. When did you tell me?"

"It's not a gang, Will, it's my brothers. And I haven't seen them for a few weeks," Kathy said, defensively. "I told you a few days ago. I even stocked up on pretzels and beer. I most certainly did tell you. Look, Will, I'm worried about that boy going downtown this time of night on a Saturday night. I mean it."

"Kathy, do we have to go through this all the time? He's growing up. He's careful. He's a responsible boy. He's got to start learning how to navigate the city."

"O.K., dear," Kathy said suddenly. "I suppose you're right. You always are."

Will looked at her. Why didn't she fight if she felt

strongly about it, he thought. She always gave in. She always agreed, echoed his opinions.

"I'm not too keen on 'The Jeffersons,' either," Will said. "Everybody seems to be yelling at each other all the time. I've never known people, black or white, who keep up that loud intensity in their voices. God, they yell a lot."

"Yes, they certainly do yell a lot on that show." Kathy shook her head. As she chewed her spaghetti, she made a sloshing sound.

"Kathy, have you ever in your life had an opinion of your own?" Will blurted out. "Just because I don't like it, why do you have to agree with me, for God's sake? If you like the goddamn show, why don't you just say so?" Will's voice shook in exasperation.

The tears in Kathy's eyes flowed down her cheeks. Her nose was running. Sean, his mother's favorite, rushed to her and gave her his napkin.

"Come on, Ma, Dad was only fooling."

"It's all right, Sean. I'm not angry at your mother." He looked at the pale blue of his son's eyes, the shadows he had placed there. This morning Will had looked into those eyes, and they were dancing. Sean was standing on the toilet as he did every morning, shaving his freckles with a beard of shaving foam and a razorless Gillette. Their morning ritual.

Will had patted after-shave lotion on his own cheeks and then on the shining face of his son.

"There, kid, you'll wow 'em. Rita Lopez won't be able to resist you," he had said.

"I don't like her anymore." Sean was sniffing at his fingers.

"What happened, son?"

Sean's eyes darted in back of Will.

"She likes Peter better, Dad. She told me. She just likes Peter better now."

Will had looked grave, and put his hand on his son's shoulder.

"I'm sorry, Sean. I really am. Maybe you'll find another girl to like."

"I gave her twenty-two baseball cards."

"Do you think you can get them back?" Will had wrapped the cord of the electric shaver around itself and put it in the medicine chest.

"I only see her in English."

"I see," Will had said, not seeing.

"And she has a lot of tough friends. They beat people up."

"What are you going to do, son? What do you think?"

"I think I don't want to think about it anymore. You know that was a lot of gum and a lot of cards." Sean was a philosopher. It's what made Will connected, so connected to him.

Sean had his arm around his mother's shoulders, patting her as though he were burping a baby. He looked accusingly at his father as Kathy sobbed, the helplessness streaming out of her eyes.

Kathy was on a waterfall, going down, she knew it instinctively. More and more lately, Will would lash out at her. More and more, she sensed his removal. She didn't know what to do about it. She didn't have a clue as to what to do. She loved him, she needed him desperately. Without him, she was nothing. She knew she wasn't too pretty anymore and that she should read a little more maybe, and definitely lose a few pounds. But she was so busy keeping the house, and mending the boys' clothes and making sure the place was clean and the food was on the table. She didn't have too much time. He never took her out anymore, and they didn't have many friends, and they didn't even go over to her folks too much on Sundays because Will got so bored and nervous over there. If only he would keep

72

loving her, everything would be all right. He took such good care of her and the boys. She couldn't stand to make him angry.

"I'm going out," Will said abruptly. He couldn't stand to see her cry. He couldn't stand the shadows in Sean's eyes. He needed some air.

Joe Cerutti had his feet up on the glass coffee table in front of the fireplace and was sitting in Will's favorite easy chair. Will could see them from the hallway when he stepped into the apartment.

"Hello, Joe." Will walked into the room and took a beer off the coffee table. "I need a glass, Kathy." Petty. He sounded petty to himself. He always drank the beer out of the can. But he would be goddamned if he'd be the slob his brothers-in-law were, guzzling.

"A glass?" Dan Cerutti looked at Will. He never did like his brother-in-law. "Who ever heard of going to law school for ten years?" he had said to Mary, Joe's new girl, freshly poured into her red jumpsuit, an oversized cross dangling in her cleavage.

"I like it in a glass," Will said evenly. He only had to see these cards once a month or so, and his evening constitutional had strengthened him for the fray.

"The kids go out?" Will asked, sitting on an uncomfortable straight-backed chair.

"Sean's in his room," Kathy looked petulant. She enjoyed her brothers. She enjoyed it when they visited. Will would rarely go over to her folks' house any more, and it was the only chance she had to be with her family. He had no right to make her feel as though they were all intruders.

"The others promised they'd be home by ten-thirty." She flashed Will a smile. She didn't want trouble. She didn't want him angry at her.

"Every fuckin' cent I earn is going to programs. Pro-

73

grams. Programs. The government is eatin' up my pay check, gobbling up my pay check," Joe said.

"Joe," Kathy said sharply.

"It's the truth. The fuckin' country's going to the fuckin' dogs."

Will felt a million miles away. Somewhere, someone was talking about going to midnight Mass in the old neighborhood, somewhere someone was talking about *Deep Throat*. Almost three dimensionally he heard the chomp of potato chips, the gurgle of beer going down. He felt as though he were enclosed in a glass paperweight. If they shook the outside of his glass prison, snow would fall, like the heavy glass round thing that sat on his uncle's desk when he was a little boy. Why didn't they go home, those strangers out there? They may as well be from Tibet. They belonged to his wife, to her world. He had two papers to do for school over the vacation. How would he ever get them done? How would he ever be able to concentrate? There was a ring of perspiration around the underarm of Kathy's dress. The apartment was overheated. He would have to speak to the super about that. And yet Kathy looked pretty in this light. Her face was flushed. She was happy to see those boors with their bellies and neanderthal ideas.

"So I hear you're leaving the little sister alone for a few days or so, Will." Dan cut through his transparent house. Will felt his glass world shatter around him into a thousand pieces.

"Right. It's just too expensive for the both of us to go."

"You've never gone to sales meetings before," Joe said, leaning forward over his belly for a handful of potato chips.

"The company wants me to go to this one," Will felt a pain over his left eye.

"Say, would you fellows mind terribly if I went into

74

the other room?" Will asked. "I've got two papers due after Christmas for school, and I don't know how I'm going to get them done."

"Sure, Will, sure. Well, listen, fella, it was great seeing you. Don't make such a stranger out of yourself, for Christ sakes. Ma was asking for you just the other day."

"Will, I didn't know you were going to work tonight," Kathy said, looking disappointed. "It's a weekend."

"I know, but I've only got these books out of the law library for a short time and I've just got to research these cases. See you around, boys."

Will got up and shook Dan's and then Joe's hand. Neither man got up but leaned forward. Mary, who had not said a word all evening, looked at Will with large blue eyes over her can of beer. Will took another can with him into the bedroom.

Walking into the room, he thought of one-word books. Just one-words stuck in his head. "Plague," "Vagabond," "Exiles." How the fuck was he supposed to crack a law book in this frame of mind? Without realizing it, he slammed the door to the bedroom so hard that the picture of Maria and Carol Cerutti sitting on the lace doily on the dresser fell flat, flat on its face.

10

Saturday morning Arnold picked Becky up early.

"Mom hates us to be late for lunch. She really makes a fuss."

Arnold's car was off-white. The seats were covered with off-white leather with a hint of green. He kept it immaculate. There was a little garbage bag in front where he threw his Kleenex and cigarettes. He had taken a piece of Kleenex and wiped the seat before Becky got into the car and had wet the edge and rubbed the dashboard to rid it of some new fine bits of dust that squeezed in.

They didn't talk very much on the parkway to the island. It was a gray day, and the Fifty-ninth Street bridge had seemed more ominous than usual to Becky. She didn't like bridges, and Arnold made her nervous, driving with one hand, the other one fiddling with a vial of Binaca which he would spray into his mouth at almost every other red light.

"Listen, do me a favor, don't bring up about that commune stuff, would you mind, hon? I don't think Dad would really dig that trip too much. Y'know what I mean?"

Becky was off drugs now, but still liked to smoke pot, but Arnold wouldn't touch it. He would barely drink, either.

"Don't you think that skirt's a little short, Becky?"

Becky had chosen what to wear very carefully. An expensive suede skirt in a rich dark brown was offset by a beige turtleneck blouse with puffed sleeves. She wore her hundred-dollar brown high boots with the outfit topped by a long fur-lined Afghanistan coat. The coat went to the floor, and Becky thought the short skirt under it was a surprise, a becoming fashionable look.

"Well, no, as a matter of fact. I sort of thought it looked chic."

Arnold took a sidelong critical glance at her long legs emerging out from the coat as she sat in the front seat with her legs crossed.

"Hey, Beck, flick your ashes in the ashtray, okay, hon? Some of that stuff really stains the rug if it's stepped on."

There was no more mention of the skirt or the ashes or anything for that matter since Arnold had put the radio on for some football scores. He listened intently, alternately smoking and squirting Binaca into his mouth. Becky filed her nails, smoothed her skirt, looked out at the lowness of Long Island things. She couldn't get over how flat everything looked, everything almost truncated.

She looked forward to the beautiful house. Arnold seemed to take it for granted, all that opulence, but to Becky, who had been brought up in a two-bedroom flat in Greenwich Village and shared a bathroom with her mother and father for all of her eighteen years, it was Shangri La. Mamie would be there. She had been the housekeeper since Arnold was ten, and Walter, her husband, had been with the family almost as long. They had three dogs and that seemed like the height of luxury and pleasure. When she lived in the commune, she tended the rabbits and had two dogs to take care of, and they had given her enormous pleasure. A city child, dogs meant country to Becky, freedom, air.

The Berkowitzes lived in an exclusive section of the Long Island suburb where they had settled twenty years ago. They had moved from a small house across the street from the school which all three Berkowitz boys had attended to what could be considered a mansion even by the upper-middle-class standards of the suburb. Louis had made unexpected money during World War II, as did many of his fellow commuters on the Long Island Railroad. All three sons were now in the textile business with him, along with one son-in-law.

A sign "Rondalay" spelled out in little bulbs that lit up in the dark was on one side of the driveway, on the other, "Berkowitz." Two stone lions guarded the entrance. The way was circular, and by the time Arnold swooped in front of the house, Becky was already impressed. It looked baronial, Elizabethan in scope, all white stucco with brown-wood trim, punctuated by masses of stone. To the left in the back was a swimming pool, to the right, down at the end of what seemed an endless sweep of lawn, was a tennis court.

"Hello, son," Louis boomed from the doorway.

He was wearing a red Chinese silk smoking jacket, white shirt and ascot. Becky couldn't make out if the pants were black or gray, but she saw how handsome he was. His cheeks were ruddy, well tanned. He stretched out his arms.

"Well, Becky, give the old man a hug."

Arnold stood by, unsmiling. He began unbuttoning his coat and taking off his cashmere muffler.

"It sure is nice to have such a pretty girl joining the family. Take off your coat and get acquainted." Louis had his arm around Becky's waist now and was moving it around almost grazing her breast.

The hall floor was stained a deep dark brown and

had a high gloss of polyurethane over it. It was covered with an exquisite oriental rug.

"Walter," Louis bellowed, "where the hell is that *schwartze*? I swear, he's never around when you want him. WALTER, where the hell are you?"

Out from behind her, Becky heard someone running. Walter, a black man in his sixties with a smooth unlined face and gray curling hair, took Becky's coat. His black shoes were polished to a high shine, and his white jacket was spotless.

"Hello, Walter," Arnold said.

Becky wondered whether Walter had a last name, but he had disappeared before she had a chance to ask.

"There you are." Sarah Berkowitz swept down a stairway that circled the hall. "How are you, Becky?" she said grandly. "I'm so glad you could come." As she offered her left cheek, the odor of Joy assaulted Becky's nostrils. Sarah's chest, a shelf-like affair, jutted out from a shocking pink satin caftan. Around her neck were three strands of Indian silver chains studded with turquoise. Long turquoise earrings hung from earlobes that looked as though they were made of elastic.

"Not everybody's here yet, so let's go on the sun porch," Sarah said. It was 11:30 in the morning by the oversized grandfather clock chiming in the hall. As they passed through the living room, Becky was struck by the tone of the room. It all matched. Everything was in shades of blue. Pale blue drapes, dark blue covering the couch, azure blue chintz on two oversized easy chairs in front of the fireplace. Everything looked as though it had been bought yesterday.

The sun porch was beautiful, all yellow and green, suffocated with light. What could probably double as a punch bowl sat on a white iron table filled to the brim with the largest shrimp Becky had ever seen.

They looked as though they were climbing over the sides. Great bowls of cocktail sauce sat alongside it, and oversized olives and celery, carrots cut very thin rested on a silver platter. Bloody Marys in large wine glasses stood on a glass bar in the corner.

"Take a load off," Louis said, indicating a chair covered with yellow-and-green silk. Outside the glass doors Becky could see three dogs frolicking on dried patches of lawn. Old snow sat in clumps, frozen into small hills, and burlap bags tied at the neck of plants made strangely ominous hoods at the far end of the garden.

"So. What's new?" Louis Berkowitz settled onto a white couch dotted by twenty cushions.

"Well . . ."

"Where the hell are those boys? They know Saturday lunch is promptly at noon. Sarah, did you call? Who was that I heard you on the phone with?"

"Marlene. She said they'd be a little late. One of the kids wasn't home from bar mitzvah practice yet."

"I don't think that's what they call it, sweetie. I can't believe that kid is old enough to be bar mitzvahed. Can you? Do you think I look old enough to have a bar mitzvah boy for a grandson? Don't answer that."

"Absolutely not, Mr. Berkowitz," Becky answered what was expected. "You really are very young looking."

"Well, first thing, young lady, for you to understand, is not to call me Mr. Berkowitz. We're very informal here and besides, it does make me feel old to be called Mister, especially by such a pretty young thing like you. Know what I mean?"

The star in the sapphire on his pinky beckoned to Becky.

There was a commotion at the front door.

"Oh, good, here's everybody." Sarah flounced up

and rushed through the living room to the front door.

So far, Arnold hadn't said a word, and Becky looked appealingly at him for some kind of connection.

Louis ignored her.

"So what happened with the Feinbergs?" Louis turned to his son. "Those sons-of-bitches would take your last nickel. They'd sell their own fucking grandmother to make a buck. I hope you gave them what for and told them we wouldn't put up with their shit anymore. They're overcharging us like crazy. Who the hell do they think they're kidding? Do they really think they're putting something over on us, for Chrissakes? So what did you tell them, Arnold?"

"Look, Dad, do we have to talk about it now? I'll tell you in the office, Mon . . ."

"Listen, kid, that deal is going to cost the firm thousands and I mean thousands of dollars, and if you think you're going to sit there and tell me that you don't want to talk about it till Monday, then you've got another think coming." Louis' voice was very loud now, and he punctuated his final remark by dipping his shrimp so hard into the silver bowl that the red stuff splashed over the table.

"Now, Louis, baby, don't start the day off by yelling. Say hello to the kids." Sarah was beaming in the doorway, holding the hand of a beautiful dimpled child stuffed into a snowsuit.

"Well, well," Louis bellowed, "if it isn't the Rover boys," as his other two sons entered the room. Suddenly, there was a flurry of activity, snowsuits being removed and loud kissing.

Becky found herself shaking hands with two other Arnolds, one younger and one older. Arnold's brother Hal, who looked about forty, was beginning to lose his hair, a sad hereditary irony, being the progeny of a father in his seventies with a fine head of hair. It was a prediction of things to come. Hal had gone to fat, and the lines that were beginning to pull down the corners of his mouth indicated the sweet smell of excess. He looked as though he had had too many women, eaten too many French dinners, drunk too much vintage wine, and hadn't enjoyed any of it.

Phil, the "baby" of the family, was in his early twenties, and had married a girl last year who came from a very rich family. Arnold had mentioned to Becky that Phil's wife had just spent $100,000 decorating their one-bedroom Park Avenue apartment, and had really not yet finished the job. Amanda was a little older than Becky. She was in Palm Beach with her parents now, Arnold had said, since Phil couldn't get away from the office and she couldn't take the hard New York winter.

"Well, what do you think, isn't she a doll?" Louis had his hand around Becky's waist again.

Everyone, including three or four black-eyed children who had finally stripped down to one layer of clothing, nodded somber approval.

"Where the hell is Ethel? That girl doesn't know her ass from her elbow when it comes to being on time. So? Where is she, Sarah?"

"Louis, dear, she'll be here. She had trouble with her car. The anti-freeze leaked out."

"That's not the only thing that leaked out."

"Louis."

"Sarah, let me talk. As you know, this is my house and I can say whatever I goddamn well please."

"All right, Louis," she patted his arm and sighed. "Now with all your yelling, I hear the car coming. Eat, everybody, the shrimp are fantastic. The fishman puts them away for me, they're the best. The best, the absolute best, he said."

"Here I am, Mother, I'm sorry I'm late. The car

kept stalling on me." Ethel Winston swept into the room. Ethel was six feet tall, forty-five years old, and her father's favorite. "She's the only one with a brain in the whole bunch," Louis would say, but Ethel had chosen to stay out of the business, spending her time traveling. Her ex-husband, Paul Winston (nee Weinstein), stayed with the firm after their divorce, until he bought into a chalet in Southern France.

Becky saw more food than she had at one sitting in her life. Even more than the last time she had come. The centerpiece was an enormous Haitian salad bowl filled with fruit. Enormous apples and oranges, green grapes swelling their skins, purple grapes draped over the mountains of pears and grapefruits. She couldn't imagine where they got so much out-of-season fruit. The sideboard was sighing under the weight of platters filled with turkey and stuffing, cranberries with nuts in them, sweet potatoes with marshmallows on top, wild rice and kasha, slices of the traditional Jewish twist from the Friday night before were piled high in a gold-ringed dish, and salad greens and crab apples, fruit compote and fresh stringbeans with almonds stretched across the table.

At everyone's place, chicken soup with noodles in gold Spode china bowls was steaming.

"O.K., Becky, you sit on my left side. You don't mind, Arnold, do you? Let's eat, everybody." Hal's three children had a contest as to who could schlurp the loudest.

"Quiet, where the hell do you kids think you are? Marlene, is that the way you train those kids? You'd think in school they'd teach you better."

Johnny, the twelve-year-old, the ringleader, buried his head in his napkin. Ellen and Nadia, eight and ten, burst into uncontrollable giggles.

"Did you hear what your grandfather said?" Marlene, a small birdlike blonde who had shocked her husband and gone back to school to get a Master's in psychology, looked sternly at the children. She flushed at Louis' remark, then winked at Johnny as the giggling subsided.

"Well, here we are, one big happy family. And to have you share this all with us, Becky."

"Thank you, Mr. . . ."

"Uh-uh, you remember what I said."

Arnold had been seated next to Becky. He kept touching her hair and putting his arm around her chair.

"So what do you think of us so far? Noisy but nice, right?" Hal, who sat across from Becky, gesticulated with his fork.

"Speak for yourself," Louis shouted. "Listen, Hal, did you ever collect from that colored guy, the trucker who was robbing us blind?"

"Yeh, Pop," Hal was digging into the browned marshmallow topping. It made a crunching sound. "The guy really had a racket going."

"I'm telling you, you can't trust 'em. I knew it, I knew that guy was on welfare and collecting a salary, too. Probably giving the money to some chippie up in Harlem."

"Lou."

"Listen, Sarah, don't Lou me, it's the God's honest truth and everybody knows it. They are bleeding this city dry. You want to know why we're in such trouble? You want to know why that Carey doesn't know what he's doing? Simple. It's the same old thing, it hasn't changed one bit. The guys are bad enough, but it's those colored girls who go and get knocked up and have about eight kids and we, you and I, we taxpayers have to pay for it. Whoever invented welfare should be shot. I'll never forget the time Susskind had some of those broads on TV, welfare mothers and they talked about how hard it was to make ends meet and

84

get shoes for the kids and hot lunches. Sure, who could support all those kids? If they'd stop screwing so much and getting a different father for each kid and go out and earn a decent living, maybe they wouldn't have any problems. Bleeding the city, that's what they're doing. We're paying for them to have a good time."

Walter was bending down in front of Becky on her left with a platter of turkey and stuffing. All Becky could see was the top of his head. There were tiny beads of perspiration on the tightly curled gray.

"It's the truth. Welfare is going to shove New York City into the Hudson River. There's going to be no more New York. Kiss it good-bye if we keep paying to support the habits of lazy good-for-nothings who just want to suck tit. The tit is the city. I'm telling you, and it's our hard-earned money that's paying for it."

Mamie, a light-skinned black in a starched black uniform with a white apron, was pouring water in the glasses.

Phil nudged Hal, in between bites. "Remember that gorgeous black model you used to know? Whatever happened to her?" Becky heard him and quickly glanced at Marlene who didn't blink an eye.

"It's the God's honest truth, don't get me on that. I'm as liberal as the next guy, you all know that. I was a charter member of the NAACP. No question they should have equal opportunity, no question. But, Jesus, they got to work for it, just like we did. I killed myself. I didn't have a pot to pee in when my folks came to this country, but I went to work at thirteen and have been working since. Why, you tell me why," he said to no one in particular, "why can't they do that? They're lazy, I'm telling you. Now granted, like that gentleman we met at that dinner one time, what was his name, Sarah? That Roy Wilkins, now he was a gentleman. He learned, he worked. And listen, Marlene, I'll tell you something, if you're still thinking about putting those kids in that bussed school, you're going to hear from me." Looks were exchanged across the table. Silence.

Ethel, sitting on Louis' right, put her hand on her father's arm. "Look, Dad, please, let's not get into that today. Come on. We've discussed it all till we're blue in the face. We never get anywhere with it, you know that."

"Now, Ethel, you know me longer than anybody here." Sarah looked up. Nobody said anything. "And you know that I'm a fair man, a liberal man. I insist that colored people should get as good an education as white. No question about that. You know I feel that way, but, Christ, then put the money into the ghetto schools. Pour money into them, that's fine with me. Build swimming pools and make them safe. But to bus little kids long distances to go to the white school is insane. Absolutely crazy. And do you know what? The coloreds don't like it either. You know that, don't you? They want to be with their own. You know that." Louis' face was getting redder. Ethel patted his arm.

"Look, Louis. We all know that, and no one is disagreeing with you. No one. Except maybe Marlene, and you know she'll come around." She smoothed the top of his white mane.

Tight-lipped, Marlene was silent. She did not look at her husband.

Hal looked at Becky. "So tell us about yourself, Becky. My brother was always known for his taste in women. I'm telling you, Arnie. You picked a winner this time. Sexy eyes. Real sexy eyes."

"God, this turkey is wet. Sarah, what the hell did Mamie do to it this time? You'd think by this time she would know the way I like it. It's wringing wet. Turkey should be crisp. Crisp skin. This is loose. What the hell happened this week?"

"I don't know, Lou. I'll talk to her. Maybe she forgot to put the foil around it."

"Did you see the David Frost-Nixon program?"

"One of the best things that ever happened to this country," Louis said, his mouth full of beans and apple. "Only one thing wrong with Nixon. He wasn't tough enough. He should have burned those tapes."

"He's insane, and he's crooked," Marlene said quietly.

"Listen, Marlene. It's very well for you to be so high and mighty about the whole thing, but as I remember, you voted for him, too. Just like the rest of us." Louis went in for the kill. "You knew that under Nixon we were making more money than we ever had. You knew that. You knew that the guy was trying to stop the war and that that Christmas bombing was the only way he could finally scare those bastards in Hanoi. You knew that as well as the rest of us. Sure, Watergate was terrible. But if you don't think the Kennedys did dirty tricks, too, if you don't think that Johnson or even your God Roosevelt didn't resort to that stuff, then you've got another think coming. They all do it. It's politics. It's what makes the ball bounce. You don't think people don't keep two sets of books. You don't think that people finagle like crazy on their income tax. Everybody does it. Why are you so high and mighty, so much better than anybody else that you can't see it?"

Marlene was not prepared for the onslaught and was embarrassed in front of her children. She would never have the strength to follow through with her father-in-law. She pulled back and took a sip of water.

"Listen, Dad," Hal said.

"Listen what? This is a big, wonderful country, and sure, Nixon made some mistakes, but so do a lot of other people. Listen, for God's sake, look what came out about the Kennedys' screwing every piece of tail

87

in sight. That's a President? That's an attorney general? Nobody's better than anybody else. You know that. I've always taught you that. And if that's the case, it's all out there for all of us. You got to go out and get it. You got to have courage and be aggressive about it.

"This is my house, and I deserve to have food cooked the way I like it. Where do you think we'd all be if it weren't for me? I made that business out of nothing. Nothing. And when I go, believe you me, nobody's getting a nickel unless I see that you know how to run the business. I sure as hell don't see any indication of it now. Paul, the ex-son-in-law's got more sense than the three of you boys put together. You got to be on your toes, you got to be ready for what the next guy is going to slip you. You got to know what it feels like to be the boss. I'm the boss, and I know what it feels like, and that's why we can eat the way we do and take trips and put the kind of clothes on our backs that we do."

Louis was indefatigable. Becky looked at him, fascinated. Everyone went on eating as he developed his theme, pausing only to put the food in his mouth.

Within moments, Mamie and Walter had cleared the table, brushed the crumbs away from the white tablecloth, and dabbed soiled spots with a cloth dipped in water. A chocolate cake, apple pie and bachla vah was put on the sideboard along with pitchers of milk and pots of tea and coffee. A large round bowl was filled to the top with vanilla ice cream.

Becky felt tight in her clothes. She ached to unzip her skirt. The children rushed to the sideboard and began filling their plates. Walter brought a sample of everything to Louis.

"Tea. With lemon," he said to Walter.

"Watching your figure? She doesn't have to worry one bit, does she Arnold," Sarah said to her son.

Becky felt as though they were speaking about some cardboard cutout of her image resting in a closet in the next room.

"I'm so stuffed, I can hardly move," Becky turned to Arnold, bending her head down to whisper to him.

"Me, too." He touched his hand to her cheek, making sure his father's quick eye didn't miss the movement.

"O.K. enough talk. Everybody finished? You girls go amuse yourselves. I got to talk to the boys for a minute. Ethel, you can come into the den if you want with us."

"No, thanks, Pop. I really came over to say hello to Becky. I'm going to the Nevelson show at the Modern at five. There's a big private party there tonight for her."

"She the one with the eyelashes?"

"Yes, Lou. I should have hoped that by this time I would have taught you a little more about modern art. She's one of the most powerful women sculptors of the century."

"Yeah? Well, they look like building blocks to me. That's the dame who's got that big piece on Park Avenue, right? With holes in it, like she forgot to finish it? Yeah, I know the one. Well, have a good time. When we going to see you?"

"Daddy, I'll keep in touch. Just take care of yourself and don't be too hard on the boys. Send my regards to Paul."

"Don't you ever talk to him?" Louis pushed himself away from the table. His napkin fell to the floor.

"Not much. Listen, Pop, I bequeathed him to you. He's yours to worry about and take care of now. Look, bye-bye, I've got to go. So nice to meet you, Becky. See you at the wedding." Ethel bent down and put her cheek on Becky's. Becky couldn't quite tell

89

whether she was expected to kiss it or not. She opted to do nothing.

The men disappeared into the den where another fire was blazing. Sarah disappeared into the kitchen to confront Mamie about the turkey moisture. Marlene was gathering up her children.

Becky, finding herself alone for the moment, the silence a surprise, went up to Marlene.

"Nixon *is* a crook," was all she could think of saying.

Marlene looked straight at her. "All I can say is, good luck. I wish you the best. Welcome to Berkowitz land." She kissed Becky on the cheek. Her lips were cold.

Driving home late that afternoon, Arnold was again silent. Becky admired his profile against the dusk. The radio was turned up very loud. He barely kissed her good-bye when he took her to her door.

11

Sunday there was a murder on the West Side. Someone had slashed the throat of a pretty young psychiatric social worker. The Monday morning papers were full of the smiling face, cut from some graduate school yearbook. The *Daily News* spared none of the details. Her young psychiatrist husband had been on television the night before, a bearded, serious looking man whose glazed look pleaded for the nightmare to disappear. There were interviews with all the neighbors who had praised the girl's friendliness and sweet disposition.

"Another goddamn murder. Do you think she could have opened the door to someone? They lived near you, Will, I think in a basement flat between Columbus and Amsterdam on Seventy-eighth. It's got to be a black or some Puerto Rican, I just know it. I'll bet she was kind to some guy in the street and he followed her home and did that." Bob's face was red. He was thinking of his Eleanor alone in the apartment, helpless in bed. If anybody did that to her, slit her throat, he would kill. "I'm a gentle man, you know that, but I'll tell you, if anyone came near Eleanor, I'd kill. Strangle him with my bare hands. That West Side is lethal, just lethal. I don't know how you can stay there. Don't you worry about Kathy and the kids over there? Look at that face, she's just a kid. Ear to ear. Too much, it's just too much."

Bob's outrage was uncharacteristic and, as Will took the paper that he thrust at him, he saw the worry etched into his face.

"Take it easy, Bob. First of all, you tell me how you know it was a Puerto Rican or a black? I want to tell you something. At Riker's Island, you'd think there was never a crime committed by a white just because they set the bail so high. Look, Bob, don't believe everything you read. Sure, there are lots of crimes being committed by blacks, but the whites are out there, too, plenty. Don't jump to conclusions."

"Well," Bob said, pushing open the glass doors with Robertson Stellars painted on in gold with black trim, "all I know is, the West Side stinks and I think you should get out."

Will was used to the West Side, but sometimes it depressed him terribly. Recently, coming home very late, the cab had let him off by mistake at Eighty-sixth and

Broadway and he had to walk the few blocks to his door.

Lying in the doorway of a deserted store at two in the morning on that freezing night was a man who looked as though his body were stuffed with rags. He was Ray Bolger in the *Wizard of Oz,* a burlap bag with no bones. Will hurried by at first, thinking it was an old discarded sack, but then he saw a wine bottle and a filthy white undershirt peeking out from a thin cotton jacket. That and trousers with slits in the knees was all the man was wearing. His bloody feet were wrapped in newspapers. There were no shoes. Someone had stolen his shoes. When he looked at him closer, he saw that the man was bleeding from the mouth.

Immediately, Will felt a rage in his throat. He was afraid it would drown him. The indignity of no shoes, newspapers for shoes on a freezing night filled him with an uncontrollable anger. He would have liked to put his fist through the brick wall against which the man was lying. Nobody cared, goddamn it. Nobody paid any attention. They're all over, he had thought, all over this fucking city, these people who nobody ever looks at, who are stepped over, looked through. He wanted to run. He didn't want to see anymore.

Instead, he bent down to the man, without thinking, without decision. The man was dying. He was certain of it. The blood had been flowing from his nose and was caked on his face from the cold. There was fresh blood coming out of his mouth. He put his hand on his heart. The man was not old, but looked fifty. His skin was very white, with dirt encrusted on it. It was cold, but he was still alive. Will stood up and looked around; the streets were deserted. In the distance he saw the light on top of a taxi coming toward him.

He began picking up the man. He smelled. Of vomit and old wine and dreams flushed down the toilet, Will had thought. As he dragged the shell of him toward the corner, trying to catch the cabbie's attention, all he kept thinking of was the little boy that man had been once. A corny, predictable, cliche thought, he observed, but this poor slob, this bag of bones, this failure who didn't have a fucking chance in this system, was once a little boy and had a mother just like everybody else.

The man could not stand upright, but was struggling to by some inner force. Will laid him down on the sidewalk and ran out into the street and flagged the cab down. It had been very late. And very cold.

"Listen, Jack, take this guy to Bellevue. He's dying. He'll freeze to death on these streets. See if you can help me get him in the cab."

The cab driver peered at him through the passenger's window. Timorously, he got out and walked carefully to Will struggling with the man.

Looking at them both, he said, "Look, man, that guy's going to bleed all over my back seat."

"Don't worry about it," Will snapped. "I'm telling you, he's going to die if he doesn't get to that emergency ward soon." He was still under control, but the cabbie could see that in one minute he would explode.

"O.K. O.K." He went to the front and took out the New York *Post* which he spread all over the back seat. Will saw a moment of pity mixed with the contempt in the man's eyes as they pulled the derelict across the back seat.

Will had taken out some bills and gave them to the man. He could barely get the words out. "O.K. Take him there, they'll come out and get him. Take him to the emergency ward."

Will had not told anyone about this. He was no hero, he wasn't anything. Sometimes he just couldn't stand how lousy things were.

He had railed to himself that night, railed at a

world where a man could die in the streets. He railed at a world where he had to get up and go to a job in the morning that was as predictable as the back of his hand. He had lain awake that night almost till dawn and the clang of garbage trucks assured him he had only an hour more of sleeping time left.

He was forty-two years old, he thought just before he dropped off to sleep. Forty-two years old. With what? With what to show for it?

When he woke an hour later, the inside of his bottom lip was bloody. He had bitten himself in his sleep.

"What a way to start the week," Bob said, searing into Will's reverie. "I feel so sorry for that poor husband. What a Christmas this is going to be for him. Poor guy. Imagine what that must be like, coming home and finding your wife murdered. You know what it is, it's those welfare hotels so close to the residential areas, that's what it is. The city's killing us with those hotels, I'm telling you, Will. Beame's got to do something about it, I don't know what, I'm no expert, God knows, but . . ."

"Hi, boys, ready for the day's big doings?" Flo flashed Will and Bob her friendliest smile. She loved Bob. He was gentle and polite. Robbins was another story. Her challenge daily was to get a smile out of him, to wipe the scowl off his face. Once or twice she had tried to talk about law school with him—they both went to Fordham—but he avoided it, and her. She was certain of it. Maybe because he had been at it ten years, much longer than she had. Maybe he was embarrassed about it. But so what? It wasn't reason enough to walk around like he just sucked on a lemon. Robbins was not one of her favorite people. Not by a long shot.

Will and Bob parted for their respective offices, both sensing the tension in the air. Office parties did that to people, offering some kind of welcome break in the endless routine, offering some kind of something to look forward to.

Will nodded to Letty Gold as she passed.

"What time is the party this afternoon, Letty, do you happen to know?"

"Sure, two. It starts at two o'clock. You planning to stay for it?"

"Awhile, just awhile. I'll see you later, Letty." Letty watched him move slowly into his office. She noticed that someone had nailed some mistletoe up on the molding of Will's office. She watched him look up, shake his head, and predictably pull it down. She knew he would.

Stan MacKail had gone all out this year, beyond the budget allotted to him by the vice-presidents. There was a full bar instead of only punch, and cold cuts and hors d'oeuvres ordered from a gourmet delicatessen. A bartender had been hired, a handsome black man with a full mustache, whose wife would help serve.

Some of the desks had been arranged to form a long serving place, covered by an enormous white cloth. Wreaths had been attached to it and holly and berries had been carefully placed between plates full of nuts and potato chips.

At 2 P.M. sharp, Flo turned off the switchboard and the girls stepped into the ladies room to freshen up. Everyone neatened their desks and put away "in" and "out" baskets, paper and pencils; a flurry, like snowflakes caused by the wind. There was a special kind of tension; everyone expected something from this day.

A whole week lay ahead for most of the office; a whole week when they wouldn't see each other, wouldn't see the same faces they had been seeing every day for the past year.

"Letty, you look gorgeous," Becky said, as they both primped in the ladies' room mirror.

"Really?" Letty took another look at herself.

"I don't know what it is. You look groovy."

"That is hardly an appropriate adjective for me. Groovy I'm not."

"Letty, Priscilla's on something," Becky said suddenly. "She sure is acting queer. Queerer than usual. I almost fell over her when I came into the john a few minutes ago. Singing. She was singing a Beatles' song at the top of her lungs. In the john. I'm sure MacKail could have heard it all the way back in his office."

"I doubt it. She's probably just feeling good, Beck, don't worry about it. How was the Berkowitzes' this weekend?" Letty asked.

"Well, it was all right. There was something I wanted to talk to you about about it, but I guess it can wait. It's getting late, and I've got to leave the party early and meet my mother at Bonniers before it closes. I'd better get out there and make an appearance. Maybe we can talk tonight. Maybe I can call you at home. Christ, the time is getting so short, Letty. The wedding's next week. I can't believe it, I just can't. You will be back for it, won't you?" Becky put her hand on Letty's arm.

"Becky, I promised. It's the day after I get back from my vacation. It's timed perfectly. I wouldn't miss it for the world, you know that. What happened this weekend? You sound strange about it. What's the matter?" Letty put the comb down after smoothing through her hair.

"Oh, nothing. Premarital jitters, I guess."

"You're going to have a good life."

"You think so?"

"I know so. Come on, Becky, let's just have a gay old time. Try not to get pinched too much and stay away from Herb. I think he's got a thing for you."

"I'm sure he's never seen what I look like. I'm sure I've been a big blur to his watery eyes all this time."

The two pushed through the door of the ladies room to the main corridor. People were coming out of offices and cubicles into the main room where the food and drink were set up.

"There you are, Becky, we've been looking for you, we can't start without you," Flo held her glass high. "Come on, everybody, get a drink."

Frank Fairchild and Fred Santini stood in a corner with Dolores. Frank leaned his arm on the wall over her head and Fred stood quietly, sipping his drink.

"Dolores, where's Priscilla?" Fred asked.

"I think she's still in the john."

"She can't make herself more gorgeous than she is," Frank said.

"I don't know about that," Fred said, still smarting from his most recent encounter with Priscilla. "I'm kind of down on her at the moment."

"I bet you'd love to be, pal." Frank punched Fred in the shoulder.

Ignoring him, Fred said to Dolores, "I hear you two are going together for your week. Just the two of you alone?"

Frank looked straight at Dolores' chest. "Well, I can't see the girls being alone too long, can you, Fred?"

"Well, I don't know if I'm going to be going," Dolores said seriously. "I know Pris is definitely going, but I got stuff going on at home I may not be able to get out of."

"Well, you certainly will have to decide soon, won't you?" Frank said, looking over Dolores' shoulder at Priscilla who was walking toward the group with Stan MacKail.

"Well, well," Priscilla trilled, "this is where the élite meet, I suppose. You've all got drinks already. I wonder if you would be so kind as to get me a scotch on the rocks, Frank. I'd be ever grateful." Priscilla flashed Frank an irresistible smile. She was trying to be on her best behavior since she had somehow ended up walking down the hall with the big boss. But Mac-Kail was all right, she thought. She'd never had any trouble with him. He'd yelled at her once or twice, but he was a good egg. He tried. He was, she thought, good looking in a weak sort of way, and years ago had probably been stunning. She'd met him as he emerged from the bathroom where, she imagined, he had just brushed the omnipresent ash off his jacket, wet his gray hair before he combed it so that it would look a shade darker. He had probably sprayed some Jamaica Bay rum cologne on the inside of his shirt under the arms where he had perspired. Stan Mac-Kail was a perspirer. When he was working, when he was nervous, when he was calm.

Priscilla didn't think he fooled around now, and "you don't shit where you eat" was her motto anyway so she had always steered clear. But he had been fair with her, and she liked him. That Robbins character was another story. There was something about him. As though he knew all her secrets.

Priscilla looked around the room at the crowd. The room was full now, the bar knee-keep in people. Luckily, she didn't see Robbins. She would steer clear of him if she did.

"Letty," Agnes said shyly, "I'm going to the Lord Windsor next week. Have you ever been?"

"Only circumcised cocks there, Aggie. I don't know if that's your speed."

Everyone laughed. Agnes ignored Priscilla.

"Letty, I just came from Loehmann's, early this morning, where I picked up a few things for the trip. Would you like to see them?"

"Loehmann's?" Priscilla exploded. "You went all the way up to the Bronx before coming to work?"

"I was an hour late," Agnes explained.

"Yipes, that is fashion consciousness, that is what I

call being chic." Priscilla knew Agnes had brought the clothes from home to show them off.

"Well, I hope so," Agnes smiled, ignoring the sarcasm. "Would you like to see what I bought? I really got some great buys. Sometimes you can't do well at all there, but today it was a bonanza, a veritable bonanza."

"Let's see, Aggie, let's see what you got. Maybe we'll go up tomorrow before our trip and get some things," Letty said kindly, not knowing whether this would put Agnes in more jeopardy than she was already.

The group of women moved to the back of the room, away from the crowd, and next to Agnes' desk.

Agnes pulled out an enormous purple box with Loehmann's written on it in bold letters. She pulled out one more beautiful garment after another.

"You don't mean to say you bought all this this morning, Aggie?" Priscilla fingered a rose-colored evening gown and looked at the label. "Where did you get all the money? This stuff is worth a fortune. There's about a thousand dollars' worth of stuff here. I'm sure that's a Stephen Burrows. Even though they've cut the labels out, I can tell by the code on the ticket. This silk shirt is definitely Dior, look at the sleeve, it's embroidered on it."

Little spots of red enflamed Agnes' cheeks as she picked up a peach-colored jumpsuit with mother of pearl buttons.

"I think this is the most divine shade I have ever seen," Agnes said. Her voice became more animated, her fingers smoothed the material lovingly. "It came in beige and light blue, but I couldn't resist this. It was on sale."

"Gorgeous, Ag, just sensational. You're going to knock 'em dead up there. You're going to do a mean hustle in that outfit," Becky said.

"I can't do those dances too well, but maybe this time I'll take some lessons." She held up a green backless long dress against her. "Letty, isn't this beautiful?"

"Oh, Agnes, your choices are exquisite. You're going to be so lovely."

Priscilla, on her third drink by now, put the rose gown up against her. "Aggie, this is sure a sexy number. All lined, too. Don't you think it will show too much boob for you?"

"It was an incredible buy."

"Worth going without lunch for?"

"Priscilla," Wilma said, deliberately changing the subject, "where did you get that blouse? It's positively enticing."

Taken off guard, Priscilla flushed. "Right. Forty-nine fifty at Bendel's." Looking up at Wilma and Letty, she realized she'd been had as they looked at her décolletage. She saw Will Robbins from the corner of her eye walk into the room. He went over to a wall covered with files and took one out.

"Will you get a load of that Robbins. I can't believe him. There's a party going on, Christmas is coming, the goose getting fat and all that jazz, and that creep has got to go over to the new business file. I can't believe him. How do you like that, he's going back to his office. He's just too much."

Will looked neither to the right nor the left and walked back into his small office. He could feel the eyes of the girls on him, but he didn't seem to care.

"Doesn't that creep drink? What's with him?" Priscilla said. "He must think he's so goddamn much better than we are."

"I think he's kind of cute," Dolores said. "The strong, silent type."

"I'll bet he's a lousy lay."

"Priscilla, is that your main criteria for everything?" Becky asked.

"Just about, kid. What the hell else is there in this world?" Priscilla looked from one woman to the other. "Good Lord, will you look at the serious pusses on your faces. Life is full of good things and bad things, and one of the best good things is getting laid. And you know it and I know it. The difference between us is that I say it and you broads don't. I don't believe in beating around the bush. I'd rather have someone beating around my bush as a matter of fact."

Dolores guffawed.

"It's the truth. What the hell are you spending all this money for, Aggie, to go up to the Lord Windsor for. Not only for the room and everything, but all these gorgeous clothes? Which, I might add, you'll never find a place in a million years to wear again to in the city. What? To find a nice loving man to support you, or to get laid? Do you give head, Ag? Have you ever gone down on a man?"

"Priscilla, lay off. You really are too much. God, you don't screen one word," Wilma said.

Priscilla was feeling her power. None of them, except maybe Letty, could touch her, and she would test it to the limit.

"It happens to be the truth. I don't believe in this women's lib and consciousness raising crap, but I know that if women were really honest with each other, that's what it would come to. We like to get laid. We like to give it and get it. Period."

"Nothing else, nothing else's important in life, Priscilla?" Letty put her hand on Priscilla's arm.

"You tell me, you just tell me. Look at Becky here, all quivering and shivering on the eve of marriage to that gorgeous hunk of man." Becky was sitting at Agnes' desk, lighting up a cigarette. "What do you think, Ag, how'd you like to snag a guy like that?"

She did not wait for an answer.

"Well, he sure is great looking and . . ."

101

"When did you see him?" Becky asked.

"A couple of times, we all did, when he came by to take you to lunch."

"Becky, he really is a dream," Dolores said. "He is the catch of all time. Those looks, and his folks are loaded, I think the whole thing is so exciting."

"Well, he's wonderful. He really is. Very kind, and very generous, too."

"Are you going to move out to the Island near his parents?"

"I think so. Their house is beautiful."

Dolores was fighting the envy. How wonderful it would be to avoid the marketplace. To have someone of your own. She had had it with being single. She would give anything to be in Becky's place.

"How many acres?" Dolores, who lived in the Bronx with her parents, had been to Atlantic Beach a few times, but had never visited any of the beautiful homes she saw on the Island.

"There must be about three, and there's a lovely formal rose garden at the end of this long lawn walk. And, Dolores, they have dogs. Three of them. Three handsome dogs."

"Becky," Agnes said, "I'm so happy for you. I really am." To be in Becky's shoes would be heaven, she thought, would be the most wonderful thing in the world. To sleep with the same man every night and to feel his arms around you, to cook his favorite breakfast for him and to plant tulips for the spring and bring in mint from the garden for ice tea in the summer. Agnes, whose glass Dolores kept refilling, saw the dream in 3-D. It was right there, in front of her eyes, Mrs. Arnold Berkowitz, Agnes Berkowitz, how would that sound? Mrs. Friedman would love him and his parents might be too grand for her family, but they would adjust. And she would have an herb garden right out the kitchen window with sage and

102

parsley fresh for dinner. She had the most divine recipe for lamb with sage. She never had anybody to cook it for . . .

"Agnes . . ."

"Yes, yes."

"Agnes, eat something, there's so much good stuff. Let me get you something," Letty said. Agnes had been staring into space for the past minute and Letty ran interference for her. Everyone was drinking very fast. Priscilla took out a joint and began to light up.

Letty went up to the bar, took a serving fork from the roast beef platter and knocked it against several glasses. The tinny sound somehow was heard.

"Listen, everybody, we have an announcement. Come on. Quiet, everybody. I want to make a toast," she shouted. Finally, the din subsided.

"Let her talk," Herbie yelled. He was looking at Agnes' yellow scarf, tied neatly around her neck.

"Listen, everybody, I want to make a toast. This isn't only a Christmas party. This is not only a time to deck the halls with boughs of holly."

Everybody groaned.

"Look. I'm not good at this so I can't be clever or amusing. Just let me say that we're also celebrating Becky's marriage next week."

Applause. Priscilla put two fingers in her mouth and let out a strong whistle. Herbie looked at her admiringly. Dolores applauded by slapping her thigh with her free hand.

"Let's toast Becky and Arnie and wish them a wonderful life together. Come here, Becky." Becky moved shyly through a hill of people up to the bar. "Bring it in, girls," Letty shouted to the back of the room as Flo and Joy brought in a cake decorated with white icing and silver balls. A miniature bride and groom stood stiffly at the center, looking as though they were barely acquainted. "Congratulations, Becky" was written freely across the top in pink. Pink and green roses dotted the four corners.

Tears welled in Becky's eyes. "Oh, Lett. You shouldn't have done such a thing. Why?"

"Shush, for God's sake."

Letty looked at Flo and Joy standing on the sidelines and motioned to them to bring in the present. They handed it to Becky, who accepted it with tears on her cheeks.

Bob McKern and Stan MacKail stood to the side, applauding.

"Cute thing," McKern said.

"She really is, a little thin for my taste, but she just has to bat those eyes and you could just melt. How you doin', McKern? How's the wife?"

"Well, she's better, Stan. It was touch-and-go there for a while and we're still not out of the woods, but she seems to be finally regaining her strength."

MacKail looked at the man with pity, and, for a split second, envy. McKern's devotion to his wife and her to him was something MacKail could never understand. Margot had gotten more wiry with age, her skin leathered from an all-year-round tan. She spent most of her time on their boat or on the tennis court or golf course. She had retained the athletic good looks that had attracted him years ago, but not only had her body become hard, but her spirit as well. He barely remembered the girl she was. The house and the country club, her tennis and golf-playing friends who were as frosted and leathered as she, who stopped off more than once or twice at the halfway house on the course on a summer or fall afternoon to drink, that's where she was today. Their lives had turned into parties. When the kids were young, they would go down to the beach at sunrise and cook bacon on the coals. Now there were dinners at the beach with Thermoses filled with martinis, hot dogs and spuds, chicken and steaks done on the outdoor barbecue furnished by the Recreation Commission of their town. They all drank too much, he knew that, but it was beginning to show on Margot more. That slim, straight, tight body now had a belly in the middle of all the bones, a belly that was as rounded and full as a six-month fetus, as though all the martinis and all that white wine from endless Fourth of July picnics had settled there. There were tiny purple veins in her nose. He barely remembered the girl she had been, what they once were, or what their promise was. They had been a golden couple. Bronzed and athletic, leonine on the tennis court. The great American dream had been theirs for the plucking, but it all had gone by so fast; the babies, the starting out in Peter Cooper Village, the bigger apartment, the first house in the suburbs, the second house. He had a mortgage on his house now that would choke a horse. Two kids in college, two cars. Money just disappeared. He liked expensive suits. Good cigars. He had to keep everything going. It was up to him.

His hair, once blond and plentiful, was thinning at an alarming rate, and no one ever remarked anymore how much he resembled William Lundigan. He was getting a belly, too, above the belt, and found that he was more comfortable playing doubles in his Sunday game. Singles wore him out. He used to be able to stay up drinking all night, have great sex with Margot and then beat old Jack Davids down the street at three sets on his court. Now if they had sex once in two or three weeks, it was a lot. Margot usually was just too boozed up to even make a pretense at enjoying it, no less making him happy.

But it wasn't a bad life, not really, MacKail thought. It's just that when he saw a marriage endure like McKern's, he felt a twinge. Granted, the guy was a loser, stuck in the same job for twenty years or whatever it was, granted the guy lacked imagination, but he was unshakable on the subject of his wife. They still were in love, and the guy probably made half as much money as he did, and even though he acted like a scared rabbit sometimes, still he had that broad at home he was always buying presents for.

"Well, the best, the best of luck to you, Bob. I'm sure Eleanor will be all right."

"Thanks, Stan, thanks a lot. I know you mean it. Have you seen Robbins around?"

"Do you know I think the guy is back in his office working. He's sure never read *How to Win Friends and Influence People,* has he? Every single person in the office loathes him, and this will give them more ammunition."

"I don't loathe him," McKern said quietly. "He's my friend."

MacKail said quickly, "Well, you know what I mean, for God's sake. He's so defensive about everything and acts so superior all the time. Well, look, that's neither here nor there," he said, retrenching, aware again that he indeed was the one in the position of authority.

"He's probably in his office," McKern said. "He hates parties. I think I'll take him in a drink."

"Don't, Bob, I will. I'll go in. What does he drink?"

"Scotch, but I'd be glad to."

"No, no, never mind, it's Christmas, it's 'Joy to the World' time."

MacKail filled a glass with scotch and some ice and, feeling no pain, imbued with good will, went down the hall to Will's office

"Merry Christmas, Robbins." MacKail knocked on the molding outside the door. Without waiting to be invited in, he put the drink down on Will's desk. Will did not look up. "Why don't you come join us, Will? It's a great party."

106

"I've really got to finish this work before the vacation, Stan. I'm trying to get a Waiver of Premium on the Goodman case. The guy will never be able to work again. Both legs gone, one eye, loss of one arm. What the hell, MacKail . . ."

"Who's arguing with you? I never disagreed with the Waiver." He glanced at the pamphlets and three books open on Will's desk. "You sure are up on the new laws, aren't you? I talked to Franklin, the insurance commissioner, yesterday and he said you had been talking to him."

Will continued writing, ignoring MacKail and the drink.

"He couldn't get over your conscientiousness on the Goodman case. Jaffee may lose his license, thanks to the research you did."

"Look, MacKail, I want to get finished and get out. I want to finish this business before we all go away."

"You said that already, Robbins." MacKail felt himself getting angry. Not wanting to.

"Listen, Will."

"What is it, Stan?" Will looked up from his work. MacKail had had a lot to drink, he could tell. He felt a confession coming on. He didn't want it, he didn't want to deal with it. Before MacKail started talking, he felt his own throat get tight.

"Look, Will, you and I both know that you're the smartest one around here. You know more than the president of the company almost, and God, I'll admit it, you know more than me. You've got a better handle on all the business, especially in the life department, than any of us. Let's face it, Robbins, you know it and I know it, you probably should be doing my job. Should probably have my job. If you'd finished that degree and hadn't gotten stuck where you are, if you'd moved up and not let all these young punks steam ahead of you, you'd be where I am and maybe farther. Maybe farther. I want you to know that, Will. I want you to know that I know it. And I'm sorry. I'm sorry that things worked out the way they did. It's not my fault, it's not anybody's fault. It just worked out that way. I want you to know that."

Sonofabitch. Will heard the words in his head. If he concentrated hard enough, perhaps the words would disappear. Perhaps MacKail would go away. Why didn't the man just go away to his house in the country and his boring wife and two cars, his tennis rackets and his three-hundred-dollar suits.

"O.K. you don't have to like me, Robbins, nobody asked you to like me." MacKail was embarrassed by his outburst, begun in good faith. Robbins was making him feel like a fool. From outside the office, loud music was blaring and MacKail could hear Priscilla's laugh high over the roar. "I just wonder why you go to such lengths to make everybody hate you. O.K., it's obvious you don't have much use for me. You think you're smarter than I am, you catch me in mistakes. O.K. But you sit here poring over the contracts, eking out a living when you've got more on the ball than any of those hot-shot loud mouth salesmen. You could take the course, probably pass the training in a minute, probably get your CLU and make four times as much as you do now. Why don't you do it, Robbins? Why don't you, instead of sitting here day after day, going to the john, out to lunch, out to the water cooler, into the filing room and back. You never have a civil word for anybody, are a total loner except for your champion McKern, who's no great shakes himself. You walk around here with a scowl on your face, and even the file clerks who would ordinarily think you were sexy can't stand you. Listen, Robbins, I'm a no-crap guy. You know that about me. I've always played fair with you. If this sounds weird, then let it, I don't care. I'd like to be your friend. Hell, it's Christmas and the New Year is coming, and maybe I'm in my cups a little, but Robbins, I mean it. I'd like to be your friend." MacKail was out on a limb and he knew it, he knew he was putting himself in a position where Robbins could chop it down and disappear.

"Look, Stan," Will said, putting down his pencil. He took a long sip of the scotch. "Thanks for the drink, I appreciate it. But you know what? I don't want to be your friend. You're my boss. You run this department. That's good enough and enough for me." MacKail felt himself go sticky under the arms.

"Friendship with you or anybody here for me costs too much. If that sounds snobbish and rotten, then that's what I am. I don't care at this point. You've got to understand that I don't care. The cost of that kind of friendship just comes too high for me. It means talking about nothing, shooting the breeze, bullshiting and worse than that, it means pretending to be buddies. I don't have any buddies. I never did, not when I was a kid or in school or in the Army. I don't want a buddy. I can get along without a buddy. I can't fake it, Stan. I can't understand the lie of it. You can backslap and bullshit from now to kingdom come, it's your life, it's part of what your job is all about. I can't do it. I can't pretend. There's enough shit out there in the world that I have to contend with . . . where we have to be, what we're not . . . but I can't do it here. I can't with you or with anybody."

MacKail looked at Will, sensing the turmoil in him. Will made him angry, he felt sorry for him, he admired him, all at the same time. The man's arrogance and independence infuriated him. Will danced to his own tune for better or worse, and MacKail knew that on the other hand, he had followed the prepared score to the letter.

"Listen, Will, there's a lot of things in life we have

to do that we don't like. God, you've learned that already. If we have to kiss ass, we kiss ass. If I didn't carry on and bullshit with the bosses, where do you think I would be? That's what life's all about, for God's sake, none of us get anything for nothing. I'm not hurting anybody, I'm not doing anything dishonest, I've just learned to be smart. Expedient. And you tell me what the hell's wrong with learning to be expedient in a tough-shit world where everybody gives you points for altruism or independent thinking. None."

"Look, Stan, that's you. I can't. I can't kiss ass. Your whole life, as far as I'm concerned, is one big sham. If you want to take it out of my salary . . . dock me because I've said it . . . then do it. I mean it. Your whole life, as far as I'm concerned, is based on air. No substance, and you know what, it could all blow up in a minute. Someday some guy up there is not going to like the way you kiss ass. The rules will change. Or maybe somebody else's ass will be the important one, and he might not like your brand of kissing. Then where will you be? You'll have to change so many times the kind of person you're going to be according to who's up there, you've got to figure out which somebody up there likes you and give him what he wants. So where does that leave you, MacKail? Where are you in all this? The whole thing is a lie. One big pretense."

The noise from the other room was rising. The smell of pot filtered into Will's office.

MacKail didn't know what to say. He looked at Will's hands. The knuckles were white. That boy's going to burst wide open some day, he thought. "I hope you can keep it up, Robbins. I'm ten years older than you and I know that you're wrong. I've found it out. You can't live that way and survive. If it's ass kissing, as you call it, then that's what it is. I think you're a fool, because you seethe and store it all up inside, all that resentment and where does it go? The world stinks and we have to make the best of it."

"Right," Will said, getting up, gathering his papers, going to the clothes rack in his office and taking his jacket. "And I am. Thanks for the drink, MacKail."

The man infuriated MacKail. So dismissed, he turned on his heel, slamming the door. God, if he gave up kissing ass, he wouldn't be anywhere. He sniffed the air. He would have to ferret out the pot smokers and put a stop to that immediately.

"Mexican guys are gorgeous. All those black eyes and coal-black hair. The brochure from the travel agent has photos of the most divine men you've ever seen," Dolores was saying. "Becky, your Arnie almost looks Mexican or Italian or something. He's got to have the longest lashes on a man I've ever seen."

The music in the background was turned up louder as Herbie and one of the file clerks began to dance. Usually, decorum was honored superficially in the office since MacKail frowned on fraternization, believing it hurt efficiency, but the liquor and the music and the thought of a week of freedom was affecting everybody. No more subways, no more sealed windows and time clocks and deadlines and stale smoke smell and Monday morning moroseness. No more winter and no more sameness. No more routine, no more same faces and predictable conversations and tuna fish sandwiches sent up. No more. For just one week.

"So, when do you leave, Wilma?" Betty asked.

"Where you going, Will?" Priscilla said with exaggerated familiarity.

"Didn't I tell you, Priscilla, I thought I confided everything in you." Wilma took one step back.

"No, where? Come on, Wilma, forgive and forget. Let's good King Wenceslas it up this afternoon." Priscilla fell backward a bit, tripping over her own foot.

"Well, I'm going to California—north. I'm flying to

111

San Francisco and renting a car and I'm going to do what I've wanted to do all my life." Primly, Wilma smoothed her skirt and sat down. She couldn't stand in high heels for such a long time. "And then . . ."

"And then what, Will . . .?" Flo asked.

"Then I'm renting a car and take that fifteen mile or whatever it is drive in Monterey. It's supposed to be one of the most beautiful places in the whole world. I've seen pictures of Carmel that make it look like paradise. Like the perfect town. And I'll see Monterey. The whole bit."

"All by yourself?" Priscilla pursued.

"Of course. Why not? Just tell me why not?" Wilma said defensively.

"Now what kind of guy, for God's sake, are you going to meet driving in a car three thousand miles away from home on the one free week you've got?" Priscilla shouted. "That doesn't make sense to me at all. Who're you going to meet, a state policeman, waiters, night clerks? If I were you, I'd rethink the whole plan, Wilma. Doesn't make sense to me." Priscilla was sitting down now, her skirt hiked high.

"My dear," Wilma said, "when you get to be my age and are imbued with the wisdom of the ages, you find that finding a man ceases to be the great search of all time. There are, unbelievable, impossible as it may seem to you, in your state of perpetual heat, other things in life."

"Name one. Just one," Priscilla said, pointing her index finger into Wilma's face.

"Look, Priscilla, I'm losing patience with you," Wilma said, pushing her away. "I don't mind being alone. It's O.K. by me. I don't have to have a man with me, around me, inside me every minute like you do. And why the hell I have to explain it to the likes of you is beyond me. If I want to go enjoy and see one of the Eight Wonders of the World by myself, I figure that's my business. Right?"

Wilma flushed. Her hands were shaking. "Why do I have to feel like a freak, why do you have to make me feel like a freak if I want to take a motor trip by myself and see the Pacific at sunset? I sure as hell don't know why I'm even bothering to explain it to you."

"Wrong," Priscilla said. "You want a guy just as much as the rest of the ladies here."

"No, you're wrong," Wilma's eyes were flaming. "You're the one who's wrong, Priscilla. I'm going to go on this trip and be myself and not worry about meeting someone. And I'm going to have a ball, and I'm going to be just fine. Just put that in your pot and smoke it." Wilma walked heavily away.

Agnes and Becky glared at Priscilla.

"Well, I guess I just will," Priscilla said, getting up, smoothing her skirt over her hips. She felt her throat grow tight. She hadn't meant all that. She hadn't meant to hurt Wilma. Why did she do that? Why can't I keep my damn mouth shut, she thought, wobbling on her heels. What is it that I want? Why do they all read me that way? It isn't just sex. No, it's not just sex that I want.

Priscilla rolled a joint and began dancing by herself. Janet, who had been drinking one scotch after another, stood next to Agnes, and watched. She felt herself propelled toward Priscilla.

She had had enough; the girl had been cruel to Wilma and even though she wasn't such a fan of Wilma's, it was a rotten thing to do to her. She'd been throwing herself around the office for months now like some waterfront whore; all she ever talked about was sex. She'd had it. Priscilla could be funny as hell, brightening up some bleak Monday morning, but so what. It wasn't worth it. She felt something building in her.

"Cut it out, Priscilla."

She walked up to the middle of the floor where Priscilla had begun an elaborate solo.

"Cut what out, babe?" Priscilla continued dancing.

"Put the joint away. You're going to get us all in trouble."

"Oh, calm down. MacKail's not even in the room. He wouldn't know one if he fell over one."

"It's enough, Priscilla, put it away."

Priscilla could see that Janet was serious. Inez and Joy, who had taken a few puffs, knew it was inappropriate but Janet's wrath was not for them.

"I've had it, Priscilla. I've had it with your flaunting and your fawning, your filthy mouth and your dissolute ways."

"Dissolute, now, did you hear that, Dolores, we're dissolute."

"You sure as hell are. I'm sick of your revolting boy friends who hang around this place. I'm scared to death to go in the hall and go to the john for fear some of those characters will be loitering outside, with their beads and their long hair and their tight pants."

"Listen, Janet, be fair, be honest. It's what's in the tight pants that's a bit worrisome, right? Is that it?"

"Just shut up for a minute, can't you just shut up?" Janet was getting shrill but it had to be said. Why hadn't she said it all before? "You have no values, you or your compatriot over there. Your little echo, your little shadow. She doesn't have a mind of her own and probably never will as long as she hangs around with you."

"Listen, Janet, cool it, just cool it. What bug got up your ass, for God's sake? I'm sitting here minding my own business and you let me have it." Priscilla put her hand on Janet's arm.

"Don't touch me. Keep your hands off me." Janet's

voice pierced the smoke and the sounds in the room. Letty moved instinctively toward them.

"It's true," Janet said. "Everytime I sit on the toilet, I think I'm going to get some kind of disease or something. I don't know where you've been or where those characters have been, either."

"What's the matter, Janet, haven't been getting it lately? Too busy baby-sitting to spread your legs? What on earth are you letting all that frustration out on me for? Finger yourself if you can't get any, do something, but shit, don't let it out on me. I didn't do a thing."

"You've done plenty." Janet was out of control now. "Ask anybody. Ask any of the girls in the office. They think you're a pig. You give the word female a bad name. You brag and boast like any macho Mexican standing on a street corner, and you know what I think, I think the lady doth protest too much . . ."

"What the hell is that supposed to mean?"

Wilma, Letty, and Becky moved next to them. The music was so loud that their voices were just beginning to be heard.

"That's Shakespeare, Priscilla."

Priscilla wheeled around to Wilma.

"Don't talk down to me, kid. I know it's Shakespeare. I'm not dumb and I'm not stupid."

"Nobody said you were, Priscilla," Letty said. "Why don't you calm down and get something to eat. Put the joint away, Priscilla. MacKail will be back in a minute. Janet's right."

"O.K., Miss Efficiency, Miss Perfect. I need my job, just as much as the next one, but one thing has nothing to do with the other. That cunt's not going to talk to me that way. Nobody is. How dare she!"

"How dare I what?" Janet exploded. "I've had it with you. You hear me? Had it. Sitting next to you and smelling your cheap perfume and listening to your endless stories about your conquests and who gives head and who gives a tail or whatever. I'm tired of it, bored with it and I don't believe half your stories. I think you're a liar."

"Listen, girls. It's enough." Letty sounded like a school teacher, like Miss Markle in P.S. 199, breaking up a fight in the girls room.

"Cool it. Everybody, cool it. This is a party."

"Some party," Janet said, "I have to listen to where everybody's going, and I'm going to be in my apartment with my kid watching 'Captain Kangaroo.' That's what the week has in store for me. Some party . . ." The room was swirling in Janet's head, and in her dizziness she saw Stan MacKail coming toward her.

Suddenly, the music stopped, the hum subsided. Herbie came over with his arm around one of the young file clerks and Letty, in one instant, saw the afternoon go up in smoke. She saw the tears in Janet's eyes, and in Wilma's, the fear in Becky's, the anticipation in Agnes', the anger in MacKail's. Suddenly, it was a freeze frame, the lava poured all over everyone, drenching them.

And Priscilla, Priscilla couldn't stop. Someone had wound her up in the back and the motor kept going. The room kept swirling, and she couldn't get hold of it. She was feeling very hot, and as she twirled around and around she began to unbutton her blouse. The top two buttons were stubborn, so she yanked at them, watching them roll on the floor. At first, no one was noticing but when she got to the third and fourth buttons, determined to get cool, determined to take off this porous thing that kept clinging to her skin, the circle around her seemed to get smaller. In a flash, the shirt was off and her bare breasts were bobbing up and down. She heard everyone clapping with a steady beat, "Take it off, take it off" was being chanted somewhere.

Letty, or somebody, she couldn't tell who, threw a sweater over Priscilla's shoulders. "Forget it, I'm so hot, I'm trying to cool off!"

"You are sure not cooling us off, baby," Larry shouted, as Priscilla pushed Letty away with a hard shove.

Letty saw the astounded, then furious look in Mac-Kail's eye. She rushed into the circle and tightened the sweater around Priscilla. "Look, Lett, I'm having such a good . . ."

"Forget it, Priscilla, let's go to the ladies room. Come on. This is it. Let's go." Letty spoke to her as though Priscilla were seven, her hand firmly ensconced in the cookie jar. The clapping had stopped, no one said anything. "I want to hold your hand" was blaring on the phonograph. Every eye was on Priscilla as Letty led her out of the room. It was so unexpected, that flash of nipple and rounded contour, so out of keeping with a cold winter day and cash surrender values, renewable terms and premium loans. It had hardly had time to register.

"That's the first time I ever felt sorry for Priscilla," Agnes said to Wilma, gathering up her clothes, folding them carefully and putting them back in the box.

"You were rotten, Priscilla. Just rotten. You don't have to be so cruel. Why do you say the things you do?" Letty was shaking with anger.

"Oh, Christ, I didn't hurt anybody."

Letty wet a paper towel.

"I was just kidding Agnes. I wouldn't hurt her or make her feel bad. And I was just trying to get Wilma to be honest. Why did Janet yell like that, why does she hate me so much? If they all think I'm a pig, then let them, I don't care," she said defiantly. "I don't. But I don't mean to be cruel. I don't, Letty, I just got awfully dizzy and felt as though I was going to faint. But I didn't mean to hurt anybody. I didn't mean to."

"I know that, Priscilla, I do."

"It's all fucking confusing, you know, Letty. It's all very confusing. Women's lib and everything. Fucks things up. A lot of things I can't figure out. Sometimes I think the girls are killing the men, using the women's lib thing to beat them over the head. You know what I mean? I mean, if they get the guys to make the coffee and bring it to them in bed, they've got it made. Liberated. Bullshit, if you ask me." Priscilla leaned against the wall, steadying herself.

"You know, I used to hear them in the bedroom," Priscilla said as Letty put the towels on her forehead. "Come on, Letty, forget about it, I'm fine. Just got a little dizzy, that's all."

"Who did you hear in what bedroom?" Letty said, ignoring Priscilla's arm pushing her away.

"The old man and my mom," Priscilla said, imitating a goose step and Führer salute. "He used to force himself on her, you know, and he was a big guy, meek as a lamb during the day, quiet, efficient, doing his job well, poking around other people's belongings. Can you imagine, Letty, poking around other people's belongings for a living, always looking for something illegal, always on the lookout for something bad that somebody was doing. That's just what he did with me. Inspecting my customs. Always on the lookout, always trying to catch me at it, always. And once . . ."

"Priscilla, why don't you sit down. You look awful."

"I feel like crying. I haven't cried in years. I don't cry. I'm not a crier. Have you ever seen me cry, Letty? No. No, sir, you've never seen me cry and won't because I'll be goddamned if I'm going to cry now. But shit, I feel it coming on now. Why do I feel like crying, Letty?"

Instinctively, Letty reached out. Priscilla didn't push her away this time. Just let Letty hold her. Priscilla's blouse was still open, the sweater around her shoulders. Letty could hear her heart beating fast. Priscilla felt the warmth of Letty.

The tears began to come. Suddenly. "Always, he always expected the worst, pretending, pretending to be so sweet and courteous all day long to his beer-drinking buddies, to his boss, but God, that guy was a fake. He used to hit her something awful, she'd have the worst black-and-blue marks and swollen eyes, and she'd never call the police or report him or anything ever, Letty, never. She put up with all his shit, just took it. He was such a goddamn fake. And he'd go out and get it from whores up and down the street, drink too much and beat her up, throw her from one end of the room to the other. Rotten son-of-a-bitch. If he came near me now, I'd kill him. All two-hundred blubber pounds of him. And she stays, she stays, Letty, just cooks his fucking fried chicken and boils up his rice. Why the fuck am I crying about it now, I haven't seen him in a couple of years. I see her alone without him, these days . . .

"Look, Letty, I feel better now, thanks, thanks a lot, I appreciate it. But I'm fine, I'm really fine, I don't need you." Suddenly, Priscilla got herself together. Her tone changed. She put her face close to the mirror.

"What a fucking mess." The mascara had washed down to the bottom of her lids as though she had black eyes. "I look like the old lady herself, for God's sake. Go back, Letty. I'm all right. I don't need anybody."

The moment had passed. Letty knew it. Priscilla would move in on her now.

Turning to Letty, facing her, she said, "Don't you ever get sick of it? The crap? Sucking up to people?

119

I'm not saying you do it. You don't as a matter of fact. You're O.K., Letty, you're a mystery to me, but you're O.K. But it goes against my grain, kills me the way people fake, the way they suck up to each other to get something out of them. I can't stand people who pretend to be something they're not.

"I'll tell you something," she said defiantly. "I'm going to have a good life. Fuck it, Letty. Some of us have it, some of us are going to get through this mess, and some of us won't. Me, I'll live. I'll survive."

"Me, too. I agree with you. Priscilla, button up. Why do I absolutely agree with you. It's crazy, but we all have to survive on our own terms. They're different ways, aren't they, but we do survive." Letty put some cold water on her own flaming face. The interchange with the girl was upsetting, very upsetting to her. The girl was like one of Shakespeare's fools, she spoke some kind of strange truth. She didn't know where it would take her, or where that wildness would lead, but she saw her differently.

"I respect you, Priscilla."

"Bullshit."

"Stop it, I do. You just act out like crazy."

"Psychological crap. What does that mean?" Priscilla was put back together. Her hair was combed, her face shone. She picked up her skirt and pulled down the blouse, now buttoned, under it. She had no panties on under her pantyhose.

"Do you know why you do the things you do?"

"Why? Do I have to? Do you?"

"No, not all the time," Letty was getting more and more uncomfortable. The outspokenness of the girl cut through. Cut through too much. "Sometimes."

"Honest. That's honest. Where you going for your vacation, Letty? Why don't you come down and get laid Mexican style with us?" Priscilla was back in business.

120

Letty laughed. She couldn't stop laughing. "Can't. I've made other plans."

"Who you shacking up with?" Priscilla was back on familiar territory. Her dizziness had passed.

"Nobody. Going on a cruise."

"A rotten choice. But good hunting. I wish you good hunting. Let's get back." Patting her hair, taking some water from the faucet and rinsing her mouth, Priscilla approved her image in the mirror.

"Listen, Letty. Thanks. That's all I can say. I'm not good at these moments. Just thanks."

And, at the door, turning around before opening it, "Be good, love. Don't do anything I wouldn't do." With a wink, Priscilla was gone. Back into the fray.

12

"Terry, let's go. The sitter is coming in a minute and you're bareassed. Come on, baby, put your pajamas on and let Mommy give you your medicine and Vitamin C. Let's go. Ter . . ."

Janet Stevens was dressing for a date. The week had been a long one. It was vacation, the first time in ages when she didn't have to get up and go to work, and she would have given anything to get away, but even if she had been able to afford it, she couldn't. Terry had been in bed all week.

"It's a new strain of flu this year," the doctor had told her, and there had been deaths reported in the city as well as all over the country. Terry had frightened her the first night he got sick. His temperature shot up to 105, and she was frantic.

"Mommy, there are puppy dogs in my bed. They're all under the covers, Mommy, Mommy, they're crawling all over my bed. Mommy . . ." Terry screamed for her in the middle of the night. He had been drenched with perspiration. She could have wrung his pajamas out. She had pulled down the covers and showed him. "Look, Terry, darling, look, baby, no puppy dogs, nothing, just some sheets crumpled up. No puppy dogs, my love."

She hadn't realized that he was delirious. Only after she took his temperature and saw the thermometer register 105 did she realize how dangerous, how alone they were. The doctor told her to give him an enema, then and there at four in the morning. And to keep in touch with him from then on. She had to get the temperature down. He said that this particular virus brought on very high temperatures, especially in children, and that it was dangerous. She had sat up all night with Terry, putting cold compresses on his forehead, rubbing his back, talking incessantly, once the enema was over and done with and aspirin given. The two of them sat there, exhausted, waiting for dawn to come. When the black morning turned into light, Terry slept, and Janet felt the dampness finally come to his forehead. By 8 A.M. he was down to 101.

So Terry stayed in bed the whole week. Janet had thought she would have some time to herself, to do some Christmas shopping, to paint some shelves, to reupholster the easy chair in the living room. She did none of this, and only by the end of the week did she feel she could leave Terry with a sitter so she could go out on a date.

Terry never got to see the men his mother went out with. Janet felt he was too young to be confronted with rivals for her affection. His father came to take him out to Central Park and the merry-go-round and sometimes the zoo and baseball diamond to watch the Shakespeare Festival players play baseball against the Phoenix Theater team. It was always a rather somber affair when his father came for his Saturday or Sunday outing since he never had very much to say to the boy. He was living in a furnished room and so never took him to a real home. They went to visit his grand-mother, or, on rainy days, perhaps to an appropriate movie. His father wasn't very much fun, Terry thought, and he'd rather be with his mother any time. Janet knew this and nurtured it, which was why she pursued her theory about never bringing men in the house while Terry was still awake.

"Hi, Francine. I'm so glad you got here a little early. I'm going to have a hell of a time getting across town, and it's too expensive where I'm going to take a cab, so I'm going to take the bus."

Francine was a student at Barnard who came from a small town in Michigan. She was five-foot-one and weighed 150 pounds. Whenever she would baby-sit, Janet would come home and find one cookie left, one sourball, one Coke, one anything sweet. Francine nib-bled and chewed, and at first Janet had gotten an-noyed. But later she felt sorry for her. Francine never went out on dates but was jolly and smiling all the time. Terry loved her, so it was worth a few candy bars and Mallomars to assuage that giant hunger in her.

"Crayons, I need crayons. Francine, thanks a tril-lion." Terry was delighted with the coloring book based on the *Six Million Dollar Man*. As Janet put her coat on and dropped a tam on her head, she was feeling good. Thank God Terry was back to himself.

"I won't be late, Francine."

"Have a great time, Mrs. Stevens," Francine said,

eyeing a giant jar of M&Ms Janet had put on the coffee table.

Janet met George Marvin in the lobby of the Sentinel Hotel. She had to take two buses to get there and then walked half a block up Lexington Avenue from the Forty-ninth Street crosstown. It was their first date. In order to convince him he should not pick her up, she had made up something about her being in this neighborhood anyway.

George was an insurance broker who often visited their floor at the agency. He was thirty, a tennis nut, and took a lot of vitamins. He had asked her if she would like to play tennis with him in an indoor court in the Village that afternoon, but she didn't know how to play.

"Hello, George. I'm so sorry I'm late." Janet glanced up at the enormous clock in the Sentinel lobby. She was over half an hour late. The lobby was resplendent with decorations. Trees with only blue lights sparkled off and on as huge wreaths lit up the room.

"Glad you could make it. Let's split from here. Too many out-of-towners for me."

George was not much taller than Janet, but because he worked out in a gym five nights a week, his body was trim and well-developed. A firm hand led Janet's elbow across the lobby and down the stairs onto Park Avenue.

"Where to?"

Already he was in trouble, although he didn't know it. If there was one thing Janet abhorred, it was a man who didn't make decisions on a date. She liked a man to know where he wanted to go, get in a cab, give directions, and arrive there. One, two, three. She liked a decisive man.

They went to the Biltmore. "How long have you been at Robertson Stellar?" George said, taking Janet's hands.

"Four years."

"Like it?"

"It's not a bad place to work. You get three weeks off a year after you've been there five years." Janet, extricating her hand gently from George's, buttered the hot rolls the waiter had brought.

"Ever been to Dionysis?" George arranged his hair carefully over a balding spot at the center of his head.

"No. I really don't care for those singles places."

"Well, it is kind of wild. The bar is always busy, but of course there's Greek dancing and fairly good food inside. It's the busiest singles bar in New York."

"Do you go to them a lot?" Janet put her hand on the table, and George promptly put it between his two.

"Well, what else can you do? It's hard to meet someone sympathetic."

It was an interesting word, Janet thought. She looked up at him. His look was an earnest one. She believed him at that moment.

"I mean it. You know, I've thought a lot about it. I was reading an article recently about India and how often the arranged marriages seem to work out. This author was saying that when members of families decided when the children were fourteen or fifteen who they would eventually marry, and the kids really didn't even get to know one another until they started living together, the chances of the marriage working out were just as good as in our culture where natural selection took place. In other words, it's a gamble either way, and now, at our age, the opportunities for meeting people get less and less. You know what I mean?"

"I think so."

"I mean, all this sexual revolution stuff is fascinating and fun, but I don't think there's too much joy in all this swinging, somehow. You know, it does get harder and harder to meet nice girls once you're out of college and not in that kind of mainstream anymore. Listen,

125

I'm not talking about just getting laid, I'm talking about somebody one might have something in common with. Right? Know what I mean?"

The dinner was being served, and George's knee and Janet's knee were moving silently together. Like some underwater ballet, their legs were carrying on their own private choreography.

"What about you? You must know lots of men."

"I don't go out a lot. I have a little boy, you know."

"Right. You told me. But that doesn't impede your meeting people, does it?"

"A little." Janet had been through this first date, getting-to-know-you, parrying games so many times. He seemed, however, to be someone she could trust.

"Listen. Your hand is awfully cold. Do you take any vitamins? The tips of your fingers are like ice. E is good for that and some C, also. It's great for circulation. How about some dessert?"

"No, thanks, George. It really was delicious."

"Coffee?"

"I don't think so. Would you like to come back to my place? We could have a nightcap there, if you like."

"Love it. I'd love to, Janet. Are you sure you wouldn't like to go somewhere else? Listen, I'm planning to have a few people over to my place New Year's Day to watch the Rose Bowl. How would you like to come?"

"That sounds like fun. Let's see what happens, though. It sounds so far away."

George kissed her in the cab. There was an aura of promise about her. She exuded a strong sexuality, and the way she kissed him, her mouth opening almost immediately, her tongue exploring his teeth, his gums, overwhelmed him. He put his hands under her coat, feeling the softness of the blue fabric. He kissed her neck, and Janet let her head fall back, giving him

126

greater access to the flesh. George loved the feeling of her back, with no brassiere cutting into her. Her kisses were more and more passionate, and cold as it was, damp as it was, George pushed the coat off her shoulders. His hands moved to her throat where he caressed under the chin and behind the ears. He was erect and aroused the minute he started to kiss her. Her perfume and the feel of her made him warm, and his hands, hard and insistent, moved down her throat to her chest. She welcomed his fingers moving into her dress, cupping her breasts. George felt the give of the dress and, momentarily fearful that he would rip the material, loosened his grip. Janet pressed against him. He moved his hand deeper into the dress, rounding her other breast where he felt the nipple point hard against his finger. Janet moved her body around to him, so he could have easier access to her. She let out a soft moan as he moved the nipple between his fingers. Janet touched his penis, which she knew would be hard under his coat. She smoothed it, feeling it grow even larger under her hand. She saw the cab driver's eye on her in the mirror over George's shoulder, but they were anonymous eyes and had nothing to do with her. George put his hand on her cheek and kissed her harder, thrusting his tongue far into her mouth.

Her husband Carl used to do that. Carl used to fatten his tongue inside her mouth; it would swell like dough full of yeast inside her mouth, she remembered.

"Loosen up, Janet," he would say, and she would push him away, taunting him.

"Everything's little about you, Carl," she would say. "A man should have big hands. Yours are small and fleshy. You look like you've never done a day's work in your life."

Carl could never figure her out. Sometimes she would be languorous as a cat, sidling up to him on the couch, begging to be rubbed and petted, and each time, each time he promised himself he wouldn't let himself go because each time she would, in the middle of an embrace, refuse him.

Janet could hear her mother's words flow out of her own mouth. Sometimes the intonation had the same singsong quality with which Alma used to taunt Janet's father. It was almost as though she had no control over it.

The night Janet told Carl his penis looked as though it had shriveled up and gone to sleep in the middle of his making love to her, gentle, soft-spoken Carl Stevens smacked her so hard it loosened a tooth. He was terrified by the blood spurting from her mouth, and Janet had become hysterical, and jumped out of bed rushing into the bathroom where she stayed, screaming. She wouldn't come out until he promised to get out of the apartment.

Carl couldn't figure her out. The harridan ballooned out of a softness and vulnerability. It was always a surprise. But his self-respect got the better of him, and he never came back.

"Good riddance," Janet's mother had said. She had brought Janet a sponge cake and split of champagne to celebrate Carl's departure.

When the cab stopped, George was afraid he wouldn't be able to get out because of the encumbrance between his legs. His heart was pounding. Janet straightened her hair coolly and smoothed her hands over her hips, pulling her coat back on.

In the elevator, George pulled her to him again, but she pushed him away.

"It's only the third floor. We'll be there in a minute," she found herself whispering.

Francine was finishing *The Catcher in the Rye* for the fifth time, and Terry was sound asleep. Janet paid the girl after introducing George to her.

"Look, I don't think you should be out there by

yourself at this hour. I'll be glad to walk you home, if it's only around the block."

"Oh, George, that's lovely of you." Janet looked at George with feeling. What a nice guy, she thought.

"I'm really just fine. Nothing ever happens to me," Francine said.

"Don't ever say that. Look, I'll be glad to walk with you. I'll be right back, Janet." George patted Janet on the shoulder. "Just pour me a scotch for when I get back."

"Well, O.K., if you put it that way. Thanks a lot, Mr. Marvin."

Within moments, they were out the door, and Janet had hung up her coat. There was something very genuine about him, she thought, getting the ice out of the refrigerator. What a nice thing to do.

After putting the ice in the bucket, Janet tiptoed into the bedroom, careful not to wake Terry. Deftly, she slipped out of her dress, pulled off her pantyhose, and put on her jersey lounging robe. It was very clinging, and her breasts looked bountiful under the material. She had aqua slippers to match, and by the time George returned she was sitting on the living room couch with a snifter of brandy in her hand.

The door was open, and George walked in.

"That was really nice of you, George."

"Where's my drink?"

"I'm sorry. I didn't make it yet. I didn't want the ice to melt." George poured himself a double and sat down beside Janet.

"You're really lovely, Janet."

"Thanks, George. I slipped into something more comfortable, as they say."

"Right." Within seconds, he put his drink down on the coffee table and his arms were around her. She had lowered the lights so that only one soft bulb lit the room.

As he kissed her, Janet thought about furnished rooms and shouting. Voices in her head were shouting obscenities. No balls. You've got no balls, floated through her head like debris on the Grand Canal. George's eyes were closed, hers were open. She watched his eyes roll. Don't fire till you see the whites of her eyes, she thought as he kissed her sweetly and pressed his hands back to the soft swelling he had become acquainted with in the cab. Janet turned to snow. She would not melt. I am the snow queen, she thought. I have a heart made of ice as thick as steel, and you have no balls. He was embracing Raggedy Ann. She would not help him, for after all, he had no balls, he was nothing. She kept her mouth closed tightly as he tried to discover again the mysteries inside. She would not move. Her body became rigid. No balls, my dear, you have no balls. There is not a ball about you, just like dear old dad, absolutely, you are nothing, you are weak, go peddle your vitamin C elsewhere. Take your cock and your balls and put them back in your pocket.

"Quit it."

Janet's tone was sharp and curt.

"What do you mean, quit it?"

"Just what I said." Janet removed George's hands from her. "Quit it."

"Look, Janet, I thought . . ."

George opened his eyes. He was erect, he wanted her, but she had turned into someone else. She had turned to stone, she was an aquamarine, a hard jewel. The fire had gone out.

"I think you had better go." Her voice was different.

"What is this, Janet? Is it the boy in the next room? Are you uptight about that? I want you. You are a very desirable woman, do you know that?"

"Of course I know that." Janet wanted to hurt him. All she wanted was for him to go. She saw the bulge in his pants and was repelled. Take your penis and go.

She had to hold herself back from shouting. Get out. Leave us alone.

"I thought you liked me, Janet. I really thought we were getting along."

"We were, George. And I do like you," she struggled to get out the words. "It's just that I'm tired, and, yes, Terry's being in the next room does make it difficult."

"Well, maybe next time we can go to my place."

"Maybe." But George knew instantly there would be no next time, that something had happened to her. She had done everything to tempt him and then had turned into ice.

He was erect again, and his penis hurt. He felt sixteen, he felt as though he was on Fiona Park's back porch a hundred years ago after necking for hours with her, and the light was turned on abruptly followed by a thousand dancing moths. He had masturbated in the car before he went home that night, his groin was so painful. Blue balls he had, and he had sworn that no girl would ever get him in that state again. It was unhealthy, he was certain of that. And he believed in taking good care of himself.

Enough, he thought. I'm a grown man. "Look, Janet, can't you tell me anything? Is it something I said, something I've done? What is it?"

"Nothing, George. Nothing. Something. I don't know. I just think you'd better go."

"Look, I'm not going to force myself on you. It's not my style. But I don't understand. I'll tell you that. And," he said, getting up with difficulty, "I'll tell you this. I'm not going to call you again. If you want to see me, here's my card." He pulled one out of his pocket and threw it on the table. "We used to call girls like you cockteasers when I was a kid. But you know what? I liked you. I really did. Besides the fact that you're nice to kiss, I liked you. So long, Janet. Good luck."

Janet picked up her glass of brandy and sat, feet tucked under her on the couch, staring at his scotch.

She had liked him. He had aroused her. She had wanted him to feel like nothing. She wanted him to feel as though his balls were made of glass. She swirled the brandy around in the snifter. She could almost see the reflection of her eyelashes. She soothed her bare breasts with the cold glass and took a deep breath. She didn't understand either, feeling close to tears, knew that she had done what she always did. What she had to do.

She got up and looked inside the bedroom. Terry was fast asleep in the cot next to her bed. He was breathing heavily and through his mouth. She leaned over and kissed him on the forehead, noticing some mucus caked in his nostrils. Leaning down to kiss him, she purposefully knocked the bed abruptly. "Oh, Terry, did I wake you? Are you feeling all right, baby?" Terry put his arms around his mother's neck and in his sleep kissed her.

"How about some milk and cookies, sweetheart? Let's go into the kitchen and have a midnight snack. It's midnight, baby, the best time for a snack."

Terry, delighted at being up so late, stood still while she put his plaid bathrobe on him, and put his feet in his slippers. Janet felt strangely exhilarated as she took the tollhouse cookies out of the jar and put them on a plate. She washed her cookie, tantalizingly sweet, down with a long, tart sip of the brandy.

13

The desk clerk behind the counter had a neatly trimmed mustache that almost hid his harelip. He was wearing a light beige suit with a red tie and a red handkerchief was peeking out of his breast pocket.

Letty, never quite comfortable with the checking in process, signed the unfamiliar name.

"My husband will be arriving soon," she said, looking directly into the black eyes of the clerk.

"Will you be paying by cash or credit card, Señora?" he said, a big gold piece staring out from his top set of teeth.

"Cash, I think. The room definitely has a king-sized bed, is that right?"

"Absolutely, Señora," the man said, and Letty was determined to overlook his leer, which may or may not have been imagined. She couldn't tell at this point.

"I do hope you enjoy your stay with us. The weather report is perfect. As you know, it rains a little bit every day here in San Juan, but just for a few minutes, and then it is superb again."

Letty thanked him and followed the bellboy into the elevator.

Later in the afternoon, Letty was lying by the pool feeling the sun's rays beating down on her. Propped up on her elbows, she watched him walk toward her. He had a terrycloth robe over his suit and was holding a bottle of sun lotion and a copy of a thick book. As he walked toward her, she felt giddy, heady with anticipation.

Will Robbins sat down beside her, putting a large hand in the center of her back before he kissed it.

They were staying in a small hotel outside of San Juan on the beach. The grounds housed several small bungalows, one of which Will had been able to get for the week. After four years together this was the fourth time Will and Letty had been able to spend any extended period of time together. Puerto Rico was still fairly reasonable, and more important, the weather was predictable.

Will motioned to a small Puerto Rican man in a

133

white jacket sitting behind the thatched hut of a bar on the far side of the pool.

"Two rum punches," he said as the man rushed over to the couple. The hotel was small, and in spite of the fact that they were filled to capacity, Will and Letty rarely saw the same people twice. Only two couples were asleep on the opposite side of the pool. Letty loved it where they were. The cottage was just off the beach, and at night hearing the waves slap the sand was comforting; like being in the attic when she was a little girl on a Saturday afternoon in the country during a storm. With Hymie and Fran downstairs with Aunt Ethel and Uncle Eli and she, lying there on the floor looking at Ethel's old trunks and books and hats and smelling the woodness and oldness of the slanted room, hearing the metronome beat of the drops. She would fall asleep there, sweetly. The Caribbean sound was softer at night, and the surf had an even gait. After a few days of sunning and eating and drinking and making love, they were both slowly beginning to unwind. And yet, Letty noticed a restiveness about Will.

"Will you play for me after dinner, Letty? Tonight, I've got to start that paper. Got to get going on that forensic paper for school. I lugged all those books down here, practically had to pay overweight for them, and the damn thing is due two days after I get back. After dinner, Lett. Let's eat early so I can crack those books. I'm beginning to get nervous about it."

Letty had disappeared for an hour at about eleven, and Will hadn't known where she was.

"Where the hell did you go?" he had said. "I looked all over for you. I was getting worried. Where did you go?"

"I was out fixing a surprise. Shut your eyes."

"Letty, this is . . ."

"Will, stop it. Just shut your eyes."

Will did as he was told.

Letty went out the door and brought in a tray. She laid a red-and-white checkered tablecloth down in the middle of the room, setting two places. She took a vase with a spray of violets in it and placed it in the center of the cloth. On two platters covered with silver covers were enormous portions of tuna salad, garnished with parsley and hard-boiled eggs. Radishes and carrots were cut up alongside it. There was a carafe of wine, some crackers and Brie cheese, and two eclairs.

"O.K. Open up."

"What? This?"

"Lunch."

"What did you do, Letty?" Will couldn't hide his pleasure.

"I did a little shopping and bribing. I cajoled, then flirted with the chef in the kitchen so I could use his domain for a minute. Don't ever let it be said you never got a home-cooked meal out of me," she said, laughing. Then, putting her arms around him, kissed his chin. "I never do that. Cook for you. I wanted to."

Will looked at the picnic on his floor. He had loved her gesture. Yet, for some reason, felt cold.

He had thought, at that moment, of Easter Sundays with ham and pineapple, without Letty. He thought of pistachio ice cream. Kathy always had pistachio ice cream in the freezer for him. It had been generous, her gesture, it touched him.

There were no ants on their picnic and no mosquitoes. But there was love, and there was silence. Letty couldn't understand his silence. He couldn't understand his own silence. But he had leaned over then, as they sat on the floor, and kissed her. Barely touching her lips. There were no words.

Their picnic had been all right, Will thought, moving his hands up to Letty's outer thighs, but he knew it was not what Letty had envisioned. And as Letty lay there, feeling her chest stick to the moist rubber of the

135

mat, she, too, was thinking about the lunch. Not one of my most successful endeavors, she thought ruefully, feeling Will's strong hands massaging her thighs, slowly, surely. Will I ever, ever cook a meal for this man, she mused? Will I ever, like every other woman in this world who takes it for granted, just be there at six o'clock with the roast in the oven and the mousse in the fridge. Sounds so simple, cooking for a man. What's the big deal. I will not think about it, she thought as he worked his hands up to her back, kneading. I will be existential. I will be a member of the "Now" generation, the "me" generation, I will think of nothing but now.

"I like you thin," Will said, feeling the pelvic bone that moved away from her hip.

"I think I've lost about fifteen pounds this year," Letty said. "It was a bitch to lose that twenty pounds I'd gained."

A rush of memory. They both remembered that terrible time. When they had broken up for the third time, a year ago. Letty couldn't eat, she drank too much. Then all she could do was eat. Piles of Milky Ways and jelly doughnuts before going to bed, pizzas for lunch and chocolate cake and peanut butter. She stuffed herself to fill up that crater inside her. She had to pass Will's desk every day at the office. She had started all over again. Three times she began putting herself on the market again, accepting dates, looking at men as potential lovers instead of just people belonging to some other sex. Three times she came to the painful conclusion, without talking to anyone, without confiding or telling her pain, that it couldn't go on. That she couldn't keep sharing this man.

Letty felt Will's warm fingers go around her toes and thought of the man Becky had fixed her up with after they had split up, who took her to dinner and a play and had brought her home to his apartment where he had kissed her feet and sucked her toes for an hour. He had worn hair spray, she remembered, and combed his graying thin strands forward to hide the bald spot. His hair had felt hard from the spray and his impersonal touch had made her want to retch. The smell of Canoe stuck to the lampshades, and in a moment after a few thrusts he was finished. It had nothing to do with sex, it had nothing to do with her. It had something to do with going out to dinner and what you do after. She couldn't remember his name, or his face, Bill something, she thought.

Will knew she was thinking about the time she had gained all that weight. When she would come to the office with her face puffy. She had resumed smoking that time, too, he remembered. He stayed at Sal's till after nine almost every night those days, hating to come home, despising Kathy for the guilt she had provoked in him, hating her forgiveness when he would be late, when he would weave into the apartment yelling at her, furious that she had not kept the kids up to see him. "What's there to come home to, for God's sake?" he would bellow at her, and she would take his coat and hang it in the hall closet and make him a cup of coffee and sit up and watch the eleven o'clock news with him.

There were days, weeks, and months of this until last December, just about a year, when this time it was Will who finally broke. He called her one morning at 3 A.M. drunk, from an Irish bar that was about to close. Letty could hear the bartender in the background pleading, "C'mon, Mac, it's closing time. I gotta open this place early tomorrow, give a guy a break, Mac . . ."

"Letty, come out and let's have a nightcap. C'mon, Letty, the night is young, and you're so beautiful."

"Will, are you all right?"

"Whadduya mean, am I all right? Of course I'm all

137

right. But I'm sad, Lett. I'm so sad. Make me feel better, hon, make me not feel so sad."

Letty had started to cry, and she had made him promise he would get a cab and go straight home. She swore to him that she would see him for dinner the following night, which was, appropriately, a Tuesday. Their whole lives were predicated on the two Ts, as Will called them, and now without realizing it, with one phone call, they fell back into the pattern. This, after all their tearful explanations and resolutions about splitting up being for the best, and he could not leave his children, since he could not bear to hurt a girl he's known since she was a teen-ager, etc., etc., etc. They had dinner that Tuesday and then, appropriately enough, the following Thursday checked into a Holiday Inn. There Letty collected a few more miniature bars of soap for her collection. Holiday Inns and Ramada Inns' matches and soaps choked the corners and caverns of her pocketbook.

And so it had begun again.

They lay there numbed by the ferocity of the rays. Lying on his stomach, Will spoke to the side of Letty's face. "You know who I feel sorry for?"

"McKern?"

"Well, him, too, but it's Gaynor I kept thinking about. I can't get him out of my mind. The kid's sensitive, too sensitive for this business, I'll tell you that."

"He's no kid," Letty said, propping herself up on her elbows, her breasts falling gently out of her suit. "He looks nearly forty."

"Can't be more than thirty-six. He's aging fast at Robertson Stellar, I'll tell you that. There's a guy who should get out before it's too late. I tried to tell him that. I tried to tell him that it will eat him alive, like maggots crawling all over him. I tried to tell him that."

Letty looked at Will. His eyes were shut, but they were twisted into a fine web of tight wrinkles.

"He's got a wife who's pushing him so far he's going

to ricochet back. I know it. I can see the signs. He should go be a teacher. He should open up an inn in Vermont. Anything but what he's doing, putting himself on the line in front of pricks every day."

He's talking about himself, Letty thought, moving closer, putting her hand over his.

"You know, Letty, McKern's better off, much better off than Gaynor. Christ, he's got no illusions. He knows what his priorities are. His life is rich in a way. He and his wife have something special, really a good thing, and the tedium and sameness of the office is secondary to him. He's learned to live with it. He's the only one in the place, it seems to me, where the shit hasn't rubbed off on him. I've never seen such gentleness before. He even made excuses for that slut, Priscilla, Letty. That takes a forgiving nature, if you ask me."

Letty was sitting all the way up now, and rummaging into her purse where she found a nail file. "Oh, I don't think she's a slut. There's something appealing, vulnerable about her," she said, filing her thumbnail. "I like her."

"Becky has more appeal than Priscilla does. The kid seems scared and sort of desperate, but there's something warm about her, something you want to protect."

"Who else?" Letty loved to play this painful game. "Who else do you find attractive in the office?"

Will pulled her down to him. He opened his eyes and looked close into hers. He put his hand on the back of her neck and opened his mouth on hers.

Opening his eyes, Will saw feet behind Letty. Black shoes with feet in them. The waiter from behind the bar. His feet must swelter and swell in those prisons, Will thought in a rush.

"It's raining, sir," he said, putting down the striped umbrella in the middle of a round white table.

And so it was. Will and Letty had barely felt the large drops that were beginning to come down. It rained a little while every day in San Juan, clearing the air, making way for the next brilliant hour. It had come a bit late today.

"Thanks," Will said as Letty giggled into his shoulder. The luxury of kissing in public.

The unsmiling waiter walked away, probably aching to get out of his black shiny shoes and into a pair of sandals, Will thought. He couldn't care less if they were kissing. The rain started to come down in torrents suddenly, and they ran for their towels and books. In a moment, sheets of slanting rain struck them as the sky became dark and forbidding. They ran for shelter the short way to their cottage.

Once inside, Letty began to feel chilled.

"You're shivering, Letty," Will said at the door, putting his arms around her.

"You're as wet as I am," Letty laughed, taking a towel and drying his hair. "You look like a puppy in a puddle," she said, tousling the wet ends.

Will took the straps sitting on her shoulders and pulled them down to her waist. "I will kiss you dry," he said. He held her by the elbows and bent his head down to her chest, blanketing her with kisses. He licked the rain away, breathed on the areola in the center of her breast, then blew on the nipple. He could feel her suck in her breath.

He pulled the bathing suit slowly down farther, over her hips. It was wet and stuck to her flesh like contact paper, but he was persistent, fingers gently pulling the brown fabric over her buttocks, cold from the rain.

Letty stepped away from the suit which lay in a rush on the floor. She loved Will to look at her. Any doubts she had about her body disappeared under his gaze. Standing there looking at her, Will broke into a full smile. She rarely saw him smile or laugh so completely.

"You are beautiful, Letty."

140

She went to him and unbuttoned his bathing suit. Silently, they moved to the bed.

"Like home," she whispered, "dark outside, cozy warm in here, as though nothing can hurt us all wrapped . . ." The rain slashed at the windows. It was more than an afternoon rain, this was a tropical storm, one that would be more intense but would not last as long.

They lay on their backs touching each other.

"Let me," Letty said as she moved her body on top of his. She began at his ears, and tasting the chlorine on him, the salt of the sea on him, tasted down to the curling hair around the small mounds on his chest, down the inside of his arm. He shuddered as she found the carved place on the inside of his elbow. She enveloped his body, cradled it, her fingers and her mouth, tongue and her palms giving. He smelled of the sea, he smelled of Will, a Will smell she cherished.

She drove on with her mouth, feeling his pleasure drain into her, wanting to give more, letting him go for an instant then driving forth, intensifying his pleasure. His joy was hers, his explosion satisfying her. The giving was plentiful, she could go on and on. His joy was her joy as he lay there, finally relaxing his clenched fingers, smoothing the tight furrows around his eyes.

They began again after he had rested, as he, pulling her up to his face, kissed the mouth that had held him inside. His hands were silently relentless touching her with infinite tenderness, finding her places, her places being everywhere, her places being caverns and creases, mounds and contours familiar yet somehow always new. It was as strong as his own release, he thought, this pleasuring her, and when she cried out and he felt her body tighten like a silk string held taut, it was as though he had come again, as though hers was a continuation of his own pleasure.

They slept in each other's arms.

An hour later when they woke, it was still brooding outside and the palms could be seen from the window, bending. Will woke first, and stared at the wind. The palms looked as though they would fall onto their houses, as though the trees would bend so far they would uproot, and as they uprooted would fall on their cottage; this quiet, temporary haven housing them. And no one would know, he thought; he would go, be washed into the sea, and no one would know who he was, who he had been. And the beautiful girl with him would be saved, but he would be washed away, and maybe Sean would be the only one who would think about him, around seven in the morning when there would be no one to shave with, no one to jaw with . . .

"What?"

Letty bent over and kissed him. Desire touched her again.

"That wind."

"It's wild, isn't it? Too bad we can't have dinner in here. Maybe the lights will go out. What, Will?" she said, looking at him. "You look so pale."

"What are you going to do if your mother dies, Letty?"

Taken totally by surprise, Letty sat up in bed. "I don't know. I think about it. She's getting old."

"What do you think when you think about it, about her dying?"

"I don't know, just thinking."

He put a hand absent-mindedly on her back, rubbing it up and down. "I don't want to die."

"Oh, Will. Nobody does. My love."

"But I think about it, Letty. Every once in a while it comes over me, and you know what, it's not so much the sleeping forever. It's not that. It's not being around anymore either, Letty." His hand stopped in the center of her back. "Letty, if I died, what would it matter?

"I keep thinking that if I went, if something happened to me, it just wouldn't matter. Even if I passed my law exams, even if I passed the bar, even if, even if I went into practice, got a job, Letty, what difference would it make? I still wouldn't have made a dent. Not a dent. It would mean that forty-two or -three or -four years of living didn't mean anything. I hate that feeling. I hate the feeling that it was for nothing, all this living."

He felt her back stiffen under his hand.

"Sweetheart, I'm not talking about us. I'm not talking about what we are to each other. It has nothing to do with that. It has to do with the whole scene. The whole picture. I feel as though I'm chasing my own tail. I mean, Christ, I don't know if I can even pass the bar, no less finish these goddamn papers due in January. I don't know if I can pass my exams at the end of this semester, no less pass the bar. I read an article in the *Law Review* that there are fewer jobs now than at any other period in history for young lawyers. I'd be a lawyer, but I wouldn't be young. So look, Letty, what am I knocking my brains out for?"

"Will, what are you saying?" Letty said, turning around, facing him. "What are you really saying?"

"I'm saying I'm thinking about dying. About just not being here anymore and not being able to touch you anymore. I haven't done anything, Letty." His voice was getting louder. "I sit in that office day after day and listen to inanities, listen to guys who have sold out, sold out their souls and the people they once were, just sold it, across the river into the trees. Over and out. Gone. And I brood about it. I brood about it, and I'm scared. Letty, is that something for a big grown-up man to admit? I'm scared shitless."

"Will." Letty put her arms around him, feeling his warm back. She felt impotent in the face of his pain. It would go away, she thought, the powerlessness, the

143

panic. "I love you, Will." It was all she could think of saying. She had no answers.

Suddenly, Will's face blurred and she saw in her mind's eye birthday cakes, hundreds of birthday cakes. Her father had doted on her birthday when she was little, and always invited the whole neighborhood to participate in his girl's birthday. The photograph album at home was filled with pictures and this big-for-her-age girl with braids and ribbons tied at the ends blowing out candles on cakes. Cake after cake. Birthday after birthday.

Last year when she was thirty-six, Fran had baked a five-layer cake and had decorated it with chocolate icing and complicated beautifully designed rosettes. "Sweet Letty" it had said on the top.

"Invite some friends in, honey. Get some of the girls from the office to come over. We'll have a party."

"They took me to lunch," Letty had said. "It's all right, Ma. Birthdays don't mean a thing. It's just another day. Just you and I will be fine. I've got to go to bed early tonight anyway." And Letty had shown Fran the scarf Becky had given her and the set of Shaw's plays Wilma had splurged on. The gifts warmed her. But it hadn't been enough. Of course.

Fran had put thirty-six little candles on the cake and had fitted in one large one. For luck and for love, she had said. And the two of them had sat in the living room, with the fire blazing in the hearth, with *Tosca*, Fran and Letty's favorite opera, playing on the hi-fi with Leontyne Price singing. And Letty had made her wish. And blown out all the candles. Except the big one. The good luck one. She missed that one.

She had excused herself and had run into the bedroom on some pretext or other as Fran cut the cake. She put cold water on her tears in the bathroom and bathed her eyes with a cloth. She wanted to be with Will. It was enough with her mother. She loved her mother. But she was thirty-seven years old, and it was enough with her mother. She wanted to sleep with Will on her birthday. After all, it was her birthday. Birthdays were important. Her father had given her a party every year. There had always been someone there to hug and kiss her on her birthday. She was thirty-seven years old, and it was enough with her mother on her birthday. The phone had rung three times that night. Once it was Aunt Tessa, her mother's sister, to wish her a happy birthday. Once it was Becky, asking her to go shopping with her at lunch the next day. And once was a hang-up. That had been Will, of course, that was the way they had celebrated her birthday together. With a hang-up. With a great loud buzzing on the other end of the line.

"Letty, what would I do without you?" Will broke into her thoughts.

"Will, I don't know how to help you. You're a good man. You're doing the best you can. Law school is a dream, and you're close. I hate to hear you talking like that. You've got spirit, you really have. Who else could have the tenacity to stick to it so long? I admire you for that, I really do."

"Play for me, Lett," Will said abruptly. "Play me something."

He wanted to change the subject, he wanted to go back to being lovers, Letty thought. Hugging him, she jumped out of bed and took the guitar out of the closet. Sitting naked on the bed, the guitar cradled lovingly in her lap, she sang the soft Joni Mitchell and James Taylor songs she loved. Letty's voice was clear and sweet, and running her fingers over the strings, she felt outside herself. As though someone else with that pure sound had entered the room. And, mingled with his fears, at that moment, with the rain insistent at the window, the light softening the room and gently surrounding the shape and sound of this woman he loved, Will was aware at that moment of a happiness he had never known.

The week was over.

They were taking separate planes to avoid problems, but drove to the airport together. The day was sticky. They were silent in the closeness of the hotel limousine.

And suddenly, Letty's plane was missed. They had misread the ticket. Will's wasn't arriving for another hour, and there were no extra seats on it anyway. They could get stand-by for a plane out later in the day if they stayed around the airport. The decision was made fast, impetuously, and in desperation.

Letty smelled her coffee. She smelled Fran's chicken, sure to be in the oven when she got home. She smelled the emptiness of her bedroom, the emptiness of dusk when she would arrive. She smelled tomorrow morning at the office and stale cigarette smoke and everyone talking about their vacations. She smelled ashes in cold coffee, she smelled New Year's Eve coming and watching the ball drop, dressed in her plain quilted bathrobe with a hot toddy on her lap and her mother's knitting needles clicking endlessly.

"Let's stay one more day."

"Will. We can't."

"It's only one more day," Will said. "What harm can there be in staying one more day?"

One more day.

They stayed.

But one more day can sometimes bring harm when you live for Tuesdays and Thursdays.

14

"And I'm telling you, boys, auto insurance is always the loser, you know that. We all have to face that fact. So we've got to concentrate on those major medicals. Last year we were 75 per cent up, around 10 mil. This year claims for auto insurance ate up 50 per cent of the profits. Now let's go, boys. Our team work can do it. If we all pull together we can do it, and the northeastern division can beat hell out of those southwestern guys!"

Stan MacKail, Frank Fairchild, and Jack Gaynor were sitting in the front row in a room on the ground floor of the Princess Hotel in Acapulco. Jack was mesmerized by the scene outside; the perfection and balance of blues and white. Pure color laced momentarily with the splash of red on a waiter's serape or the brightly streaked flags decorating the tables lining the pool. Acapulco rested languorously outside.

Inside the Princess Hotel, it was business as usual. The New York men were attending their third seminar of the day while the other regional offices were meeting on the second and third floors of the hotel.

Some of the men had brought their wives, and Stan MacKail's had barely gotten off the tennis court since her arrival. She would refresh herself with rum punches or margaritas in between sets, and even in the heat of the day would rally with the pro who looked like a young Pancho Segura only taller with longer, more graceful legs.

Jack's wife had finally persuaded him to take her and leave the children home with her mother. Elise had spent a fortune on clothes the week before they left, knowing this was an opportunity of a lifetime, knowing that the big brass was going to be there and that it was now or never as far as moving Jack up.

Jack barely heard what Mr. Sanderson, corporate vice-president from Hartford, was saying. He was wondering how he was going to get through these four days and how he was going to pay for the trip once the credit card bill came. The hotel was something out of an Elizabeth Taylor fantasy, all pinks and purples outside, and chandeliers and heavy dark Spanish woods and steel lattice gates inside. It was outrageously opulent, and Elise Gaynor had swooned when she saw the enormous bathroom with gold faucets and two sinks. The terrace looked out onto the serene Gulf, and sitting there, watching the sunset, she was aware of having attained the impossible.

But for Jack, it was a terrifying attainment, so conscious was he of the tenuousness of it, so sure it would never happen again. To Elise, it was a beginning, just the forerunner of opulence to come. Jack had it in him, she always told him. He just needed a little push every now and then.

Jack couldn't stop perspiring. Ever since he had arrived, he could feel his armpits sticking to his shirt, and he kept patting his upper lip with his handkerchief. He could barely hear what Sanderson was saying as he watched outside the window as a Mexican governess starched into a white uniform was playing with a plump beetle-brown baby.

". . . and before I introduce Joseph Cuomo, the salesman of the year for the northeast to say a few words to us, I just want to reiterate that our division can do better next year. And now, let's hear a few words from the guy who made it big this year, Joseph L. Cuomo."

Jack felt the sweat trickle into his eyes and noticed his handkerchief was soaking wet. Only a few minutes till lunch, poolside, he thought, sensing an uncontrollable need for a drink. Tomorrow was the last night of the sales meetings, and he couldn't wait to take off the badge with his name on it whose small safety pin was making a hole in all his shirts. Everything was so bright, the perfect resort world out the window was *Playboy* centerfold, larger than a cut-out paper doll 3-D world of leisure and acquisition, two unfamiliar words in his life's vocabulary.

The men leaned forward as Joseph Cuomo walked up to the front of the room. Many of them had notebooks and pens, anxious not to miss a word, anxious to find the secret of Joe's success. They had moved the giant posters that had festooned the lobby with photographs of prominent salesmen of the year into the meeting room, and there was Joseph Cuomo's face smiling out of the middle of a silver star.

His hair was just long enough not to be abrasive, cut in stylish layers. Despite the heat and the relaxed Mexican ambiance, he was wearing a gray lightweight suit, a yellow shirt and black tie with yellow stripes. His nails were manicured and his shoes shone. It was Joseph Cuomo's year and he was enjoying it to the hilt. He looked forward to these sales meetings as a child does to Christmas. He had worked long and hard all year. It had practically broken up his marriage. It was so long and so hard, but he had been determined to write way over the top this year. And it had paid off. He finally bought the boat he had been coveting for years and he had promised Denise a month in Europe. He was smooth and he was articulate as he explained to the men that a curt rejection on the

149

phone, a company vice-president turning him down for an appointment, all meant nothing to him.

"I barrel right in. I never let it get me down, fellows. That's the trick; once you've got your foot in the door, you've got them. And once you sell them one kind of insurance, you're destined to sell them more. You've got to believe in yourself. That's the key. To thine own self be true, and if I may, I'd like to recommend *Winning Through Intimidation*. It's my Bible . . ."

Jack Gaynor watched Stan MacKail take voluminous notes on Cuomo's talk. Frank was sitting back in his chair, taking it all in. But Jack couldn't get his mind off the woman he had seen nursing her baby on the beach yesterday. Since it was a public beach, the owners of the hotel had no right to keep people from trespassing, and so cordoned off a small portion of the pale white sand for its residents. Just beyond the demarcation was a family of Mexicans. They traveled on horseback to sell beads and shawls to the tourists. They were in rags. The mother, who seemed exhausted, was sitting down in the middle of the sand at the water's edge, and had taken out her swollen breast to feed her greedy infant. There were four or five little children around her who did not play in the water. They did not make sand castles or dig to China. They stood listlessly at their mother's side with huge brown eyes staring up at the Shangri-la of the hotel in the background.

No one seemed to notice any of the stragglers who walked by the hotel every day, Jack thought. The salesmen were so intent on their meetings, and everyone seemed so involved in the elaborate luxury that no one noticed. Jack had been standing close to the Mexican woman and could see the blue veins puffing out of her breast. She had looked sullenly at him and then struggled up off her feet as she saw potential customers coming her way. None of it made sense to

Jack. Looking at Joseph Cuomo, Jr., he saw the woman's breast, blue-veined, instead of the stylish haircut and freshly shaven face. He kept blinking his eyes but it would not go away.

". . . and so, fellows, that's about it," Cuomo was concluding. "The rewards are many. There's a lot of you that can do it. I know it. Just build up those sales and when you get to the top and have earned enough points to join The President's Club, I'm telling you, you won't have to work more than four hours a day and will get two months off. These are the possibilities. This is the land of opportunity, man.

"It's a technique that I mastered," he added, "and if I could, you can. I'm telling you. You've got to learn how to change the customer's attitude, you've got to learn how to get him to leap-frog. You've got to learn how to put yourself in the proper posture. If it means a five-dollar calling card, then so be it, if that's your bag. You've got to be a self-starter. If you're not, forget it, you're in the wrong business. You know what they taught us in the TAP? I look back on that Training Allowance Program and remember the wisdom of some of those lessons. I started out by being Agent of the Month, and grew along with each incentive. Just coming to Acapulco had always been an incentive for me.

"And speaking of Acapulco, we're not here to only work, and forgive me for taking up so much of your time. You're here because the meetings are geared to a campaign, but, if I'm not mistaken, Mr. Sanderson, you're here to have fun, too. Right? So go to it. As I understand it, the afternoon is free for swimming, tennis, fishing. Whatever your heart's desire is. See you tonight when the mariachis start beckoning."

Joseph Cuomo smiled and the men stood up as they applauded. As they filed out of the room amid the hum and chatter of dreams and envy, hopes and challenges, Jack couldn't take his eye off the window. The Mexican governess was holding the plump child by the hand. The child had on a white dress that was trimmed in what looked like real lace. They both looked so white and so perfect. I feel so dark and so imperfect, Jack said to himself.

"Hey, Gaynor, chowtime, let's move it," Frank shouted at Jack.

"See you later," Jack said without looking up at Frank, without taking his eyes away from the window.

Jack found himself walking on the beach. The sand was getting in his shoes. He had grabbed a straight scotch at the bar and had disappeared to the beach. He wanted to see the woman again. He wanted to buy something for her; he wanted her to have something. He felt badly that he hadn't given her anything yesterday.

Looking back, he could see Elise, hand-shading, her eyes scanning the pool area for him. Scotch in hand, he sat down on the white sand and removed the white bucks Elise had bought for him. They had gold buckles. He hated gold buckles. Jack felt the hot grains of sand between his toes. Holding his shoes and socks in one hand and his scotch in the other, he walked toward the water. His shirt was sticking to his back so standing at the edge of the surf he put the glass inside one shoe and removed the shirt and sat on it. Jack looked out at the brilliance of the blue-green out there. It was all so sharp it hurt his eyes.

Looking down at his feet, he noticed a bunion. His father had one in the same place. He had his father's feet. His father used to talk about go, go, too, he thought, about getting there first before the other guy beat you out. It was impossible. How did he get into this? He wanted to read. He wanted out. He wanted to do anything but what he was doing, and he was getting in deeper and deeper. He hadn't told Elise that a week ago he had started crying when he was trying to get an appointment with the executive of a big company. The man never knew, of course. Jack had covered up the muffle in his voice with a cough and a blowing of the nose, talking about the flu that was going around. But it had come on him like that, the fear. The tears. He just didn't have it. He never had it. A salesman's lot is not a happy one for me, Jack thought. I do not belong here. What am I doing here?

"Where the fuck have you been?"

Frank loomed over him.

"Elise is looking for you everywhere. There's a thing for the wives that you really should go to. I've been looking for you everywhere. MacKail's and Sanderson's wives hit it off really well and I told Elise she'd do well to get in with them and she wanted to talk to you about it. What the fuck is the matter with you?"

"Tired. I'm just a little tired, Frank." Jack leaned over into his shirt pocket and pulled out the handkerchief and began mopping his face.

"Forget that, Jack. Forget the tired. Once you decided to come to this thing, you got to toe the mark, man. Do you know there was a guy from San Francisco I heard, who addressed one of the other seminars who's been their top salesman for the past seven years. Has a cabin in Tahoe, takes two months off a year, has made almost ninety thousand for all those years, and only works four days a week?

"It's all out there, man, if that guy can do it, why the hell can't we? Come on, Jack, where's the old pizzaz?"

"I want to sit here, Frank. I want to look out at the water and feel the sand on my feet. And I never had any old pizzaz."

Frank said, unrelenting, "I'm telling you, you're doing the wrong thing. W-R-O-N-G, Jack. You go mingle, you go to stand by your wife's side. Sanderson's the biggest wig we've ever had come speak to us, and he's an important guy to get to know."

"So get to know him," Jack said. "You haven't been in the water once. You haven't gone into town to see what Mexico is like. You might as well be at Coney Island."

"What are you talking about?"

"Get to know Sanderson, Frank. Do that."

Jack walked away, holding his shoes in his hand. I do not belong here, he thought. What am I doing here?

When Elise came back to the room, she found Jack sitting on the patio looking out at the water.

"Where the hell have you been?" she shouted. "I've been looking all over for you, Jack. I had a great foursome for tennis. What's the matter?" she said when she saw his face.

"I met the most charming couple from Arizona. He's that attractive tall man with the prematurely gray shock of hair. I've never seen such beautiful hair. He can't be more than thirty-five with that full head of gray hair. It's very striking. We had a nice afternoon. Jack, where were you?" When Jack didn't answer, Elise went out on the porch and sat down next to him. "What is it, Jack?"

"I don't belong here."

"What are you talking about? Of course you belong here. What do you mean? This is the best thing we ever did, come here. I knew it, intuitively I knew it would be the right thing to come. Just to get to meet all these other salesmen, I have a better picture of the whole scene, and I want to tell you, you are as smart, if not smarter, than some of these men here, Jack. I know you are. I heard some of the wives talking and the possibilities for large incomes are fantastic. We could retire, for goodness sake, if what they say is true. It can be done, and I know you can do it. Jack?"

Jack was staring out at the Gulf. I am not as smart

as they are, he thought. I never was in the running, ever. Ever. I wonder if the woman on the horse with all the children will come by and breast feed the baby. The sun will go down soon and it will get chilly so perhaps she will not come, the baby might get cold. How lucky they are, they don't live in a cold climate, they would die in those rags. They were breaking his heart, that family.

"Jack, are you going to answer me, or what?"

Elise was standing over his chair. Someone named Elise was talking about dressing for dinner and wearing a tuxedo and little diamond earrings.

"Jack, you're frightening me. Stop it. Answer me." Elise walked around in front of him, and stopped short when she saw the tears, one on each cheek.

That night, dinner was set up around one of the four pools at the hotel. Swimmers could still be seen half-immersed in water, having drinks at the bar inside the pool. Many of the faces had the swollen eyes and scorched looks of New York skins gluttonous for the brown hope of the Mexican sun. But, treacherous as it was, the sun gave the illusion of health to the sallow faces.

Elise Gaynor looked very beautiful in the tie-dyed wisp of a nothing dress that had cost her three hundred dollars. She had wisely kept her sunbathing to a minimum and was touched only briefly by the most benign late afternoon rays. She glowed. Candles flickered on each table and the soft night air tantalized the guests with its promise. The Mexican band traveled unobtrusively from table to table, playing the sensuous yet monotonous mariachi music. The moon, as though suspended from some perfect perch, hung benevolently over all.

Frank had managed to sit next to Sanderson and his wife, outmaneuvering Stan MacKail who was concentrating more on keeping his wife sober. Frank had somehow arranged for Jack and Elise at the Sanderson table.

"A toast," Frank said, standing up looking at the brightness of the moon, "to the two most beautiful women at the convention, luckily seated at this particular table."

"Hear, hear," Sanderson said, "to you, my dear," he said, addressing his blond wife, "and to you, Mrs. Gaynor. That certainly is a becoming dress," nodding pointedly at her modestly displayed yet appealing cleavage. Elise flushed. Jack could feel the perspiration coming through his white tuxedo jacket.

Mrs. Sanderson fluttered away as one of the executives asked her to dance.

"Go over and take her seat," Elise whispered to Jack.

"What?"

"You heard me. Go over and sit by Sanderson. There's a vacant chair by Sanderson."

"I see. I see, Elise."

Leaning over so that all the rest of the table could see was the top of her head, Elise squeezed Jack's knee hard. "Jack, just trust me for once. Do as I say. Go over there. Talk to him. Get to know him; he thinks I'm attractive."

The *non sequitur* did not get by Jack. "Why don't you go sit there?" He excused himself and walked off to the men's room.

Fred Santini came over to the table and asked Elise to dance as Frank leaned over in intimate conversation with Charles Sanderson.

"Absolutely fantastic speech this morning, Mr. Sanderson."

"Charley, Frank. Call me Charley." There were gardenias in the middle of the table, the sweet smell complementing the music and the moon.

"Well, thanks a lot, Frank. I appreciate that. I

wanted to spur the men on. I think it's so important for them to know that they start from a clean slate every year, that they're really competing with themselves. That's the American way, you know. I think of myself as the Knute Rockne of the team, you know," he said conspiratorially. "I guess you're too young to know who he was, but damn, that was one fine man. He spurred those players on to incredible heights. It's what I try to do, in my modest way, with you fellows."

"Yes, sir, I saw the picture."

"Do you know this Santini fellow? He seems to be a guy with something on the ball. He's a friend of yours, isn't he?"

Frank paused an instant. Just an instant. "Sure. Terrific guy. Just terrific."

"Family man?"

"Definitely. Has three kids. Just had another one."

"You married, Fairchild?"

Frank flushed. "Not just yet, Mr. . . . Charley. Haven't quite met the right girl yet."

"Right. Well, this is a business frequented by a lot of young men, and these days I suppose most young men don't feel they have to get married. Can get it all for nothing, I suppose. But I am interested in this Santini fellow. We've been getting terrific reports on the man in our home office; he was Rookie of the Month, wasn't he?"

"Yes, sir." Frank felt the ball slowly being taken out of his court.

"He was some kind of football star in college, wasn't he?"

"Yes, sir, before he hurt his wrist."

"Right. How about a cigar, Fairchild?"

"Thanks, thanks a lot, Charley."

"Right. Well, we're thinking of pushing him upstairs, you know what I mean, Fairchild, and I'd appreciate it if you could tell me something about him. We've been hearing some great things about him lately at the Home Office."

Frank felt as though someone had put a wet washcloth on his neck. Cold. He felt cold all over.

"Well," he said, puffing on the cigar, surrounding himself in a house of smoke. "He's one terrific guy, Fred is. Sensational. A real friend. As I said, we've been close for years. And his wife's a doll. A living doll."

"Yes, she's a pretty thing."

"There's only one thing, and," Frank took a deep breath. He had no other choice, he thought. "Lately he's . . . well, Charley, I don't know if I should tell you this. It's sort of like betraying a confidence. I feel strange about that."

"It's the team that counts, Fairchild."

"Well, lately," Frank said, bending close to Sanderson's ear, "Fred's been acting a little edgy."

"Edgy?"

"Yes. As a matter of fact, I've been a little worried about him."

Sanderson leaned back in his chair and took a long drag on the cigar. "Edgy?"

Frank felt trickles of sweat on his upper lip.

"He's been a little nervous lately about making calls. I'm sure it will pass, just something he's going through at the moment. He's under a lot of pressure, you know, a pretty new house in the country, one kid who's dyslexic and has to have expensive tutoring, you know."

"Right." Sanderson looked expectantly at Fairchild.

"He hung up on Blake and Johnson," Frank blurted out.

"What do you mean, hung up?"

"On the phone, talking to an account. The vice-president of the company, as a matter of fact."

"What are you talking about, Fairchild?"

158

"He's just tired, I think. I'm sure it's nothing," Frank said, retrenching for a moment.

"Well, that sounds kind of serious to me. What was the situation?"

"He was just talking to an account and he started to shout, and . . ."

"Thanks, Fred. You're a fabulous dancer," Elise said as Fred returned her to the table. Flaming torches now illuminated the outdoors.

Sanderson and Frank stood up as Elise slipped into the chair Fred was holding out for her.

Frank moved over behind Fred and put his hand on his shoulder. "I'll see you later, buddy," he said. "Good evening, Mr. Sanderson. Fine speech this morning."

In back of Sanderson, Frank could see Jack Gaynor stepping out of the hotel lobby onto the pale pink marble of the patio surrounding the pool. He had changed into a black jacket and was leaning against a marble pillar, looking up at the stars, out into the darkness of the water.

15

Frank had rented a convertible from Hertz, a light blue Mercedes. It was expensive, but it was only for a few days. He met Fred in the lobby an hour later when many of the men were playing cards or sitting at the bar. It was only 10 P.M., and he was wide awake, full of energy. He felt the blood in his veins, he felt an unfamiliar power. Things were starting to happen for him. Sooner than he expected. He wasn't going to scrounge for one more penny in his life, he wasn't going to have to kiss anybody's ass soon, ever again.

Driving along the coast near Acapulco, wearing a red and white sports shirt, tan slacks and loafers, he felt like a king. The only thing missing was the girl, and that would be taken care of very soon.

A few minutes later, Fred and Frank found Priscilla sitting at a ringside table in the night club. She was wearing tight white slacks and a white open-necked blouse. There were red and green Christmas lights that blinked on and off over the bar where mustachioed men were standing five deep.

"Where have you been, Frank? I've been fending for myself for the last hour." In the dim light, she looked about fourteen.

"Sorry, kid. Really sorry. Got into a confab with Charley."

"Sanderson, the big shot? You certainly are trading up, aren't you, dear?"

"Look, babe, let's make a truce from the beginning," Frank said, kissing her on the nose. "This trip was my treat, my idea, right? So be nice. Let's have some fun. You been swimming and sunning down the road apiece while we fellows have been slaving away at the convention, right? So the least you can do is be civil and sweet and lovable. Right, Fred?"

"If it isn't Santini, the family man. You said you were bringing a friend. I didn't know it was my good sparring partner, Freddie boy."

A beautiful Mexican girl seated at the next table was rubbing the chest of her escort. She had a long black braid that hung all the way down her back. Frank ordered three beers since the night clerk at the hotel had told him not to order mixed drinks or anything with ice which would probably get them sick.

A three-piece band announced the arrival of the star stripper with a flourish. She was fleshy.

"They sure like them fat here, don't they?" Priscilla whispered. The rolls on the woman's hips looked like cookie dough ready to be flattened. Miss Martinez, as she was introduced by a frantic MC, was wearing five-inch heels and a flower in her hair. Her costume was framed in fur, and when the bodice was removed, revealed an intricately constructed Theda Bara bra. The girl listlessly meandered back and forth on the stage, taking off her gloves, then her top. The grand finale revealed her with pasties bobbing on her breasts and flesh-colored pantyhose.

"This is supposed to be raunchy?" Priscilla turned to Frank who had taken her hand.

The next stripper was fatter, was wearing a blond wig, and began her act by singing "Havah Nagilah" with frenetic energy.

Priscilla had her glass between both her palms. She was twirling it like fluting on an apple pie. The men watched her, fascinated. She took her third finger and absent-mindedly circled the rim of the glass. The rim of the glass became her circling her own nipple, the torso of the glass their own cocks swirling in the glory of her practiced palms.

"Who wants a smoke?"

Both men nodded.

Frank moved his hand from Priscilla's knee up into the softness on the inside of her leg. Priscilla did not move, or acknowledge the touch. She finished rolling the cigarette and took a long drag before passing it to Frank.

The combination of beer and the marijuana made the trio giggly and silly. Priscilla, in her haze, was enjoying her own aura, the power she had over the men vying for her. She put both her hands behind her neck and pulled her hair up on top of her head. "How's this, boys? Hair today, gone tomorrow. Guess what? Who wants to guess if I've got collar and cuffs?"

"I guess blond," Fred said, entering in the spirit of the evening finally. "Yellow blond on your cunt or maybe strawberry blond, yellow with a hint of red. What do ya say, Priscilla? Going to give us a look or what?"

Priscilla ignored him.

"What about you, Frank?" she said, a seductive tilt to her head. "What's your guess?"

"Black, my dear. Black is the color of my true love's hair."

Priscilla roared. She laughed so hard, tears came to her eyes.

"Wrong. Give that man forty-nine hard-ons!" Priscilla said.

The swinging flesh of the next entertainer came on, and Priscilla said, "Who let that broad in?"

In a moment they were out on the street, where Frank immediately went over to a man leaning against a taxi. He was wearing a white turtleneck sweater with a maroon suit, had no teeth and red boils over his face. Frank chatted with him in halting Spanish. They spoke for a while as Fred and Priscilla went into a nearby shop and looked at leather jackets and pocketbooks.

"O.K., kids, follow me. I've got us some action," Frank called to them.

The cab driver motioned for them to follow him up the stairs of a nearby hotel. It was seedy and smelled of urine. The lobby floor was green-and-yellow tile, and the night clerk, a paunchy man with a large mustache, stood stroking his belly in front of a sign that said, "Drop your key when you check out," in English and Spanish. He grinned openly at Priscilla.

They followed the man in the maroon suit up three flights of stairs. He knocked on a door where the paint was peeling in curls like the bark of a tree. A Mexican woman of about forty opened the door a crack and shook hands with their guide. She put out her hand and Frank gave her twenty dollars. There were small couches set up in a corner of the bedroom with sheets on them.

"She says she wants six dollars more for the room," Priscilla whispered to Frank as the woman held out her hand unsmilingly. Priscilla smelled the potential danger of the room.

An enormous man with his shirt open to the waist and a Zapata mustache emerged out of nowhere. Priscilla translated what he wanted: two dollars more for the prophylaxis. They started to argue but his menacing stance and the fact that they were an obvious captive audience dissuaded them. They all paid the two dollars.

A moment later, moving into the room with the smell of disinfectant surrounding him like a halo, was a young swarthy Mexican, with a towel around his waist. A beautiful girl of about sixteen joined them on the bed. She had olive skin and even white teeth, and her body so far spared the swelling trauma of endless childbirth, was slim and straight. The man removed the towel, revealing a heavy tan. The white of his small rock buttocks looked uncommonly pure.

"He's got a crooked dick," Priscilla whispered to Frank, who was squirming uncomfortably in his seat.

Passionlessly, the two began making love, the man kneading the girl's nipples as though they were television dials. Priscilla admired the boy's body and surprised herself by her calm. The girl moaned loudly and exaggerated her movements and gyrations. She thrashed on the bed, throwing her head from side to side at almost the moment the boy touched her. She had only a small patch of hair over her pubic area.

"That's what I call a weird looking snatch," Priscilla whispered. Priscilla was dispassionate as she looked at the boy, pumping into the girl. It reminded her of young virgins atop giant marble slabs being sacrificed to some voracious Aztec god. The girl had a strange kind of beauty writhing there, and Priscilla was fascinated. Frank and Fred could not pull their eyes away from the coupling.

In a moment, it was over and the girl jumped up, threw her wrapper around her and smiled sheepishly at the audience, revealing a mouth full of gold.

In a moment, two more women suddenly appeared out of the bathroom. One wore high heels and pantyhose with nothing underneath and a Frederick's of Hollywood push-up bra, squeezing out puffs of peacock flesh from her chest. The other woman had scrolls of fat and wore red underpants. Her breasts were bare and lay like pancakes on her pigeon chest where unexpected bones featured prominently. She was carrying a roll of toilet paper which she rolled out in long strips over the bed.

The women tousled each other's hair like the varsity team before scrimmage and began kissing and embracing each other. From out of nowhere, the fat woman found an enormous rubber dildoe which she held up for the audience to see. Frank and Fred were mesmerized by the woman's huge flanks.

She pushed it into the woman's vagina. The woman underneath kept crying out in Spanish in mock pleasure, and the grunting, the heavy odor, the chunkiness of the flesh, the shouts, the obscenity of those huge legs open like some spread eagled cowboy captured by the Apaches was alternately compelling and revolting.

"You like suck pussy?" the tall mustachioed Mexican appeared from out of nowhere and obsequiously approached Frank. He said it as though it were one word.

Frank waved him away as the couple on the bed choreographed the finale. The women shrugged and disappeared into the bathroom again.

Walking down the stairs, Priscilla felt weak in the knees, moist in the groin. Frank put his arm around her waist.

"I told you I'd find some action, baby," Frank whispered.

"I've never seen that before," Fred said, dropping his pose for an instant.

"Second time for me, chum," Priscilla said, rumpling Fred's hair. "It gets better every time." She was feeling strong again, titillated.

"Listen, fellows, why don't you come back to my little hotel. I've got some booze and great grass and my little record player that I never travel without. What do you say? Let's have a party."

They were all shaken by the sordidness of the hotel room. But it had excited them.

Fred looked at his watch and thought of Ellen back home nursing the baby. She was probably reading *New York* magazine and some woman's article about how middle-aged men were not matched as lovers for their middle-aged wives. They weren't in that category yet, not by a long shot, but Ellen was beginning to believe, young as she was, that she was reaching her peak and Fred was beginning the long spiral down to *non erectus est*.

Priscilla rolled them a joint which they shared on the drive back to her hotel. Frank had found her a small pension with outdoor dining and a pool. Priscilla had been enchanted and it was worth it, putting up with Frank's pomposity to have the days there by herself, swimming and sunning, surrounded by such beauty.

By the time they reached Priscilla's room, they had tripped over each other's shoes and put their fingers to their lips in forced hoarse whispers ten times. They were all convulsed with giggles as Priscilla fumbled for the key.

"This place looks like a fucking hospital," Frank said, throwing his jacket on the couch in the small sitting room. Priscilla went over to her tiny portable stereo and put on an Al Green record. It was slow. She kicked off her shoes. She had decided to waste no time. She swayed her hips back and forth, embracing herself around the arms. Humming, she shut her eyes and danced by herself. The men watched her silently. She was graceful, and for the moment, lost in herself. She put her hands around her waist and went to the back, unzipping her slacks. With deft, quick movements, she removed them over her hips. She threw them at Fred. She wasn't smiling. She had on a pair of pantyhose with no panties underneath. She continued dancing by herself, sinuously. The flash of pubic hair and her plump thighs disarmed the men. Priscilla was living up to her reputation, more than they could have imagined.

"What the hell are you staring at, Fred, it's just a cunt," she said angrily. "You know, just like the one that married dear old dad. Just like the one wifey has at home in the suburbs or wherever it is you're going to creep home when this is all over."

A contempt had glided into Priscilla's speech and Fred couldn't figure out whether she was making fun of him or provoking him. Whatever it was, it made him uncomfortable.

He decided not to take offense.

"Scarsdale, kid, Scarsdale, home of the free, land of the supermarkets."

"Oh, God, I should have known. That or Valley Stream, one or the other, for God's sakes." Her tone

166

suddenly became softer. She turned to Frank and purred. "I wonder if you could scratch my back, hon. I've got an itch right about there below the shoulder blade."

Frank began to scratch her back, below the shoulder blade, as instructed. It was a strong young back with no straps or encumbrances.

Priscilla began to moan. "Mmm, that's super, man, simply super." She moved her body around so that the rounding motion of his hand caught her breasts instead of the shoulder blade. "Mmm, that's just fine, kid, but really kid stuff. Don't you think?" Her voice changed and she sounded like a ten dollar whore reciting her litany of prices. "Anybody here see *Deep Throat?*" Both men nodded. Frank still was rubbing her back.

"I just loved that beginning part, didn't you?" With that, Priscilla hopped up and sat on a table in the corner of the room. She pulled off her pantyhose. She spread her legs. "Now do you remember?"

Her pubic hair did indeed match the gold on her head. Both men sat on the couch, Al Green moaning in the background as Priscilla fingered herself. She opened her blouse and shook her breasts free. The nipples hugged the air. With one hand, she lovingly caressed her own cunt, with the other she smoothed her breast.

"Now do you remember?" she cooed, "at the opening of *Deep Throat*. Remember this dude was going down on this broad with black hair. It was a horny scene. I sat through it twice just to get to see it again." She didn't skip a beat on her own breast as she was talking. Both men had started to perspire. Both wanted to move over to her but were inhibited by the other's presence.

Frank was the first to break the spell.

"What do you say, Pris?"

"I thought you'd never ask," Priscilla moved down off the table, slipping off her blouse which revealed her breasts, round apples with hard sharp stems pointing at each other.

Within moments, Frank was nude in the bedroom, and had thrown off the coverlet.

Priscilla was sitting up in bed, her back against the pillow. She had both her breasts in her hands. Slowly, she was moving her fingers around each nipple, slowly pulling them out, extending them and the breasts. She moved her hand over her belly and into her inner thigh with round slow motions.

Frank, who had had a lot to drink and had smoked some strong grass at that moment saw Priscilla with Picasso-like four breasts and cunts the size of Vesuvius. He grabbed for her. He pushed her down flat on the bed and tried to find her nipple with his mouth. He missed, finding a mole instead, just under her armpit. He licked it ravenously. His erection was tentative, he couldn't tell that immediately from all the booze and the brazenness of the woman, but he tested it. One hand on her breast, the other guided his member into her. He was heavy and was sweating. Priscilla, who had brought herself to a pleasurable pitch, became bored almost immediately. She felt as though he were a tootsie roll, so timorous and hesitant were his thrusts.

She rolled him over her. He was panting.

"What the fuck are you panting for?" she asked, "you didn't do a damn thing."

"Hold on, baby, I just have to go inside for a drink. Be right back. Don't start without me. Hold the fort."

Frank grabbed a towel on the back of a chair and pulled it around him, and walked out the door.

Priscilla lay back. Knowing what was next.

The door opened and a streak of light showed a figure with a white towel around the middle. He threw the towel over the chair and flung himself on Priscilla. He didn't fool her one bit.

"Hi, there, Freddy boy, finally got the nerve to give it a whirl. Well, let's see if you're better than your friend."

Priscilla felt Fred put his penis into her. In a moment it was over.

"Christ, what a pair," Priscilla shouted.

"Shhh, baby, it's just that you're so sexy. You get me too excited."

Priscilla so far had found herself the most exciting member of the threesome. "Fuck off, Fred, get a load off, get lost." Her voice was tired.

"No, baby, look, let me help you get off. No sweat, be glad to."

"Fuck off, I said," Priscilla's voice was harsh. "Who needs a deadhead like you and your pal? A friend in need is a friend indeed and I've got my own fingers, for Christ's sake. Lie back, pal and watch how it's supposed to be done."

Fred rolled off her body, and through sleepy eyes, watched the girl take both hands to both breasts and knead and rub their tips with short strokes. Her expertise was not lost on Fred's squinting eyes and he felt himself get hard watching her.

In the doorway, the light at his back, Frank had a drink in his hand. He was watching. It was what he liked to do best.

Priscilla took one hand away when she found herself ready and found the button below that protruded like large waxen lips. She pushed her finger deep inside her and then withdrew, brushing the tip of her button, establishing a rhythm and counterpoint with her nipple. Fred touched himself as he watched her skillfully bring herself to a crescendo. The back of her head went from side to side on the pillow. Frank was soaking wet, standing in the doorway.

When she was finished, Priscilla raised both arms above her head and stretched. She got out of bed, went into the bathroom like Alexander the Great after a battle. Haughty, contemptuous. Her own body had been high scorer. That was one thing she could always trust, she thought, bathing between her legs. The one thing she could depend on.

Two deadheads. With all their talk. Who needed them. She'd gotten her rocks off and got a little tan. Maybe she'd stay down here South of the Border, maybe she'd take up with one of those black-eyed waiters, maybe she'd stop fucking altogether. Maybe one damn day she'd find out what it was she was looking for.

16

The hills were purple. Driving in her rented car from the San Francisco Airport, Wilma was overwhelmed by the tint of this Western world. It was as though her windshield had been painted with luminescent paint and the roofs and trees and especially the hills surrounding the houses had all turned pastel.

She had left in a raging snowstorm. New York was a good place to get away from, she thought. She had left grays and whites for more gracious colors. The plane had sat on the ground for one hour contemplating its navel, wondering whether it could take off or not. By the time the wings had finally spun their promise of flight, it was anticlimactic. She had come to terms with dying in this storm, crashing into a telephone pole or plummeting into the Jamaica Bay followed by thousands of scurrying snowflakes. But, the captain, bless his soul, within minutes had risen above the clouds. Suddenly, the storm had subsided and a brilliant sun was greeted by a burst of applause by the not so fatalistic passengers who were determined to reach their destination.

Wilma was like a little girl. She loved to fly. She loved the movie, she loved the cardboard food, she loved the earplugs. It was an adventure. She had never gone so far from home alone. She was proud of herself, yet no matter how accomplished and self-sufficient, she was a little timorous about the proposed itinerary. She didn't drive often and had decided to do the seventeen-mile drive herself. She was not on any tour, so if she met anyone it would have to be as a result of her own assertiveness. She didn't know a soul in the state and didn't have one telephone number to contact. It was a test, a self-imposed test of her ingenuity, her ability to fend for herself, her capability of being truly, inexorably alone.

She was aware of her ambivalent feelings. Part of her felt stimulated by the challenge of it, being behind a wheel, watching a city open up to her. New York constricted her vista, her chest felt tight and small in the city. She never looked up or around, rushing the streets. Here she found herself looking in every direction. She felt a sense of freedom; of being her own person, here behind this wheel in this new place.

She checked into the Stanford Court Hotel that night. It was a clean well-lighted place with a lobby that exuded an understated elegance. Her room was beautifully furnished, and the bathroom, she decided, was worth the whole trip. There was a second color television there, a phone on a long dressing table, and there was steam and a sunlamp overhead. She never wanted to leave.

Wilma ordered a martini up to the room. The elderly bellman was respectful and kind, putting out the little nuts in a dish on a small coffee table for her. She luxuriated in the excitement, determined to dispel all fears. Although she had asked for a view, they had given her an inside room and she overlooked a rather uninteresting court. But it didn't matter.

Laboriously, she made up her eyes. After forty, cut the hair; after fifty, use very little make-up, was her motto. She knew she was a handsome woman, but she also knew that she was going to be fifty-one years old next birthday and there was no use getting too gussied up. Any man who looked at her would know she was fifty and that was that. There wasn't much she could do about it. Even if they would chop off a few years, it would be splitting hairs. She didn't mind being fifty, she didn't even mind looking fifty. What she minded was that other people minded.

Wilma had brought about ten books to read, works she had been trying to get around to for months. Some best sellers, and she had decided to reread Jane Austen and George Eliot. No one ever had time to do things like that, she decided, so she brought along *Middlemarch* and *Pride and Prejudice*. There was something seductive about sitting in this sumptuous hotel room, surrounded by television sets and steam, martinis and cashew nuts reading Jane Austen.

She had asked the desk to make a reservation for her at L'Etoile. And at 8:30, a fashionably late enough hour she thought to eat, the place was still only half full. The *maître d'* looked behind her for her escort, but she swept grandly by, giving him the most austere withering glance she could muster. She dined grandly, eating, chewing, sipping slowly. She felt strange, but sat upright, determined to be proud, determined to ignore the eyes that looked quizzically at her table. In the old days, when she was young and would be sitting alone in a restaurant or in a coffee shop or airport, someone would catch her eye or notice her trim ankles and stare. It didn't happen any-

172

more. Only once in a while would a man, waiting for the red light to change on Fifth Avenue, make eye contact with her that would be followed up by an invitation to coffee or at least a conversation. It didn't happen anymore, and it hurt. It was a loss. No longer did she walk into a room bathed by the glances of approbation from men and women alike. No more. Silver threads among the gold. Screw it. So what? She was still the same person inside; better, as a matter of fact.

She had the fresh Rex sole, the limestone lettuce salad, ordered a half bottle of *Chablis* and savored the brandy crisp with grand marnier sauce. She dawdled over her demitasse and had a B&B. The waiter did not flirt with her, the *maître d'*, knowing she would not slip him a five, surreptitiously ignored her once the initial contact was finished. But she enjoyed the meal. She had taken some notes, jotting down thoughts between the courses. It was something to do rather than stare ahead or at the dishes other people were eating. She walked around a bit after dinner, but the air was chilly. It had been a long day.

It was all right. She had gotten through the first day rather well, she congratulated herself. I can do it, she thought. Where is it written that I have to have a man by my side all the time? But back in her room, between a brandy, the late show, and Jane Austen, it still took a long time for her to fall asleep.

The next few days were filled with sight-seeing; she marveled at the Golden Gate Bridge and drove her car across the Bay, into Sausalito where she had lunch at a restaurant overlooking the water. The gulls came and perched on the wood deck, and she enjoyed the forced quaintness of the town. She spoke to a couple from Ames, Iowa, who had left the children home, and struck up a conversation with the waitress, a doe-eyed girl who looked like a ballet dancer. She went to Santa Cruz College and was studying anthropology. Past

Sausalito, Wilma drove to Muir woods and took pictures of trees that were thousands of years old, whose enormous trunks had silently, stolidly observed a world changing. She was awed by the ramifications of their age. What sights, what storms, what changes they've seen, she thought, looking endlessly up into the sky. The woods were darkly mysterious, and she yearned to nudge someone's elbow and tell them so.

She shopped and took the cable car in San Francisco and went to Chinatown, buying gifts for her nephews and nieces. By mid-week, she took the car and drove to Big Sur and Monterey. Carmel was gingerbread. The perfect place. It was clean and neat and original and so far from the dirt and disorder of New York that her body was filled with relief.

The next day was dessert. It was what she had come for. She had learned about Monterey and the Seventeen Mile Drive in college when she had read Robinson Jeffers' poetry. Years ago, it had stuck in her mind; this is the place to see, the place of such formidable beauty that, before I die, I will see it so I will be able to conjure it, have it before my eyes whenever I want it.

She set out hours before dusk, timing her trip so she would see a sunset through the spaces in the jagged trees lining the cliffs.

She snapped picture after picture until, stopping at a spot on the drive where seals were frolicking in the water across the way, she sat down on a grassy area. There were no other cars around. For a moment, it was very still. The seals were undoubtedly croaking, but were too far away to be heard. Like some orange lantern dangling in the sky, the sun began its descent. Steadily it began to fall, as though someone had cut its strings connecting it to the sky. The Pacific would swallow it in seconds. For that moment, Wilma was barely aware of her own breathing. The gnarled branches of the stripped trees reached for the sun, and there was no sound. In one last defiant "we who are about to die salute you" gesture, the sun lit up the sky with rays of reds and yellows. Wilma was washed in its palette.

Like an orgasm that makes you think you are going to die, like a blinding pain, the exquisite sky overcame her. She had never felt so alone. The sky was burning, and she had no one to tell. At least Chicken Little went screaming into the barnyard, telling the animals that the sky was falling, she thought, tears wetting her face. She hadn't realized she was crying, and couldn't stop. All this beauty. No one to nudge. No one to tell. All her composure and all her strength and determination that she had so carefully compiled the week long, crumbled as the sun, with infinite grace, made a path for itself into the water. Without a splash, she thought. At this moment in this world, she thought, searching for a handkerchief in her pocket book, at this moment in this world, there is no one more alone than I. No one to nudge. How will anyone ever know how beautiful it was. The tears lasted a long time, and Jane Austen proved small comfort.

17

From seven-thirty till midnight, Thursday, Agnes packed. She was a careful person. She had saved the cleaning bags for weeks so she could wrap her shoes before packing them at the bottom of her suitcase. Tis-

sue paper from gifts and old Lord and Taylor and Alt-
man's boxes from Christmases past had been neatly
piled at the top of her closet. She had been able to
collect all colors, and lovingly wrapped in green paper
the green copy of a Bergdorf original she had seen in
the window with a cut-out back and shawl to match.
She had found the same thing at Loehmann's in the
Bronx for half the price, and it gave her a surge of
pleasure to see it folded at the bottom of her suitcase
on top of the shoes, tissue paper hidden in each curve,
each layer and lap of the dress.

She folded the new flowered bikini with the little
fringed skirt designed to minimize the swelling of her
upper and outer thighs. Agnes had been dedicated to
this mission ever since she was thirteen and they had
ballooned out of proportion to the rest of her. She had
small but shapely breasts, a fine straight torso, but like
tires inflated from an air pump, her thighs seemed
stuffed, puffed out from below hips of reasonable
size. They seemed to have appeared overnight ("What
happened to you, Agnes?" her mother had asked one
day, sitting in the small dressing room in Filenes in
Boston where they had come in for the day from
Brookline. "Where did you get those stretch marks?
We'll have to put cocoa butter on them immediately."). But it was too late, and Agnes, like Mrs.
Friedman, had a pretty face but heavy rounded flanks,
just as Mrs. Friedman's mother had. Ever since Agnes
knew her mother and grandmother, they both had had
heavy rounded everything, flanks and breasts, shoulders and ankles. Edith Friedman was a mountain of a
woman, shapeless, always surrounded by one of three
flowered cotton dresses she always wore. It seemed as
though there was always a scratched imitation leather
bag around her wrist and black cloche with an un-
timely feather on her head. "He'll come along, your
prince," she would say to Agnes. "Some day your

176

prince will come." She would say it in the way Snow White sang in that saccharine sweet voice of hers. And Agnes believed her. And it would be this weekend. He would come. This is the weekend of my prince, Agnes thought.

Twenty dollars a day extra was a lot, but she had saved for it. Bringing her lunch, walking one way to work. Every Friday she had put the money away in the Chase Manhattan branch at Twenty-third Street. The thought of not having to share a room was titillating. Some girls in the office had gone away last Christmas and had saved a lot by sharing a room with three other girls; with one bathroom, one closet. No, sir. Not for her. Agnes was going to do it right. "If you're going to do it, do it right," Mrs. Friedman always said.

At 11:30, Johnny Carson had just finished his opening monologue and was introducing Burt Reynolds. Agnes glanced at the TV. She looked at the actor's sleek, sly looks, his flat stomach and long legs stretching casually in front of him where he had plumped himself in his chair with studied ease. Agnes caught her breath. She tied the ribbons tight around the bulk of the clothes in the suitcase, pressing them down, and struggled it off the bed. Burt Reynolds was essaying some double entendres, his chest bursting out of his cowboy shirt. "A man like that," she mused, slipping out of her slacks and sweater, a man like that, kissing you and holding you, protecting you. What would it be like?

Agnes slipped her flannel nightgown over her head after folding her clothes and putting them away. Everything was in order. She straightened the hand mirror and brush set embossed with silver sitting on the white ruffled cover on the bureau.

Reynolds was still taunting her from across the room. He had shaved off his mustache. She wasn't so sure she liked it. He had just made some starlet blush, leered at Carson, then at Agnes. She blushed, too. If only there were such a thing as a Jewish Burt Reynolds, she thought; with that twinkle, that wickedness, that promise of strength.

She blew Burt a kiss before shutting off the set.

The Port Authority Building made Agnes uncomfortable. Everyone looked dirty to her, unsavory. She didn't feel safe. She understood the logic of having a bus terminal so close to New Jersey, but she couldn't understand it being on Ninth Avenue with its darkness and garbage-strewn streets where bearded blacks looked her straight in the eye and nudged their companions when she passed. They terrified her. She finally found someone to help her with her large bag. "Short Line," she told him, and he waited till she bought her ticket. She tipped him seventy-five cents, a quarter more than she usually did because she was feeling so good.

She was finally seated in the back of the bus, near the bathroom, and before she knew it they had zoomed through a dark tunnel. The skyline of New York, shining in the morning sun, was behind her. She was on her way. Agnes put the return ticket into the zippered portion of her wallet. The round trip had cost $15.70. She couldn't bear the thought of returning home. She knew it would be over so fast.

"Tom Genent, the Swingingest Discount Dealer in Hudson County" the sign on the left said. Then, out the window in the middle of a cluster of forlorn naked trees, a larger-than-life poster of Raquel Welch emblazoned itself against the sky. "Coming to the Lord Windsor late in January." Agnes felt her ears popping. Resort land. The land of resorts, she thought, watching the billboards rush by; Nevele, Browns, Tamiment, names she had heard all her life. Places her parents

178

could never afford. Did you ever see a dream walking, she thought. I am. I am walking in my own dream.

The girl next to her had a tiny button nose with X's from the stitches at the corners of each nostril. She had on a full-length raccoon coat which took up most of the seat, including Agnes' half, carried a Vuitton bag and held a very small dog wrapped in a purple scarf. Her nails were long and painted dark red, and her black hair, cut in the fashionable short bob with bangs, still had residual red dye in it.

Agnes had tried to make conversation with her, but she wasn't interested. She seemed to have her own dreams.

As they turned off the thruway into Monticello, her excitement began to mount. One sign in front of a bank said the temperature was fifteen degrees. A few yards down, in front of the lumber company, it was seventeen degrees. Whatever it was, it was much colder than in New York. The girl next to her gathered up her dog, her Vuitton bag, her raccoon coat, and her hairbrush which had fallen from her pocket. With great hauteur, she swept out of the bus. Agnes followed, a bit envious at the dash of the girl.

They transferred to a small blue school bus that Agnes thought should have been dismantled for the graduating class of 1925. Rickety and hardly the entrance into the wonderful world of resorts she was anticipating. The travel agent had told her that she would be met at the depot by a limousine from the Lord Windsor. But Agnes and the twenty or so guests good-naturedly got on the bus after the driver took their bags.

She found herself next to the raccoon coat again, but this time she talked to her.

"Single, or double? Triple, or what?" The voice was rasping, the flat A's and nasality startling out of the well-groomed facade. New York shone in every vowel; every consonant trembled with Manhattan streets.

"Pardon?"

"Single or double? Do you have a roommate or what?"

"Oh, I'm alone. I've taken a single room."

"Me, too. Make out much better that way. Especially since I have to sneak the dog anyway. Ever do this singles bit before?"

"No. First time. Have you?"

"Sure. I was here a few months ago, had a ball, an absolute ball." She pulled a cigarette out of her purse despite the "No Smoking" sign at the front of the bus. "You do better when you come alone. Know what I mean?" Without waiting to hear an answer, Arlene, her handkerchief had the name embroidered in pink, turned to the young man across the aisle. "Got a light?"

After checking in and going with the bellboy in the elevator to her room, Agnes sat down on the bed. The lobby had been a disappointment, the Musak blaring Beatles songs out into the vastness of the room. "Yeah, yeah, yeah" bounced off the red flowered carpet. "Yeah, yeah, yeah" careened off the ceiling.

Agnes felt warm in her slacks suit. Arlene had brought with her essence of Priscilla, eau de Dolores, the odor of girls in their twenties. They made her very, very nervous. Arlene's aggressiveness frightened her. Intimidated her. Just as Priscilla's did. No assertiveness training course for this one. She could get across Alaska in a glass-bottom boat.

She got up, carefully hung up her coat, ran water in the tub for a bath, pouring in some Jean Naté bath oil, and began to unpack. It was 2 P.M., and from three to five a singles get-acquainted cocktail party was slated downstairs.

180

An hour later, Agnes was standing at a punch-bowl dressed in her cherished pair of Jax slacks cut carefully to imply less roundness, her cheeks pinkened with Revlon's blush-on, a beige sweater over a flowered Lauren shirt. About several hundred people converged on a long table. The board was groaning, after all, Agnes thought, with meatballs, thousands of little frankfurters with toothpicks on the side, surrounded by mountains of mustard, peaks of Dijon.

As Agnes sipped the pink stuff served in a small paper cup, all at the moment seemed right with the world. As she looked around, she felt a bit overdressed. Most of the younger women had on skin-tight jeans and casual shirts or sweaters. Most of the men seemed to be wearing jeans as well. A very short pretty girl with platform heels and a tight-fitting skirt was standing next to Agnes. "I love your sweater," she said. "Oh, thanks so much," Agnes said, glowing. "I know this little shop downtown that sells only name blouses. Just blouses; Laurens and Blasports and even Diors. I got three Dior shirts there with the Dior insignia embroidered onto the cuff for thirteen dollars each just the other day." The words rushed from her. It was the first time she had spoken here and she was grateful for the interchange. The girl smiled. She came up to Agnes' chest. "Downtown where? New York?" "Yes. Where are you from?" "Washington, D.C. Just moved there from Chicago." "Why did you move?"

"I got a better job," she said, her eyes going to Agnes. Her hair was frosted and flipped and she had round blue eyes. She was very pretty. And very young.

"What do you do?" Agnes asked, refilling her glass with the sweet wine punch.

"I'm a lawyer. What about you?"

"Insurance," she said. Not going into detail.

"Have you ever met anyone at any of these things?"

"Never," the girl answered. "I came here with a

181

few girl friends because none of us had anything going for the holidays. I never really do expect to meet anybody terrific. Just some new faces. Somebody new. What about you?"

"I've never done a week or weekend before."

"Listen, what did you say your name was? Mine's Karen, Karen Stern. Listen, don't expect anything. Remember. The guys want to get laid. That's what they come up here for. You'll see they won't even buy you a drink at the bar if you won't put out. And if he's attractive, and will spring for dinner back in the city, why not? I just come to unwind and have a good time. Forget about really meeting someone worthwhile. It's a flesh factory, and if you don't expect anything more, you'll have a great time. There's a lot to do, tennis and swimming and ice skating, and if it doesn't snow, they'll make their own."

Why was she telling her all this, Agnes thought? Did it show? Could she tell how she had been saving and dreaming for this week? Was it written all over her face, for heaven's sake? She couldn't believe the cynicism of the girl, whose angelic demeanor implied something else.

"Well, hope we bump into each other sometime. There are my friends." She left Agnes in a swirl of skirt and fragrance of Charlie.

Hilda Schneiderman, recreation director at the Lord Windsor for the past fifteen years, stood up and adjusted the microphone behind the hors d'oeuvres table. Hilda wore a three-piece suit with the jacket lined in the material of the blouse. She had candlestick legs, hair dyed red and a voice like Lionel Stander.

"Welcome to the Lord Windsor." She peered at the group through thick glasses. "This is going to be the best, the very best time of your life, believe you me, and if it doesn't work out, we don't want to hear about it. Listen, I'm good at match-making. I introduced a

182

brother to a sister." She looked around the room expectantly. A few young girls giggled. A striking looking young man standing in front of Agnes stroked his beard. "Now remember," Hilda continued, "this is a get-acquainted party. That's the purpose of the whole thing, you know, to get acquainted here. Later, there will be champagne and dancing, and what happens is, you go in one and come out two. And next year, come out three. And listen, we help the needy, not the greedy. So married people, if there are any, just keep out."

There was a small round of applause as Hilda went on to say something about the card room being always open and the bridge tournaments would be starting tomorrow morning. Agnes was beginning to feel the punch, realizing that she hadn't eaten lunch yet. People were milling about circling, eyeing each other like cats in an alley.

"Hi, there."

Mel Feinstein found her.

"How about a real drink?"

There he was. Before it even started. Her Jewish Burt Reynolds. So what if his nose had the same stitches as Arlene in the bus, so what if his Icelandic Fisherman's sweater and custom-made jeans looked as though *Gentlemen's Quarterly* had hired him for the fall back-to-school issue.

"What do you say?" Mel Feinstein breathed into her left ear.

"Pardon?"

Boston and Friedman breeding and Sunday school and Rabbi Feldman fashioned the word.

"Pardon?"

"You heard me, Freckles. How about a real drink?"

"Freckles?"

"Two of them. The glorious ones at the bridge of

your nose. Hasn't anyone noticed them before? From now on, you're 'Freckles' to me."

Agnes wished she had put on her red plaid ski skirt with the black turtleneck. She wished she hadn't put so much hair spray on her hair. She wished this moment would stay suspended like a snowflake on a branch before the sun shone.

"Mel Feinstein. What's yours?"

He was talking some more.

"Friedman. Agnes. Agnes Friedman."

"Well, Agnes Friedman, what do you say we go into the Owl Lounge for a drink? Let's split the punch and Judy show here and get some real booze. Whatdya say?"

"Fine. Just fine."

Mel Feinstein was a man who needed these weekends. He needed the glances of the girls, the tightly encased crotches bending into his way as they did the hustle, he needed the hungry looks and the adoring repartee. "A dime a dozen" he would say to Herb and Frank, his bar-hopping pals, or Felix and Dan, the walking weekend wounded, as he called them. Getting laid to him never palled. He had been married briefly when he was twenty-two to a Jewish-American princess who, he would tell anyone who would listen, was a lamb chop in bed, but a veritable virago at Bonwits. Jewish girls, he would say, after seven drinks at Bradley's down in the Village before, during and after the jazz set, had bad backs, and never swallowed it. He was thirty now, seasoned, a successful garment center maven who considered himself a true aficionado of womanhood. Years ago, he had weighed 202, had his father's strong Hebraic nose and had acne from his forehead to below his shoulder blades. Today he eschewed all ownership to that Mel, glorifying in the new consistency of his Harry Reems erections, the velour of his matching jeans set, the round custom-made bed in his apartment with round brown custom-made fur to cover it. Under all the *savoir-faire* was still a fat boy for whom his mother wore her deepest décolletage when pressing him to bed. "It's like the New Deal," he would say to Felix and Dan, candlelight flickering in some East Side bar waiting for the girl singer to come on. "It's the CCC, creature, comfort and cunt, that's all that matters. Once you've had a Jewish princess, you've had them all," he would say, the fat boy smarting.

He put his arm around Agnes' waist and led her across the floor to one of the many rooms off the large lobby. The Bear Lounge next to the Carthinian Room which was near the Royal Room. Each room promised unknown mysterious delights to Agnes. She was determined to see the inside of them all.

She tripped over the carpet as she walked into the Bear Lounge, Mel's arm firmly around her waist. Erskine Hawkins, in a business suit, was playing the trumpet with his small combo at the back of the bar.

"What'll you have?"

"A Rob Roy, please."

A few people were dancing in the aisle and Hawkins, looking like a college professor, was blowing "Days of Wine and Roses" across the room, little musical kisses straight to Agnes' cheek. Long, thin tables in front of the small bandstand were filled with groups of girls in twos and threes, shoulders straight, eyes darting, heads unmoving around the room. The lights were low. Agnes was glad she had put a piece of Kleenex dabbed in Chanel into her bra. She could sense her own odor.

More couples got up to dance as Hawkins quickened the beat. Several girls were dancing together.

"So, and what do you do, my dear?"

"Insurance. I'm in insurance. And you, you're a lawyer I'll bet." Wishful thinking. Someone this hand-

185

some and suave would have to be a lawyer, Agnes reasoned.

"Nope. Guess again. Here, babe, have a nut." Mel pushed the salted peanuts to her. He picked a few up, with his fingers softly opened Agnes' lips and fed them to her one by one. Agnes shuddered.

"Chilly, babe?"

"Not at all," she said, recovered. "Have you ever been here before?"

"Last year. Last year I came up twice and had a blast. Then last summer a bunch of us went to Grossingers. More choices on the menu. Have you?"

"Have I what?"

"Ever been here before."

"Never." Agnes saw her reflection in the mirror behind the bar. Not a hair out of place. She patted her head, taking comfort in the taut teased top. It made her feel in control. When Donny Lawder used to come by and take her to the movies when she was in eleventh grade, even though he wasn't Jewish and even though she didn't approve, Mrs. Friedman was grateful Agnes was beginning to have dates. She would stand behind her in the bathroom clucking approval as Agnes would tease the top of her hair. "Remember now, a movie and a soda or something is fine, but Donny Lawder is hardly the living end. He is just a boy to go to the movies with. Just think of him like that."

Agnes had liked Donny Lawder. He was quiet and had introduced her to the poems of Walt Whitman. His father was a policeman and he wanted to be an English teacher. "He's short, he's puny, he's a goy, and he has pimples," Mrs. Friedman would scoff. "What kind of boy friend is that, I'm asking you? A girl like you with your brains and your skin. Have you any idea, any idea of what's out there waiting for you?

You save it, kiddo, you get somebody worthy of you. I'm telling you. I know from whereof I speak."

It wasn't that Agnes was a virgin. Once she had moved out of the house, was graduated from junior college, gone to secretarial school and moved to New York, she was on her way. There had been a few men. Just a few. She had never admitted it to anyone but she hadn't been to bed with a man until she was in her late twenties. It never seemed appropriate. Her first had been Martin Edelman, an adjuster from Newark who came to the office for meetings once a month. Martin was attractive, dressed well even though the large plaid patterns on his suits were overwhelming to Agnes, and a solid gold cigarette case was a little much. But he wined and dined her for a month every Wednesday.

When he took her to bed finally, she didn't understand why she had felt so cold. It had been painful because she wasn't lubricated, because she didn't love him, because he wasn't special enough. Perhaps she had gone on too long, perhaps she had stayed too long at the fair, perhaps she was, indeed, "dried up," as Martin accused her. He stayed around, however, every Wednesday for another few months, putting vaseline into her vagina, trying to make her nipples stay hard, tickling the inside of her mouth with his tongue. He liked her fleshy thighs and soft bottoms. His wife was a thin woman.

Agnes found out about the wife from Flo, the receptionist, one Wednesday morning when a call came in from a hospital in New Jersey. The wife had slipped on the ice with a bag of groceries in her arms and had broken a bottle of vinegar all over the Jersey Turnpike or something. The story lost a lot in translation from Flo's Brooklynese, but the essence of the tale was there. Martin had a wife, who walked, who shopped, who fell. And that was the end of that. Agnes didn't

187

get out of bed that whole weekend after she found out, hair unteased, eyes unmascaraed. She felt betrayed, sullied. Her bruises healed slowly. She had almost convinced herself she felt something for Martin, but after finding out he was married, she broke all six of the milk glass vases he had brought her, one by one, straight into the kitchen garbage pail.

There had been only one other. She had had no illusions about Bernard Stone whom she met on the Crosstown bus one night. They had chatted, exchanged pleasantries about the cold and the potholes of New York when he asked her for a drink before going home. She had to water her plants and do her nails that night, and that was all. The apartment was an empty thing to come home to. She tried to hide the grateful look in her eye when she accepted. Not Mr. Right certainly, and even though she was determined to wait for Him, there were times after she turned thirty that she would get that cold empty pain in her stomach, when she thought about being alone for more years.

She couldn't take sex lightly as the younger girls did. It was beyond her. She knew somewhere that there was more pleasure, more spiritual comfort in it for her than she had experienced. But it was elusive. Bernard turned out to be an accountant, prematurely bald and self-conscious about it. He didn't have enough hair on the back of his head to get a transplant. That was the great disappointment of his life, after putting aside a little money every week for the plugs, to find there wasn't enough for the plastic surgeon to work with. He and Agnes became friends, and he took her to Shakespeare in the park, and since he was into transcendental meditation, to hear the Maharishi at the Felt Forum at Madison Square Garden.

He took her home to meet his mother, a bony woman of seventy-eight who was confined to a wheelchair but still gave thirteen piano lessons. Agnes let Bernard fondle her as they would lie naked in bed Saturday nights, listening to her Pops Concert tapes with the lights out, watching the reflections of the headlights dance on the ceiling. Only once in the year she knew him did she have an orgasm, and it had crept up on her, before she could catch it, savor it. It was her "falling star" as she ruefully referred to it in her diary.

She had stopped seeing Bernard a year ago when she realized that he was indeed the farthest thing from Mr. Right there was; that his touch had begun to disturb her. She wanted so much more.

"A penny for your thoughts, babe."

Mel had taken her hand and was tickling the inside of her palm. "Ever had your palm read?"

"Yes. A long time ago a gypsy told me my heart would crack in two."

Bite your tongue, Mrs. Friedman was saying to the Agnes in her head. Bite the tip off, you fool.

"Know the fortune telling scene in *Carmen?*"

"Oh sure, it's one of my favorite operas."

"Yeah, me too. I see it once a year at the Met."

"Really?" Her eyes were wide.

"Sure, and I used to have a season ticket to the Philharmonic, but something was always coming up on Thursday nights. You like music?"

"Oh, enormously." Agnes played with the charms on her bracelet.

"Me, too. But what I love is musicals. *Chicago* was unbelievable, a classic."

"Oh, I didn't get to see it, but I loved *Chorus Line.*"

"Me, too. Get to read Mailer's book on Marilyn Monroe?"

"Oh, yes. I love the way he writes."

"Me, too. But James Michener's my favorite, my absolute favorite. His *Centennial* is a classic. A classic."

"I liked *The Source.*"

"Never got into that. There was an interview with him in *Playboy* a while back and he seemed like quite a guy. Does every bit of his own research, you know."

Agnes found herself unable to pull her gaze away from Mel's brown eyes. His eyes were small and very brown. Birdlike, blinking continually. His hands never stopped moving.

"Ever have the bumps in your head read?"

Mel took both hands and began to massage Agnes' temples.

She jerked her head away abruptly. A twenty-dollar wash and set.

"Calm down, babe, just investigating a little phrenology." Mel started to laugh and Agnes joined him. She was feeling the drink, light and heady and awkward and foolish all at the same time. She felt very warm under her arms. Mel was holding her hand again and she never wanted him to let go.

"How about another?"

"One more. Fine, Mel."

"O.K. Jack. Another round."

"How're you doin', pal? How've you been? Remember me from last time?" the bartender said, polishing some glasses.

Mel leaned over and shook hands with him.

"Sure, I remember you, you live around here. Own a farm, as I recall."

"Wow, pal, what a memory. Sure do. Moved from Astoria to the mountains. Can you imagine? Who's the pretty lady?"

"Agnes. A dream."

"Sure. Listen," he said, lowering his voice, "how's the action so far?"

"Give it time, give it time. How's the cows?"

"Well, you know the government came and bought my parcel of land, gave me a good price but left us only a small bit to farm. My brother runs it and

190

works with the Gurnseys now. You know, you got two tits here, but me I go home and get four tits and they give milk, too." The bartender looked apologetically at Agnes, but roared. It was obviously one of his favorite lines.

"How about a dance, Agnes?"

"I'd love to." Agnes found it difficult to get off the bar stool. It seemed so far away from the floor.

"Let me help you, my dear."

Mel put both hands around her waist and attempted to lift her off the chair. She felt enormous and bottom heavy, wishing for the moment to be as minuscule as Tinkerbell. She arrived at the floor with a thud. As she started for the dance floor, Mel pulled her to him. "Let's do it right here, baby." He put his arm around her waist and put his cheek next to hers. "The Godfather" theme struck its mournful notes as Mel pressed himself straight up against her. Agnes closed her eyes, feeling the warmth of his hand on her back. He wasn't actually dancing, but swaying back and forth with the music, holding her very tight. He moved sinuously, maneuvering her into a long, slow dip. She felt slim and light. Circular. Everything swirled inside her head. This was indeed what it was all about.

The music stopped but Mel continued to hold her. His cheek smoothing hers.

Reluctantly, she moved away, putting her hands on his shoulders.

"That was nice."

"You're telling me. Listen, got plans for dinner?"

Agnes caught her breath.

"No, not yet."

"Well, listen, I've got to see some guys, the guys I came with, in the card room. So why don't you go on up and get dressed; dinner's in about an hour. Meet me in the lobby and we'll do a dining number. What do you say, honey?"

"Fine, Mel. Just fine. I'd love to."

"Great. What's your room number?"

"C-101."

"Great, kid. I'll give you a ring if there's a change of plans. I got to go now. See you soon."

Mel patted Agnes on the rear with a proprietary touch.

" 'Bye now."

Agnes couldn't decide what to wear for dinner. Back in her room, she looked in her closet for something slimming, something seductive, intelligent, smashing.

God, she wanted to look perfect. She would take another bath. She would put on a face mask, a tightener, she would stand on her head and let the blood run to her cheeks. For Mel. Yell. Mel. Pell Mell. I've fallen for Mel, the fellow with the fisherman's sweater and warm hands. Mel. Mellow. Marshmellow. Mel.

Soaking in the tub, her hair carefully preserved by a pink showercap, her face richly lathered with cold cream, Agnes tried to control her excitement. It was no use, she would give in to it, give in to the joy. She felt things loosening inside her, all the tightness of the past year oozing out of her. Perhaps she would find him, the man she could trust. And love. Comfort you with apples, everybody, comfort me with love, she thought. She had denied the need so long, she had gotten so out of touch with it, so out of touch with being touched.

18

Mel was nowhere to be seen. The lobby was almost empty since nearly everyone was in the dining room.

Agnes had decided on the green backless dress, even though it was only Friday night and it would have been more appropriate for Saturday. Still, she wanted to continue her soaring mood. She was in a green mood. A green backless mood. She had taken meticulous care with her make-up, wearing the false eyelashes she saved for important occasions. Her hair still retained its contour and she found the high tease particularly becoming. She wore no bra. There was no way to wear that dress with a bra, and even though it made her feel dangerously unencumbered, she was determined to try. Her thighs were mercifully camouflaged under the folds of the dress. And she wore green-dyed shoes and the real pearl earrings her grandmother had left her. Pale pink glossy lipstick shone on her lips. Her stomach contracted as she looked around the lobby. He had said the lobby, hadn't he?

Agnes decided to walk over to the dining room. Perhaps she had misunderstood. Timorously, she stood on the edge of the door as the host pointed to empty seats.

The dining room was enormous. It looked like an airplane hangar. The clatter was deafening with the cacaphony of dishes and talk competing for attention. About ten people were seated at each round table, served by ubiquitous waiters who were rushing, circling, piling the tables with chicken and ribs, roast beef, strudles, soups and breads. The air was frantic with sound. She didn't know what to do. There was no Mel.

"Just take an empty seat anywhere, Miss. Be sure you have your coupons." Yes, she had her coupons, but where was Mel? Oh, where and oh where has my little Mel gone, oh where, oh where can he be with his hair cut long and his tail cut short, oh where, oh . . . She was getting dizzy.

"There you are, kid, I've been looking all over for you."

He had on a blue suede jeans outfit, studded with California nails. The white turtleneck simplified the look. Agnes touched his shoulder.

"I've been here."

"We were in the bar for a while and had a few in the meantime. Hope I didn't keep you waiting. You O.K.? You sure you're not going to catch cold in that dress? Wow!"

She watched his eyes touch her breasts.

"Let's go, girl, we'll find two places."

Mel took her arm and led her into the room. The hollow hum sounded like the ocean.

He led her to a table with eight women. They all were wearing slacks.

"My, my, look at this bevy of beauties and just two seats left."

He pulled out a chair for Agnes with an exaggerated flourish and took a low bow.

"Hi, girls. I'm Mel, and this vision is Agnes. Mind if we join you?"

"Sit right down."

It was Arlene, the raccoon girl. She was wearing

tight jeans, a low-cut black sweater with deep cleavage, a jeans jacket thrown over her shoulders. She had a lot of blue on her eyes. Her eyelids seemed lower on her face than on the bus, Agnes thought.

Arlene sat up straight at the sight of Mel.

"Well, if it isn't Mr. Seventh Avenue."

"Hi, Thirty-third Street. How ya doin'?"

"Flyin', man, just flyin'."

Mel patted her on the shoulder. "Everybody acquainted?"

Everyone went around the table and gave their first names. Mel was the master of ceremonies, basking in the inequities of the game.

Agnes toyed with the menu, drawing her shawl around her.

"O.K., O.K.," the waiter sang, "anybody else on the noodle? And who may I ask is a lentil? I think the little lady is a lentil."

"Soup, honey," Mel leaned over and whispered to her above the din, "soup. He's pushing soup."

"Aha," the waiter shouted at Agnes, "I do think the little lady is a lentil."

Agnes let him put the bowl of steaming lentil soup on her plate. She had never tasted it before. Mel was leaning over the slip of black that peeked out of Arlene's sweater. Her eyes looked heavy as though some strange power was forcing them shut.

Agnes was beginning to feel as though she were the invisible man on television, bandages around her head, unraveling to reveal nothing there.

"So listen, babe, what're ya going to order?"

"I thought I'd have the roast beef."

"Now listen, ya know you can have as much as you want. You can order five entrees, if you want."

"Last time I was here, I ate every entree and every dessert at every meal," Sarah, the economist said.

"Can you imagine what they must throw out there,"

a plump redhead on Agnes' left said. "People just nibble and sample and then they just have to throw it out."

"Well, that's what you're paying for. Right, girls?" Mel had his arm around Agnes' chair. He touched her bare shoulder lightly.

Like Kamakazi pilots two photographers circled, then plummeted. They thrust their cameras in the faces of the diners, by twos. In a second, Mel tightened his grip on Agnes' shoulder, smoothed back his hair, moved his face closer to hers, as the young boy zoomed in to flash the bulb in their faces. Agnes didn't have time to lick her lips or tuck in her stomach. Sarah and the girl next to her remonstrated with them. "We don't want our picture taken, get lost. Scram. You poor man's papparrazi."

The boys paid no attention to them but continued to circle the table like Indians outside a wagon train. "Look outside the dining room tomorrow, everybody, and you can order whatever you want. Thanks for being co-operative." The maneuver completed, they retreated to the next table.

Agnes found it difficult to eat. She only picked at the piece of roast beef looking like the map of Italy sitting on her plate. Boston cream pie, chocolate cake, peach Melba, the waiter brought them all, slinging them hard on the table with exquisite good humor. Like an undulating octopus, the table seemed to grow arms as the desserts were attacked, sampled, and discarded. Agnes kept taking small sips of water.

"What do you say we blow this place and find something else to do," Mel said, after a final sip of coffee. He stood up, winked at Arlene, waved to the other girls, and helped Agnes on with her shawl.

Dancing had begun in the Little Club, a room Agnes had not noticed before. "Let's dance before the show, but how about taking a little walk?"

196

"I'd love to, Mel." Dinner had been so rushed, so public and impersonal that Agnes would have given anything for a quiet place. With Mel. His arm moved down from her shoulder to her bare back which he cupped as he led her through the lobby.

"Better put that shawl around you, honey, it's very cool in these passageways."

Agnes was moved by his concern. She ached to sit in some silent secret place with him and find out who he was. So far, she was sure he was the closest thing to exactly who and what she wanted. He read, he loved music, he was sensitive to her feelings. Go slow. Go slow, Mrs. Friedman was instructing from the firm foothold in her head.

They found a couch in a far corner near the entrance to the Health Club.

"Let's get a load off the feet here," Mel said. "So. Having a good time so far?"

"Yes." Agnes found herself tongue-tied with Mel. She heard herself drowning in monosyllables, but couldn't help herself. She was dazzled by his assurance, compelled by his sure pursuit of her.

Mel stretched his arm over his head and let out a full sigh. "It's hard to just have a decent conversation at a place like this. Know what I mean? I mean people are so involved with small talk and meaningless jibberish. Know what I mean? Now take that Arlene, for example. She's only a kid, I've seen her around on Seventh Avenue. Cute chick. A model. Now I'm in my thirties and a little old for that kind of action, but don't you know, before dinner she gives me a joint at the bar?"

"When?"

"While you were upstairs dressing. I was sitting at the bar near the card room with Barney and a few of the guys and she comes along, and after a few hellos and how are yous brings out the pot. That's the younger generation for you."

"Did you smoke it?" Agnes was smoothing nonexistent wrinkles off her lap.

"Sure, why not? That kid was so stoned at dinner, she could hardly keep her head up. I can take it once in a while but Christ, these kids live on it. Ever try it?"

"No. A lot of the young girls in my office are into it though."

"Well, that's the trouble with the young ones, they're on pot so much you can't have a decent conversation with them."

"Right."

There was silence as Agnes scrambled for something to say.

"I do. I hate small talk, too," she managed.

"Right. Hopefully, when you come to a place like this, what you'll find is a friend. Someone you can talk to."

"Oh, absolutely. Absolutely."

"Because really, frankly, it's a downer for me to see so many women around flaunting themselves, eventually going to bed with guys, no matter what. It's a downer. A real downer."

"It must be. As for me, I'm not a flaunter or a flirt like the young girls, like Arlene, or Priscilla, a girl in my office. I just can't be that way. It may be old-fashioned, but I believe in love."

Mel's arm went back to her back.

Warmed by the contact, encouraged by his receptivity, she let the words flow.

"I've always believed that there was someone somewhere special for me. You know, sex is, after all, something so private and so beautiful. It's the merging of two beings, the spiritual connection of two hearts and souls. I always knew someday it would happen, that I would find someone who would understand me, who I would understand and give so much to." She flushed at the avalanche of feeling. Mel was staring at her.

"Right. Go on, baby."

"Well, it's just that, silly as it may seem, I believe there is such a thing as Mr. Right. My mother always used to say that for every woman there is a man waiting for her, her counterpart. I believe it. No matter what Priscilla or Arlene or any of the young girls say."

She hoped she didn't sound prissy, she hoped she didn't sound silly or romantic. She trusted him at that moment; no one had ever made her shiver the way he did.

"Sure, Agnes. I know what you mean." He kneaded her shoulder with his hand gently. "I know exactly what you mean. Say, listen, what do ya say we go have a little twirl around the floor and then take in the show? I hear the comedians are supposed to be pretty good."

"Oh, lovely. I'd love that."

They strolled back to the Little Club, where Mrs. Schneiderman was holding court in front of the door. "This is get-acquainted dancing time," she was saying to no one in particular, and groups of men and women moved in, drawn by the staccato lights on the ceiling and discothèque music. Mel and Agnes stood inside, Mel's arm firm on her back. He waved to a couple who were dancing, and guided Agnes to the floor. It was very dark in the room except for the flashing lights and, although the music was very fast and jumping, Mel held her close and continued his swaying. He slid his hand from her back to her waist and lightly touched her buttocks. Agnes could hardly breathe.

The music stopped. Hilda Schneiderman broke the mood.

"Now look, everybody, let's give a hand to this marvelous band and promise to meet here tomorrow night, same time, same place. There will be rock-and-roll dancing to the wee hours of the morning. And we want every gentleman leaving here escorting a lady. We're going to lock the doors, if not. Come on, fellows, this is a singles weekend."

There was some laughter during the grand exodus into the large night club. Here an orchestra was playing, as people arrived for the show and some were dancing. Agnes noticed a very heavy woman with tight black slacks over her swelling rump dancing with a slim young girl, like the aunts and great aunts did at Bar Mitzvahs, with no self-consciousness, only a realistic acceptance of their slim chances of being asked in the first place. The heavy woman was light on her feet, Agnes noted, in the way that heavy people have, like Mostel or Gleason, whose bulk turns into air the minute their feet touch the floor.

"Did you get a load of that?" Mel said. "What hams. Probably two leses."

"Oh, I don't think so," Agnes said. "They just want to dance."

"Well, I don't know, I've never been to a place where the management let them. If there's one thing that turns me off, it's lesbians. I can't even use my imagination to figure out the way they do it to each other." He led them to seats at long, rectangular tables in front of the stage. "Fairies, that's something else even. They slay me. If one came up to me, just for a second I'd knock him dead. God, they make me mad. We've got some designers at the firm that make me really uncomfortable. Listen, kid, what'll you have to drink, you haven't wet your whistle for quite some time now."

"I'd like a scotch on the rocks."

People were beginning to get acquainted. Agnes noticed men sitting at tables where only girls had congregated. An overly energetic girl singer whose nipples

200

pressed through her see-thru dress was straining through a rendition of "Learn to Live Together Till We Die." Red, green, and yellow spotlights heightened the contrived intensity of her delivery and when she finished with "There's a New World a Comin'," Agnes found her ears aching. Mel was applauding enthusiastically.

"What a pair," he said to the man next to him. But he concentrated on Agnes. During the singer's act, all during the comedy duo (the suave singer whose face seemed three-quarters teeth, one quarter dimples, and the bushy-haired silly one reminded Agnes of early Allen and Rossi), Mel concentrated on Agnes. He nuzzled her ear, nibbled at it. He never moved his hand away from her bare back, touching it with light circular movements. Bushy hair ran through his repertoire of Polish jokes, Italian and Jewish jokes and Mel pressed Agnes closer to him, kissing the tip of her ear softly.

"Only an Italian would bring his wife to a singles weekend," the comedian shouted, and Mel moved his knee closer to Agnes.

She sipped her drink until the glass was empty, and with a wave of his hand, Mel ordered two more.

"You're really sweet, Agnes, really. A doll. You're a lovely girl," he whispered into her ear.

"Y'ever hear the way a Mississippi frog talks; bigot, bigot, or a frustrated frog, he says; needit, needit . . ."

"You're really a fine person, Agnes, I can tell, even after such a short acquaintanceship. I like you, I really do."

"Me, too, Mel. I like you, too."

"Y'know, the Jew's idea of being separated? He leaves his wife in the room . . ."

"You're not like the rest of the girls I meet who are frivolous and dumb. You've got a brain, Agnes, and sensitivity, and I like that. I like you." He turned her face toward him and, after moistening his lips, put them on hers. A soft slow kiss.

"I don't want to leave her now," Dimples was singing, after turning into Robert Goulet. Agnes didn't move as Mel ran his tongue over her bottom lip. Suddenly self-conscious, she withdrew, putting her hand on his cheek.

"Listen, the Mafia is merging with the Gay Lib these days. It's called 'The Kiss of Death,'" the comedian threw out to the crowd as Mel and Agnes got up and pushed their chairs under the table.

"What do ya say we sit at the bar for a while," Mel said.

Agnes was not used to drinking so much but she liked the way it made her feel. She couldn't quite figure out if it was the liquor or the headiness from Mel's compliments that made her feel so utterly loose, so positive she was very desirable.

"One more, I'll have one more drink, Mel."

"Swell. Too bad Raquel Welch wasn't on the bill, I sure would have preferred her to those two clowns."

"I know, they were awful. So corny."

"Well," he said, helping her on the bar stool, standing behind it while he ordered the drinks, "the point is, so many comics got their start here. You know that, I'm sure. This is a breeding ground for the Red Buttons and Norm Crosbys of today. They all got their start here, you know."

"Right. I'd heard that." Agnes took a long swallow of her drink. She could see that other Agnes in the mirror, whose face smiled back at her from back of the labels on the bottles lining the wall. There was a glamorous creature there in a green dress and pale white skin shining out of it. She was a glowing thing, that Agnes in the mirror, all confidence and poise breathing in the perfume of the chase, the scent of romance. The mirror was clouded with smoke and misty faces and bartenders' backs but she could make her own face out clearly. It was the way she always wanted to look, wearing just the right thing, high color in her unblemished skin, hair high, fingers circling a glass with ease, an attentive, marvelous man whom she could love at her side, whom he knew she could love and who might very, very well love her. The mirror was a montage of a dream come true and the office and the ridicule and the monotony of her routine seemed so far away.

". . . you really are. You have a softness about you that is very appealing."

Mel had his hand so far around her back that he was brushing her breast. She fought the tears that had formed in her eyes.

They had one more drink and Mel, like a New York Knick, made a basket of his mouth and scored every time he threw a peanut in.

"It's getting late," he said, looking at his watch. It was after 2 A.M., but there was still a lot of activity. The bands kept playing. Agnes saw some girls pass through the bar in tennis clothes. They stopped to explain that after midnight, playing tennis was free and was very expensive at all other times. They expected to play all night.

Agnes was a little dizzy walking to the elevator, but she felt secure and warm wrapped in Mel's arm. At her door, she took out her key but had trouble finding the keyhole. Mel took charge. From the doorway, they could see that the chambermaid had turned down her bed, put out fresh towels and her nightgown and slippers. Mel leaned on the molding of C-101, and smoothed her hair. "We could have a nightcap if you have some booze, Freckles. There are two other guys at my place." He was touching her hair but it didn't matter. She didn't mind anymore if he messed it.

203

"Come in," she said, summoning all the Joan Crawford she could muster.

One small night light gave the room a soft glow. Agnes put her bag and shawl on the dresser, taking a quick glance at her image which had stayed remarkably intact.

"Swell room. We've got pretty much the same but with two extra beds in it. Listen, Agnes, excuse me just a minute, I'm going to the john."

Mel went into the bathroom and Agnes heard the toilet flush and the faucet go on simultaneously. In the mirror her eyes were shining.

Mel had taken his jacket off and Agnes could see his ribs through his turtleneck. He was very thin. He moved over to her and put his finger on the tip of her nose. "That's right, Freckles. You're a Freckles to me." He cupped her face in his hands and pulled it to him, giving her a lingering kiss. He kissed her nose, her cheeks, her forehead, and moved to her neck, holding her lightly but firmly. She felt him get hard as he pressed against her, holding her.

She felt his back, damp from perspiration, counting each rib as she smoothed his sweater.

"What do ya say, Agnes, what do ya say?" his voice was hoarse as his hand moved insistently down to her buttocks. She hadn't intended for everything to happen so fast; dreams have a way of staying dreams for such a long time, that she wasn't prepared for the quixotic few hours she had just experienced.

"I'm a fairly serious person, Mel. I don't do things lightly and . . ."

"Listen, babe, don't you think I know that? Don't you think I respect the kind of person you are? I can tell that, don't you think I know that?" he was purring into her ear, trying to find the zipper in the back that would facilitate a green avalanche falling to the floor.

". . . and I like you, I really do, and . . ."

"So trust me, baby, trust me." He found the zipper and began to slowly pull it down.

". . . and you know what, Mel, you know what, this is such a silly thing to say, but it's what keeps running through my mind, it's a house, a little house that I want. I'm so tired of apartments and doormen who grunt at you and not being able to control the heat and sirens at night and elevators that break down . . ."

The dress lay like pale jersey petals at her feet. Agnes, standing facing the mirror, could see Mel's back straining as he put his arms around her. Past her shoulder she could see her face, feel the air of the room on her bare back, her naked breasts. Putting both hands on her shoulders, he pushed her away from him.

"Beautiful, you're beautiful."

Her thighs rose out of her pantyhose like a cake before the oven door opened, but she forgot. She forgot about the thighs and the teased hair and her grandmother's earrings that Mel was struggling to pull off. She forgot about everything but Mel as he guided her to the bed.

She held on to him very tightly as he kissed her, touching his hair, smoothing his cheek. She moved her hands down shyly, feeling his thigh, caressing the small mound of buttock. Mel had read his Masters and Johnson well, he had learned all the plays: foreplay, byplay, after play.

This was where he felt whole, this was where he felt the big man, because if he didn't make out with this chick, he reasoned, if it didn't work out, then Christ, there was a line a mile long of girls with whom he could. So he could relax. He hadn't been impotent for a long time, not since he'd finally gotten rid of the wife who, with one word about his fat stomach or the irritated pimples on his shoulder, could make him lose his erection in a minute. No more. He could do it anytime, anywhere now, hanging from a chandelier, in an elevator, on top of the Statue of Liberty. He had nothing to worry about. She had no tits to speak of and he was turned on by girls of *Playboy* proportions, but she had a great ass, and soft white skin. He was enjoying himself.

There was someone moaning in the bed and suddenly Agnes realized it was she. Mel was everywhere. On her breasts, in her ears, little butterfly kisses on the insides of her arms. No one had ever been everywhere before.

As he touched her nipples, she started, jerked forward as though in a bad dream, but he was unrelenting, rubbing them, eating them.

She felt the whole lower half of her come alive. She felt as though she would wet the bed. And then Mel put his hands on her. Found some magic place down there at the same time he was stroking her nipples, whose combination began to build in her a terrible tension, a terrible love for this stranger. She would go to the bottom of the sea with him, she would find a secret cave with him, build the highest most extravagant sand castle with him, with wet sand and drippings on top, making towers and intricate architectural designs out of soft sandy beaches, castles of delicate drips of wet turning into steeples . . .

Agnes came. The orgasm flooded her. She tightened her legs instinctively to make it last, to make it more intense. How she loved him. She had come. Friction, the right combinations, trust had made her come, and fall in love with Mel. Pell mell, she thought, I have fallen in love.

"Thank you," she murmured, her eyes still closed. "Thank you."

Mel entered her then, and with a few short bursts, his hand still tightening on her breast, he came himself. He poured himself into her.

Agnes stroked Mel's back. She wanted to make

206

breakfast for him, she wanted to go swimming with him and to the supermarket and the neighborhood rental library with him. He wanted to sleep for a while and then get out. It was hard for Mel to spend the night anywhere. He liked to wake up in his own bed. He had a rule about that.

19

It had snowed during the night. Large flakes were still coming down as Agnes accustomed herself to the strange room.

She remembered. She remembered Mel and his touch and the whole evening. She had slept long. She threw off the blanket, surprised at her nakedness. She had asked Mel to stay, would have liked him to stay the night with her, but he had insisted on leaving. He hadn't said anything about breakfast, but Agnes was sure they would spend the day together. He had been so loving, so tender, she hadn't wanted to get out of the bed when he left.

She ran a bath and looked at her face in the mirror. She looked rested. She put on her new French slacks with a pale pink turtleneck, and put her ski jacket over her shoulders. Opening the drapes all the way, she was almost blinded by the reflection of the sun on the snow. It was clean and untouched. And silent. It always amazed her that snowing was such a quiet thing. One could almost hear the soundlessness.

Downstairs was steaming with activity. Skis and skates were piled in the lobby and the Musak was louder than ever. At the door to the dining room a new coupon taker smiled at her and beckoned her in. The place still had all the serenity of rush hour on the BMT as Agnes scanned the faces for a sight of Mel. She didn't see a familiar face anywhere and shyly took the first empty seat she saw, near the door.

"Hi, Helga Santos. What's your name? My friend here is Lisa. Lisa Capstein."

"Oh, Agnes, Agnes Friedman. So nice to meet you."

The friendly ladies were over fifty, foreign language teachers from Teaneck, New Jersey.

"No bagels today, kiddo," the waiter bellowed, "it's Saturday and they don't use the steamer. Kosher kitchen, you know." He went off and brought back sweet rolls and stacks of butter and jam.

"It's humiliating," Lisa was saying. "First, they look you over close to see how old you are, that's before they ever even think about talking to you."

Agnes was still searching the dining room for Mel. They were both widows, both had Masters degrees, were colleagues in the same high school. Agnes wasn't hungry and wished she wasn't so distracted. She would have liked to talk to the women some more. There was probably some middle-aged man somewhere in the room who would find these women ideal companions. But she couldn't worry about that now. She took a sip of coffee and walked out of the dining room. Wondering where Mel was. He was probably sleeping late since he had left her room past 4 A.M. She walked around the lobby for about an hour, bought a New York *Times,* read it twice, and was tempted to call his room. Let him sleep, she thought.

Agnes decided to take a sauna and steam bath, and then a swim in the indoor pool. The thought of so much heat around her with all that cold and snow outside was inviting. She went up to the room to get her bathing suit, hoping against hope the little light would be on the phone with a message that Mel had called; that he wanted to take her to lunch, or tobogganing, or that he wanted to come back into her room and touch her again. The phone was dark, the bed had not been made up yet.

Wrapped in a sheet, a towel around her hair, Agnes lay on the top bench of the steam room. No sooner did she lie down when the water poured from her body. She much preferred the sauna, which started slowly, that didn't seem to assault her body with its wet, damp heat.

There were three other girls in the room. Perspiration was dripping into Agnes' eyes so it was hard for her to see them. By squinting, she noticed that two of them looked very young, the other was over thirty. The older girl was lying flat on her front, naked. Agnes had never been in a steam room where women were allowed to go naked. In her health club around the corner from the office, a few of the patrons had complained when some of the European women would be there all exposed, so they had posted a manifesto on the door, gently worded about not wanting to affront some of our ladies and how it was a health code so please wear a bathing suit or keep yourself safely wrapped in a sheet. The European women had grumbled, but secretly, Agnes was glad.

It made her uncomfortable, to see other women's breasts so boldly bare, and other women's pubic area made her lower her eyes. She found it difficult to look. This girl had blond hair covering her down there, she had never seen that before. She closed her eyes. It just all seemed so open, women's bodies displayed like that, brazen. Opening her eyes again, she looked at the girl's breasts. The nipple was a large circle with hardly a tip on it, and in this horizontal position, there

209

seemed to be no fat tissue at all around the nipple. She almost looked like a boy there, lying down. The girl sat up and looked at Agnes staring. "Hi."

"Hello," Agnes said, feeling herself blush through the moisture. When she sat up, the girl's breasts were large but empty. They hung limply on her chest like some African necklace aching for insides.

"What a drag," the girl said, gathering her excessive flesh around her.

"What?" Agnes said.

"This whole thing. It's getting so even the creeps don't talk to you."

The other girls, who were deep in conversation, paused to look at her.

"It's the truth. Who needs it?" She was wiping her face with a towel. Patting her chest and legs. She was not very pretty, and her mouth turned down long before gravity's time.

"I don't know why I bother to come. I swear. This is the last time, the very last." She stood up and patted her behind. Her body looked soft. Unused. She wrapped her wet sheet around her, and looked at the two girls seated in the lower tier. "Be honest, are you having fun?"

"Not particularly. It's a way to spend a weekend."

"Well, I don't know about you girls, but I want someone with a head, a brain. Not here, baby, not here, not under a haystack here are you gonna find anybody having anything vaguely resembling a cranium. Not a chance." She gathered up her towel and her glasses, her wash cloth and her timer. "Luck to you girls," she said. "See ya."

Agnes felt sorry for her, abrasive as she was. At the moment, Agnes felt more secure, more loved and attended to. There but for the grace of . . .

"She's dumb to take it so seriously."

"All that sourness. Her face is going to set that way.

But I tell you, sometimes I feel the same way. I know how she feels."

"How old are you?" the younger of the two asked.

"Twenty-nine."

"She's probably about five years older. It makes a difference. I think a few years make a difference." Agnes figured the young one was about twenty-one, so she really didn't have anything to worry about anyway. "Do you know that I was supposed to get married this week?"

"You're kidding."

Agnes kept her eyes closed. She didn't want to seem to be eavesdropping, but she couldn't help listening. All the while she kept thinking she should get out of there and phone Mel's room. It was past lunch time now. She would miss him, and in the chasm out there, she was bound to miss him. He must have left a message for her. She would look in her box.

". . . and I just couldn't go through with it. My folks were marvelous. Relieved, even. Do you know that every single one of my friends are married, and I'm only twenty-one. Everyone. At school and at work. I swear, I think some girls marry the first guy who asks them, they just think nobody else will."

"I thought that was all supposed to be changed now, what with women's lib? I mean, not for me or my friends, but certainly for you."

"Well, it hasn't. I'm telling you. Listen, a lot of my friends married real young for sex. And after four years of marriage realized it's not all it's cracked up to be, and they want out. I swear, I don't think any of that will ever change." She took the towel off her hair and shook it out. She looked different, Agnes thought, all doe-eyed and soft with long black hair falling over her face. She arranged the towel back on her hair, sheikh style, and began filing her nails. Her face was almost dry.

211

"About ten years ago, I got married at nineteen for the same reason. Only for me it was rough. Really rough."

"What?" The other girl leaned forward sympathetically.

She had a tired look, the girl who was talking, and she spoke painstakingly. "Well, he turned out to be an alcoholic and I, I who don't have a penny, had to pay to get out of the marriage."

"No kidding. Did you have any kids?"

"Two. They're eight and five now. Live three hundred miles out of New York with my mother."

"Why? How can you be away from your kids?"

"What do you mean? I have to. I can't earn a decent salary in the hick town I come from in Pennsylvania. I've got a good job in New York that pays well. If it weren't for my mother, I don't know what I would do."

Agnes couldn't keep silent anymore. She sat up.

"Look, sorry for eavesdropping, but I couldn't really help it."

"Oh, don't be silly. We knew you were there."

"But how do you manage?"

"I go home every other weekend, it's all I can afford. And I manage. Listen, whatever it is, it's better than the way it was. Because you know what?"

Agnes and the twenty-one-year-old were an eager audience.

"It wasn't so much the alcoholism that got me, it was his tearing me down, you know. We all have our weaknesses, but he would go right for the jugular with me. Right to my most vulnerable part. It took me one year with a psychologist and two with a psychiatrist to find my sense of confidence again." She was talking softly now, surprised at the intimacy she had developed with two strangers, so soon.

Agnes was moved by the girl. She had a quiet dignity and lack of self-pity that she admired. She had

212

picked herself up and made do. Mrs. Friedman had no use for anyone who didn't just "pick themselves up and make do." She was a no-nonsense person, Mrs. Friedman was practical. She had pushed and shoved Sol Friedman to and fro for the past forty years and, although Sol made a living, he never made it anywhere near big. She had never forgiven him for that, but at least when he would get depressed, like when he lost his job as a diamond setter, and felt the failure, he had Mrs. Friedman. "Take it on the chin, kid, you can take it. You'll get another job," or "Mr. Friedkin is no good. Why do you let him get under your skin? Ignore. Think about something else. Make do."

Agnes had heard about making do for a long time. There were times, though, when it wasn't so easy. When courage came in eye droppers. She remembered crying bitterly when she and a friend had seen a production of *A Streetcar Named Desire* and when the man in the white suit came to take Blanche away, she couldn't stop sobbing. Her friend Laura had been embarrassed by Agnes' nose blowing and heaving shoulders, but Agnes was out of control. Blanche had tried so hard to make do, to live by her wits, to stretch herself into something fine and it all fell down around her, and when they tried to fool her at the end when they carted her off to the looney bin, it was too much. All the way home Agnes had cried for Blanche and for herself and for those people who at a certain point just can't make do anymore, who just let go.

". . . well, it's not so bad, something will happen. But I'll tell you one thing, it would take someone awfully special to get me to marry again. What about you?"

Agnes decided not to wait for the answer. The whole conversation had given her a sense of uneasiness and malaise. The heat and the steam had fostered a sense of pseudo closeness, as though there were no world

213

outside of those sheets and those towels, those open pores and bare feet.

Without a word, she got up, smiled a hesitant good-bye and walked out onto the white tiled floor of the Health Club. A Jacuzzi was nearby and several naked women were sitting in it. Agnes fled into the bathroom and put cold water on her face. She was beet red. Her skin shone.

She took her bathing suit out of her bag and went into the toilet to put it on. Her skin had red splotches on it as though the steam had attacked her body through a collander. She took a fresh towel and then her sandals with the thin heels on them out of her pocketbook and put them on. One looked so much better in a bathing suit with heels on. At least her leg wouldn't seem so short, the thigh so heavy this way. She combed her hair, but didn't put any make-up on. I'll let my skin breathe, she thought, like *Harper's Bazaar* tells you to once a week. On second thought, she put a little green over her eyes, and pencil and mascara, thinking ahead. One looks so drab getting out of a swimming pool with stringy hair and naked eyes. At least her eyes would stand out.

Agnes walked from the women's health spa down an underground corridor. Suddenly she came upon it, a mammoth pool surrounded by what seemed to be thousands of deck chairs under a giant glass bubble. Surrounding the pool were Caribbean type straw hats and papier-mâché palm trees. Tentative tropics. And at the left, outside beyond the thousands of deck chairs through the hundreds of paned windows, was an ocean of snow. It was beautiful. Agnes caught her breath, loving the incongruity.

There were a lot of people swimming and diving, and some lying in little cubicles with sunlamps overhead. Shyly, Agnes walked in the direction of guitar music and singing. A beefy man was surrounded by several girls and was singing a medley of Israeli songs. She was self-conscious as she walked in front of couples lolling on the couches, but she was flushed with the confidence of her high color. She stepped lightly, slowly, determined to be graceful and poised.

And then she saw him. She couldn't miss his back. He was wearing a brief bikini, buttocks tucked neatly into it. He had a tennis jacket over one shoulder and was holding it with his fingers. He was talking to somebody.

Agnes felt it in her stomach. As though someone had taken one of those big bags they load on the docks and slung it at her belly button. No one had ever elicited such a response from her before. She would walk. She would not run. She would measure her steps. She would quiet her pounding heart. A rush of memory of legs wrapped around her and last night's love moved her.

Mel was standing with a group of men. One, whom she heard him call Barney, was very plump, his chest fleshy as a girl's, his legs round. He pushed his hair off his face with puffy fingers. There was a star sapphire on the pinky of the hand. The other man was handsome, with blond hairs sprouting on his chest. Agnes saw that he didn't have a jock strap on, and his penis glared defiantly at her out of his green trunks. Barney had his hand on Mel's shoulder and was whispering in his ear.

Agnes walked quietly next to Mel.

"Hello, Mel."

Mel looked at her briefly, put up his hand as though to say, "just a second, kid," and went on listening with his eyes to Barney's secret. Barney gave Agnes a quick appraisal, his eyes dismissing her at a glance. For a moment, Agnes felt she was in the fifth grade when Stanley Weintrab had led a band of boys in the class against her at lunch time. They had run after her with

215

water pistols, and what had started out in fun ended in her running hysterically into the principal's office. She had never felt so violated or so frightened in her life. Barney's look reminded her of her helplessness then, and she felt her feet welded to the tiles in the floor.

"Would you like to swim?"

Mel put his hand on Barney's face and pushed it away from his own ear.

"Oh, hi, Agnes, how ya doin'?"

"Would you like to swim?" Agnes felt forward and too aggressive, but she forced herself.

"Gee, no. Sorry, Ag, we gotta go. The fellas and I have a tennis date."

Stunned, Agnes put her hand out to touch his arm.

"See ya later, doll."

Thus dismissed, Agnes automatically retreated. The chairs and water, snow glare from outside and bright lights overhead formed a kaleidoscope, a shattered mirror in front of her eyes. As she watched Mel and his friends swagger away like Teddy boys after a slashing, she put her hand on her heart. "Be still, my heart, be still," she heard someone whispering.

Karen Stern, the small lawyer with the frosted hair, came up to Agnes.

"Hi, Agnes, how are you? Is anything the matter?"

"He was probably trying to be a certain suave way in front of his friends."

"What? You look awfully strange. Why don't you come over here and sit with us and compare notes about last night?" Karen's tone was friendly, but Agnes wanted to be alone.

"No, thanks. Swimming. I'm going swimming."

"O.K., hon, we'll see you later. 'Bye, now."

Agnes put her bag down on the spot, slipped out of her sandals, and walked over to the ladder of the pool. All she could think of was water, and wetness, submerging herself. Mrs. Friedman said she was always giving herself water therapy ever since she learned about it in her psychology course in high school. How they just dunked you in water, preferably warm, to soothe you, to wash your troubles away, to wash that man right out of your hair, or whatever. Perhaps because she was a Pisces she gravitated to water, always taking two baths a day.

He was trying to be suave and cool in front of his friends, that was it. He would definitely try to contact her alone. There would be, there would definitely be a message from him at the desk or in her room. The water assuaged the whiplash of his departure.

She lay on her back and shut her eyes. Of course, that was it. Men are just like boys, he didn't want his friends to know. He didn't want them to tease him. They didn't know how intimate Mel and she had become, they didn't know the extent of his tenderness.

She felt better. She would go up to her room and get his message, it was getting to be dusk already, and across the room the snow glowed with a pink softness. Agnes dried her body with the towel, and combed her limp, wet hair. She would be dazzling for him tonight, she would wear a rose and it would make her skin glow; she would go to the beauty parlor and have her hair done. He would touch her again.

Mel and his friends sat at the bar downing martinis, eyeing the two secretaries from BBD&O four stools down. They had put tennis trousers over their suits. Each one wore another color in deference to the new liberated fashion in tennis clothes which relieved the obligatory white look. Mel wore brown, Barney blue with a white stripe and Ben yellow with a brown stripe.

"So, let's have it, Mel, who was the broad?" Barney was vacationing from the rigors of Weight Watchers this weekend, so he smeared hills of Cheddar out of a brown jar over an unsuspecting Wheat Thin.

217

"I spent last night with her," Mel said with calculated simplicity.

The two others stared at him.

"You're kidding. You've got to be kidding."

"No, sir. Why should I be kidding?"

"I don't know, old bean, your taste is in your ass. You sure are slipping. Plain Jane with legs like a hippo."

"Wrong, my friend, wrong," Mel was enjoying this. He had not intended to let on so soon about his conquest, his first conquest, but since it came up, he would share his expertise.

"What you guys don't realize is that that kind of girl is not the easiest, but the best lay there is. You know why?" He stroked his chin like some humanities professor about to hold forth on the Aegean civilization. "Because they're grateful. The absolute best lays in the world. They know what they're missing. They resent the fact that the girls who are more hip are getting their share, and they'd give anything to get it regularly."

Barney spluttered on his drink, spitting it over his jacket. Ben looked enviously at Mel. He hadn't been able to score last night because the girl he ended up with was taking her Ph.D in college administration, and even he could tell she was so bored with him she would rather go to her room and do some studying. Which is exactly what she did.

Mel sipped his drink and looked across the bar into the mirror. Arlene's eyes stared back.

Agnes did wear rose, convinced it was her most becoming color. The dress was deceptively simple, cut very well, accentuating her long torso and so tight below the breast that it appeared to increase her bust size. It was not low-cut, but little rose-colored buttons climbed up the bodice to the neck. It was ladylike,

218

yet, she was convinced, very sexy. She wore simple black pumps, and a pink wool shawl. The beauty parlor had set her hair too tight, and probably by tomorrow, it would be perfect. But this was now, there had been no message from Mel and she wanted to look her best to clear up this misunderstanding. She put on more rouge than she was accustomed to since she seemed pale to herself.

Downstairs in front of the dining room, the photographers were holding court. Hundreds of tiny flashlight-like receptacles were lined up on the table. The pictures they had taken the night before were for sale. Agnes found hers easily, and felt strange as she squinted at the Mel and Agnes living inside there. Mel had a toothy smile and Agnes looked as though she were sitting in back of herself, looking strained and uncomfortable. She ordered four photographs.

Agnes moved toward the dining room. She was wet. She would stain her beautiful dress under the arms. The room was a blur of fish-eyes as she sank into the nearest empty chair.

She couldn't eat a thing and the avalanche of food made her stomach turn. A slow panic was beginning to build. She couldn't swallow. Like apples in a tub at Halloween, the faces in the dining room bobbed up and down, grabbing at the food. Agnes' nausea was moving up out of her throat, and she excused herself and ran from the room.

She found a ladies room, and threw up into the toilet. She had hardly eaten anything so all that came up was a tart liquid. A touch of it got on her dress. Breathing heavily, Agnes struggled to the sink. Under the spots of rouge, her face was white. Oh, God, she hoped that spot would wash out. Gratefully, there was no one in the ladies room, especially no orderly solicitous attendant. Like some wild animal, Agnes wanted to put herself back together in her own cave, by herself. She repaired her make-up and dabbed cold water on the spot over the bodice. Dinner was over and people were milling about. Looking.

Agnes went from room to room, bar to bar, looking for him. She couldn't imagine where he could be. Perhaps he had fallen on the tennis court and hurt his ankle, perhaps one of his friends had taken sick and he was sitting up with him. She went to a house phone near the reception desk and called his room. She let the phone ring fifty-three times.

At 10 P.M., the show was going to start. New acts had been billed for Saturday night and people moved out from the various bars and dancing rooms to find a table. Agnes could not find Mel. She stood at the door of the night club, as though taking tickets, as though checking coupons, as though on a reception line. Some people smiled, some looked at her rather oddly, as she scanned their faces assiduously.

When he walked in with Arlene, she thought it was someone else. He looked familiar but thought perhaps it was someone with whom she went to high school. Only when he got within a few feet of her did she realize it was Mel.

"Well, there you are," she said, attempting a lightness. "I must have missed you at dinner."

Mel had his arm around Arlene's waist, which was bare, which didn't have an ounce of flesh on it. Her midriff indentation was pronounced by a white jersey halter top. Mel gave it an extra squeeze at Agnes' words.

"Hello, there."

"You know, I think the comedian tonight is supposed to be much, much better than last night, you know the corny ones we saw last night, the little bushy-haired short one and the good-looking Irish singer. Mel, do you remember the show last night, when we sat in there . . . ?"

Agnes heard someone babbling on as Mel turned

and faced that girl with no underwear on, that girl with nothing around her waist but skin. They were walking away from her and she hadn't finished. She hadn't told him that she would be there in her room waiting for him later, ask him how did he like her sweet little rose-colored gown with the spot over the breast where she had thrown up because she was so nervous because she couldn't find him.

Agnes did say all these things, to no one in particular as it turned out, because Mel had long since gone inside. Agnes kept hearing someone talking about little houses and sunshine all around it and secrets and making do.

She couldn't stop talking to herself as she walked into a small lobby where Sammy Small, a fledgling Mel Brooks, was alternately entertaining and insulting the guests. He was playing "Take a Giant Step" with twenty people, shoving the microphone into their faces and introducing them to the throngs, and making jokes indicating he wanted to be discovered and catapulted to the "Johnny Carson Show" instantaneously.

"Hey, girlie," he shouted, eyeing Agnes who couldn't stop the flow of words. "Hey, sweetie, you with the soft gorgeous bod, come on up here, baby and play with us. Come on, sweetheart, we need a tootsie like you to liven things up around here. Listen, lovey, do you believe in sex before marriage? Not if it interferes with the ceremony . . . Here he is," he said, pointing to a man in the first row, "the minute man, that's the story of his sex life . . ."

The jokes flowed like water down a mountainside and Sammy refused to come up for air.

"There's something about this girl. What's your name, pussycat? Come on, don't be shy. I just can't put my finger on it. Listen, I find vaseline very important in sex, don't you, sweetheart? I put it on the doorknob to keep the children out . . . O.K., now we need some more players up here, come on bubby. What about the lovely lady in red? Come on, let's have a hand for the lady in red . . ."

He started humming, gesturing toward Agnes. She felt the heat in her cheeks and turned away.

But Sammy was relentless, quick.

"Oh no, you don't, little lady," he said, running up the aisle to where Agnes was standing. "Here's my big chance to meet this beauty. And you are a beauty, my dear." He took Agnes by the hand and dragged her up to the front of the room while everyone laughed and applauded. "You're a *sheinda meidle,* yes, you are," Sammy said, pinching Agnes' cheek.

She wanted the floor to open up, she wanted a net to come down from above and envelop her, carrying her off to some haven in the sky; she wanted him to go away.

"So, pussycat, what's your name?" Sammy was about to put his hand on her hair as Agnes recoiled.

"Agnes."

"Speak up, babe. By the way, everybody, don't you think Agnes here has some bod? Stacked, that's what you are, Aggie, absolutely built."

Guffaws and scattered applause greeted Agnes as she tried to pull her hand away from Sammy's. She was terrified Mel would come into the room at this moment. Her legs were sticking to each other.

"So, my friends, we are now going to play a little game. Sort of like 'Simon Says,' but better. Come on, Ag, don't be a spoil sport, give us a smile."

Sammy put his hand around Agnes' shoulder and brushed her breast. The men in the audience stamped their feet and howled. She felt rivers running down her back, she looked up and was blinded by the hundreds of cut glass Agneses dancing up there in the chandelier in the ceiling, then she heard the sound of nylon thighs rubbing together as she propelled herself up the aisle, hearing someone with Agnes' voice shouting, "Don't touch me, don't touch me." As Sammy Small shrugged his shoulders and breathed *"yenta"* into the microphone.

20

"Your job as an underwriter is to protect the company from a poor risk," MacKail was shouting into the phone. "I can't understand how on the basis of the medical and credit report, this guy was given the 'go-ahead.' According to the report you wrote, this guy had three operations and was due for another one. You better get into the office now. What a way to start the week, for crying out loud." MacKail's earlier good humor was spoiled. He was already aggravated, on only the second day back to the office after vacation. Yesterday had been awful with Letty out and he was already behind.

He had taken two weeks of his three earned after working at Robertson Stellar for fifteen years, playing tennis and golf in Mexico. The weather had been perfect and MacKail had a ruddy color. He had stayed up drinking with his wife every night and the tan hid the tiny red veins decorating the sides of his nose. MacKail had staggered the vacations for his department this year, but several of the employees had earned their weeks and wanted to take the same winter period instead of during the summer. Many people on his floor had already been with the company for over five years and were entitled to two weeks.

"Letty," he barked into the intercom. "Come on in. I need your help, that idiot Sloane fucked up a whole account and there's been hell to pay. Find out for me if he took the doctors' course for underwriters, and listen, double-check that the salesmen all have their tickets and hotel reservations for the seminars in Hartford. And get the file on Larry Fletcher. And where's Jack Gaynor? I want to see him. Who needs all this *tsuris* so soon?"

"All this what?"

"*Tsuris*. How come a nice Jewish girl like you doesn't know what *tsuris* is? You don't have to be Jewish to know what *tsuris* is all about, that's for sure. I gotta see Gaynor. Consumer Affairs has two complaints on him."

MacKail hung up the phone and started muttering to himself. Ten minutes later, Letty walked into his office.

"You look great. The cruise must have agreed with you."

Letty felt herself blushing, but used to the man's attempts at good-humored contact, she ignored it. She knew he was still annoyed that she had missed the first day back at the office.

"O.K., Mr. MacKail. The salesmen are all set, the conference is at the Sonesta Hotel, the rooms have all been booked. I haven't had a chance to check up on Sloane yet, and Gaynor called in sick."

"Christ. Listen," he said, subdued now, "don't pay any attention to me. I think I'm getting the flu or something. Between tennis and golf, the planters punches really got to be a way of life. I swear I'm going into withdrawal pains now. Can you imagine,

224

it's ten degrees outside. I can see my own breath on the street and I'm dying for a planters punch."

There was a knock on the door.

"Come in," MacKail shouted. "Yes, McKern, what's the story?"

"Something's the matter with the computer. The magic box doesn't seem to be working properly. I put in a policy number and got some very odd information; the premium payment couldn't be right. I think it just needs a small amount of adjusting, but it's off, MacKail."

"O.K. Letty, call the computer service. Listen, how's Eleanor?"

"Well, she really seems so much better. I think just having me home for the week was a vacation for her. We're just hoping like hell she won't have to have another operation. The doctor doesn't think she could survive it. And, MacKail . . ."

"Yes, Bob?"

"A woman called a few minutes ago and somehow I got the call. She's got problems with her agent. He was rude and not giving service. I transferred it to upstairs, to Consumer Affairs, but the agent was Gaynor, and I thought you ought to know about it."

"Christ. O.K. I'm glad you told me. Write me a memo on it. Listen, how long does Eleanor have to stay in bed?"

"God, another couple of weeks, for sure. She really could use a private nurse now, but we just can't. There's a woman in the building who comes in an hour or so every day, and I try to make it home by five-thirty every day."

"Listen, McKern, good Lord, if you finish your work, for God's sake, take off early, these days. Do the figure stuff at home. Don't fool around."

"Thanks. Thanks, MacKail," Bob said quietly.

Letty noticed that the lines from his cheekbone

225

down to his chin were deeper, as though someone had taken a chisel and chipped away at the skin around it. "Do you need me anymore, Mr. MacKail? I'll come in as soon as I hear about Sloane."

"O.K. Buzz me the minute you know," MacKail said.

"Bob, wait, I'll walk out with you," Letty said.

"Letty, come in with your steno pad in about an hour," MacKail remarked as she walked out with her arm on Bob's shoulder. "I've a whole stack of paperbacks and magazines for Eleanor, Bob," he said. "Come by my desk before you go home this afternoon. Does she have enough to do to occupy herself?"

"She's the most self-sufficient person I know. And she's a reader. Incredible. She reads about three books a week, even when she's not bedridden. She's a reader. That's awfully nice of you, MacKail. She'll really appreciate that."

There was a group of women around the coffee machine which Letty joined as Bob went into Will Robbins' office.

"So, how was it?" Bob asked.

"How was what?" Will said, his glasses perched on the edge of his nose, his cap like something out of *Front Page* twisted on his head. He was in his shirtsleeves and his desk was piled with papers.

"St. Petersburg?"

"O.K. It was O.K.," he mumbled into his papers.

"So, what did you do?"

"Not much. Got a tan. Listen, Bob, tell me, how's Eleanor doing?" Will said, changing the subject. "That last operation must have knocked hell out of her."

"It did. Listen, I can't deny it, I'm worried, damn worried. Her color is so bad. It's her color that worries me. She was always so ruddy and pink-cheeked. Will, she never had to use much make-up, never, she always had this high color, you know, but now she's so sallow. It's as though her skin had turned yellow overnight. That worries me. You know, Robbins, you know, sometimes when I think of what it would be like if something terrible really happened to her, I think seriously, quietly, not dramatically or anything, Will, sometimes I think I would just take an overdose and just chuck the whole thing. This is a maudlin way to start the week, but I swear, I've been thinking. Is that so awful, to be so close to someone that life just wouldn't be worth living without them? I don't know."

Will looked up. If Letty had been there, she would have put her fingers on the furrows between his eyes. He was getting deep indentations.

"Bob, don't talk that way. Don't. Look how well she's done. Look how she's been able to get through the worst of it. Her color will come back. She's strong. And Bob, you know the thing I envy about her, from what you tell me? The thing I envy the most is that she is determined to live. She wants to live so badly, Bob. That's going to pull her through. That plus the fact that every day they are discovering new ways to deal with heart surgery. There was an article in *New York* magazine the other day by a guy who had the most intricate heart surgery, and he's playing tennis, for Christ's sake. Look, Bob, you've got to be optimistic. You can't show Eleanor your doubts. You've got to be supportive with her now."

"Will, are you crazy? I'm so busy protecting her from my feelings, building her up and giving her hope. And when I'm alone, or talking to somebody, that's when I let down. She doesn't kid me, either, you know. That's just what she's doing, too. She's cheerful and trying not to have me worry and never lets on how scared she is. I found her with a hand mirror the other day, just putting her hand over her face, staring at herself. Incredulously. As though she couldn't

227

believe it, as though that person in the mirror was a new terrifying acquaintance. Look, Will, I'm sorry, I really am. I didn't mean to go on like this, I'm sorry." Bob, suddenly aware of his outburst, was embarrassed.

"McKern. What the hell's the matter with you?" Will said gruffly, "we're friends."

"I know. I know. I tell you, I'm almost grateful to be back in the office. There's something about the routine, deadening as it is, that helps. I don't know."

"Well, I tell you, I sure as hell don't feel that way. It's deadening all right, and I sure as hell try to do my best. These new accounts are piling up like manure on my desk, but I tell you, McKern, me, I'd rather be someplace else. That's for sure. I'd rather earn my three hundred thirty-odd bucks a week someplace else."

Will saw Bob blanch.

"What's the matter?"

"That's what you're still making?"

"So what?" Will was irritated.

"Robbins, I've been in this company for twenty years. I've seen them come and go. Do you know that some of those hot-shot salesmen make $50,000 a year? If they sell a million, they can make a cool fifty grand a year, at least. Will, you're smarter than any of those guys. I thought sure you were making more by now."

"Forget it, McKern. Forget it. You're the fucking bookkeeper. I thought you knew everything. It's the only reason I even said anything. Look," he said, feeling the familiar throbbing moving from his temples to behind his eyes, "let's end this. I don't know how we got into it, as a matter of fact." Will reached into his desk and took out the pain killing suppository the doctor gave him to block the onset of his headache. They had been diagnosed as histamine headaches, and at their worst he felt almost blinded. "I have to go to the men's room, Bob," he said abruptly. Will struggled up and, bumping into a chair at his desk, walked out of his office.

"They were going to bring an animal in, a donkey, I think," Letty heard Priscilla say, "but I figured it would be hard for them to get it up the steps in the hotel room, and we might have to pay more, so I begged off. Well, Letty, how ya doing, or better yet, how did you do? You sure look sensational. You must have had a ball."

"I did, Priscilla. It was a lot of fun. How about you?"

"Sex. It's all over the place. In the bars, on the streets, in the stars."

"Come on, be serious."

"Did you get a load of Aggie this morning?" Lorraine said.

"She looks so peculiar. You know how unbelievably perfect she is all the time. Well, Christ, this morning she's wearing pants, for one thing, and she's got a big ass, you know, and she shouldn't wear pants. I know, I know, I should talk, my ass, after all those tacos, is getting to look like a rumble seat. But she never wears pants. Never, did you ever notice that? Well, she's wearing pants today, brown pants with a brown sweater. I know that doesn't sound like much, but there's a hole in the elbow of the sweater. And she doesn't have any eye make-up on. And the hair, you know the way it always stands straight up under all that spray, well, Christ, it's flat. No spray. She just didn't look like Agnes to me. When I trilled hello to her, she positively ignored me. Looked right through me. Weird. I felt sorry for her. It was on the tip of my tongue to find out if she scored over the week, but I didn't say a word. Stopped dead. Nothing I could put my finger on. She just seemed weird."

Letty moved away from the group and, concerned,

walked in the direction of Agnes' desk. She could see her sitting in her chair, feet planted firmly on the floor like they taught her in typing school, fingers poised over the typewriter. Only she wasn't typing. Just staring into space.

"Hello, Agnes," Letty said, cheerfully. "How was your vacation?"

"Yes. Letty, I'm glad to see you." Agnes didn't look at her, but Letty noticed the nakedness of her eyes, how the lack of make-up did affect her whole face. She looked younger. Vulnerable.

"Yes. I had a superb time. It was everything I thought it would be." She said it in a monotone.

"Agnes, I'm glad," Letty said softly. "How did the lovely rose dress look? Beautiful, I bet. I'll bet you looked beautiful in it."

"It got a spot on it. I threw up. Letty I'll have this work for Mr. MacKail and Mr. McKern after lunch. I seem to be typing so slow today. After lunch, okay?"

"That's fine, Agnes. I don't think there's a big rush on that. I'll be at my desk. I'm not even going out to lunch, I've got so much work to do."

Agnes, still not looking at her, took some papers out of her "in" basket and began shuffling them. It was her way of dismissing Letty.

Somewhere, Letty felt Will's eyes on her. Somehow in the middle of the cacaphony of the lady talk, the shrill and the staccato, she felt him. It was only a day since they had parted and she could hardly remember the color of the wallpaper in their room. She could hardly remember his face in the morning when she would wake up and reach out to him. It had to be a dream. It never happened. It was only one day since they had parted and she already forgot how his nakedness looked. How his body felt under her hands and her mouth, how he felt inside her. The chatter faded, a freeze frame of sound. She felt Will's thoughts surround her. Strangely, it did not make her feel warmed. It did not make her feel nurtured. She resented it. She was aware, as she walked back into the middle of the large room, she was aware of missing him desperately and being furious with him. All at the same time. I don't even remember how you smelled in the morning before you brushed your teeth, she thought. She had not thought she could make it to the office this morning. Fran had looked at her strangely at breakfast and was so silent. She hadn't thought she could face it. The sameness. The brief glimpses of him. The formality with him, the hiding, after so much intimacy. After such nakedness together. She couldn't bear it. She almost wished they hadn't gone, she almost wished he would let her be, so that he wouldn't love her and that she wouldn't love him, so that she wouldn't feel this empty letdown.

She saw Will looking at her through the glass. The sounds of typewriters clattered in the room, phones were ringing, people were holding phones on their shoulder, typing. Will beckoned to her. "I have some papers for you, Miss Gold," he said to her as she stood in the doorway. "Could you come in, please?"

She could tell he was in the throes of a headache. His face was contorted and he was speaking painstakingly.

"Yes, Mr. Robbins. Here I am."

Will thrust a sheaf of reports at her. Clipped to them on top was a long white sheet. "Memo from Will Robbins," it said. Underneath were three words. Three words: "I love you."

Letty sighed, looking into his eyes. At least tonight is Tuesday, she thought, at least tonight we will be with each other. At least tonight I don't have to be alone.

21

"You're not eating a thing."

Fran looked over her glasses at Letty at the table. The spaghetti sauce was steaming on her plate, untouched.

"I'm not hungry, Ma."

Fran didn't know how to begin. Her relationship with her daughter was satisfactory to her, but it was hard for her to creep inside Letty's head. There were places she could not go. She could never tell what she was thinking. And now this. Wilma's phone call had completely unnerved her. She didn't know how to bring it up to Letty that she knew she had been away with someone. But she had to. Fran was glad Letty did perhaps have someone, but she was hurt that she had not trusted her enough to tell her.

"Letty, Wilma called yesterday for Mr. MacKail, wanting to know why you hadn't come into the office."

"I know, Mother, she told me."

"Where were you?" The words came out sharper than she meant. Less guarded, wrong. All wrong. Fran was not used to this. She didn't know how to handle it. She looked at Letty and noticed some gray curling at the sides of her temples.

"Mother." Letty looked at Fran. She had been expecting this all day. She had already had the conversation in her head with her mother. This part was anticlimactic.

"Mother, I'm almost forty years old."

"Letty. Letty. I'm not sitting in judgment on you, I would never do that. God. If you're involved with someone, there's nobody who would be happier about it than I would. You know that. It's just that you've never really lied to me. There really hadn't been any need to. I'm pretty modern for a mother and I know what goes on these days and . . ."

Letty looked at Fran. She couldn't stop feeling sorry for her.

"Mother. I've been seeing a man from the office for four years. He's married and he's got three sons." Letty took a long sip of the wine and poured herself some more from the Chianti bottle on the table. She did not want to look up. Ever.

Letty felt herself go cold all over. It was none of her business. Why didn't she be still? What business was it of hers? She was a grown woman, capable of doing what she wanted to do. She was too old to have anyone tell her what to do, even give their opinion of what she should do with her life.

Fran couldn't identify the look in Letty's eye. She had never seen it there before. A married man. It would ruin her life.

"Jessie Greenbaum's affair with Jim Stone has been going along fourteen years. She can't break it off. And now she's getting to a point where no one else is going to want her anyway. Letty, you're too good to go sneaking around back streets and . . ."

Back streets. Old-fashioned expression. Still, true, Letty thought, unable to stop a crooked smile. Back streets.

"Mother, I don't want to talk about it. I'm in love with this man. There's not a damn thing I can do about it. I just love him. So he's married. So big deal.

233

What am I supposed to do about that?" She was beginning to sound shrill. "Have you been out there lately? Have you been in that jungle out there? There's nobody. There's guys who just want to go to bed with you and don't care if you have a brain or a bit of sensitivity in your body." She didn't know where all this would lead. She was resentful that she had to explain Will to her mother, and at the same time the words came rushing out; she was grateful at last to be able to talk about him to someone.

Letty filled her glass again. She wanted it to loosen her tongue, she wanted the wine to make all the heaviness in her chest go away.

She looked at her mother's face. It was white. She knew she was hurting her, that Fran was used to a more benign exchange. But she would have to learn. She was a big girl now, why she had lived so long with her anyway. Whoever heard of a grown woman living with her mother anyway? Letty was defiant in the face of angels. Her mother was offering no protest, no recriminations. Still, she decided then and there she had to make some kind of stand.

"He loves me. And he's troubled. He's a troubled bitter person. He feels he's gotten a rotten deal from life and wants to give his kids a better one than he's had. His mother abandoned him and it scared him. And I make him feel better, I give him life. He's the smartest person I've ever known, and he's wasting himself in some dumb underwriter's job while everybody around him is just sprinting by. He's afraid. He's afraid, Mother, of losing the security of that pay check every week. He can't take a risk because he feels he has too much at stake, and it paralyzes him, torments him. And he gets these terrible headaches."

"He sounds sick. What are you doing with a sick man?" Fran blurted out.

"God, Mother. He's not sick. He's good. He's a

234

good man. When is the last you ever met a good man? A decent man who was bright and made you feel bright?" Letty had fought the tears long enough. They were hot in her eyes.

"What does his wife look like?" Fran didn't know what questions to ask.

Letty looked at her mother incredulously.

"What on earth does that have to do with anything? Mother, I can't believe you," Letty shouted.

"Oh, Letty, I'm sorry. I don't know what to say. I don't even know what I'm saying. I just think you're worth so much more than that. I can't see you like Jesse Greenbaum. Fourteen years, Letty, ending up over forty when you'll never get a man of your own. Don't, don't, baby, don't throw your life away on a married man. Look, look, just look here, Miss Smart. Look what I cut for you out of the paper today. You won't believe this, like sent from God it was. Right out of Dear Abby."

"Mother, I don't want to hear it," Letty got up to go into the kitchen for a Kleenex.

"Oh, yes, you will, you'll hear this and you'll listen to it," Fran said, following Letty into the other room. She sat down at the kitchen table and began to read.

"You know what the headline is? 'What to expect of a married man,' that's what the headline is. And what it is is a letter from one of her readers talking about what it's like to go with a married man, and you know what? She says, it makes my heart sick. 'I address this to any woman who is in love with a married man,' it says. Now stand there and listen, Letty Gold. You just listen."

Fran began to read. " 'Never expect to see him on Sundays or holidays. Never call him at home. Don't ever expect him to take you out in public but be prepared to entertain him at your place. Never depend on him in times of personal crisis . . .' "

Letty stared at her mother, blowing her nose.

Fran continued. " 'Don't believe him when he tells you that his wife is a shrew, cold, homely, too fat or thin, and she hasn't slept with him in ten years. Don't expect his wife to divorce him if she catches him. She knows that you aren't his first affair and won't be his last. Also, she's not about to give up her social status, financial security and retirement income because of you . . .' Have you ever thought about these things, Letty?"

"Mother . . ." Letty tried to tear the clipping out of her mother's hand.

"Let me finish just a litle more. 'However, her discovery will probably terminate his affair with you, so be prepared to get some new clothes, circulate and find another man whose wife is a shrew, cold, homely, too fat or too thin and hasn't slept with him for ten years. And it's signed, His wife.' So?"

"So what, Mother? Just, so what?" Letty ran back into the living room after tearing the newspaper out of her mother's hands. "Just stop this. You sound like a soap opera, you sound like a story out of a B movie. I'm not a character in one of those. I'm me. Letty. And I know me."

Fran started to cry.

"Letty, you could have anybody. Anybody. There's no one more beautiful more thoughtful in this world. You have so much to offer, baby, so much. I can't see . . ."

"Mother, don't say it. Don't say it. You know what. I know that. I happen to know that there is something special about me and that some day I will do something special. I don't know how, but somehow, some way. But so what? Because on the other hand, I'm just an ordinary girl. There are millions like me. And I can't. I can't have anybody I want." Letty was crying hard now. "Maybe I'd like a brilliant physicist

236

who spends hours in the laboratory contributing his life efforts to mankind. Maybe that turns me on. But you know what? I can't have him because he wouldn't want me.

"I'm not so young anymore, either, Fran. Not by a long shot. There's gray already in my hair, and lines, and my breasts are beginning to sag. I never for the life of me thought that would happen to me. Not me. Not my boobs. And now, all of a sudden, I'm just like everybody else. And don't think I don't think about getting to be forty." Letty looked at her mother's wide eyes as she spoke. God, she wanted her mother to understand. If this was the first and last time she could ever unburden herself to Fran, when she could tell her what was in her innermost self, it would be worth the pain she was inflicting on her mother.

"I think about that a lot, Mother, and I'm scared. And I look at my life and I wonder where it's going. You never married again. You had me. Somehow, you've survived. But me, I want to more than survive. I want to make my life more worthwhile than it is. Will enriches my life and at the same time squelches it, constricts it. I know that. We've broken it off, Mother, several times, and it's always so painful, I think I'm going to die. Do you remember the time you couldn't wake me that Monday morning? When they rushed me to the hospital and I said I'd been so sleepy I took too many Seconals with my wine? I said I didn't know what I was doing. But I knew. I knew exactly what I was doing. I couldn't stand it, Fran. I couldn't stand this needing him and at the same time knowing it wasn't going anyplace, that it goddamn well may never go anyplace. And I know, I know deep down that what the women's lib people are saying is right, that to build your life around a man is stupid, non-self-realizing. I know that. I haven't found a way out of that yet, but I'm trying. I'm damn well trying and somehow I'll find the answer. But right now, that's what it is. Will. I've seen him Tuesdays and Thursdays all those times, all those years you thought I was with the girls from the office on those regular dinners, I was with Will. Every time."

"A waste. A waste. You've wasted those four years. You're right to worry about forty. This is a young people's world. Look at TV. Read the magazines. To be young is everything. It will be there before you know it. Before you turn around. It's been a waste. I'm sick. I'm sick about it . . ." Fran was shouting. She knew she was saying all the wrong things, but she couldn't stop. Letty was all she had, but she knew about this. She'd known so many women who threw their lives away waiting around for a man to divorce his wife. How did it happen to her Letty?

"Don't yell at me, Fran. I'm a woman. I'm not a child. I have to be able to take responsibility for myself. Do you hear me? It's my life." Letty was screaming. "I'm not saying it's perfect, that it's not a compromise. But at the moment, he's the one I want. There's no one else. There's no one else who wants me. Who needs me. He needs me, and I have to be needed. It's as simple as that."

"Wrong, you're wrong. That German boy wanted to marry you."

"Mother, you're talking nonsense. I'm talking reality, cold, hard facts, and you're talking fantasy. Gene Grossman did not want to marry me. He wanted to sleep with me and pick my brains. Both of which he did." Letty watched the words glance off Fran's face as though they were the back of her palm. "So, don't glamorize that one. And Mother, I didn't love him. I didn't feel what I feel for Will. That's the difference. That's what's so killing. But I'm telling you, if I met someone else, if someone unmarried would give me what Will does and I felt the same way, maybe

I would walk away for good the next time. But this is better, much better than nothing. And nothing you can do or say is going to change my mind."

The phone rang.

Letty and Fran stared at each other, then at the phone. The sound cut through the silence like a sliver of steel.

Defiantly, Letty picked up the phone.

"Letty, what's the matter? Your voice sounds so odd," Will said.

"Nothing. Nothing, Will." Letty's words were staccato. She could barely get them out.

"Letty, I can't make it. I haven't been home in a week, and . . ."

"Obviously. I know that."

"Letty, what the hell is the matter with you? Are you all right?"

"Of course I'm all right. What makes you think I'm not?"

"Cut the shit, Letty. I'm sorry, you didn't let me finish the sentence. Sean has a temperature of 102, and I would feel awful to cut out now. Look, we'll see each other Thursday for sure. I'm sorry, Lett, I really am. I wanted so to be with you tonight."

"Sure."

"Letty, I haven't got any more change, can you call me back at this pay phone?"

"It's not necessary."

"Is someone there? Is your mother standing right on top of you?"

"Yes, as a matter of fact, that's true."

"I'm sorry, Lett. Look, I'll see you at the office tomorrow. Maybe we can get a few minutes together somehow. And Thursday, we'll be together, Thursday. Christ, there goes the damn buzz. Call me, call me back."

"I don't want to. I'll see you tomorrow. Goodbye."

Letty had wanted to see him so badly tonight. Tonight especially. She didn't want Fran to see her disappointment.

Grabbing her bag off the couch, she ran to the hall closet and pulled out a spring coat too light for the weather outside. She ran out of the apartment.

Fran automatically began to clear the table, scraping the uneaten spaghetti into the garbage.

She's going to catch her death of cold, she thought. The wine spilled out of Letty's glass as Fran knocked it over. Paralyzed, she watched it trickle down off the red and white checked oil cloth onto the kitchen floor.

22

The week flew by for Becky. It seemed as though the details multiplied daily, and she was sure she wouldn't be able to get every last one of them accomplished. But she did.

The wedding was slated for nine, Saturday evening. The Berkowitzes had rented an entire floor of the St. Moritz Hotel for the wedding party, and Becky had an exquisite room with a view of the park all to herself.

Looking in a mirror in her room, her mother adjusted her veil as the photographer, a friend of the groom's, Anthony Scaturo, took the traditional pose for what would be prominent in a white velvet photograph album to rest on some future coffee table in front of some future fireplace.

Natasha Krause, Becky's mother, wore no make-up. She never had. She was short, shorter than Becky, and plump. Her heavy, unplucked black eyebrows stood in sharp contrast to her short white hair, hair that had been white as long as Becky could remember. The Krauses had had Becky late in life, the only child of a relationship that had lasted since they were in their teens. They loved her, and had always treated her as an equal, not ever knowing or caring much about small children.

Natasha Krause had been a beauty when she was young, with heavy unplucked brows that stood guard over searing black eyes. She had been a dancer, and Sam Krause was a mediocre painter. The years had added excessive pounds to her frame. Sam's work had always been associated with ballerina types, and Natasha had been his favorite model for years. Her calves still bulged from years at the bar. As a little girl, Becky remembered the slim girls in leotards and ponytails who climbed the four flights to the studio. She was never allowed in when her father was drawing or painting, but the models would stay in the studio long hours while her mother was uptown at ballet class.

Sam had been a Trotskyite since he had first come from England. Natasha had met him one day on a cold street corner in Washington Square. There he was a skinny, pimply Trotskyite standing on a soap box with newspaper in his shoes and clothes with holes, ranting in a heavy Cockney accent to everyone who would listen. He would paint and sleep on park benches. Natasha brought him home, and they lived together ever since. They had brought Becky up permissively, out of strong conviction, yet with love and great pride in their beautiful daughter.

"Mom, how do I look? Maybe daisies were silly for the headdress, Mom. Oh, Mom." Becky threw her arms around her mother.

"No crying, no crying," the wispy photographer cried out. He pranced over to the two women and straightened Becky's dress. It was high-necked and had old-fashioned puffed sleeves. Thousands of tiny seed pearls had been sewn into floral designs on the bodice and skirt. She was wearing lace gloves, with one finger cut off, third finger left hand, its nakedness anticipating the ring. Becky's tiny waist was accentuated by the billowing fullness of the skirt.

Anthony Scaturo then gathered his photographic equipment. "You're a sensational-looking girl, my dear. If you ever get bored with the housewife routine, the Long Island Lethargy, and running to the hounds or whatever you plan to do, here's my card. Look me up. You'd make a great fashion piece."

"I can't believe I'm going to be married, Mamma. I'm scared. I'm scared, Mom. I want to know somebody's going to come home every night with the newspaper tucked under his arm. I want someone to be there, someone I can depend on. I want it, Mom, but I'm so scared."

"You know," Natasha said, turning away, smoothing her hair in the mirror, "I always let you go. Maybe I let you go too much. Maybe you were a little too wild. Some of those guys of yours used to give me the creeps. But I always thought, if you had a choice, if you experimented and then found a man you really wanted, then it would be worth everything."

Natasha dabbed the tears away from her cheek. "You know, you're doing what I did. You're marrying at eighteen. I swore no daughter of mine would marry so young, and here you are, just eighteen, doing the same thing I did."

Becky looked at her mother. She couldn't make up her mind. Of course it was all right, and yet there was something terribly wrong. She couldn't put her finger on it.

"Mamma."

The door burst open, and Mrs. Berkowitz walked in. Her painted lips were pulled tightly over teeth tightly clenched. Her thick body was covered in a baby-pink gown, the kind Lane Bryant carried for overweight matrons always in childlike pastels. Her hair was teased into a Barbie doll mold. She smelled of too much Joy perfume. Her diamonds sparkled with the ferocity of street lights on plump, soft hands and thick ear lobes. She looked at Natasha with open contempt as she studied her gown knowingly. Natasha's deliberate colorless, inexpensive dress floored and angered her. It was an affront to everything she felt most important.

"Where are you ladies, for heaven's sake?" she cried. "Didn't they buzz you? We have to go to the ballroom. Rebecca, my dear, you look exquisite. Mrs. Krause, you look lovely. You must now call me Sarah. We're *machatenesta*."

"What do you mean?" said Natasha.

"We're relatives now."

"Relatives?" Natasha looked at Mrs. Berkowitz dubiously nonetheless, and as Mrs. Berkowitz opened the door for them, she couldn't help shaking her head from side to side as she noticed Natasha's boots whitened by dried salt from the snow crush into the down of the golden wall-to-wall carpet.

Thousands of candles flickered on cut glass chandeliers hanging from the ceiling in the ballroom. Becky, standing in the back about to enter the room, held tightly to her father's arm. The corduroy felt rough to her touch, and amid all the glitter the texture was vaguely comforting to her. Bring on the clowns, she thought. She and her father would have to travel down a long red-velvet carpet thrown over the floor for the occasion. Rose petals had been scattered along the way. The room was stuffed with people on either side of the carpet. Through her clouded eyes, Becky could see pill box hats looking like tops of mayonnaise jars and pearls around the backs of necks with hundreds of diamond clasps. And as an organ from somewhere began the music, hundreds of heads like jacks and jills in boxes, swiveled in her direction. At the rehearsal, she had been told to look straight ahead but had decided secretly instead to look from right to left, smiling. She would be a rose in bloom, a dazzler. She would start this thing off right.

From the back of the room, Becky strained to see the unfamiliar horn-rimmed glasses and large pearl earrings that were Lorraine's trademark. She did see Wilma and Letty seated near the aisle in the back. She could just make out that Wilma had her handkerchief out already.

Arnold's three cousins were bridesmaids and wore identical gowns of ante bellum design with pale beige shoes and hats to match. By the time they reached the altar, Mr. and Mrs. Berkowitz, beaming, had started the long march. Louis Berkowitz swaggered as though it were he who was winning the hand of the young maiden in the story. He looked from right to left, greeting and welcoming with his eyes, a silent mouthed "hello," a raised eyebrow.

When the wedding march finally sounded, Becky felt her stomach turn, as her white satin shoes stepped into the rose petals. The walk took forever; in retrospect she couldn't remember it at all. What she did remember were sighs and sounds of approbation, turning of heads, whispers, the rustling of silk, blankets of

244

fur, the odors of hundreds of perfumes mingling in the air. Arnold was down there somewhere at the end of this mile, she remembered thinking, my husband, Mr. Berkowitz, is down there at the end of this magic carpet. Her eyes had blurred and only when she finally arrived at the *chupa* did everything clear and did she see him. Arnold looked perfect. His thick black eyebrows seemed almost trimmed and perfect for the occasion. His eyelashes, long and lustrous, looked longer and more lustrous, more perfect. The tuxedo with tails fit him perfectly, the white carnation perfect in the lapel. She looked at the perfection of him. His mother, expensive in pink, was looking up at him with tears in her eyes, the Rabbi was solemn and serene, Natasha and Sam were to the right, dry-eyed.

She felt a terrible sinking in her stomach as she heard the first words of Hebrew. They had broken their promise. The Berkowitzes had sworn that there wouldn't be a religious ceremony. They had sworn that there wouldn't be a Rabbi. Through her veil, Becky could see her father tensing; her mother clenching his hand. They were offended. The Berkowitzes had promised. How could they break their promise?

Suddenly, they came. The tears. Becky couldn't stop crying. Everyone looked at her lovingly, assuming they were tears of joy. But Becky was aware of being in pain. She put her hand up to her eyes, and through her fingers, through the veil, it was as though Arnie was being photographed in 3-D, as though he were painted with phosphorescent paint. Why hadn't she noticed his puffy ineffectual hands before, she thought. Why hadn't she noticed the tufts of hair growing out of his knuckles. Those hands are useless, she thought, they are not the hands of somebody I want to spend the rest of my life with.

Her eyes moved up to his face, and it was as though she were looking into the future and she could see the way he would look years from now. His face looked fleshy, there were jowls. The face was weak. The hands looked as though they had never done anything in their lives and the face looked craven, soft.

Becky was out of control as her shoulders heaved up and down. She had difficulty getting her breath. She looked down at the green-velvet cushion resting on the altar. She looked back into Arnold's eyes, hoping to see the old vision of him. She listened to a voice from the deepest recesses of the back of her mind that told her this was a mistake. That this was not a good man. That this would not be a good life. And that's what she wanted more than anything, a good life.

She was in a daze, and when the Rabbi looked expectantly at her for the I Do's, she could barely hear him. Arnie smashed the glass with his foot. He missed at first, stamping down on the wine glass, losing his balance because of the force of the blow. The second time he landed on it straight-on, the splinters splattering the carpet, the *mazel tovs* rising as one voice from the guests. It all became a blur after that, Arnie lifting her veil, her smelling his Binaca lips, the swirl of the reception line, where a long line of relatives, including Hal's flower girl daughter, stood in line to shake hands.

She heard the bottles of champagne cluck and pop and saw the waiters immediately converge on the crowd with silver trays laden with hors d'oeuvres. There were cheese balls enclosed by the lightest, thinnest dough and steaming platters of meatballs piled high, and there were trays of chicken liver formed into the shape of a heart and delicately fried cornucopias with mysterious concoctions inside. The waiters ran interference with their cargo.

There were so many aunts. It seemed to Becky that uncles were at a premium. But aunts were in excess. She was introduced to Rose and Leah, Sarah and Ruth.

They kissed and hugged her, and stroked and petted her. Many of the older aunts wore white gloves and sensible shoes, but the majority of the well wishers were in taffeta or satin, long slinky black or shiny off-white. "I only hope you'll be as happy as Herb and I," Aunt Essie was saying, adjusting the rhinestone studded glasses perched on her nose. Uncle Herb added to the cache of white envelopes protruding from Arnold's pocket with a wink and an elbow nudge to his favorite nephew.

She was still crying softly at the reception line but was slowly regaining her composure. Finally, her face felt welded into a smile, the nuts and bolts screwed tight at the corner of her lips. Even her jaw felt locked into the perennial smile of thanks. Arnold barely looked at her but smiled a dazzling smile to the guests. Becky noticed that his second pocket had envelopes now.

Becky started to cry again when Wilma and Letty came to their turn in line. Letty was crying, too, overwhelmed at the beauty and fragility of the girl.

"Baby, you look so lovely. It was beautiful." Becky threw her arms around Letty's neck and held on. Letty could feel her bones through the fullness of the dress. They were holding up the line, but Letty couldn't tell everybody, all those relatives and well wishers how her heart was breaking. How a wedding, this kind, any kind of wedding, would never be hers. She didn't need the trappings, she thought, trying to extricate herself from Becky's arms. She didn't need the canapes and the champagne, the hall or the relatives. She just needed Will to be free. As simple as that. She felt ecstatic for Becky. She felt empty for herself. Just one of those things. Just one of those things she would never have.

She put Becky back in her place in line and took a Kleenex out of her bag and wiped the girl's eyes. Everyone around them applauded. At that moment, Letty wanted to be Becky's mother. Letty wanted to be glowing and proud and hopeful for her daughter. But there would be no daughter. There would be no wedding.

"Let's go, Letty, you're a bottleneck," Wilma moved Letty gently on to Arnold and the parents.

"Becky, you were a dream walking, you just floated down the aisle. You look sensational. Be happy, dear." Wilma gave Becky a hug and moved on to the grateful stare of the gentleman in back of her.

Finally, the end of the line was in sight and the room barely emptied as the guests were led into another room where tables had been set up. Each table had a lush bouquet of pink and yellow tea roses in the center and yarmulkes in white satin with Arnold and Becky printed inside in gold were placed at each man's place.

A dais had been set up in the far corner of the room, rimmed in wreaths of fresh flowers. A small orchestra enlarged its ranks and moved into the large room. They rolled an impressive introduction, then repeated "Here Comes The Bride." The guests applauded and stood up as Becky and Arnold made their way to the dais. Becky saw her mother and father sitting at the head table, and she could tell that her father had had his quota of champagne already. She smiled to everyone and waved to Lorraine who had been placed at the "young people's table." She threw kisses to Wilma and Letty who unfortunately were with the aunts.

When the buzz and hum subsided, Louis Berkowitz rose, holding up his glass. He offered a hand to his wife as he helped her out of her chair. With one arm around her waist and one reached out toward his guests, Louis Berkowitz proposed a toast, "Here's to the best damn looking couple in all of Long Island,

Manhattan and every single borough. I wish them health and happiness and lots of grandchildren for the old man. Enjoy yourselves, everybody, and be of good cheer. This is going to be a swinging party and we want, the wife and me, we want you all to swing. *Mazel Tov* to us all!"

The applause was deafening and Becky reached over to catch Arnold's hand. He was fumbling in his pocket for his Binaca vial, a new solid gold one his friend Reuben had given him for a wedding present.

"This is really something, baby. Did you ever see such a shindig?"

"Arnie, it's beautiful."

"Here, baby, do you have room in your bag for these checks? I've got more loot here than I know what to do with."

"It's too tiny, Arnie, I'd never be able to fit them in."

"You broads never have the right size things. Well, never mind. Did you have some champagne?"

"Not yet."

"Hey, waiter, how about some champagne over here, don't we rate?" he motioned to a young waiter who was passing by with a tray filled with champagne glasses.

Natasha, with Sam on one side and Mrs. Berkowitz on the other, had a hard time getting a glimpse of Becky who was being monopolized by her father-in-law. In the center of the room the dance floor glistened from a recent waxing and the orchestra began playing "Oh How We Danced on the Night We Were Wed."

"Take your bride to the floor, Arnold," Louis commanded.

Arnold and Becky danced the first dance, Arnold's arm barely touching her waist. Becky floated into the waltz. She looked up into Arnold's eyes but couldn't catch them as his glance wandered around the room, nodding to the myriads of relatives lining the floor. In a moment, Louis Berkowitz cut in and Arnold was dancing with his mother. Then Louis was dancing with Natasha and Sam stumbling with Mrs. Berkowitz. Arnold and Becky were together again. The waltz became faster and faster and Arnold twirled Becky around the floor, her full skirt billowing about her. She could see Mrs. Berkowitz's diamond shining on her finger as it rested on Arnold's shoulder. She felt her veil swelling in back of her like sails on Long Island Sound. She wished Wilma could dance with Mr. Berkowitz. She wished she could aim her bouquet right at Letty and let it fall in her lap. By this time, the entire floor was filled with dancers. Young nephews in form-fitting blue suits and striped ties last worn at their own bar mitzvahs were dancing with their mothers or twelve-year-old cousins with braces and uncomfortable shoes. Aunt Leah was dancing with Aunt Ruth and Aunt Sophie with Aunt Essie.

Becky ate very little of the dinner as guests came up to the head table to shake her hand, and when it came time for them to wheel in the mammoth wedding cake, the orchestra repeated their drum roll and Arnold and Becky moved to the center of the floor. A waiter handed her a large cake knife and she cut into the top tier, where the bride and groom standing stiffly like toy soldiers gazed at her stonily. The knife slipped and she cut off the groom's top hat down to his meticulously designed sugar spats. She took the piece and put it in Arnold's mouth for Anthony Scaturo who was hovering about with his flashbulb over his head like a helicopter contemplating a rescue mission.

The evening reached its crescendo about midnight. Then, slowly, the exodus began. The aunts moved to the check room to get their minks and sables. Lorraine came over for a brief moment and kissed her on the cheek. "You're going to have such a wonderful life," she whispered to Becky, determined to obliterate the envy from her eyes, determined to wish her friend well.

Wilma and Letty were dry-eyed and hoarse, having spent the evening shouting to Arnold Berkowitz's two deaf aunts. Aunt Leah had a hearing aid but refused to turn it on because the buzzing irritated her. They kissed and hugged Becky good-bye, and Letty, shy about kissing Arnold, shook his damp hand warmly. She was certain he didn't know who she or Wilma was.

Suddenly, the room was almost empty. Suddenly, everyone had taken their toys and gone home. Suddenly, as spontaneously and gloriously as it had begun, it was all over. The orchestra was putting its instruments away. Mrs. Berkowitz was kissing the last cheek. Mr. Berkowitz, indefatigable, was patting his last behind.

Suddenly, Becky turned cold. She ran to her parents who were collecting some of the baskets of flowers on the tables to take home. "Becky, baby," Natasha held her. Sam patted her on the back. "It was beautiful, baby, beautiful. You were a beautiful bride."

"Mom. I'm sorry about the Rabbi. Don't go yet. Don't go. It's only twelve. Stay, have a last glass of champagne with us. Please."

Natasha looked up, surprised at the plea in Becky's voice.

"Sweetheart, it's over, baby. The Rabbi wasn't your fault. You tried. I've calmed your father down. You're a married woman now. Sweetheart, these flowers are so beautiful, Arnie's mother said we could take some home."

"Mom. Dad. Don't you think you could stay a little while longer?"

251

"Silly. Don't be silly. It's still the same jitters, baby. They'll pass. I promise. Come on, Sam, let's say good night to the Berkowitzes and let the kids be alone. Good-bye, baby. Please call me when you get back from the Bahamas. First thing."

"O.K., Mamma, O.K." Becky was afraid she would give in to the sobs she felt massing in her throat. She hugged her mother hard.

"Sweetheart. You're pulling on the earring."

"Sorry, Mom. Sorry."

"It was a beautiful wedding, Becky."

"Yes, Mom."

"Becky," Sam put his arms around her. "Be happy, baby," was all he could muster. He smelled of turpentine and there was still charcoal under his nails.

The bridal suite was framed in flowers. Baskets of fruit and bottles of champagne were lined on the chests and tables in the living room. A stocked bar had been set up in the small kitchen.

"I feel like we're going on a trip to Europe instead of getting married," Becky said, surveying the room, dropping into a chair. She kicked off her shoes. "My feet are all swollen. I must have danced every dance. Arnie wasn't it fantastic? A wonderful party?"

Arnold sat down on a pale yellow silk couch in front of the television set. He threw his jacket in the corner and loosened his tie. "Hey, babe, do me a favor, will you? Dash in the kitchen and fix me a Dewars and water. What do you say?"

Becky struggled up, unzipping her dress from the back as she went.

"I'm going to get into something less constricting. I can hardly breathe with all these skirts."

"Hey, sweetie, get me the drink first, O.K.?"

Becky realized she hadn't talked to Arnold for most of the evening and now saw that he was quite drunk.

He pulled his gold Binaca case out from his pants pocket and sprayed his mouth.

"I'll be out in a sec," she said, running into the bedroom.

Inside, she stepped out of the ruffles and flounces of her dress and hung it up carefully. She put on the white jersey negligee from her trousseau.

When she looked up, she saw Arnold standing in the doorway.

"I thought you were going to get me a drink?"

"Arnie, dear, I just had to get out of the dress. Here I come."

"It could have waited. The dress. It could have waited. I wanted a drink." Arnold's hands were filled with white envelopes. He threw them up in the air and they came cascading down on the middle of his shoulders like confetti in the Lindbergh parade. "Look at this loot. Just look at this loot. Is this going to come in handy. The old man will die when he sees how much we made."

"I can't hear you when the water's running," Becky said from the kitchen.

"Forget it. Come on out here."

Becky, barefoot, handed Arnold his drink. She had poured herself a glass of champagne. Arnold was sitting on the floor surrounded by the envelopes. He looked like a child at Christmas morning looking at the Lionel trains. He opened the envelopes, tearing off the seal, pulling out the checks.

"Those cheap bastards, do you know that the Marxes only gave us $500? I can't believe the gall. The firm gave his kid $1,000 when he was confirmed. That settles his hash. Jesus, the Feinsteins broke down and wrote a check for $750, things are looking up. Aha, here's one from Dot and Dan Fogel. If they gave us less than a thousand, I swear I'll stuff it up his nose."

253

Becky stood in the doorway, looking at him. She didn't know how to break the mood. She wanted to go back to the dance floor, she wanted to go back to dancing with her daddy, she wanted to go back an hour feeling her veil swirl around her.

"Arnie, why don't you do that in the morning? Let's go to bed. It's so late." She felt a strange shyness overtake her.

"Sure, Beck, sure. Look, why don't you just turn down the bed, take a tub, and I'll be in in a flash. O.K.?" He blew her a kiss. "Hand me my calculator, hon, it's in the top drawer. I want to add up this stuff."

Becky gave him the calculator and went into the bedroom. She ran her bath. She could still hear the rustling of the checks when, sweet smelling and dressed in a long satin gown, she pulled down the covers and got into bed.

23

Janet thought she heard Terry stirring in the bedroom. He had been sleeping soundly when she came home with her date, involved in that heavy, deep all-encompassing sleep that only a child, only an innocent can have.

Lying there on her couch, a bottle of brandy on the coffee table with only the light from the kitchen shining into the room, was a familiar vantage point.

The man with his hand under her dress was whispering something into her ear. Janet couldn't make it out, since part of her attention was directed toward the bedroom door. She didn't like this man whom she had met the night before at a singles bar three blocks from her house. He had told her he was some kind of executive with an oil company and had worked in South America on a project, but she didn't really believe him. She had checked him out with the bartender, because she certainly wasn't going to bring anyone who would in any way be considered dangerous into her home.

The man was a fool. At dinner he had held forth about how sexy it was when a woman didn't wear a bra and how he could tell the minute he had laid eyes on her that she was a sensual woman since her breasts were unencumbered.

"Let's get on the floor," he said hoarsely since the couch was beginning to become untenable for him. As she moved to the floor, Janet deftly removed her flowered blouse. She watched Ben Marden's eyes widen as she shook her breasts free.

"Suck them," she whispered as she lay on the floor, pulling his head down to her chest. Instead, Ben, on his knees, unzipped her fly on her slacks and pulled them off in one stroke. She lay there naked with only her black pumps on. She had removed her pantyhose when she came home in the bathroom. Feeling the soft down of the carpet beneath her, she pulled Ben down to her again, pulling his hands away from the buttons on his shirt as he was beginning to undress. She did not give him time to release the bulging penis straining to burst from the trousers.

"Suck them," Janet ordered, putting one breast into Ben's mouth, as she felt the welcome relief, his tongue pulling on her, carrying the intensity to her groin. She felt her buttocks move automatically from side to side on the carpet. Janet pulled Ben's hair away from her and, both palms on his cheeks, stared into his eyes.

"Go down on me. Eat me," she said. "Hurry."

Ben, overwhelmingly excited by her heat, still tried to get into a position where he could loosen his belt. Janet would have none of it.

She jerked his head down and with both hands buried his mouth into her. Ben put one hand on her thigh and with the other continued kneading her breast and nipple. Janet was hurting him. She dug her fingernails into the top of his head, and even though her head was back, she could see her own pubic hair acting as a beard for the panting man.

She was strong and Ben could not loosen her grip on his head. She was in a frenzy, shaking her head, taking his mouth in her fingers and moving it to the spot, the only spot that could complete her.

Janet put the back of her arm against her mouth to muffle her scream. Ben, breathing heavily, rested his head on her thigh. He smoothed it as he rose up to start unbuckling his belt.

"You've got to go," Janet said, suddenly, regaining her composure in her voice.

"What are you talking about?"

"You heard me, I've got to go to work tomorrow. It's getting late."

"Listen, Janet, I don't get you."

"There's nothing to get," Janet said, struggling to stand up, bolstering herself with the edge of the coffee table. "It's done. Over. That's it."

"Just who do you think you're kidding," Ben said, as he continued to unzip his fly and remove his belt.

"Put your clothes on," Janet said in measured tones. "I want you to go home."

"Forget it, sister," Ben said, pulling her down to the floor. She had already put on her blouse.

As she started to struggle out of his grasp, he pulled

the shirt off her. The ripping sound startled them both, but enflamed Ben.

"Who the hell do you think you are?" he said, pushing her down.

Janet tried to get up but he pinned her to the floor.

"Maybe with other guys, but not with me, kid."

Janet was afraid to scream, afraid of waking Terry, but with her knee, she butted Ben in the groin.

"Listen, you little bitch," he yelled through his pain, "get the fuck up, you hear me, get the fuck up," he jerked her up, almost pulling her arm out of the socket, and they both struggled to their feet.

"I don't like to hit women, but you're the pits, kid, the pits. I wouldn't want you if you looked like Raquel Welch, you know that. Just listen to this, though," he said, tucking his shirt into his pants, picking up his jacket, "some day you're going to pick up somebody who's going to beat you to a pulp, just take your cunt and wrap it around you. What a bitch."

He fumbled with the double lock on the door and went out, slamming it. When Janet looked up, feeling her aching shoulder, she looked straight into the eyes of Terry Stevens, who was staring at her. She would have to put a patch on his doctor dentons, she thought, that knee has a hole in it.

24

Letty was waiting for Will in front of the Plaza Hotel. She had been there for an hour. Periodically, she would go back inside the lobby, then to the ladies room, then to the phone. Something must have happened. But she couldn't call his house, she couldn't do anything but stand there and wait.

Two men in business suits and Chesterfield overcoats looked admiringly and expectantly at Letty as she stood just inside the door away from the cold. She turned away. Tomorrow was Christmas Eve.

It was far from Dickensian, she thought. It was cold, but there was no snow. Crowds jostled and jousted for position on the sidewalks. New York was frantic. 'Twas the night before Christmas and all through her house, was silence, Letty thought. No tree, no wreath. I'm Jewish and Christmas means nothing to me. But it does, she thought, sitting in a chair in the lobby, huddled into her coat, watching the furs and the gloves, the laughter and the suave hand-kissing by the *maître d'* in the Palm Court. She tucked her legs under her and felt overwhelmed by that familiar malaise.

Will had children and a tree and presents in the morning day after next, and she would have Fran and her coughing. Fran spit a lot now. She used to run for the toilet when the phlegm came into her throat. Now she just spit into a handkerchief. That would be her

Christmas morning. Her books. Her studying. A bialy, perhaps, her mother's kiss peppered with toothpaste smell. That would be her Christmas morning.

She hated it, Christmas. She couldn't wait for it to be over. Perhaps Wilma would come over for lunch. She would make a chicken. Families should have kids and tinsel. Will has that, kids and tinsel. Christmas is the worst, the very worst.

She got up abruptly, refusing to stay anymore. "Fall on your knees, oh, hear the angel voices; Oh night divine, oh night when Christ was born . . ." a Salvation Army band was playing in front of the hotel, with two young rosy-cheeked singers standing by the pot where the donations were expected.

Just as she was descending the steps, she saw him. He was rumpling the head of a blond boy and putting him in a cab. She watched him take some bills out of his pocket and give them to the boy.

Will loped up the steps with his characteristically wide stride. He caught sight of Letty.

"Oh, honey, I'm sorry. Sean and I had to wait almost two hours in the doctor's office. He had to have the penicillin shot and Kathy had to take the other boys someplace. Baby, I'm so sorry. Have you been waiting long?"

"Will, what kind of question is that? Of course I've been waiting long. Over an hour, as a matter of fact. I was about to go home."

"You would leave. You would go home?"

Only after the words were out did Will realize how childish they sounded.

"Lett, I'm sorry, I really am. There was no way of my getting in touch with you. I was going crazy sitting there in that doctor's office. I never read so many back issues of *Today's Health* in my life."

Will leaned over and kissed her on the cheek. His eyes moved quickly around behind her.

"What's wrong? What's wrong, Letty?" he said, putting his arm through hers.

"Nothing. Everything."

"How about Chinese food tonight?"

"Fine."

It became dark suddenly. There was no inbetween with New York dusk. It was light. Then it was dark. No nuance, Letty thought.

They walked down Fifth Avenue, looking in Bergdorf's window at the mannequins assaulting passers-by with their insolence, past Rizzoli's where they wandered in, listening to Vivaldi's "The Four Seasons" which was blaring from the record balcony above. They spoke little, wandering in and out of the book stalls, fingering the prints and posters in the back room.

Out on Fifth Avenue again, Will said, "Let's splurge on a cab, let's go down to Fourteenth Street, there's a great inexpensive place near the office."

"O.K., Will. That's fine with me."

Will did not know how to handle this mood.

"A week ago today, a week ago today, baby, we were making love in the middle of a tropical storm. Remember?" He tightened his arm on hers.

It was the wrong thing to say.

"Right. I remember."

"Letty, what is the matter with you? I said I was sorry. I said I was sorry about last week. What could I do? The kid was sick. His fever was so high. Would you have any respect for me if I just left them there? When they needed me? I tried to get out. I really did. I couldn't for the life of me get out Tuesday or Thursday. Come on, Letty. We're supposed to be glad to see each other. We're the ones who are moving heaven and earth to make time and space to see each other. I get enough flak at home. I don't need it here."

In the cab, Letty looked at Will. Right, she thought,

you don't need it here. Neither do I. I don't need it, either.

Will ordered a lavish meal. Two full dinners which they shared. He kept looking at Letty, trying to break into her mood.

"What did you do Tuesday after I called? Did you go to a movie or something? I called back later with a fake voice and a fake name and talked to your mother."

"I know. She told me. You don't make a very good woman. She thought it was somebody making a joke."

Will toyed with the fried rice, picking out the mushrooms. Kathy always left the mushrooms out, he thought. What the hell am I thinking about Kathy now? I can't even count on a predictable thought. This is hardly the time to think about Kathy, for God's sake, he thought.

"So what'd you do? Go to a movie or something?" He couldn't stop.

"I went out and took a walk. Then I came home and started a paper I should have started long ago. Will, I don't think I should have to answer to all this."

They struggled with the chopsticks, and ate silently.

"How's your mother feeling? Is she all right?" Conversation, he was making conversation.

"She spits. Coughs and spits." Letty pushed the food away from her.

"Why? What's the matter with her?"

"I don't know. Bronchial something, the doctor says. All of a sudden at that age things start to go. Little things. She has a lot of little things."

Tomorrow is Christmas Eve and your kids will hang up their stockings alongside some mock mantle and maybe you'll sing some Christmas carols or something and I'll watch Perry Como or Andy Williams and all those kids and brothers all looking so American, so family. And Fran will sip her tea and talk about her mother who hid behind her grandmother's skirts during a pogrom in Russia. How Christmas Eve was always the worst night for the Jews when the Cossacks would get drunk and brandish their swords and sometimes catch a head on them.

"What else besides the spitting?"

"What? Oh, I don't know. She's just getting old."

"Letty, are you all right? You look tired. Was it a hard day for you? I saw you giving it to Dolores. God, that girl is dumb. She had to do something for me three times over. Letty, I wish we could go away again tomorrow. You know?"

"We can't, though. Can we, Will? I'm not tired. I did lose my temper a little at Dolores. And Agnes worries me. She's so odd since she came back. It's as though someone pulled a thread from her and she's started to unravel."

"I didn't notice. She seems as plump and perfect as ever to me," Will said, pouring some tea for the two of them.

"Not at all. You're the one who's supposed to be so sensitive to others' feelings, Will. She's . . ."

"Look, what's that all about? I never said I was. She's a scatter-brained clothes horse, as far as I'm concerned."

"Oh, Will, you don't even know her. You don't even know her." Letty felt like crying. There were miles between them. All of a sudden, they were strangers.

"Letty. It's getting late. I want to hold you."

I want to hold you, too, Letty thought. Tomorrow is Christmas Eve and not a creature will be stirring, except that mouse and me. I will never sleep. I will wait for the clatter of the reindeer's hooves on my roof and will wait for the Ho-Ho-Ho as Santa tries to find a chimney and he will get halfway down and say, "No, sir, wrong place, I will pass over this house." Go to Will's house, Letty said to the Santa in her head, as

262

Will took her arm and led her out of the restaurant. Go to Will's child-filled house where you will be welcomed with open arms.

"Merry Christmas," Letty whispered as Will put the key in the lock of Room 809 of the Ramada Inn after they checked in. Letty whispered, "Merry Christmas, Will, Merry Christmas."

25

Letty inadvertently bumped into Ed Coyne the day after Christmas. They stood and talked at the corner of Eighty-sixth Street and Lexington Avenue, and Letty was aware that Ed was curt and seemed to want to avoid her. She knew she had acted rudely the time she had gone out with him, and, exhausted by the thought of spending another evening alone with her mother and her studies, she behaved as charmingly and seductively as she could.

Delighted by her change in style, Ed asked her to go bowling. She hadn't bowled in fifteen years but decided to go anyway. She saw Ed on Friday, Saturday and Sunday evening. Monday night they went bowling again.

Entering the alley, Letty put her hands over her ears; it sounded like D-Day at the Normandy beach. Ed's arm around her waist was reassuring, and she liked the fact that she didn't have to look around to see who was watching, but she wished it were Will's arm.

"The shoes are over there. Just lay out the money. I'll pay you back," Ed said, pointing to the women's shoe rental in a corner of the mammoth alley.

"Ed, don't be silly. I can pay for it."

"I insist," he said gallantly. "Meet you in aisle four. Phil has it all reserved."

Ed was glowing. He liked being with Letty and was delighted she had agreed to bowl again. His brother, Phil, and his wife, Sally, were old hands at this. They had a steady date every Monday night, and although Letty wasn't very good, the idea appealed to her.

Ed's sister-in-law had put on a lot of weight with the last baby who was only a month old. It was her fourth in six years, and as she pointed out to Letty ruefully after being introduced, they certainly kept her on the go. Sally had a big round Irish face with uncommonly fair skin and laughing blue eyes. She had a nun's face, Letty thought, a face that would look serene and beautiful in a habit with the black and white headdress framing her face. Her hands were rough and red from so much soaking in water, and it looked as though the nails were bitten down to the nub. Sally's hair was dirty blond and very short, and looked as though it hadn't been washed in weeks.

"I'm so glad to meet you, Letty," she said, giving her a hug. "Would you like a beer? This is Phil."

"Hi, Letty. You've met the mother of the year, I suppose." Phil, as wide as Ed was tall, patted his wife on the behind. She slapped his hand.

"You'll still have to wait a few weeks, bozo, so forget about patting my behind, kid. Come on, Letty. Let's bowl."

"I get the feeling I'll never be able to get my fingers out of this ball," Letty said, as Ed showed her how to hold it.

Letty was having fun. It was an unfamiliar experience for her. Times with Will were stimulating, but they were heavy. There was a heaviness about the concern about being seen, an unseen tension that hovered. But now, she felt light, and the sips of beer in between her hurling of the ball and its inevitably landing in the gully on the right side of the alley sent her into gales of laughter.

"Gorgeous you are, a bowler you will never be," Sally roared, having racked up her own score of 150 with ease.

"Knock it off. With a little practice I could make her a star," Ed said. "It's her knees, she locks her knees. Letty, you have to bend more."

"I could make a comment, but I won't," Phil said with a guffaw.

"Don't," Ed glared at him.

Letty didn't care. She felt relaxed, and it felt good to laugh. Nobody was talking about Proust, that's for sure, or Carter's latest trip, but Ed was dear and attentive and she liked Sally. She bored her, but she responded to her unpretentiousness.

"Well, we got to go," Sally said after an hour of bowling. "Baby sitter's too young to leave too late. Coming, Phil? Listen, babe, you don't have to, I can go home alone. Why don't you stay and bowl a few more, I don't mind going at all."

"Knock it off. Don't be a drag. I want to watch the eleven o'clock news. O.K., sport, see you around. Great to see you again, Letty. Don't be a stranger now." The brothers shook hands. Sally gave Letty a hug and they were off.

"You tired, Letty? Want to call it quits?"

"I think so, Ed, if you don't mind. I would love another beer, though. There's a little cocktail lounge in there, I see."

"Swell, let's get rid of these shoes first." Ed took his

265

own ball and put it in the bag he had carried over to the alley.

He's a good man, Letty thought, watching him walk away. He's not bright, but he's good, and he makes me laugh. I don't have to pretend anything. He accepts me just the way I am. He doesn't want to change me. His touch was comforting. But he wasn't Will.

"Did you have fun, Letty?"

"I really did, Ed. Really. I feel loose."

"It's really good to see you laugh. I love being with you." He leaned over and touched her hair.

"Me, too. Ed, I've really enjoyed our times."

He ordered two beers as he spread himself out in the chair. He put his hands together as though praying.

"You're getting to be a habit with me," he said. "Look, I'm not good with words. I wish to God I was. I really do. And if I could write well, I'd send you a letter, but I'm beginning to care for you, Letty. I really am. I don't want to make a fool out of myself, and you know, I have a lot of pride. I know we don't know each other very well, but well, the first time we were out together, you were strange, abrupt like, and it cooled me. You know. And well, you know I've never . . . can I go on, Letty? Can I tell you how I feel?"

"I know, Ed," Letty said softly. Dreading the next. Knowing it was coming, knowing she owed him some kind of explanation. She couldn't tell him she was using him, she couldn't tell him that being with him made the days go by faster, the nights less heavy, that it passed the time. Till she would see Will.

"Ed, I'm seeing someone. I'm serious about someone."

Ed knew it. Somewhere inside him, he always knew it.

"Then why do you see me, Letty? Why do you go

out with me if you're serious about someone else?" He couldn't hide the hurt.

Letty wouldn't hurt him for the world.

"Look, Ed. He's married. I can't see him all the time."

"So, I just fill in, right?" the words slipped out. He really wanted her. He had been building up hopes somehow.

"No, Ed." Letty was speaking so softly that Ed could hardly hear her.

"I truly like you. I wouldn't see you if I didn't. And you've been a real friend to me. And I need a friend."

"That's the kiss of death. Friend. I don't like that word."

"Ed, that's precious, friendship." She didn't know how she was going to get out of this. She had known this would come, that he rightfully would want to make demands.

"Well, is he going to leave his wife? Is he planning to divorce her and marry you?" he said with feeling.

Letty looked at him. She heard the music blaring from the jukebox, the low roll of the balls rumbling down the alley, the crashing into strikes, the muffled squeals from outside the lounge.

She was beginning to get a charleyhorse in her calf already. So soon after bowling. You never use those muscles in anything else other than bowling, she thought. I'll have to take a hot bath as soon as I get home.

"No, Ed. I don't think so. He won't. I don't think he'll ever be able to get a divorce." The words came spitting out of her mouth like watermelon seeds, like pits of oranges.

26

A few days later, the phone rattled Will out of a deep sleep. Peering at the clock radio that was lit, he saw it was 3 A.M. Kathy didn't hear the phone. She didn't stir.

"Yes," was all he could muster.

"Will?"

"Yes."

"It's me. Bob. I'm sorry it's so late . . ."

Will was awake immediately. Some burst of adrenalin shook him.

"What? What is it, Bob?"

"I'm taking Eleanor to the hospital. I just called the ambulance. I called you automatically right after. I don't even know why. Will, is it awful to ask you to come to the hospital? Do you think you could meet me at St. Claire's? It's in the fifties off Ninth. Is that a terrible inconvenience? I'm scared, Will." It was hard for him to get the words out. "I don't want to be alone."

"I'll be there in five minutes."

Will woke Kathy, gently shaking her by the shoulder. "McKern's wife, something happened. I don't even know what. I'm going to St. Claire's. I don't know when I'll be back." Kathy was awake immediately.

Will slipped on a pair of jeans and heavy turtleneck sweater.

On the other side of town, Bob McKern was riding in a screaming ambulance. He was holding Eleanor's hand and watching the black ambulance attendant write some notes on a piece of paper attached to a clipboard. The fear was so tight in his chest, he could barely breathe. He knew Eleanor could not survive another operation. She had woken up, clutching him, and when he turned on the light and looked at her, her face was almost blue.

They wheeled Eleanor upstairs, whisked her away from him as soon as he arrived at the hospital. Will Robbins was standing there, by the information desk.

"What is it?"

"She was turning blue. The doctor is upstairs waiting for her. I can't go up until he comes down to talk to me."

"Come on, Bob, there's a coffee machine over there in the corner."

"I can't . . ."

"Of course you can. O.K., you sit over there, I'll get it. How do you take it?"

"I don't want . . ."

"Well, I'll bring it black."

Will returned with two cups of coffee. The round white-faced clock said 3:30 A.M. Bob's hand was shaking when he took the cup.

"Thanks, Will. I'm giving myself lectures all the time."

"I know, Bob," Will said, lighting a cigarette.

"I've got to believe that she's going to be all right. But she can't, I know she can't survive another operation. She's just not strong enough. Remember I was telling you about her color? How she used to be so rosy. She's all different colors now; yellow, yellow and sallow. And before. Blue. Her lips were blue." Bob's eyes filled with tears.

Without realizing what he was doing, Will put his arm around Bob. It was an awkward but firm gesture. He ached for Bob as the man fought for composure.

"I don't know why I keep thinking about that. Her cheeks were always red. You know, that high color that fair people sometimes have. Will, sure that goes when you get older, but ever since she's been sick, it all faded. I don't even care, but it hurt her so much. She felt so bad about losing that natural rouge. Will . . ."

"Right, Bob." Will moved his arm away, lighting another cigarette.

"I've really been thinking about it."

"About what?" He hated the smell, the hospital smell of disinfectant and ether or whatever it was. He would like to get out of this hospital, Will thought.

"About what I was talking to you about the other day. About my not being able to go on without her. She is really my life. I know that sounds melodramatic and everything, but the thought of sleeping in that bed alone, the thought of coming home from work and her not being there, the thought of knowing the finality of it that I would never see her again is just too much for me.

"Once, only once I was tempted by another woman, Will. Eleanor was out of town, you know," Bob said, determined to confess at this time. Will didn't want to hear, and turned away, but Bob pulled his arm. "All of a sudden, sex took on such an importance for me. I don't know what got into me that time, Will, but I let a woman pick me up. Eleanor was away for a few weeks that time. I can't remember why, somebody was sick or something. It was such a long time ago. But I went to bed with her, Will, with this woman who was my wife's inferior. She wasn't as pretty or as good.

She was cheap, you know what I mean, but it was like I was crazy that time. I would talk to Eleanor every night on the phone and I missed her like hell. But I needed a woman. And it got to be any woman. I felt rotten about it, always have. And I never did it again, never let myself get tempted again. The woman's body repelled me even, but I needed it. I had to have it. I felt so bad. I still do."

"Bob, drink your coffee. Look, I really think it's going to be all right. I have a feeling. Vibes. Just vibes, Bob. You've got to believe that, you've got to believe that she's going to live for a long time."

If it was Letty upstairs, if Letty had been his wife, how would he feel? Will looked at the elevator, watching the lighted numbers climb.

Bob was leaning back on the bench, his head against the wall, his eyes closed. Will took the coffee cup out of his hand.

If it were Letty upstairs, if he could never see Letty again, if Letty were his wife. How would it be? What would it be like? How those two loved each other. It was old-fashioned and there was a powerful dependence, but I'd give anything for the absoluteness of it, he thought. The commitment.

Will looked over at his friend. The weariness and fear were shadows on his face. As painful as it was, what Bob was going through, there was a part of Will that envied, a part of Will that envied Bob McKern more than anything.

27

"The doctor said it was a miracle. A simple miracle. Will, she'll be home in a few days. I was up there at the hospital last night and she was sitting up asking for a glass of wine. Can you imagine? The doctor said she passed some kind of crisis or something. Will, I can't tell you, I can't explain how joyful I feel." Bob McKern was extravagantly happy. After a week of touch and go, Eleanor had begun to make phenomenal progress. She was going to get well.

The two men were sitting in a delicatessen around the corner from the office. Out of the corner of his eye, Will saw Letty sitting alone at another table in the back. He was trying hard to share Bob's joy, and at the same time make eye contact with Letty. As they so often arranged, Letty had lunch at the same restaurant. They never sat together.

"Bob, you know how glad I am for you. Can I go visit? How much longer is she going to be in the hospital?"

"Just a few days. She'll be home again. Christ, what a great way to start the New Year. Perhaps," he said shyly, "you can come over sometime. You've never been to the house, and she would love it, Will, just love it.

"I'm telling you, the doctor said he never saw anything like it. It was as though she passed from one country into another. Miraculous. Look, Will, would you mind taking the check? I've got to go to the bank.

272

I don't have a cent on me. I'll pay you back this afternoon."

"Sure, Bob. No problem."

Will sat at the table, took out a cigarette and began to light it. He looked across the room at Letty. There was something wrong. He could tell from the way she held her coffee cup, from the tightness of her shoulders, the way she was sitting.

Picking up his cup, snuffing the cigarette, Will broke his own ground rules and walked to Letty's table. She was startled when she saw him sit down.

"Listen, I got tickets for the play you wanted to see, Letty, you known, that new Tom Cole play, about Vietnam. *Medal of Honor Rag*. It's at the Theatre de Lys on Christopher Street." He took out another cigarette and began to light it. Through clenched teeth, he continued. He was talking quietly, simulating a certain formality. The most casual onlooker would assume they had just met.

Letty didn't answer. She stared into space.

"Don't you want to go? I thought you wanted to see that play?"

"I do. I do want to see it."

"What's the matter, Letty?"

"I don't think I can go tonight, Will. I can't go to the play. I've got a conference with my teacher."

"You never told me anything about that, Letty. Tell me what's bugging you. Tell me the truth, Letty. Where are you going?"

"Will, what difference does it make? It's true. We made appointments for private conferences about the papers we handed in."

"O.K., Letty, who is it? Who are you going to see?"

Letty put on a smile, assuming as relaxed an air as she could.

"Will. Come on. Let's not get into this. Will, I can't talk about it here. People are all over the place."

In a hoarse whisper, Will said, "I can see people are all over the place, as a matter of fact, Lorraine and Dolores are in the back booth. But that doesn't have anything to do with anything. Tell me what it is, Letty. What's bothering you?"

Letty couldn't stop the tears from forming in her eyes. "It's me, Will. It's my life outside these two days of the week. It's getting to me, Will, it's beginning to get to me. My life outside of Tuesdays and Thursdays. There are five other days of the week that I have to contend with. You have your wife, you have your kids. I've got an old lady I have to . . ."

"This seat taken?"

A very short, very round woman with a babushka on her head and glasses sat down between Will and Letty. She was almost as old as Fran, Letty observed, but she was very spry; she exuded energy.

"Just came from the Welfare," she said. "You wouldn't believe those lines." She proceeded to take her plate of frankfurters and beans, cole slaw, and Jell-O off her tray.

"Mind putting that tray over there, son?" she said to Will, who obediently put the tray back on the counter. He sat down again, looking at Letty.

"They sent me out on a job last week, you know," the woman said, addressing both of them, "so they forgot that I wasn't entitled to a check. Now I'm an honest woman, so I just gave them the check right back. The young man was so surprised, I thought he was going to fall right off his chair. So anyway . . ."

Letty was staring into space. Will ran his fingers through his hair. He wanted to reach out and hold Letty's hand. They couldn't touch each other. The woman sat between them, chattering like a chorus in their own private Greek play.

Letty felt like a character in a mask theater. I am not really here, she thought. The only person here is

this woman. I am a shadow. I've got to fill in the out-
lines of myself. She got up abruptly, taking her coat
from the back of her chair. Will looked after her as
she walked out of the restaurant, but she didn't,
wouldn't look back.

28

"O.K., Letty, now what was all that about yesterday?"

"What was all what about?"

"Listen, you know what I'm talking about. What's
the matter with you?"

"You know how difficult it is to talk on the intercom. I can't talk, Will, I really can't."

"Letty, what's going on?"

"Look," Letty had begun to whisper. "There are all
kinds of people around. I can't . . ."

"For Christ's sake, come off it," he shouted into the
phone. "All right, all right. Look, meet me at the bar
at Bradley's after work. Letty. Letty? Are you there?"

"Yes, I'm here."

"O.K., then. About five forty-five, all right?"

"I've got school at six-thirty."

"O.K. O.K. It's right around there, isn't it?"

"I've got to hang up." Letty put the receiver down
as Priscilla sat on the edge of her desk.

"What the hell is level premium?" Priscilla whispered. "MacKail gave me a whole lecture on it, and
I don't understand a word of it. Fill me in quick,

Letty, I've got to go back into his office. What's up, you look ghastly." Priscilla was wearing a cinch belt that accentuated both her small waist and swelling hips.

"Nothing, I'm fine. What is it you wanted to know?"

"Level, level premium. What is it? I've got to know fast. I've been pretending for the last half hour that I'm an authority, and I don't know what I've been talking about."

"Oh, well, it's when the cost is distributed evenly over the period during which the premiums are paid."

"Is the cost the same from year to year?"

"Yes," Letty recited as if by rote, "and it's more than the actual cost of protection in the earlier years of the policy and less than the actual cost in the later years."

"Well, but I still don't understand how it works."

"The excess paid in the early years builds up a reserve to cover the higher cost in later years."

"Oh."

"What do you mean, oh?"

"I mean, I think I get it."

"Good."

"You still look like a truck just hit you."

"I'm O.K., Priscilla, really." Letty patted her upper lip with Kleenex sitting in a box on her desk.

"How about a drink after work, Letty? Me and Dolores are going to a new swinging bar. We found i last week. New crowd."

"No, thanks. Give me a raincheck, Priscilla. I'll g next week, I promise."

"O.K., hon. God, I hope I can remember that leve stuff by the time I get back to my desk. See ya later. With a bump and a grind and a bounce of her head she walked away.

"Why don't you cut school tonight, Letty?" Will wa

leaning with both elbows on the bar. The mustachioed bartender shoved a container of cheddar cheese and crackers in front of them.

"I wonder what time the jazz starts?" He looked over at the piano in back of them in the corner. "Barry Harris is here. I've heard him, he's sensational. So what do you say, Letty? We could stay here for supper. It's nice and dark way in the back there and we could listen to some jazz."

Letty looked at Will. His top two buttons were unbuttoned, the tie plumped out. He needed a haircut.

She was trying to sound very firm.

"Will, I can't. It's Wednesday. What got into you anyway? How come you deviated from your Tuesday and Thursday syndrome? Have I ever in my life seen you on a Wednesday?"

She took a long sip from her scotch, and slid the glass forward to the bartender.

"O.K. here we are. There it is. What's with the snickers? That's the purpose for this drink. To find out what's eating you. Come on, Letty. Forget the sarcasm, for Christ's sake and let's talk."

"I'm not happy. I'm confused, and I'm tired of the set-up. That's it, pure and simple." Letty spoke slowly, looking at the clock over the bar. It was after six already. She did not want to miss class.

The bartender gave her another scotch.

"Give me a double," Will said. "What do you mean?"

"Will, you know what I mean. I'm talking about yesterday. I'm talking about the delicatessen. I'm talking about sitting at a table with a stranger in between us so somebody from the office in the back of the restaurant wouldn't realize we were together. I'm talking about talking to you out of the side of my mouth, so nobody would realize I was talking directly to you. I'm talking about . . ."

"I got the message." Will downed his scotch in one gulp. He beckoned to the bartender.

"Letty," he said, swirling his finger into the new scotch, then putting it to his mouth, sucking it, "I don't believe you."

Letty looked at him. "I'm telling you the truth. Why wouldn't I tell you the truth, Will?"

"How come you're so anxious to get to this class? Who's in that class that you're so anxious to see?" He couldn't help himself. The drink was going to him. He hadn't been able to eat lunch.

"Who is it, the teacher, some eighteen-year-old? I don't know, I don't trust you anymore. I can't depend on you. I believe that after that perfect week, after all that togetherness and loving, you would go out and get yourself laid with anybody."

Letty shook her hand free.

"So what if I went out? So what if I see someone else? Do you actually expect me to sit home night after night whatever hell the day or night of the week it is, waiting for your call? Waiting for you to extricate yourself from this wife or that child. Four years. Four years, Will. I have to figure out seriously if it's been a waste, whether I've wasted all that time. Because there's been more waiting around than spending time together, that's for sure."

"I can't believe you," Will said. "I can't believe that after that week, when we both were beginning for the first time practically since we know each other, to let down and unwind, to have some possible sense of normalcy, I can't believe you'd hand me this shit now."

Letty was crying. It was as good a place to cry as any, she thought. Chinese restaurants, French, Indian. Once she made the curry far more salty than it should have been, seasoned by her tears.

"You're impossible. You're irrational. Do you honestly expect me to sit home all the time?"

"I don't believe there's a faithful woman left out there," Will shouted. "I don't believe there's a woman in this world who wouldn't sell her cunt for the right price. I don't believe there's a woman in the world who knows what it is anymore to be faithful. I swear. The women's lib movement has made whores out of you."

Letty couldn't stop the tears now.

"Will, stop. I know you don't mean it. I know you don't. But you're weak. You're so weak, sometimes I can't stand it. You're good and you're the biggest hypocrite I've ever met, all at the same time. You're the one who's married, or have you forgotten that? You're the one who's tied up, not me. I'm free. Free, Will, to all intents and purposes, you have no right to say one word about what I do with my life.

"I can't believe you, Will. I can't believe you're serious. I feel hemmed in." She lowered her voice and put her mouth to his ear. Her eyes started to jump. They did that when she was upset. It would be a few minutes before she could focus again. "Will, I love you. What's the matter with you? That doesn't change. But I think we should . . ."

"We should what?" he said, breaking away from her abruptly.

"I don't know, Will, just take a rest for a while. Maybe not see each other . . ."

"We've tried that, kid." Will took a cracker and piled a spoonful of cheddar on top of it. He held it to Letty's mouth.

"I don't want any."

"Eat it."

"Will. I'm tired of it," she said, pushing his hand away. "It's four years, Will. Do you know that next year I'm going to be thirty-eight?"

"I don't want to hear about it. I survived it."

Letty looked at him. They'd been through this before. This was all familiar territory. The breakup. The anger. Will's temper. The making up. She understood him so well.

"You're cruel. You know that? Look, I've got to go. I'm going to be late for class." Letty began gathering her things, her notebook and pocketbook were resting on the bar.

Will gripped her elbow.

"You're hurting me."

"Stay. We've got to talk this out." His own elbow knocked over his drink, and even though there wasn't much scotch in it, his shirt was drenched. "Stay. Just stay, Letty. Let's have another drink and talk this out."

"Why are you drinking so much? I've never seen you drink so much. I just want to have some time to think."

"Why do you give me this bullshit?" Will said, putting his face close to hers. "Why do you give me, hand me this crap? You've got another guy. You can't kid me, Letty. You've met somebody in that goddamn class. Maybe it's the teacher. I don't know why all of a sudden you're complaining, it's part of the deal. You think I like it, for Christ's sake? Do you think I like the sneaking around, begging, borrowing time to see each other?" He was beginning to raise his voice. "I don't like it, either. It's rough. Real rough on me. Don't you think I feel hemmed in, as you call it? It works both ways."

"All right. So maybe it can't work. Maybe love isn't enough . . . maybe . . ."

"Don't give me that." He began to shout. "Don't give me that crap. We'd settled it. We made a bargain to live with it because we cared, because we loved . . ."

"What? Where? What bargain? We never made any such bargain. We both hurt. Differently. But I'm

280

struggling out from under it, Will. I'm trying to survive for myself." She reached into her bag and pulled out her compact, dabbing powder under her eyes.

"Come on. Let's get out of here. I can't stand it here anymore," Will motioned for the check. He stumbled as he extricated himself from the high stool. Squinting at the bill, he felt into his pockets.

"Letty," he mumbled, "Letty, do you have any bills? I seem to be a little short." He vaguely remembered giving Kathy his last twenty dollars that morning, not thinking he would need any money until pay day. He hated not having enough money. He hated asking a woman for money. He hated the whole fucking world.

Letty pulled some bills from her wallet and left them on the bar. It was after seven already. If she rushed, she could make the class before the break. The break. She was breaking. Her heart was breaking.

Will took her elbow roughly and guided her out onto Sixth Avenue. It was dark already.

"Do you have any more money?"

"Yes."

"Let's go someplace cheap and have a bite. We haven't finished."

"Will, I've got to get to class. I've got to get the assignment for next week. I've got . . ."

"You've got to settle with me," he roared. He whirled her around to face him. "What is this crap you're giving me? We're together, we're together. We need each other. How can you think of not seeing me, unless you've got some other guy. Is that it, Letty, do you have some stud under wraps?" He put his hands on her shoulders and began to shake her. She was dizzy from too many scotches, she was embarrassed as passers-by glanced at them, she was worried about the look in Will's eye. "Will, stop it."

"I want to tell you something, Letty. If somebody puts his cock inside you, I'll kill him, tear him apart. I could do it. I could do it now. It's what I feel. And just let me find out who it is. Who have you been fucking, Letty? Tell me. Who is it? Since when are you so goddamn interested in psychology? You've got some cocksucker you see after class, I know it."

He kept shaking her as though she were filled with salt, as though she were a small child who had to be punished because she hadn't listened.

He has no right, she thought. He doesn't dare to do this to me.

"You have no right," she screamed. "How dare you. I am a person. I have dignity. What the hell are you doing to me? To yourself? Let me alone. It's too much. There isn't anyone. There should be. I should be fucking an army. But there isn't. At the moment, at this very moment, there just doesn't happen to be anybody. I'm going to be thirty-eight years old and you're worried who I'm fucking. But I can't vouch for tomorrow. Don't you ever shake me again. Don't you ever." Letty was crying now. No one stopped as they walked by, just looked curiously. A city happening. A usual thing.

The slap took her by surprise.

She felt her mascara sting in her eyes. I'm going to have a bruise, she thought. How will I explain a bruised face to Fran? The next thing she knew, she was punching his chest. She couldn't stop crying. She was a Mack Sennett policeman with big feet pointing the wrong way, flailing a billy club around. She was the man in *The Cask of Amontillado* nailed up in the wine cellar pummeling the wall to get out. This man was crazy, this man whose chest she was beating. This man was ruining her life.

"Get out of my life!" she cried. "It's over, it's no

good! You can't talk to me that way. Who do you think you are? You talk about my life, and what I do. What about yours? What about law school and finishing? At least I'm trying. At least I'm trying somehow to get out of this morass. School has some meaning, some goal for me. You know that. And you know what, Will? You know what?" She couldn't stop punching him with her fists, as hard as she could. "You'll never finish. Never, never. You'll never get out of law school. Ten years in law school and four years with me and none of it, none of it consummated, finished, nothing to show for it!"

There. Now it was out. The truth. Will looked at her. He knew it was the truth. He knew he had been telling himself lies. Now the truth was out from the person he felt the closest to.

Letty looked at him, ashamed of herself, ashamed for saying this. She felt a criminal. "We're finished. Finished. No more. Stay away, Will. Stay away from me. Don't call, don't come, don't look at me. We're over. We're finished. Leave me alone."

"Who do you think you're kidding?" He said it to no one. He wasn't making any sense. He could feel that somewhere. Somewhere he could feel that he had hit this friend of his, this girl that he loved, and this harridan in front of him with black running down her cheeks, banging on his chest, was someone else. Where was Letty? Perhaps he had better borrow some money from this lady in front of him who was beating on his chest. He wouldn't have cab fare home. He would have to take two subways or maybe two buses. Tomorrow everything would be all right.

Letty ran down the street, unable to control the sobbing. This is it, she thought, the last time. We are killing each other. She ran into a restaurant that said burger something. She had to go to the bathroom.

She had to fix herself up. She had to take stock. But she couldn't stop crying. Even in the bathroom, her head under the tap, the cold water running over her face, the tears just wouldn't stop.

29

Don't say anything. Just be quiet, some secret voice inside Kathy whispered. If you don't say a thing, perhaps it will go away, perhaps this really isn't happening after all.

Kathy watched Will as he sat opposite her at the dining room table. The lace tablecloth from her grandmother's hope chest had a stain on it. She would scrub it tomorrow. But you can't chlorox lace, she thought. It would fall apart, disintegrate. Like now. Like me and Will. It was New Year's Eve and like a piece of old lace, her world was beginning to fall apart.

She sneezed. Five times. Kathy never sneezed once. Will stopped talking and waited for the sneezes to be over.

"I've got another cold," she said. "Perhaps I'd better get flu shots or Vitamin C shots or something." Kathy blew her nose.

A large crash came from the front of the apartment. Followed by a wail.

"I'll go," Kathy said, gratefully.

"Leave it. Let them settle it themselves. People

have to do that sometimes, Kathy, settle things themselves. It's what we have to do."

"O.K., Will," she said, resigned. "I'm listening."

"You can't tell me you haven't sensed anything." Will was uncomfortable. He wanted to be somewhere else. He couldn't bear the look in Kathy's eyes.

"Of course I have, Will, of course I have. I know you, you know. I've known you practically all my life, you know. I don't know if you noticed, but I tried, I tried to please you in so many ways."

Don't let her cry, Will thought. Please, God, don't let her cry.

She wasn't going to. Kathy was determined not to cry.

"I lost some weight, Will."

"Kathy, stop. You're lovely. You always were. It's not that. It never was."

"What is it, Will? Did you just outgrow me, like the magazines say? Did you read more and accomplish more while I stayed home and kept house and brought up the kids? Was that it? Are we just statistic number five million and two? Is that it, Will? Did you just outgrow me?"

"Kathy . . ."

"Tell me. Tell me who she is, Will. Is she somebody wiser? Somebody prettier? Is that it . . . ?"

He was waiting for her to cry. Maybe it would be better if she would. Maybe it would be better if she clawed at him, flailed. But she sat there. Looking at him. She looked like a wayward child, a waif. What was he doing? He should take her in his arms and comfort her. She had lost some weight, and the loss made her eyes seem enormous. They were surrounding her face. But it was Letty he loved. This woman, this child, was someone who needed his protection. She was not a woman to love.

"I never felt pretty enough for you, Will. I know I

285

was pretty, but I never felt pretty enough. I knew I had a good head, but I wasn't intelligent enough. For you, for anybody. But I try. And I'm a good mother. Aren't I? Aren't I a good mother, Will?" Kathy couldn't keep the whine out of her voice.

"Yes, Kathy. Yes, you are."

"And I keep this house immaculately, and everybody eats well."

"Kathy, stop this."

"What is it that you want, Will?"

"I don't know. I'm just not happy. I need some time. Some time, away . . ." He was waiting for his head to throb. He was surprised that it had taken so long.

It was different to suspect, Kathy thought. It was different to look for lipstick on handkerchiefs and hairs on his blue jacket. But she knew without his telling her. She knew there was somebody. What did he take her for?

"Do you want to leave? Is that it?" She could barely hear her own voice.

"I don't know, Kathy. I just don't know. This way is killing me. I'm rotten to you."

"I'm not complaining."

"You should, for Christ's sake, you should," he shouted. "Why do you just sit there and take it? You take everything."

"Because I want the marriage. I can't think of life without you. It's unthinkable." Kathy was gripping the arms of the dining room chair.

"But I can't go on this way. I'm no good to you. I'm no good to the boys. My headaches are getting worse at work. I think I should move out for a while."

"I followed you one day," Kathy said abruptly.

"What do you mean?"

"I mean, I followed you. I waited at five o'clock after you got out of work one Tuesday and followed

286

you. You went into some bar across from the office called Sal's. You had a drink, and then you met this tall girl five blocks beyond. You put your arm around her. You got into a cab. I followed you to a restaurant in the Village and I waited outside. Then you went to a Holiday Inn. Then I went home." Staccato.

Hundreds of tiny beads of perspiration dotted Will's forehead like raindrops resting on a leaf.

"So I know."

All those Tuesdays and Thursdays, all those excuses, he thought. All that subterfuge. A paper bag with a hole in it. He noticed some gray coming in at Kathy's temples. He had never seen it before. What would she do without him? She did not know how to make love. Why in hell was he thinking about that now? His mind was racing. Whether it was the nuns and their early fear inducements or her nature or her preoccupation with getting older, it didn't matter. She didn't know how to do it. She wasn't good at it. It took so long to arouse her. He just had to breathe on Letty and she was moist and ready.

"Kathy, why didn't you tell me you knew?"

"Because I was afraid you would leave me."

Kathy took a napkin and dipped it in a glass of water still resting on the table. She scrubbed the stain. Will watched her. Out, damn spot. Out, damn pain, he thought. I want to go. How can I go, how on earth can I leave those boys? He watched her fighting for composure. He admired the dignity she was trying so hard to achieve.

"I want you to know something, Will," Kathy said.

"What, Kathy?"

"I want you to know I'm going to fight for you. I'm not the naïve little girl I used to be." She was scrubbing the lace spot hard. Will was afraid she would tear a hole in it.

Kathy had a feeling of unreality. She looked at her

fingers rubbing the cloth and felt coldly, dispassionately that the fingers did not belong to her. Those fingers over there belong to somebody else. Kathy Robbins has no part in all this, she thought. She is an innocent bystander.

"He took my microscope and won't give it back. I've got tons of bio homework, Dad. Make Sean give it back." Robert and Sean galloped into the room. Sean ran around behind his father's chair. Will was exasperated.

"Listen, Sean, quit it. Enough is enough. It's late, and I've got an hour's work to do."

"Where did you put it?" Robert shouted.

"Give it back, Sean," Will said.

"I never had such a thing. How do you know I took it? Just because he says so? Christ, when you don't know who to blame it on, good old Sean will always do."

Later, after the boys chased each other out of the room, Kathy said, "I mean it, Will. I'm not going to let you go."

"I think we should separate. For a while, Kath. I've got to get my bearings. I've got to do some clear thinking. I can't do it here."

"Where would you go?"

"Kathy . . ."

"Do you want a divorce, Will?"

"Of course not. I don't know. I don't know. Kathy, I need some time to think."

Kathy didn't know what to say. She looked at Will. At how tired he looked. She could tell he had a headache. The wrinkles around his eyes were deeper in the grimace. She felt numb. She was determined not to give in to panic. She hated him. She felt sorry for him.

"But where would you go? We can hardly afford to keep this place going. How on earth could we support two places? Which reminds me, Will. You've been at me for so long to get out of the house and do something. I thought I'd sign up for a practical nurse training course. Elena Santos upstairs told me about it when I met her in the drugstore yesterday on Broadway. She knew that I might be interested, so she got me some information. I'd love to do it, and you really have been right all along . . . all the kids are in school till three, I've got all that time. And the money would be wonderful. Two incomes instead of one . . ."

Pitiful. She was pitiful, Will thought. But she had spunk. He had to give her that.

"Kathy, that's fine. But it has nothing to do with what I'm talking about. I'm bursting out, Kathy. It's no good. We're no good. Something's wrong."

"Will, honey. It will get better, I promise. It can only get better. Imagine, if I could maybe go to work . . . well, I know the training takes a long time, but before long I could be working and the money would be such a help."

"It's not the money," Will was shouting. He didn't care who heard him. "You haven't been listening to a thing I said. I'm dying, Kathy. I feel as though the walls are closing in on me. The same damn thing every day at the office, the same damn . . ."

"Thing at home," Kathy said, finishing his sentence.

God, don't let me hurt her, he thought. In his anger. In his shouting.

"It's not that, for God's sake. I need a rest. I need a change. Nothing's happening to us, Kathy. Nothing's happening to me. I'm in a hole and sand is falling on top of me. It's getting in my eyes, in my ears."

"Will, what are you talking about? I don't understand you."

"I know you don't, Kathy, that's just it." God, I want out, he screamed inside his own head. He thought of

Letty beating his chest in the middle of the street. He thought of Letty's mascara streaking her face.

"Night, Ma." Sean appeared and put his arms around Kathy's neck and kissed her. "How do you like the Fonz hairdo, Ma? Jimmy's mother lets him wear it to school all the time. What's the matter, Ma?"

"Nothing, baby. Say good night to your father."

"Night, Dad. Meet you in the bathroom in the A.M."

Will was looking at his hands.

"Good night, son," he managed.

"You two having a fight?"

"Go to bed, Sean."

"It's New Year's Eve, Dad. Remember, the family who fights together stays together. You gonna stay up and watch the ball drop? Let's go watch Times Square." He slid out of the room as though he was wearing ice skates.

"Since when did that kid turn into a comedian?"

"It's Fonz. He's got a whole new image all of a sudden. Walks around with his thumbs up all the time." Kathy got up and began clearing the few remaining dishes off the table.

Will watched her, looking at the familiar swing of her body. The ineffectual duck's ass hairdo on his son, encumbered by the thick blond curls, remained in front of his eyes.

He knew he could never do it. He knew he couldn't leave him, any of them. He knew it.

Kathy put down the cups and saucers when she saw Will get up out of his chair. She felt his tears on her forehead when he put his arms around her.

She stood stiffly. She didn't know what to say.

"Happy New Year, Will," was all she could muster.

30

The tables were made of butcher board and the customers sat together, picnic-table style, watching the cook, festooned with a giant chef's hat, standing in the center. He was tall for a Japanese and he sliced and chopped, stirred and sautéed with the finesse and fortitude of a Samurai swordsman. Letty sat fascinated as he chopped the onions for their steak, never missing. Over his head was colored crepe paper and beautifully designed dragon masks.

"Watch how fancy he's going to get now," Ed said, squeezing Letty's arm. The cook used the knife as though it were a baton and he the drum majorette leading the home-coming parade. The knife went behind him, under his knees, over his head.

"It's a wonder he doesn't chop off his finger," Letty whispered.

"He's the greatest. They have a few others here, but this guy's the best. Pretty tall for a Jap, isn't he?"

Letty looked around quickly, concerned that the cook would have heard Ed, or any of the other diners at the community table, but everyone was concentrated on the culinary flourishes in front of them.

"I really like this place, Ed."

"I knew you would. I've been saving it as the peace de resistance, a New Year's treat." Ed grinned.

291

Letty was moved by how hard Ed was trying. New Year's Eve. What was Will doing?

"Ever had sake?"

"Just once, a long time ago." She and Will had had dinner at a Japanese restaurant in the Village the second time they went out together. It hadn't been as elegant as this restaurant, but it was more intimate. An exquisite young Japanese girl had put them at a table in the back, and the room had been so dark Letty could barely see what she was eating. They had gulped their hot wine as though it were lemonade, out of nervousness and heat. It was a small space and Letty could feel the warmth of Will's body next to her. She wanted him to touch the wetness between her legs right there. She knew that if she got up to go to the ladies room, she would fall, her legs felt so weak. She wanted him to write his name on her breasts with the chopsticks, she wanted him to put her down in the middle of the floor and put his tongue on her eyelids, inside the curve of her waist. She would paint her face white like the geishas, and pencil her eyes. They had sat burning out of their clothes that night, and left before they finished eating, bowls filled with steaming rice sitting untouched on the table as they fled. Will splurged and they slept that night appropriately in a Japanese hotel, on Park Avenue in the thirties. They had started undressing each other in the elevator that time and made love standing in the vestibule with the key still in the lock.

"I love these little long-necked jars they bring the sake in, don't you?" Ed poured her some of the wine in the tiny eye cup of a receptacle.

"Yes, it looks as though it were made for one rose." It wasn't the time to think about Will. She ached when she thought of their blowup. She would think about something else. She would think about school. Lately, taking the Fifth Avenue bus down to Twelfth

292

Street, she had gotten an attack of dizziness. Her class fascinated her and Dr. Brandon fascinated her, but she had uncontrollable fits of nausea up until the moment she slid into a seat, always unobtrusively in the back row of the class. It was like fifth grade and Miss Franklin when she couldn't do the math, she thought. It was like ninth grade and Miss Griswold in geometry. You never lose those fears, she thought, the room triggered it, the smell of sweat on a rainy day triggered it, the teacher stalking up and down, writing on the blackboard. But she missed him. God, she missed Will.

"A penny for your thoughts." Ed took Letty's hand.

"Ed. Would you like to go to bed with me?" She had to, she thought. She would ring in the new with Ed. Ring out the old with Will. Perhaps it would be overwhelming with Ed, perhaps he could be someone she could depend on. She had to try.

A short time later, after three carafes of sake, Letty and Ed opened the door to his apartment. Unprepared, he had left it in chaos. His overalls stained with grease were thrown over a chair in the living room, and a pair of blue socks and undershorts were knotted up in a ball on the couch. Dishes were still in the sink from the morning, and open issues of *Popular Mechanics* and *Playboy* were over the floor.

"I'm sorry for the wreck of the room. Obviously, I wasn't expecting anybody," he said sheepishly.

"Don't be silly." Letty looked around the room. There was a blandness to it, a colorlessness coming from unseeing eyes. A blow-up of a racing car was on one wall, and on the mantel over the imitation fireplace were photographs of his parents and brother's family.

"What would you like to drink, Letty?" Ed said, taking off his coat. "I've got scotch and beer."

"Nothing. Not a thing, Ed."

Ed moved over to her and put his hands on her

293

cheeks. "I'm glad you're here, Letty. I love having you here. I've thought about it. I really have." He put his arms around her. Letty could feel him shaking.

His breath smelled of sake and soy sauce and his hands were big on her back. Letty threw back her head and let him take off her coat. It fell to the floor. He rubbed her back softly, and seemed almost to be humming as he moved his hands down to her buttocks. They stood that way for a while, Ed hiding his face in her hair, Letty moving her head into his chest. He was so tall. She liked the fact that he was so tall.

Ed led her into his bedroom. The room still had a morning smell to it, stale shaving cream odor. The bed was rumpled and the sheets looked like cream whipped to a point. It almost looked as though someone were still sleeping in the bed.

Ed disappeared into the bathroom. He doesn't want to embarrass me, Letty thought, he wants me to undress without him. Sighing, she removed her clothes swiftly and folded them neatly on a chair. She straightened the sheets and got into the bed. Her toes felt cold. She shivered.

Letty heard the toilet flush and Ed came out smelling of cologne. He had washed his hands.

Lying there side by side, they were tourists in each other's lands. Ed fumbled for her. His hands were not sure, but were searching. His touch was tentative, waiting. Letty closed her eyes and kissed him, opening her mouth slightly, exploring the insides of his gums. She fluttered her tongue and put her arms around him, pressing her breasts against his chest. He had almost no hair and what there was was blond and very fine. There was something callow about that, Letty thought, something untried and young about that thin empty chest.

But he was aroused immediately. They lay there, caressing. Suddenly, his touch became authoritative

294

Deftly, he began to relax the rigidity of her body. He understood women's bodies, she thought. As a girl, she had always had a fantasy about truck drivers. There was something strangely sexual about them, she had thought, the attractiveness being the sexuality of the non-thinking animal. As Ed petted her breasts and put them in and around his mouth, he made more short humming noises. There must be a tattoo on him somewhere, she thought.

"Your body is unbelievable, Letty," he murmured. "Your skin is as smooth as silk. God, you feel so fucking good. God, if you knew how many times I've thought about this."

Ed kissed her mouth softly, then moved to her neck, hard. His hands explored every part of her, and he was not silent, he kept whispering his delight to her. His body was hard and, despite the cologne, smelled of sweat and the outdoors. He was harder than Will. He must work out in a gym, she thought, feeling the tightness of his back muscles, feeling the bulges in his legs on her own calves. On top of her, he was heavy. Will was lighter, gentler, more tender. But Ed was skillful and attentive. He anticipated her movements, and when he heard her breath come shorter, her pleasure taking over her head, her associations, he moved into her. He thrust into her body, never letting go of her breast, moving his tongue deep in her mouth at the same time. He was surrounding her with himself, her head was still whirling, but her body had given up the battle. Her body succumbed to the pure pleasure of him. She heard someone screaming, crying out "more, more." And when she came, the relief was overwhelming. Seconds later, he poured himself into her, pressing his full weight down on her. It didn't matter, she could barely feel him, he was light as a cloud. He lay, his mouth open at her throat, breathing heavily. His body was covered with sweat. Letty tried to move her legs.

"Too heavy?"

"No. No. It's all right."

"You're a surprise, kid. No sweat. You look so lady-like, but you're something else. You're some . . ."

"Lay?" she said, unsmiling.

He rolled off her. "I didn't say that, kid."

Letty lay there, wiping her chest with the sheet. Her body was soaking wet.

"Ed, do you have any cigarettes?"

"I didn't know you smoked?"

"I don't. I'm just in the mood for one now."

"I used to smoke a cigar. I used to crave one after balling."

Letty marveled at his choice of words.

Ed got up and Letty watched his rock buttocks in the middle of a large mass of flesh walk to the other room.

"I've got some left over from a party. They may be stale."

"That's O.K."

The moment Ed was out of the room, Letty got up and went into the bathroom. She didn't look in the mirror but walked straight into the tub and the shower overhead. She let the water stream over her and turned it on as hot as she could take it. She tried to avoid getting her hair wet, she didn't want to catch cold out on the street. Maybe I'm not so out-of-date after all, she thought. Maybe I can have sex for sex's sake, just like a man. My body is all velvet, I am released. Then why do I feel so awful, she thought, why am I washing it all off? She scrubbed her breasts and her vagina until they hurt.

While she was drying herself, she saw Ed's brown

terrycloth robe hanging on a hook on the door. She put it on and belted it, throwing back her head and shaking her hair.

Ed was sitting in the living room with a towel around his middle. He had made coffee and put two jelly donuts on a plate.

"Hey. That robe never looked so good. You sure fill it out better than me."

You are a bore and a bigot and I don't know why I am here. Wrong, she thought. I am here because nobody asked me to bed and there is no more Will in my life. That's why I am here. So I won't be alone on New Year's Eve. That's why I'm here.

"How about some coffee? The cigarettes are really stale."

"I'd love some, forget it."

Letty sat in a large easy chair across from the sofa where Ed was sitting. She was quiet as she tucked her leg under her, warming her hands on the cup.

Ed looked at her with open admiration.

"Wow," he said.

"I've got to go, Ed."

"Eat and run, Letty?" Letty did not smile.

It's no good, she thought. I can't pull it off. How do they do it, Priscilla and the rest? How? Will, damn you. Damn you. It's just not the same.

"Wasn't it good for you, Letty?"

"You're a marvelous lover, Ed."

Without knowing why, Ed winced.

Letty got up and went into the bedroom and began to get dressed. When she came back in the living room, Ed had powdered sugar all over his upper lip. There was, after all, a tattoo on his left upper arm, she noticed. A bore he might be, she thought. But he's not stupid. She could tell he knew what was in her mind.

She could tell he knew that expedient as it was, it still couldn't work for her. She touched his tattoo and walked to the door. There was no point in saying good-bye.

31

"So he hit me."

"Where?"

"On Sixth Avenue." Letty started to laugh. It was inopportune, the laughter, she thought, but soon her psychiatrist was laughing with her.

"I mean, where, on your shoulder? On your back?"

"In the face. He hit me in the face. On Sixth Avenue." Neither of them smiled this time.

Dr. Brandon had recommended Dr. Saul Schraeder to Letty. She had arrived at class the night of her fight with Will after the break, looking so distracted and strange, that when the class was over, the teacher went up to her and asked her if anything was wrong. She had tried desperately to keep the tears back during class, but they returned, the minute Dr. Brandon looked with concern at her. He took her for coffee in the New School cafeteria without asking questions about the ugly red welt that was puffing out of the right side of her face. He told her he knew a fine doctor, if she needed someone to talk to. He had written out the address and telephone number and after a fitful week of not being able to eat or sleep, Letty called him.

Saul Schraeder was forty, but looked older. He was smooth-skinned and trim. His shoes shined. He sat in a leather chair under a magnified photograph of two hands sculpted by Rodin. He wore glasses and his sports jacket looked cashmere. Letty liked him. He seemed dedicated and caring. She liked him because he appeared kind.

"And how long have you been together?"

Letty shifted in her seat. She was uncomfortable, despite the fact that Dr. Schraeder was doing everything possible to make her feel at ease.

"Four years."

"That's a long time, Letty."

"I know. I know, Dr. Schraeder. And a lot of it has been wonderful. I love him. He's probably the only man I have ever loved. But this is it, I don't see how we can get back together again this time. He's hurt me too much this time. But . . ."

"But what, Letty?"

"But, Doctor, at the same time, I understand him. I understand him so well. I can't bear to see him hurt. I know what drove him to the frenzy he was in that night. I know that he's a man in a box. He feels trapped everywhere he turns. In the office, at home. I'm his only safe place. I'm his harbor. And that's why he blew up at me. His mother left him. She . . ."

"What do you mean, she left him?"

"Well, I guess I'm using his phrase. That's how he always puts it. She left him with relatives and took off. It's so classic, it's almost pat. I mean, even I've only just started reading some psychology, and I can figure that out. He thinks all women are going to abandon him. Dr. Schraeder, I want to be his safe place. It makes me feel good to be the place he can come to. But," Letty rummaged in her bag for a

Kleenex, gave up and took one from the box resting on the table next to the chair where she was sitting. She blew her nose. She felt as though she could cry for a week.

"But what, Letty?" Dr. Schraeder lit a cigar.

"But it's getting me down. Dr. Schraeder, I've never felt anything about age before. I always looked pretty good. I'm not boasting, but I've always known I was attractive. But all of a sudden, I'm not thirty anymore. All of a sudden, I'm going to be thirty-eight, and there are changes in my body. And . . ." she paused, embarrassed.

"And," she said, taking a deep breath, "men don't look at me as much as they used to. I notice it. I miss it. All of a sudden, it's going, that sort of power. And I'm beginning to get scared."

"What kind of things scare you?" he asked, shifting his position in his chair.

"Children." She didn't know where the word came from. It popped into her head. She smoothed her skirt. Picked the dirt out from under her nails.

"I've always wanted them." She felt choked up. "Not anymore. It's too late. It's all right, though," she said, tossing her hair back, "it's really all right. There really isn't anyone else I can think of whose child I would like to have. And I don't think, no, I know Will will never get divorced. That's what's killing me. Eating me up inside."

"Well, how does that make you feel about him?"

She couldn't stand all these questions. Letty had come for answers, not questions.

"I'm angry at him," she said, defensively. "Is that what you want me to say?"

"I don't want you to say anything, Letty. It's for you to say."

"Of course I'm angry at him. I told you that. Anyway, we've broken up. I'm seeing other men. It's over.

I came here to exorcise him. To get him out of my system, and all I ever come to is that I still love him."

The room was silent.

"Yes, I wanted children. Always hoping against hope that I'd give Will a girl. He has three boys. It was always my fantasy to give him the thing his wife never did. He'd fall apart over a little girl. But I'm too old now. I'd probably have a Mongoloid or something if I got pregnant. Never mind. That part of my life is over. I'm resigned to that."

More silence.

"You sound annoyed with me, Letty."

"I am, Dr. Schraeder. I told you. It's all right. You know what? And I mean this, that's almost the least of it. It used to bother me a lot, a few years ago, when I was younger, when I felt thirty-four, thirty-five was not so old to have a first child. But I'm a funny person. I've figured it out. It's O.K. now. And I've gone back to school now. I'd rather take those energies and put them toward building a career. I don't feel too old for that. All of a sudden, along with my fears of my rear end sagging and men not looking at me, at the same time I have this burst of energy toward training for a profession. I feel good about that."

After the first month, Letty got the courage to talk to the doctor about his cigar.

"Dr. Schraeder, would you mind terribly putting out that cigar? It's getting me a little dizzy."

"Not at all. Why didn't you say something sooner? I'm sorry I didn't ask you if it disturbed you. I am sorry."

"It's all right. I just hate the smell, that's all."

"So what about Will, Letty?" Dr. Schraeder extinguished his cigar.

"I don't know what to do about Will. I'm suffering. I miss him, but I know that if we get back together again, the same thing will happen all over again. And

301

we'll see each other two damn days a week till the day we die.

"And," she added, unable to hide the sarcasm from her voice, "that's how it's done when you go with a married man. I'm sure you've had other patients who have gone through it."

"This might sound strange to you, Letty," Dr. Schraeder said softly, "but I have a theory that if a relationship goes on for over a year without anything happening, nothing will ever happen."

It was a departure for the good doctor, Letty thought. He must be exasperated with her to make such a firm opinionated statement.

"I don't understand what that means."

"What do you think it means?"

Letty thought for a minute. "If you mean that Will is taking advantage of me, that I am a bright, attractive, appealing woman and there are many men out there who would appreciate my quality, then I would say you sound exactly like my mother."

Dr. Schraeder laughed. It was, indeed, the first time she heard him laugh.

"Be that as it may, Letty," he said, leaning forward in his chair, "it sounds to me, from what you've told me, that Will is the kind of man who wants you to be a mother or even a daughter rather than a lover or a mate. And from what you tell me, it would seem that his wife is the same kind of figure. Perhaps because he was left alone with his mother taking the father-husband role when his father died prematurely, perhaps after she abandoned him so cruelly, he just keeps repeating those patterns. I don't mean to sound so pat, but you asked for my opinion. You should, it seems to me, Letty, begin thinking about yourself now, about who you are, not related to Will, but what the ultimate potential for you is in life."

"That's quite a mouthful. Especially from someone supposedly 'nondirective.'"

"You came here asking my advice, Letty. You wanted to hear what an objective third ear had to say."

Letty continued to see Dr. Schraeder for several months. She liked him, and respected his straight talk. But one day, after telling him a dream she had, about being an understudy in a play and being called to go on for the leading lady and not knowing the part, not knowing the other actors, she suddenly told him that she didn't want to come anymore.

Saul Schraeder looked shocked.

"Letty. We're really just beginning to get started."

"I don't know, I don't think so. I feel good about myself. I like myself. I've got my fears and foibles, I know that. But what brought me here and what was, and in some way still is making me miserable is that I'm in love with this married man. This man who you may say is taking advantage of me and my youth and my warm nature.

"But Dr. Schraeder, I can't help thinking, and I think about it all the time, no matter what happens, God, we may never get together, but no matter what happens, I've learned something. I love him. Married. Unmarried. Drunk, sullen, sad, funny. I just love him. I just do, it's as simple as that. He is the man I love. I've been with other men and I may be with more. But Will is the man I love. And Will loves me. We love each other.

"We work in the ridiculous office together and play this game, this excruciating game of avoiding each other and not being where the other will be, or just the opposite, being exactly where the other will be. And we're both dying, and we're both trying to make this separation work. But there's nothing more that you can do to help me. You're a good man, and you've been very kind to me and I am grateful for it. But no matter what happens, Dr. Schraeder, we love each other. We just do. I've learned that much. There's nothing I can do about that."

Letty got up and handed the doctor an envelope with the money she owed him. She shook his hand and went out the door, looking at the clock in his waiting room on her way out. There were still ten minutes left to her fifty-minute hour.

32

Sunday.

Letty couldn't sleep late anymore. When she was a little girl, she could sleep till noon, the sun slashing zebra stripes through the venetian blinds. But people didn't have venetian blinds anymore, she thought, sitting naked on her bed, squinting at the clock on the night table.

The day loomed ahead of her.

In the bathroom, she took a long, hard look. If there ever was a panic time, it was when she took those long, hard looks. Like the back of her arms, for example. Letty shook her arm and watched the flesh move. Not fair. Men never get that. She loved to feel Will's arms. Will's arms were sexy to her, the veins pushing through the muscle. She wouldn't feel his arm anymore. There was Sunday to get through. Then Monday.

Letty looked at the droop of her breasts. They had altered just a bit since last year. It was like an assault on her body, this invasion, this aging. Imperceptible the changes, but nevertheless, there they were. Reminders of her mortality, this inevitable decaying.

Quiet. Quiet, she thought. These thoughts are for the birds. Revolting. I am not decaying, I am entering my prime. Kinsey says women in their forties are in their sexual prime, hormonally, psychologically, they are at their peak. She had that to look forward to. She couldn't believe she was approaching thirty-eight. Forty was for other people. Putting her face close to the mirror, she pulled the darkening skin under her eyes up toward her cheek-bones. She looked carefully, clinically at herself. Not bad. But beginning to wane.

There were some benefits to this not living with a man, she thought, scrubbing her face with a sponge. He doesn't have to see this ghastly morning face every day. Why do these eyes puff like this in the morning? It seems that mornings do things to my face. Wrong, she thought, stepping into the shower, I'd settle for it. I'd put up with his looking at the puffy face, if I could see Will every day. She would not think about him.

As the water scoured her, she leaned her head so that the hair fell down her back. She thought of the first time she and Will showered together. When? When was it? She could barely remember. It had been in this very shower, she recalled. Right here in her bathroom, the first time she and Will had been together. Fran had gone to Syracuse that week to see her dying brother. A whole week. Letty often wondered if Fran had not gone away, if the apartment had not been empty then, whether she and Will would have ever gone to bed at all.

It was a pill, a pill that had started the whole thing. Letty, coming into Will's office to hand him some reports four years ago, found him with his head on his desk, his fists clenched.

"Mr. Robbins, what is it?"

"It's nothing, just my head," Will had said into his arms, not picking up his head.

"Can I get you anything? I'll get you a glass of water."

"Nothing. Cut it," he had said harshly, raising his head and pressing his palms on his temples. "I just want to squeeze the damn thing out."

"I've got some codeine in my purse."

"Forget it."

"I'll be right back," she had said, not paying any attention to his dismissal of her.

In a moment, Letty was back with the water and the pill.

Will's eyes were glazed and hurt. He looked like a frightened child, she thought, as she put the pill into his hand and handed him the water.

He just stared at her.

"Take it. Take it, Mr. Robbins," she commanded softly.

Dutifully, he put the pill at the back of his mouth and, throwing back his head, drank the water.

"Thanks, thanks, Letty. Just close the door when you go."

Letty, who had never gotten more than a growl from Will Robbins before this, who had never had a personal word from him, had touched him then. She had put her hand on his shoulder without thinking. He had looked up and had stared through her. Letty could not blink, she could not take her hand off his shoulder. It was as though they were children and had been frozen into statues. It started at that moment, Letty thought. If she had been able to pull her stare away, if she had been able to move her hand. If he had put his head back down into his cradled arms,

306

perhaps. Finally, the phone rang. And, jumping, Letty answered it.

It had been Kathy, Letty remembered, and "who was that?" she could hear through the earpiece after Will took the phone. She walked out of the office then, shaken; she couldn't tell why.

Will had taken her out for a drink after work that night; a "thank you" drink he had written in the note he dropped by her desk.

"I'm very grateful to you," he had written rather formally. "Those headaches come upon me sometimes so fast that I'm taken unawares. And you came in at the propitious moment. Thank you."

She liked the word propitious, she liked the fact that he appreciated what indeed was only a natural gesture.

That night, drinking the scotch in the bar, she remembered clearly thinking, as the lights hit Will's forehead, the rays dancing off the wrinkles in his brow, I would like to be his friend. I would like to make his headaches go away. I would like to take care of him and make him feel better. It was all irrational and perhaps crazy, but she had been struck by the contradictions of his sullenness and his vulnerability.

Will needed her, she thought, interrupting her reverie. She felt indispensable to Will. But it can't work. Kathy was indispensable, too, she supposed, his needing to be needed by her. And round and round it goes, where it stops, nobody knows. There was a Yiddish expression her mother used to use that was appropriate for Letty. That fit her to a tee. (There were blue veins on her breasts, she thought, scrutinizing herself once again in the mirror. They never used to be there, those veins, either the skin on her breasts was getting thinner or the veins were getting bluer.) *Herenisht dernisht.* Neither here nor there. That's me, she thought. Neither here nor there. A thirty-seven-year-old woman who is just beginning to fade, who is just beginning to get blue breast veins and loose back of the arms, yet who feels lovely and young and yet not young enough. *Herenisht dernisht.* Neither here nor there. She realized now that her mother's heart-to-heart talks when she was a young girl, embarrassed forays into elaborate rationalizations for staying a virgin until she was married, were philosophically obsolete. Dead. The concept was dead. Long live freedom, up with liberation, woman power, blah-blah.

But that didn't apply directly to her, either. There had to be some middle ground for her. There had to be something between being a libertine, taking her pleasure where she found it, and the restricted dicta of her youth. Hell, she never felt soiled, she had been finally delighted to discover that her own body was such an infinite source of pleasure. The human potential movement had blared it to her, the touchy, feely incantations prevalent had exhorted her and every other person to glory in their own senses. She didn't have to go to Esalen to find that out, gratefully she found a man who taught her to live in her own skin. But so what?

She stroked her belly with circular motions. Calmly, without pain, she thought, will there ever be a baby in this belly? Will a head ever stretch down that canal and pour out of me. Will I ever ever feel life in me? Will I ever feel those kicks from the inside, will I ever feel another heartbeat inside this body?

Her belly looked white to her, untouched, except for the barely visible line of down leading the way to her opening. There were girls she knew, young girls in the office in their twenties who eschewed motherhood. They truly did not want to have children. Sure, better than bringing babies into the world whom they might cripple with their own pain and neurosis, some people should never have them, for sure. But this belly seems so untouched. So ready. And there are no seeds and there is no chance. Thirty-seven. No babies. Will has his. I have none.

Letty went into her bedroom and lay on the bed. The sheets felt cool to her back, which was burning. Her thoughts were consuming her. Will, it is Sunday. Are you in the park, are you reading the Sunday *Times?* I would like to have lox and bagels with you and cream cheese and white fish, and I would like it to be spring and walk through the park with the baby, our baby, and spread a plaid blanket on the ground and lie in the sun and let the baby crawl on our bellies.

No. Pipe dream. Hopeless fantasy. There will be no babies with Will. There will be no babies with anyone. I love you, Will. You are bad for me. But you are a good man. But I can't settle. I won't. You're what I want. You're the other side of me. But still, it isn't enough, is it?

"Letty, a fuse blew. Call the super."

Fran was knocking on the door, crashing into Letty's thoughts. She forgot where she was. What day it was. Sunday.

"What is it, Ma?"

"Dark. It's dark as anything out here. No lights work, even the fridge has no lights. The food will spoil. Letty, do something. Call the super."

"Mother, why can't you call the super?"

"That intercom confuses me. Letty, come out."

Letty looked at the clock. She had been ruminating for over an hour. And there were still so many Sunday hours to get through.

Throwing on a robe, she went out the door of her room.

"Put your slippers on, Letty. You'll catch your death."

Sighing, Letty pushed the button next to the inter-

309

com and, putting her face close to the mouthpiece, shouted into the screen.

"Mr. Flom, we have no lights."

"Right. It's the whole building. Don't worry about it, it will be fixed in a while." The super's wife answered. Letty had an image of her with fat curlers nesting in her hair and a flowered bathrobe swirling her bulk.

"Mother, what on earth was the emergency? You were knocking like there was an earthquake or something."

"I don't like no lights, Letty."

"The sun is shining outside."

"I don't like the idea. And there is lots of sour cream in the ice-box."

Letty looked at her mother. She would be seventy-five this June. Suddenly, it began to show. Last year she was straight, her step was firmer. Suddenly she had gotten old. Her mother was really old all of a sudden, and it was like being closer to her own death really. It was something they didn't talk about much, except that recently Fran kept talking about the plot out in Queens where Morris was buried and how Letty had better put aside some money for its eventual use.

"Where are you going?"

"Out. It's nice out. I think I'll go to the museum."

"I wish I could do the walk."

"Me, too, Ma. It would be nice if you could come."

"Too many steps. I get too tired. Bring home the Sunday paper and some pot cheese. The deli on the corner will be open."

"All right, Ma."

"And listen," she shouted to the shut door of the bedroom. "Don't fool around. It's bitter out there. Just bitter. You could bring a few pickles, too, you know."

Letty put on a pair of heavy wool slacks and a bulky sweater. She didn't feel like it, but she forced herself to make up her eyes and put base and rouge on. She would walk over to Fifth Avenue to the Metropolitan and see the Lehman exhibit.

Letty walked over to the museum, intimidated a bit by the crowds, the families. The lovers. So many people with their arms around each other. Alongside of the museum on Fifth Avenue, people had set up booths where they were selling jewelry and crafts. They would stay there until the police made them move along. She walked down to Sixty-fourth Street and went into the zoo. It got very cold. There were many children in strollers holding balloons and many more people with their arms around each other. Some were nuzzling.

She bought the pot cheese and pickles for her mother, the New York *Times* and the *Daily News*. When she was home, she took a hot bath, hoping there would be something good on PBS.

Inside her bed, it felt like sheets of ice.

33

For the next four months, Letty tried. She was determined to transcend her own pain. She knew that she had to sit it out, experience it, not run away from it. That much she had learned from Dr. Schraeder and all the reading she was doing. Intuitively, Letty knew that to run away from it, to drink herself into oblivion or sniff coke like Herbie was always slyly encouraging her to, or to bury herself in sexual encounters were not the answer. She knew it, and yet the temptation was there. Nights after work became almost unbearable, her mother's chatter made her irritated, and she took refuge in brandy. She would sit in her room smoking, waiting, pleading in her own head for the phone to ring.

Finally one night, after she told Dr. Schraeder she wasn't going to see him anymore, that she had to get through this thing herself, it rang; cut through her like a stiletto. When she heard Will's voice, music in the background, the chatter of voices like chickadees sitting on a telephone wire, she thought she would faint. She broke into a cold sweat. And hung up. It was against her rules. No more Will. No more. She loved him. So what?

"Letty, what about some sponge cake?" Fran was at the door. She was trying to be kind.

"No thanks, Ma."

"Letty, can I come in?"

"Come on, Mom."

Fran had on a flowered housecoat. She had taken off her corset and had taken out her bridge.

"*Mitindrinin,* I decided to make a cake. Have a piece, baby."

"No thanks, Ma. I'm not hungry. Did you make it from scratch?"

"No. I wanted to, but I didn't have the patience. I used a mix. You sure? It's out of this world."

"No."

"What's with the brandy bottle?"

"Nothing, I just feel like a little drink. It will help me sleep."

"It's still that fellow. Your young man?" Fran sat down on the bed.

"Mom. I'm not in the mood to talk. I've got class tomorrow and I've got some reading to do."

"School. That's good. You should. School is what you should have done."

"Let's not go into that now, Ma."

"You want some advice?"

"No."

"Forget him. Go on about your business. He's not worth it. A no-good bum, carrying on while he's got a wife and children to sup . . ."

"Ma, please go away. I want to be alone. I don't want to talk."

Fran sat at the foot of the bed sucking her gums, forgetting her teeth were not there. "Look, Letty."

"I mean it, Ma. Please."

The phone rang. Letty looked at the instrument. Fran rose to pick it up as Letty brought it to her ear.

"Letty, don't hang up. What's the point of hanging up? I want to talk . . ." She heard Will's voice on the other end.

Letty put down the receiver softly, and poured herself a few drops of brandy.

"You're going to get shicker."

"I'm going to be all right." Letty got up abruptly from the bed and went into the bathroom. "I'm going to work now, Ma. Do me a favor and put up a pot of coffee for me. And then, have a piece of sponge cake for yourself and go to bed. It's getting late."

The next night after school was over, Al Pomarentz, who sat next to her usually, asked her out for a drink. They went to the Lions Head since Al, a packager of industrial shows, said a lot of literati hung out there.

"Pete is always there, and Joe, a lot of the *Village Voice* crowd goes there. It's a trip."

Al was earnest. He stared intently into Letty's eyes when he spoke, and told her that since he left his wife in Westchester, he had moved back home four times. This time, it was for good, though, he said. He had a pad near the New School where he could take a bus right uptown to his office. Over drinks at the bar, where no recognizable writer seemed to be imbibing, Al confided to Letty that he had this obsession about topless waitresses. He used to hang around Forty-second Street and finally made a date with one of the girls whose breasts had felt as though they had inner tubes inside. Al and Letty had a lot of drinks and he invited her at one in the morning to see his pad.

It was in a brand new building with tiny rooms and one closet. She could barely turn around inside the bathroom. Al had not yet begun to furnish, but there was a well-stocked bar and lots of plants. There was a sleeping platform upon which he coaxed Letty. She was a little drunk, and as he pored over her body like a near-sighted student studying for college boards, she noticed a long crack in the ceiling. In a new building. For which he was probably paying a fortune.

It was nothing. Al Pomerentz's mouth on her was nothing, his breath smelled of gin, and he had rolls of fat around his middle.

He was so busy pleasing himself with her that he didn't notice that she wasn't moving. That her face was wet. He rolled off her and went to sleep, muttering something about setting the alarm.

At 4 A.M. in the taxi on the way home, sobering, Letty remembered that before they went up the narrow ladder to the bedroom, he had asked her to stand topless for him, with her bra pulled off her shoulders so her breasts would be pushed up. Provocatively. The city was beginning to go to sleep or to wake up depending on your income bracket, she thought, looking out the window at the sprinkles of rain on the window; like perfect circles they spotted the pane.

She would take a boiling bath at home. She hoped the running water wouldn't wake Fran. There was no way of avoiding the Als of this world, she thought.

314

One-night stands made her sick. But there was nothing else she could do. She was trapped into her own scene just as much as Will was.

One night a week later on her way to the subway after work, she heard someone running behind her. Thinking it was a shop-lifter, thinking it was someone in trouble, she stopped and looked back. It was Will. He was panting and his eyes were wild.

He grabbed her elbow. "Come on, Letty. I want to talk to you. Quit this. We've got to talk. I'm going crazy."

She shook herself free.

I want to kiss you. I want to hold you, she thought. You need a shave and have lost weight.

"Leave me be. I have to go home. Good-bye, Will. It doesn't do any good. You're only making it worse. Please."

"Letty . . ." He squeezed her arm so that she cried out. A man in a gray suit with overcoat and hat to match stopped and looked in concern at them.

Letty broke away. "Stop it. Just stop it." She felt as though he had almost torn her arm off. Letty broke into a run and weaved in and out of commuters going down the stairs to the subway.

When would this end, she thought? She was going crazy. Last week Dr. Brandon told her she should enroll in the regular undergraduate program. That she could be whatever she wanted to be. If she wanted to help people, she could. That she could be her own person. That she could have a profession and could be a help. Help in a rotten world.

Will, help me. Help me, she cried inside herself, swaying, holding the ring above her head. This man. She couldn't build her life around this man. She rode past her stop and had to go upstairs at Ninety-sixth Street, and pay another fare and go back downtown one stop in order finally to get home.

34

The Connecticut town that Jack and Elise Gaynor lived in was flanked by the Saugatuck River and Long Island Sound. Water was an indigenous force to the town and its recreation. Boaters and swimmers flocked to those towns in Fairfield County for the beauty and ease, if not for the prestigious association to those ex-urban communities immortalized in the works of Peter de Vries and Max Shulman.

Elise, who had come from Topeka with Jack to a cramped New York apartment, found in Westport finally the epitome of her dreams. The schools, the beaches, the town-owned country club, the cultural thrust, all satisfied an intense yearning for status and arrival.

They had lived in their small ranch house for a year. There was room for a swimming pool in the less-than-an-acre back yard, and she had been badgering Jack to take out a second mortgage for it. It would save on vacations in the summer, she reasoned, and they wouldn't have to send the kids to camp.

In April, with the snow finally melting its hardened clumps on the back lawn, and the ground softening she had been involved in a concentrated campaign for the pool. She had gotten four estimates, each one assuring her that with the price of materials and labor

316

going up as they were, she had better get going because next year it would really be prohibitive.

She had been attacking Jack all week about it. One night at dinner, their eight-year-old went crying from the table, screaming, "You leave my daddy alone," when Elise had gotten so exasperated with him. It was when she had screamed "You're a loser. You can't hack it. You'll never make it. In college you were a hot shot, what happened to you?" that Mandy had fled from the table, seeing in her father's face something unexplainably terrible.

Elise hadn't spoken to Jack for three days after that and didn't budge from her side of the bed in that time. He kept getting indigestion and couldn't stop perspiring.

The police found his body Monday morning.

Nobody could understand how he did it; just walking into Long Island Sound. He always liked to go for a walk on the beach after dinner and sometimes would take the kids, but Sunday night, he had been drinking heavily at Marios by the railroad station, surrounded by women who had stopped by for a few drinks after golf and hadn't gone home yet, and men who didn't want to go home at all. Elise told the police that he had left the house about seven. They arrived at the house at seven Monday morning to tell her. The worst part of it was, she hadn't missed him. She hadn't known he wasn't lying there in the bed next to her. She had gone to sleep thinking he would be home later, and had slept soundly.

The policeman, one she recognized by his handsome face and neatly trimmed mustache as a father of a child in Mandy's class, was kind and solicitous. Jack, numbed by drink and perhaps pills, had just walked into the water. Just went to the beach. And walked into the Sound.

The last guests had just left, and Will, who had ar-

317

rived late after borrowing a car and driving up to Connecticut, was alone in the living room with Elise. A neighbor had put the children to bed and had cleaned up the kitchen and put away the casseroles and cakes people had brought. In back of the pale blue couch where Elise was sitting, Will noticed three portraits of the children done in pastel. Why do so many ranch houses have so many portraits of the children, pale photographic likenesses hanging over sofas, he thought?

He was embarrassed that suddenly he was left alone with Elise. He didn't like her. He blamed her. Elise was dry-eyed, Jackie Kennedy incarnate, Will thought. In control.

"I've got to keep busy, Will. Jack didn't keep the life insurance really up-to-date. I mean, I haven't even talked to anybody about that. I don't even think we can collect. I'm sure we can't. As an insuranceman's wife, of course, I know that," she said, looking down at her fingers. "He knew that, of course, didn't he, Will? He knew that if he took his own life, we wouldn't get a penny. You know. That was, when you come right down to it, pretty rotten of him, wasn't it? I mean, what am I supposed to do with three kids and a mortgage to pay? I called up this morning and enrolled in the Real Estate School. That's something. Maybe I can keep the house that way. I'm going home to Topeka for a while. My parents insist I do. But we'll be all right," she said fiercely, her eyes filling with tears.

"He hadn't been happy for a long time. He was showing some strain in the office," Will said. He didn't know what to say. It was clear that to Elise, Jack was gone, but she had to survive. She would move on.

"I know."

After an uncomfortable silence, Will rose out of his chair.

"Well, Elise, I just wanted you to know Jack was my friend."

"That's nice of you, Will. He spoke of you, I must say, as the only one in the office with a heart. I'm sure that was an exaggeration, not to take anything away from you, but I know so many people in that office, and, of course, Fred we've known since college, and there are some lovely people at Robertson Stellar. It's just that it was hard for him . . ." she was hesitant to continue.

Will looked at her expectantly.

Elise took a deep breath and continued as she led him to the door.

"There was so much out there," she said, looking at him straight in the eye. "Why couldn't he have been salesman of the year? Why couldn't he make it? He was my husband, but he didn't have it. I can't help it, and I don't care how terrible it sounds. He couldn't push. All he could do was walk into the goddamned water and leave me with three kids to support. That's all he could do." She stood, with the front door open, tears in her eyes. She thrust out her hand.

"Thank you for coming," she said, composing herself. "Jack liked you. He would have been pleased."

There was something the matter with the lights on the Connecticut Thruway; there were large stretches that were completely dark. Will put his brights on since there seemed to be no cars coming the other way.

He felt his rage welling up. The speedometer was over 60, and the limit was 55, but he couldn't help it. Life insurance. Pusher. Pastel portraits. Real Estate. Making it.

Poor Jack. What a waste. Why hadn't he gotten out? Why hadn't he listened to him? Why haven't I gotten out, he thought as he approached the Hutchison River Parkway. Jack was only there a few years. It only took him a short time to let it get to him. Look at all the time I'm there. Look at my waste. So what did he leave, Will thought, a bitter wife and three kids asleep upstairs. No traces. There will be no traces of Jack Gaynor. Jack Gaynor who sweated so much and hated what he was doing.

Will didn't remember going through the last toll. Did he pay it, had he gone through? New Rochelle already. He hoped Kathy would be asleep when he got home. He wanted Letty. God, he wanted to talk to Letty. His friend, Letty.

Poor son-of-a-bitch. Poor Jack, climbing up a beanstalk planted by his wife. Poor son-of-a-bitch walked into Long Island Sound and didn't even take off his shoes.

35

Tony Cohen taught creative writing in the room next to Letty's at the New School. Tony was slim, divorced, and just recently had let his hair go curly. It had been a liberating thing, not straightening it, not going through the whole routine of wetting, blow drying, and combing it into the straight look. He was more accepting, more comfortable with himself now. His hair was curly and it was high. And it even made him look younger than the thirty-three he was. Tony had published stories and poetry in the *Hudson Review,* the *Paris Review,* the *Southwestern Review,* and the *Atlan-*

tic had kept one of his stories for six months once, dickering about whether to publish it or not. They had decided against it, but were very encouraging, and the editor to whom he talked told him he should definitely spend his energies writing a novel.

Letty noticed Tony in the cafeteria and in the elevator and responded to the quickness about him. He moved fast, talked fast. He was always surrounded by his students, and Letty kept catching phrases like "motivation" and "character development."

One Wednesday evening when Tony sat next to her before class in the cafeteria, Letty was flattered when he began flirting with her.

"Good writing has to do with words," he said after they had talked nonstop about *Humboldt's Gift* which he was carrying. Before she knew it, they were talking about eroticism in literature, and Letty found herself very drawn to him. "Anybody can graphically describe the sexual act in print. Anybody," he said. "That's not erotic. Did you ever compare the masturbation scene in Joyce's *Ulysses* with the one in Philip Roth's *Portnoy?* It's the difference between art and imitation. Colette's erotic because she writes so sensitively about leading up to the act. Well, I do go on, don't I?" he said, "I didn't catch your name."

"Letty. Letty Gold."

"Right. Well, look, Letty, how about continuing this after class? Want to meet me here, same place for a bite? If you're not busy or anything."

"No. That's fine. I'd like that."

All through her psychology class, Letty couldn't concentrate on Dr. Brandon's lecture, and when he called on her, she had blushed and stammered her way back into the room.

Letty went out drinking with Tony Cohen that night, and her head whirled with his words. He loved words. And he juggled them in front of her like the court jester, with appropriate color and gesture. She strained to be clever, to appear more well-read than she was. He seemed interested in her in a mild way. Tony was different from anyone Letty had ever met. He was exciting, and unpredictable. There were days, when she was waiting for his call, that she would get by without thinking of Will. It was blessed, the distraction. But painful, she realized, because Tony made her feel not quite smart enough, not quite young enough, not quite quick enough.

The second time he asked her out, they went to a poetry reading at the Y on Lexington Avenue and Ninety-second Street. The audience was a group Letty had never encountered before in New York, and the poet was someone she had never heard of. She didn't understand the poetry, but Tony was enraptured, and kept scribbling notes during the reading. Even though she lived nearby, Letty did not ask him up to the apartment for coffee, as Fran had asked. But Tony invited her to his place for a nightcap. He lived near Columbia on 120th Street and Riverside Drive. It was a studio apartment where the room smelled of incense and there was an absence of hard furniture. Enormous pillows covered with madras and Persian rugs warmed the floors, and the walls were filled with Nepalese paintings, lush erotic figures. Tony collected Chinese erotica as well, and had elaborate hi-fi equipment.

He offered her a brandy after lighting the incense and candles. Mozart chamber music was playing on the hi-fi. Letty offered no resistance when Tony silently undressed her and made love to her on his mattress resting on the floor covered with a bright coral Indian cloth. He was a skilled lover and whispered to her in the middle of their love-making, "You're a walking erogenous zone and don't know it. Relax. Touch yourself. I'd like to see you touch yourself." She did. The encounter was lovely, she thought, lying there, looking at the phalluses decorating the walls, breathing in the too sweet incense smell. This was lovely. But lonely. His hand on her was stimulating, but detached. It didn't matter, she decided.

Tony only called once a week, sometimes every other week. And at times she thought of herself as Miss Masochist of the Year, as she would take his taunts about what she hadn't read, what she didn't know.

"How can anybody get through life without reading *The Magic Mountain?*" he said to her over a glass of wine at a jazz place on 122nd Street, and that night after making love, he read aloud from *Tonio Kroeger* and he gave her a copy of Nabokov's *First Love* to take home and study.

Tony made her feel stupid and uneducated. Which she wasn't. Which she knew she wasn't. But she also knew she wasn't in his league. She was a fish out of water. When they would drink with his friends, she never said a word, afraid of sounding dense and not bright enough.

Women would call when she was visiting, and he would ignore her and spend hours on the phone. Tony was enamored of cocaine and called her a square when she wouldn't try it. "It's the purest escape," he said. "Pure sensuality. Undiluted. The ultimate orgasm." She was out of her league, she knew it.

The night that turned out to be their last together, Tony had been talking to a girl on the phone. Letty was lying on the floor, listening to some English madrigals that were playing. She was sipping a glass of wine, feeling marvelously decadent and decidedly out of place, all at the same time.

"Hilda's coming over."

"Who?"

"Hilda, a friend of mine. You'll like her. Maybe we can all make it together. She really gets turned on by that." He said it casually, tossed it off, Letty thought.

Letty sat up and attempted a full lotus. She could only get one foot to do it.

"No, Tony."

"God, Letty, I'm getting exasperated with you. You look like such a swinging chick, and you're a square. You sure as hell are deceiving. You seem independent but it's a pose. You know that? That's what I've learned about you. You belong to another generation. What's with you, kid? This isn't a monogamous age, this is the age of the alternative life-style."

"I know that," Letty said, looking at him defiantly. Knowing that phase number thirty-three of being away from Will was coming to an end.

"Then what is your *schtick?* Read Gide, read Sartre, if you can't be existential about your life, then what is it all for? Have you ever read Sartre? Or Gide?"

"No."

"Look, Letty. I don't want to be cruel. I'm not a cruel person. But, you know. Nothing's happening here. Existential or not. We live in different worlds. You know?"

That was her cue to leave. Pick up your marbles and leave like the lady that you are, Letty said to herself. But she sat there. Paralyzed.

"Go, Letty. O.K.?"

Letty picked up her bag and her coat, and, without turning around so he could see the humiliation in her eyes, slammed the door, hard. This was, she thought later lying in her bed licking her wounds, an appropriately poetic leave taking in deference to Tony's frame of reference, since she had left not with a whimper but a bang.

Trying to find something to fill her off days and her weekends, Letty worked at Rockland State. It is a kind

324

of half-way house for people coming out of mental institutions.

She had worked with Dr. Brandon as a trainee in group therapy, helping people adjust back into the world of sons and daughters and supermarkets and policemen and muggers and television and noise and loneliness.

But she never was sure how much she helped them. And at times she felt she was preposterous, like Dr. Joyce Brothers, or a hostess on a late night talk show who might give bits of advice to people, no better than a stranger they might pass on the street might give. And she began to doubt Dr. Brandon, too. It seemed that sometimes he helped; but so many times people slipped back. And she was sure there were psychiatrists in the world that were helping, that were making gigantic strides. But she didn't feel she could ever be one of them; and neither did she feel that Dr. Brandon could.

Then Barbara McMullen, one of the girls at the office, the very fat girl who was promiscuous and rather a joke at the office, talked to her about her work with retarded children.

The institutions with retarded children were so desperately in need of help that experience was not required. After a cursory interview, if you did not have a drinking problem or had not a criminal record, you were accepted as a volunteer worker.

Letty worked at Hillcroft, a state-run institution. At first she was put off by the children; by the way they looked, and by the seemingly hopeless plight of their lives. It seemed to her it was the most depressing work one could do.

One evening she was there when a boy was deposited by his family, and she spent the first night with him. He went through the most unbelievable hell, walking, pacing around the dormitory house all night, crying for his mother. Letty had been able to help him get through that night and his pain of the following days.

She began to feel a kinship to these children who had been abandoned. Abandonment had always struck a very deep chord in Letty, and she felt needed for the first time. Perhaps this was the answer for her.

She felt she was able to break the falls of some of the children, and that she was doing quite well.

Until Dr. Ben Proteau, a man in his sixties who she disliked intensely, said to her, "You may think you're doing well with these children, but you're not. You're imposing your own values on them. And unless you do better, you're not going to be able to continue to work here."

"I didn't think I was doing so badly, and I didn't think the children felt so, either," said Letty defensively.

"Are you married?" asked Dr. Proteau.

Letty didn't answer. She knew that Dr. Proteau knew the answer to it from the interview she had had with him before.

Dr. Proteau continued. "You've never had any children, have you, Ms. Gold?"

"No," said Letty stunned.

"You're looking at them as though they were your own children. Perhaps the children you can never have."

Letty searched inside herself.

"But they're not your children, and they never can be," he continued. "Something worse. You're using them as objects of pity. It's as though you want to take some of the falls for them. But they need more than that."

"I'm sorry I haven't been very good at it," said Letty, though feeling she had been.

Letty left Hillcroft feeling the sense of another defeat.

36

Nine months to the day after he hit her on Sixth Avenue in front of Bradley's in the Village, Will convinced Letty to have lunch with him. It was September now and, although it was still warm, the suspicion of fall was in the air. September was probably Letty's favorite month in the city; not quite cool enough for fall clothes, not hot enough for light pastels of summer. But fall was a hopeful time. Will had sounded so urgent on the phone. There was something in his voice that made her listen. And he was wearing her down. Life was wearing her down. It had been rotten without him.

She was going to take two courses this semester. Getting an A from Dr. Brandon in psychology had given her courage. She had not expected the grade but he had praised her final paper on Robert Lindner's *Fifty Minute Hour*. "You have a natural innate understanding of this material," he had written underneath the A, "your additional reading on Adler and Jung were relevant and fruitful to the ultimate understanding of what Lindner experienced with his patients. Good work." She had wanted so badly to share with Will her success. She had sat on it over the summer, knowing every day at the office that this wonderful thing had happened to her. But they were finished. There was no point. It was an empty victory. But finally, she acquiesced to lunch. They met in a small Italian restaurant on Eighteenth Street across town from the office. She noticed he didn't have anything to drink. Neither did she. She felt her cheeks grow warm. She was home again.

"So, how's it going?" he said. He looked at her hair, her cheeks. He was remembering her face with his eyes.

"I'm all right. I got an A in my course." She blurted it out.

Will beamed. "That's great. Why didn't you tell me?"

"Because we're not talking. Because we don't see each other anymore."

"Well, that doesn't mean we can't be friends. You would tell a friend about an A in a course, wouldn't you?"

They both smiled, and both had chef salads with oil and vinegar.

"How are the children?" Letty asked.

"You sound so polite."

"I am. I am a polite lady."

"You look wonderful, Lett. You look thin and it's becoming. Marvelously becoming."

"Thank you, Will." She picked at her salad.

"The kids are fine. The two youngest went to a day camp up in the Bronx and the big one had a scholarship to Andover this summer. A terrific summer school program."

"Will, that's fine. Really great. Did he like it?"

"God, he came back so fired up. He wants to go to Harvard. I told him he had better get all A's from now on in, and he reminded me that he already has. And at Bronx Science. He's a bright kid."

"What about law school?"

"Quit," he said abruptly. "You were right, Letty. It turned out to be a fool's errand. One of those things."

Letty could read behind the lines in his forehead. She could hear her own screeching, pummeling his chest . . . you'll never finish law school. Perhaps it skips a generation. Perhaps his boy will go. Oh, Will.

"How about some dessert, Letty?"

"No, thanks. We really should get back." After a pause, "I'm sorry about law school, Will."

"Let's walk across town, it's so beautiful today. How's Fran?"

"She's really only fair. Sometimes I think I should forget about my guilts and my terrors and put her in a home. But those places are enough to make you sick. And they cost a fortune. I couldn't afford it even if I decided to do it. She'll be fine for a while, and then all of a sudden, just won't make any sense. I should take her to the doctor and see just how far the arteries have hardened."

"Letty, I love you." Will put his arm lightly on her shoulder.

"I know, Will." Letty leaned down and sniffed a hyacinth, pink and sweet smelling resting in a box outside a florist's window.

"How much?" Will motioned to a man with a white apron smeared with dirt who was arranging some plants.

He held up three fingers.

"Sold." Will presented it with a flourish to Letty.

She carried it back all the way across town in silence. Neither of them said anything. They both knew it was like coming home.

As they approached the building, Will kneeled down to tie his shoelace.

"I'll see you inside, Letty."

"Thanks for lunch, Will."

"How about a movie Tuesday?" he said it casually, calmly ignoring the loaded implications.

"I don't know, Will. I . . ."

"Just a movie." His hand was on her elbow. Gently this time.

"All right, Will." Her heart was beating fast. How would she live till Tuesday? Whether it was wrong or right didn't matter. She only knew one thing. She had to see him again. She had to sit across a table from him.

They held hands in the movies Tuesday and as he smoothed each finger slowly, as though fitting some invisible glove, she knew they would again be in bed. After nine months without him, she knew that out there in that big city, there had been no one else for her. She had tried. Perhaps their two days were worth more than a lifetime of Ed Coynes. Or Tony Cohens. Her head whirled as he rubbed her palm, then took the fingers and put them to his mouth, finger by finger, the darkened theater a velvet cushion for them. She felt herself grow unbearably moist between her legs, and by the time the film was almost over, she was softly cupping his penis in her hand, feeling the harsh metal of the zipper against her fingers. They never looked in each other's eyes, just groped softly for one another.

Neither of them said anything. Just lunch, or just a movie seemed out of the question.

Later, they made love in the familiar antiseptic solitude of a room at a Ramada Inn, the glasses in the bathroom covered by the familiar tissue paper, the familiar landscapes hanging on the wall that looked as though they were painted by a computer.

Will had laid her down gently on a bumpy tweed cover. Even though they had not been with each other in so long, he went very slowly, undressing her quietly. He stayed long in the curve of her neck, and when the last stitch of clothing was removed, began the long exquisite journey down her body. He savored every swell, every indentation, he played with the inside of her arm with his tongue. He took what seemed hours to Letty before he even began to explore below her groin. She moaned and moved her head from side to side on the pillow; his tongue was everywhere, on her knees, under her knees, on her calves. Slowly he turned her body over and began again, remembering with his mouth the warm curves leading to her buttocks, the sweet fullness of the back of her thighs.

When finally he was inside her, it was a first time, a last time, a place where they belonged.

They both cried. Their faces were still wet when Will woke Letty and showed her his watch. It was 3 A.M. They had to go home.

They made an appointment to see each other the day after next. Thursday.

37

"I can't believe this. I can't believe this is happening. My own daughter. *Mein Kinde*. My own flesh and blood. I'm an old lady and you do this to me. I can't believe it."

Fran was watching Letty pack her books. She was almost hypnotized by the thin slivers of papers Letty had torn up for cushioning. Her newly acquired psychology library, her complete set of Shakespeare, the Greek plays, Shaw and the over a hundred novels she had collected over the past several years were resting in cartons in her room. Fran was sitting in a rocker, rocking back and forth.

"At ten o'clock Saturday, October 10, you have

broken my heart. I will write it down for all the world to see. I will carve it in tree trunks. 'The day my daughter deserted me,' the day my daughter deserted me for a no-good married goy."

"Mother, stop it. Stop it, immediately." Letty looked at her mother like a kindergarten teacher, appalled by a five-year-old tantrum. "I am not deserting you. I should have done this long ago. I am not deserting you. I am taking a place for myself where I will stay a good deal of the time. Not always. Not forever. Just when I want to be alone and be by myself or be with Will . . ."

"Don't. Don't mention that name to me. He is ruining your life. He is ruining my life." Fran felt for a crumpled piece of Kleenex in the pocket of her house coat. "He has broken your heart and you have broken mine. God is not going to forget this too easily, Letty. He'll not forget nor forgive you, believe what I'm saying. I know what I'm talking about. Who will go for my pot cheese?" she said, the last with a whine.

Letty was determined to be strong. It was the only way. The only way to lead some kind of decent life; it would cost as much to put her mother in a home, and she couldn't. She had already decided that. She could not put her mother in a home. She knew she had to find another alternative, another option that she could live with in good conscience.

"I won't be downtown all the time. I'll still be here a lot. I'll still do the shopping for you and go to the park with you on Sunday, Ma. I've already gone over this with you a thousand times. You've got my new phone number, I can be up here in ten minutes if you need me. Mother," she said, quietly, still with patience, "remember how you always kept telling me about forty . . . that forty was coming, and where was I? What did I have to show for it? Ma, I decided to keep on going. If I keep at it, I can get my degree in a few

332

years, if I can afford it and have the energy to take some more courses at once, I can do it even faster than that. And with all the supervisory training I'll get with the courses, which give me credit, by the time I'm forty-one, forty-two, I'll be making twice as much money as I'm making now and I'll be a professional person, Ma. Aren't you proud? Isn't that what you wanted?"

"Don't change. Who do you think you're kidding, kid? Don't change the subject. I'm not talking about schooling. Who's talking about schooling? I'm talking about him. I'm talking about throwing your life away on a married man. I'm not talking about living in that jungle down there in the Village. I'm talking about leaving your poor mother alone. That's what I'm talking about. And don't give me the business about my pouring guilt on you. I'm not doing no such thing. I'm going to be seventy-five, and I want to live to see some grandchildren . . ."

"Now who's changing the subject?"

"He's no good. Why don't he leave his wife and marry you? Let's put it that way."

"He can't," Letty said quietly, taking some sweaters and blouses out of her bureau and packing them in her suitcase. "He can't afford it. He can't leave his children. Not now." And, as though she was explaining how Noah found two animals of each species and led them, two by two, up the ramp to the Ark, she carefully, painstakingly described for the thousandth time that she had made her decision.

"I didn't like it the other way. I was miserable. I'll be all right. I've thought about it and thought about it till I can't anymore. And I know it's the right thing. I will have my own place. I will somehow be able to keep this place going and another apartment, too. You'll come, Ma, you'll see. It's not in the greatest neighborhood, but it's cheap and convenient to the office and school. I painted it last weekend and it's fresh and clean. Today I'll hang the curtains . . ." Letty's face was flushed.

She had a pain at the pit of her stomach. She ached for her mother. How could she do it? What a rotten person she was. No, she wasn't. Gritting her teeth, she knew she was not rotten. She knew she had to fight for whatever joy and reward life was going to give her. She wasn't sacrificing her mother. She was convinced of that. Her mother would be all right. And there would be no more motels and no more soap collections. She and Will would have their own oasis. If it was only two days or one day, it was better. She just knew deep down inside her she was doing the right thing.

Fran screamed at her down the hall when she pushed the "down" button in the elevator, surrounded by her boxes and her suitcases. And she could still hear Fran's voice ringing in her ears, even as the driver helped her unload her things into the third-floor rear apartment just off Tompkins Square.

38

The New York *Times* was spread all over the floor in Becky's and Arnold's den. Becky had ripped out several items from the theater section about plays she wanted to see. Arnold had combed the sports section and had left it in pieces on the floor.

Becky lay on the floor in a pair of slacks and a sweater, wondering whether she should call Letty or not. In a few months, she and Arnold would have been married a year.

They hadn't moved to the country which Arnold had promised. He hadn't let her continue working, as he had promised. He hadn't continued taking her to the museums and to plays. Before they were married, he said he loved them. He turned out to be a jock. Nothing else. Sundays he was glued to the television set with his brother Hal, or his friend Reuben. He was out four nights a week playing squash at his gym. He let her buy whatever she wanted, but only if it suited him. Only if he felt it would look good standing next to him.

In a few months, they would have been married a year, and Becky felt more confused than ever. She took a gourmet cooking class. He said it wasn't necessary for her to go to college. He wouldn't give her the money for it. She was gorgeous and had everything she wanted, what did she need college for, he said.

She dialed Letty's number. Her mother told her she was out for a walk. "You must be so happy," Mrs. Gold said.

Not at all, Becky thought, hearing Arnold and Reuben in the other room scream at the touchdown somebody made.

"Becky, is there any salami in the fridge?"

Sighing, Becky got up and went into the newly decorated kitchen with Mexican tile surrounding the six-burner restaurant stove. She sliced some cheese and salami for Arnold and Hal. They grunted as she put the plate down on the coffee table.

She was determined to talk about it tonight. Her mother was really worried about her since she had lost eight pounds. "You're too thin as it is," she had told her at lunch yesterday. "You eat. What's the matter?"

She just couldn't tell her mother. She couldn't tell her mother that there was something about Arnold that frightened her. She had made a mistake. She knew that now. But she didn't know how to get out of it, she didn't know what to do. It was as though he had proved his point, he got a girl that his parents approved of, got to be treasurer of the company now that he had the girl his parents approved of. And that was it. It was an end, this marriage, not a beginning. They saw each other in passing.

And he never touched her.

Abruptly, Becky threw down the papers and went to the closet and took out the heavy bulky-belted sweater Arnold had bought her. Its mate hung next to it. Changing her mind, she hung it back up and took out her old pea jacket and put it on. She yelled into the TV room to Arnold. "I'm going to a movie."

"Come in," Arnold yelled back.

Sighing, Becky picked up her purse, slung it on her shoulder and moved to the doorway of the TV room.

"What time you think you'll be back?" Arnold asked.

"I don't know. I don't even know what I'm going to see," she said, trying to keep the accusing tone out of her voice.

"Well, we'll be here, this game's going to go for a long time, don't you think, Reub?"

Reuben Stein was Arnold's blond counterpart. He was tall and muscular, his body sinewed by daily workouts at the gym. His eyes were brown and his fingers long and slim. Becky preferred his fingers to Arnold's. Reuben was in his father's business also, pocketbooks, and periodically took trips to South America to buy leather. Last time he brought Becky back a pony rug and an exquisitely colored wall hanging dyed and woven by a remote Indian tribe. "See you later, Becky," he said, without looking away from the set.

Becky closed the door quietly, suppressing an urge to slam it so that all the pictures would fall down, so that the two tall men lounging on couches would fall with a thud to the floor.

Outside, she found herself chilled. She hadn't even taken the Sunday *Times* with her to see what was playing. She really didn't want to go to a movie anyway, she thought, pulling up the collar of her jacket.

Becky found herself suddenly on Madison Avenue and Seventy-eighth Street. Passing the huge prisonlike squares of the Whitney Museum, she impulsively went in, noticing a sign outside advertising a collection of sculpture and mobiles on view. The artist was someone named Alexander Calder, she read, and as she walked through the enormous rooms filled with the large structures, some hanging from the ceiling, some stationary on the ground, she didn't know why, but she began to be filled with good humor. There was something so good-natured about the pieces, and while she couldn't quite explain it to herself, she found her tension being released; she was beginning to lose her anger.

By the time she came out of the museum, she was feeling better. She passed a man with a cart full of flowers and plants and bought a bouquet. She would make a lovely dinner for them. Hopefully Reuben would go back to his bachelor digs, or perhaps would have a date, and would leave them alone. She would light the candles in the *skanzas* screwed into the wall in the dining room. She would wear a beautiful bouffant ante bellum negligee she had just bought, she would light a fire in the fireplaces in the dining room and in the den.

Becky almost skipped home. She felt like a little

girl again. When had she been a little girl? she thought. She had grown up so fast; men's hands had been on her so soon, she had sniffed coke before her fourteenth birthday and been smoking pot since she was twelve. Her friend Selma was an alcoholic at thirteen. Childhood just wasn't. It was hard to conjure up what it felt like, being a child. Skipping helped.

"Good evening, Harold," she smiled at the aging Irish elevator operator. Harold had wonderful red cheeks, and now, in these few months before Christmas, was always especially solicitous to his residents. He had worked in the building thirty years, he had told Becky, and had seen them come and go, including the two suicides from the penthouse, but aside from them, it had always been "good old-fashioned family people."

"Have a nice evening, Mrs. Berkowitz," Harold boomed as she got off at her floor, and Becky flashed him a big smile.

"I intend to, Harold, good-bye."

The apartment seemed quiet and dark when she walked in. Becky turned on the lamp on the marble table in the hall wondering why she didn't hear the blare of the football game from the TV room. She walked into the kitchen and put the collection of mums she had bought into a vase. She slipped off her boots and brought the vase into the dining room where she put them in the middle of the table. I guess they went out for a walk, Becky thought as she collected her boots and headed for the bedroom.

The clock over the mantel chimed four. The game must have ended early, Becky thought. She couldn't imagine their leaving in the middle.

It gets dark so early this time of year, she thought, as, feeling for the switch on the wall, she illuminated the room. In the middle of the bed with the mahogany headboard and eyelet canopy were Arnold and

Reuben. They were naked and they were in each other's arms.

When the light went on, they pulled the sheet up to their chins. They look ludicrous, she thought, before she started screaming. They look like ladies caught in *flagrante delicto* in some B movie.

She heard herself screaming, "Best man, best man, you were the best man, Reuben. You were the one who stuck your finger into that little pocket in the tuxedo vest and pulled out the ring, and Arnie put the ring on my finger and has probably been screwing you ever since."

Becky couldn't stop. It had been bottled up in her for a year, the hurts and disappointments, and the humiliation.

"And I thought it was me. I thought there was something the matter with me. I thought I was ugly, and that's why you wouldn't touch me. I thought I smelled. I haven't been able to eat because I thought there was something wrong with me and that's why you wouldn't make love to me. And it wasn't me all along, it had nothing fucking well to do with me. It was you. It was you all the time, Arnold Berkowitz, all along."

Becky began tearing off her clothes. What did it matter, she thought, they're fags anyway. She threw the Jax slacks at Arnie, and the cashmere sweater from Bergdorf's she flung at Reuben.

Arnold was speechless. He didn't know what to say.

As Becky tore around the room looking for her jeans, the ones she had brought with her from the Village, she couldn't stop screaming through her tears. "You always had an excuse," she shouted. "You were tired from playing squash or paddle tennis or swimming, and every time your father made one of his dirty cracks about how come there was no little Berkowitz on the way and how come I wasn't going to

339

make him a grandfather again, you just sat there with your arm around me. And I want to tell you that every Friday night sitting there around that table after the *brucha,* after your mother finished lighting the Friday night candles, I felt like bellowing to them that their precious, gorgeous son never touched me. Never, never, never made love to me."

Becky was hysterical as she pulled clothes out of her drawer. She would leave the same way she came with her Christopher Street clothes, her sneakers and her father's old college shirt. She went into the bathroom and collected the electric toothbrush for her bleeding gums she had paid for from her salary.

Running from the room, she passed through the dining room and flung the flowers down on the table. The water made neat little puddles on the eighteenth century wood. Sobbing, Becky screamed back into the room, "I'll be back for my clothes," as she heard them scrambling out of the bed.

Becky ran down the thirteen flights. She couldn't face Harold.

Several hours later, after Arnold had had two straight scotches, had said so long to Reuben, had wiped up the dining room table and put Becky's clothes back in the drawers, he was sitting in the chaise lounge in the bedroom watching Lee Leonard's sports analysis. It had been quite a scene. His heart had just about begun to settle down to a normal pace when the doorbell rang

They were there, the two of them, Becky and her father.

"What do you want? You walked out. What'd you do, bring reinforcements?"

"I came for my clothes," Becky almost whispered

"You walked out, kid, you walked out, you said you just wanted the clothes on your back, isn't that what you said?"

Becky's father brushed past Arnold with two suitcases in his hand.

"Just one minute there. I pay the rent on this pad."

"What's that got to do with anything, Arnie?" Becky said, becoming upset again, "You won't have to see me again after this, I promise you. I just want my clothes."

The sight of Becky back, the remembrance of her seeing him and Reuben in bed together was a trigger. "Listen, cunt, nobody leaves me," Arnold screamed. "Nobody. What's the old man going to say? Go home," he shouted to Becky's father. "Go home. Becky and I will handle this ourselves. We've just had a little spat, that's all. All newlyweds do, we'll patch this up ourselves."

"I want my clothes."

"You're not getting a fucking brassiere, for Christ's sake, until we talk. You think you can just come in here with your father and just take over my apartment? Screw that, kid. Come in here and let's settle this like mature people."

"You call yourself mature, you call yourself mature when you treat me the way you have? I never want to see you again, you fag. I want my clothes. I want out." Becky was screaming at him.

Arnold, enraged, pulled her by the shoulder and flung her against the wall. Then, rushing her, uncontrolled, he hit her full force in the stomach.

Doubled over, Becky moaned an animal sound and ran screaming out the door. Her father looked at Arnold, not knowing what to do. He was frightened; he was frightened of Arnold.

In a moment, the apartment was silent. Empty. Arnold was shaking as he heard the sports announcer discuss his prediction for the upcoming Ali fight.

The old man was going to have a fit.

39

Wilma's car was old. It was her major extravagance in New York City. She had to pay for a garage, and gas and insurance were exorbitant, but she couldn't give it up. It was her joy to drive into the country weekends up to Connecticut or across the bridge to New Jersey. She had friends in Princeton and in New Canaan, and in the fall when the leaves were changing, she loved to get in the car and just go; leaving behind New York and its stimuli and its terrors, the job and her memories.

Saturday morning she drove into the gas station a few blocks from her apartment where she had been dealing for several years. A tall spare man with a red and black lumberjack shirt with a turtleneck under it approached her.

"Morning," he said pleasantly.

"Hello. Where's John?" She hadn't meant to sound disappointed, but John was an attractive twenty-five-year-old who was always cheerful and friendly. She was getting too old to start making new contacts with tradesmen, she thought.

"Disappointed?"

"No, of course not. It's just that I'm a regular customer here and I just got sort of used to seeing John every day. Fill it up with unleaded, please, and check the oil."

The man looked at Wilma intently.

"Nice day for a drive," he said.

"Yes, I'm really looking forward to seeing the leaves. They're glorious this time of year."

Wilma decided to get out of the car and take off her coat.

"Allow me," the man said, smiling as he helped Wilma off with her coat. She was wearing one of her tent dresses which she had in four colors. Today she wore the rust in honor of fall.

"That color is beautiful," the man said, "like autumn."

Wilma took a second look. He was very tall and very thin. His eyes were kind, she didn't know how she could tell, but she could. He rolled up his sleeve to put the gas in the tank, continuing his conversation.

"I guess I'm one of the few people in this world who likes the smell of gas," he said. "I really like it. Reminds me of when I was a kid and used to help my uncle in his gas station in New Mexico. He was a good man. Those were good days."

"How long have you worked here?" Wilma asked.

"About a month. I was living and working in Brooklyn for a long time and then things got sort of sad and I moved into Manhattan. Pace is faster than Brooklyn."

"Why did you move away?" Wilma asked and was suddenly sorry when she saw the cloud in front of the man's eyes.

"Wife died. Good marriage. Couldn't take the old neighborhood anymore. What's your name, Miss?"

"Wilma. Wilma Scott. What's yours?"

"Sapphire, like the jewel. Howie Sapphire. You going to pay cash or charge?"

"Master Charge, please."

"Sure thing. John got married. Moved away. Went

back to school. The boss says this place is a real stepping stone. I don't know. But today has certainly been my lucky day, Miss Scott. I truly enjoyed meeting you. Do you live around here?"

"Yes. A few blocks away. My garage is on this street."

"Right. Well, you should have your transmission checked. It sounded kind of funny when you drove in here. I'll be glad to check it for you next time you come in."

"Well, thank you, Howie."

"Sure. Well, I guess that's about everything. Have a wonderful trip. Enjoy the leaves. They must be out in full force now."

"They are. My friends who I'm going to visit say it's the loveliest year yet, but they say that every year."

"Right. Come again, Miss Scott. I like talking to you."

Me, too, Wilma thought, as she drove away. Something compelling about the man. A gas station man and he had the kindest eyes she'd ever seen.

Two weeks later, when Wilma brought the car in to have the transmission checked, Howie Sapphire opened the door for her.

"Can I say something?" he said, pulling her over to the corner of the garage, near the pay telephone.

"Of course, Howie."

"I thought about you a lot these past two weeks, and I asked the boss about you, and he said you were one of the nicest customers he had. And if this sounds ridiculous, forget about it, but Miss Scott, I'm going ice skating tomorrow at Rockefeller Center, and I would love to take you with me."

Wilma couldn't believe it. He was a gas station attendant, and he had a plain face, but he looked positively glowing as he asked her for a date. And me,

Wilma thought. I'm a fat fifty-year-old who hasn't been out on a date in months. Who hasn't seen that look in a man's eye in my direction in years. A gas station attendant. He probably never reads. He probably . . .

"Howie, I would love it. I'm a terrible ice skater and I'd probably fall all over the place. I'm no lightweight, as you can see." She had to get that over with, in case he hadn't noticed that she weighed a ton.

"Terrific. Terrific, I tell you. You'll have a great time. I'm a good skater. It's a hobby of mine, so I'll help you. And listen, weight doesn't matter, I swear. And you know, Miss Scott?"

"Wilma . . ."

"Wilma. Forgive me, you're lovely."

Wilma wrote her address on the back of an envelope.

Wilma fell down on the ice a lot but she laughed a lot, too, and Howie had pink in his sallow cheeks and was delighted every time he had to help her up. He relieved her self-consciousness about herself. I feel thin, for God's sake, she had said to Letty. The man makes me feel thin, can you imagine.

"What's he like?" Letty had asked.

"Look, the man has never heard of Plato or Pinter that's for sure. He pumps gas for a living. Look, Letty, no joke, I'm embarrassed, snobbish about admitting what he does. To you, it's all right, but when it comes time to introduce him to the rest of the world, I don't know. He's got this dumb job, which is to me the dumbest of the dumb. But somehow, all of a sudden, it doesn't seem to matter anymore."

"Wilma . . ."

"No, wait. Let me talk. Can you imagine me ice skating? Me? Graceful lissome lithe me was floating around Rockefeller Center doing the most painful figure-eights you've ever seen. You know what? I loved it. And I loved the hot toddy after. Just simple things. It's a new thing for me. That man just likes to live. I've never met anyone like that. Uncomplicated. He's terribly uncomplicated. Too much so in a way. The complications are what makes sensibility, I know that, but somehow it just doesn't seem to matter. I'm having a good time.

"I know it's ridiculous to go on and on about someone I've only gone out with a few times, but I don't know, he seems to make me feel alive again. You want to hear something silly? He likes butterflies. Can you imagine? He never heard of Nabokov, but Nabokov would probably love him. Look, stop me from running off at the mouth."

After a month, Howie was coming for dinner a few times a week and Wilma loved shopping and cooking for someone besides herself. She wrestled with worrying whether she liked him because it assuaged the loneliness or for the person, Howie, himself, but she was determined not to deny herself the joy he gave her.

Friday night, Wilma moved with untypical speed, puffing up pillows, pulling the drapes in expectation of Howie's arrival. One entire wall of her apartment was covered with books and there were three trees and perhaps twenty plants throughout. The leaves were shining and the plants looked well taken care of, well spoken to. Wilma played music for them the whole day while she was at work, and they showed the results of her loving care.

When Howie's knock came at the door, she was ready, but she was certain the stew wasn't. She offered him a drink and went back in the kitchen to putter.

Howie came into the kitchen with a fat volume of

bound programs from Broadway plays Wilma had on the coffee table.

"God, I remember this," he said. *"The Shrike,* with José Ferrer, remember that one? And *Tea House of the August Moon* with John Forsythe. I saw them all."

"I used to work for a man, a producer," Wilma said, "and I used to see every play on Broadway then. Every one."

"I go to every play I can. I love the theater," Howie said. "It's one of the reasons I came East, to be able to see theater."

Wilma took the book of programs out of Howie's hand and absent-mindedly leafed through them. Julian used to say she never threw anything out, but the programs reminded her of him.

Now somehow with Howie she was able to remember her relationship with Julian as it was, not as she thought it was, but as it was. Julian Frank was a thin, ascetic Jew who came from modest circumstances and had innate taste. When Wilma had first come into his office he had three plays running simultaneously on Broadway. Two of them had won Pulitzer Prizes. Arthur Miller, Lillian Hellman, and other equally distinguished playwrights sought his company, his advice, and found a certain cachet about having Julian Frank's name above their titles.

Wilma had to laugh at herself when she thought how gauche she must have looked the first time she entered Julian Frank's office. He was looking for a private secretary. Perhaps it was her excellent shorthand. Perhaps it was her total naïveté and complete ignorance of the theater and Broadway. Perhaps it was because he enjoyed seeing all of the bizarre aspects and the glamour through the eyes of someone who had never seen them before. But he used to enjoy stopping in the middle of a conference with a Jed

Harris or an Arthur Laurents and say, "What do you think, Wilma?"

Wilma knew part of it was a put on. She knew part of it was the amusement he got from looking at one of the famous playwrights and directors and wonder why he would be asking this gauche-looking girl from Iowa her opinion.

There would be lunches at "21," phone at the table, decisions made as Jose Ferrer would drop by, or Olivier when he was in town. It seemed he could do nothing wrong. He made her an integral part of his business and his personal life. He introduced her to the literature and excitement of Broadway. Twelve years with a man whose name was associated with intelligence, class.

He had made her indispensable to him. No one could handle clients the way she did, he told her. No one could take notes on conferences and discuss them with him with such lucidity and constructive criticism. No one could soothe him when he was working at a frantic pace as she could. Twelve years of being next to the best.

Then one night, when they were in London together taking a look at a show that he was thinking of importing to Broadway, and they were staying at the Savoy in one of those suites that face the river, he was very drunk, and they made love. It was the first and only time.

She decided that there was no one else in this whole world who could excite her and teach her and be so infinitely kind to her. No one. He had been her mentor. Julian Frank had stretched her, introduced her to books and plays and people she never knew existed.

Then, suddenly, an import that was a great hit in London and a disaster on Broadway changed his image. Julian Frank himself adapted *The Cherry Orchard* and set it in the ante bellum South. After that it seemed that as surely as Julian Frank could do nothing wrong, it seemed he could do nothing right. He began producing plays that were too esoteric for Broadway and not bold or new enough for Off-Broadway.

Wilma continued to work for him, first for a cut in salary, then for no salary. His wife and he had long since parted, and he wound up living on Riverside Drive on the west end of New York, which was once fashionable but now was populated by old European Jews living cheek by jowl with Puerto Ricans and young couples with no money.

The last evening she came to see him was in that apartment with a small terrace overlooking the river. She knew he had plans for years to revive Sean O'Casey's *Within the Gates,* and direct it himself. He had always felt it had never been done properly in this country. Wilma had saved money during the last twelve years. Wilma had always been able to save. She offered it to him to produce *Within the Gates.* She offered him her bank book and proudly showed him her balance.

Julian laughed. She could never get over her surprise in his laugh. Wilma looked at him, not understanding what he meant.

"Are you offering yourself, too, Wilma?"

Wilma looked at him realizing that was exactly what she was doing.

"I don't want you, Wilma. I don't even want to go to bed with you."

It was the cruelest thing anybody had ever said to her, but she understood the truth of what he was saying, too. She had felt no matter how many other women there were, in spite of his wife, in spite of everything, that he had really cared for her alone. There were tears in Wilma's eyes. "I don't want anything from you. I just wanted to give you this because I think you're a great man."

"Great man," he said contemptuously. "There are no great men in this so-called business. Maybe a couple of plays. Maybe one or two by Miller, passages by Williams. A couple of actors who run to the movies at the first offer and never come back. And then there are the rest that prey on the talents. The agents, the business managers. The publicity men. The producers. Con men. All of them. What did I ever do? Use a little bit of seedy charm to manipulate them, use them? A con man like all the rest." He laughed to himself. "Take that pathetic bank book and go home."

He didn't even seem to see her when, blinded and almost hysterical with tears, she left the apartment.

That was the real story of Julian Frank and Wilma Scott. Not the story she had told herself or the story that she had told Letty or other people when she had needed to talk to someone. That was being the non-wife—the indispensable, beautifully organized, dependable secretary, unquestioning mistress, totally accepting non-wife.

For Wilma Julian Frank was now reduced to David Merrick and Robert Evans and Jacqueline Kennedy and Joseph Papp and all the other names in *Women's Wear Daily* and the New York *Post*. She wasn't part of that world anymore.

That night, after dinner, Howie took Wilma to bed.

He undressed her slowly, gently touching each part of her body as it became exposed. Wilma was trembling and near tears. Howie was gentle and loving. She could tell, a woman can tell, she thought, that he loved her flesh. She knew her skin was beautiful, very fair, unblemished, smooth, albeit excessive, and every touch of his fingers and his palms told her that her flesh enchanted him. Its bounty gave him pleasure.

And he made her feel desired. He made her feel relieved. He was a good man to have in her bed. They made love all night long.

40

Priscilla was sitting on her favorite park bench feeding pigeons. Every Saturday she came to the Seventy-ninth Street entrance to the Park off Fifth Avenue and sat on one of the benches that lined the wide walkway just inside. She carried bags full of bread and cookie crumbs

How divine not to wear a coat, she thought. How groovy not to be involved with winter any longer. This was a secret thing she did, almost every Saturday morning, sitting on this bench eyeing the matrons and straggling shopping-bag ladies flung far from their familiar stamping grounds. The air smelled of summer, and Priscilla took off her sandals and wiggled her toes in the sand, hoping some dog off the leash hadn't peed there moments before.

"Let's go, gang," she shouted to the birds who appeared to be waiting for her arrival. "Chow time!" And she threw up handfuls of crumbs so high they almost touched the leaves on overhanging wide branches covering the bench. The crumbs fell like rain closer than Priscilla had planned; they sprayed her blouse, the bench, and the shoulders of the thin, bespectacled young man she finally noticed at her left.

"Sorry. God, I'm sorry," she giggled, moving over to brush the bread off the top of his head and shoulders. She could feel the boniness.

"It's all right. It's all right, already," the young man said. "What do you think you're doing, dusting the piano?"

Priscilla took a good look. Round black eyes peered out through horn-rimmed glasses. The brows were night black and thick. The nose was long, the lips wide. She liked the face.

"God, you got some swatter there for a hand. You could play for the Rams, for God's sake. You almost took the shoulder off with the crumbs. David Stryker's the name, what's yours?"

Caught off guard, Priscilla was not prepared. Her legs had not been crossed to advantage, her eyes were not narrowed and sultry, her lips were unmoistened. Up to the moment, he hadn't looked like pickup material—more like a candidate for someone's mother to feed chicken soup to, judging by his bony shoulders and cavernous cheeks.

"Busy?"

"Sure I'm busy. Don't you see I'm feeding the birds?"

"Yes, lady but aside from that. I mean, well, how about letting me help you feed them."

"Sure. Here's a bag of your own."

Priscilla liked him. He wasn't coming on. He just was. Treated her easy. Different. She was feeling different with him.

"You have a hole in your jeans," was all she could think of saying, as a pigeon came up to her, waiting patiently to be fed.

"Oh, Christ, the patch came off."

"How come you wear patched jeans?" she said grandly.

"All the Brooks Brothers' suits got moth holes in them," he said seriously.

"What do you mean?" The pigeon waddled away.

"They were in storage for a while, and I guess they weren't sprayed enough. Anyway, shirts and ties are out for me these days."

The man was beyond making a pass, Priscilla thought. He was looking her straight in the eye, and she could tell he liked talking to her.

"How come? You are a little old to be a hippie."

"Probably."

He took out a pack of cigarettes and offered one to Priscilla.

"No. And you probably shouldn't smoke yourself," she said, noticing the yellowed fingers.

"You're right," David Stryker said. "I shouldn't smoke, and I shouldn't smoke joints and I shouldn't drink beer and I shouldn't bite my fingernails. But what can you do? We become selective after a while about the bad habits we choose to keep, don't you think? We retain what hopefully are the least destructive of the myriads of corrosive things we can do to our bodies. What do you do, and what's your name?"

"I work in insurance and my name is Priscilla." For once in her life, Priscilla found herself growing shy. She was acutely conscious that she wanted this man to like her.

"Want to share my sandwich?" David pulled a paper bag out from behind him on the bench. "Cold meatloaf. Not too soggy, the bread crumbs keep it in one piece. What do you say, Priscilla of the insurance business."

"I'm not very hungry." She looked into David's eyes and, concerned she would lose his concentration, continued, "but maybe I'll take just a bite. Did you make it?"

"Sure. I like to cook."

Chewing carefully, Priscilla added, "What else do you do?"

"Law. That's my bag."

"You're kidding?"

"Would I kid a pretty girl like you? That's it, kid, I'm a lawyer. N.Y.U., Class of 1969. You know, you have gorgeous hair. Really gorgeous. It's the color of wheat, you know that? Anyone ever tell you that?"

"No. They talk about other things, but not my hair."

"Well, that's a shame, because you should be told. Your hair just shines in the sun." Her other remark was not lost on him. "That's not to denigrate your other attributes, but your hair is beautiful. And you're funny. Did anyone ever tell you that?"

"Right. It's one of the two things I do well."

"O.K., Priscilla, you made your point. Listen, you want a balloon?"

A passing vendor selling balloons was about fifteen blocks out of his territory. He was obviously looking for the Sixty-fourth Street Zoo.

"Sure, why not?"

David gave the man a dollar and told him to keep the change. The balloon was bright red, and Priscilla felt ten years old as she put it up to her face and looked at a red David through it.

"Thanks."

There was silence as Priscilla played with the balloon and David finished his sandwich.

"How come your suits were in storage?" Priscilla asked.

"You don't miss a trick. Sure you won't be shocked?"

"I'm shockproof."

"Time. I did time."

"A lawyer?"

David laughed.

"What did you do time for?"

"What is it about you? Ingenuous underneath all that— I don't know. Something about you I like. Something about you I'm going to like more."

"Come on. Why were you in jail?"

"You really want to know?"

"Yes."

"Harboring a fugitive. A client of mine was a Weatherman, and . . ." By Priscilla's quizzical look, David could tell she thought he was talking about Tex Antoine or Frank Field.

"A radical. He was involved in the bombing last year in Salt Lake City, in the headquarters of Kennecott Copper on the anniversary of Allende's downfall in Chile . . ."

Priscilla's eyes were wide. She was silent.

"And so," David said, stretching his long legs out in front of him, "he had no place to go when they were looking for him, and I put him up at my pad. And they caught him. In my place. So I did time for harboring a fugitive. So I had put my suits in storage, and so they got moth eaten because . . . because I don't know why. Whether it was my fault or the storage people's fault."

Priscilla was quiet during David's explanation.

"The Weathermen were breaking the law, weren't they?"

"Yes. But I couldn't turn him in. How would you feel? You start to defend a kid. He's convicted. He goes on the run. Knock, knock. He's at the door. The police are after him. He has no place to hide. What would you do?"

Priscilla thought a moment. "Let him in."

David looked at her and smiled a moment. "Of

355

course you would. Listen, what are you doing for the rest of the day?"

"Well, I thought I'd do a little shopping. Then I was going to meet a friend for drinks later, and . . ."

"I've got the day planned for us. First we walk all the way down Fifth, pick up maybe a hot dog and some sauerkraut from one of those vendors along the way, then end up at the Sixty-fourth Street Zoo. We kick around a little in the monkey wing, if you can stand the smell. God, I love to watch the monkeys. How does it sound so far?"

"I'm waiting for the punch line."

"Then we're going to a meeting downtown in the Village, the Lower Manhattan group that's working for Caesar Chavez." Noticing her blank look, he explained. "Anyway, that's my schedule for the day. I'd like to share it with you."

David took Priscilla's arm, and as she looked down and saw the hole in his jeans she thought thoughts like I'll have to find a patch and sew one on there if he insists on wearing them.

41

"So he took me to a meeting. That was our first date. Can you imagine?"

Priscilla took long slow sips from the container of coffee. She was sitting in a chair next to Letty's desk. The clock above them said ten minutes to five.

Letty pulled the paper out from her typewriter. Priscilla looked different. Letty had noticed over the past few months that she was dressing less flamboyantly, that she never hung around the office after work chatting with the men, that she was in bright and early in the morning. She seemed at ease.

"Your eyes look so bright. What's happened to you?"

"Visine, Aziza, and David. What can I tell you. I'm busy, I'm occupied. Letty, you know what?" Priscilla leaned over with a conspiratorial tone.

"What?" Letty smelled the soft scent of the girl.

"We get home so late from some rally or something, and then he gets into some deep discussion with some guys at a bar and there I'd be, horny as ever, drinking my beer, and then forgetting about it because it was so fucking interesting, what they were talking about. Did you ever, in your wildest dreams, ever, ever think I'd be talking this way."

Priscilla crossed her legs, plump at the thighs, curved at the ankle. She's still a morsel, Letty thought, this new intensity making her all the more appealing, all the more attractive.

"I'm not surprised, Priscilla. I'm really not. We all change, thank God for that, we all change. Life is, always has been, more than . . ."

"Than what? Than fucking? Is that what you were going to say? I can tell you something that will make you roar," Priscilla said. "David's not so hot in bed. Ironical, right? You know what? It doesn't matter. I swear to God, it doesn't matter."

Letty was taking her checkbook out of her purse and began writing a check for Priscilla. "To whom do I make this out?"

"Leave it blank. I'll fill it in. Caesar Chavez, I think, but I'll ask David and make sure. Whatever it is, it's tax deductible, so don't worry about that. Listen," she said, taking a pencil that was resting on Letty's desk and putting it in her mouth, "don't tell anyone, Lett, I'm giving notice."

"Priscilla."

"I figure I can live on unemployment for a while. Then, I don't know. We'll see. I'm just into other things now. And you know what else, I haven't screwed another man in months. Letty, I don't miss it. The variety. There's a fucking monotony in numbers, you know that? Have you ever noticed that?"

Impulsively, Letty leaned over and hugged Priscilla. "Here's your check, with my blessings. You look just terrific. I'll be so sorry to see you go, Priscilla. When do you think you'll be leaving?"

"I don't know. I have to figure it out with David. He thinks I should do something more useful with my time, and God, so do I. Look, I'm just happy, that's all. Things are good with me. That's all I know. I don't even do coke anymore. Grass, sure, and not even that so much anymore. Every time I think about that Christmas party, I could die. What a fucking fool I made of myself, right? Well, that's then. This is now."

Letty put the cover over her typewriter and began gathering up her papers and purse.

"Come down in the elevator with me, Priscilla. I have a six o'clock appointment uptown and have to rush. Can I drop you in a cab somewhere?"

"Nope. I'm going downtown. Where are you going?"

"As part of a course I'm taking, I work at a Halfway House on the Upper West Side. The instructor of the class runs a program for recently discharged mental patients there, and some of us work there three days a week."

"Wow. I think that's super. I mean, really super Letty. How long have you been doing that?"

"Several months now. I'll have my degree soon, I can manage more courses. The head of the department is really trying to convince me I should get a Masters Degree in social work," she said shyly.

"I can't get over it, girl. And you never said a thing. I can't get over it. Wait till I tell David. Letty, that's terrific. Do you think you'll do it? Go for the degree?"

"I don't know," Letty said, pushing for the "down" button, pulling her coat on. "It's expensive, but the professor seems to think I could get some kind of scholarship. He's been training us to run groups with these people involved in the Recovery Program. It's the most exciting thing I've ever done."

Letty swallowed as her ears began to pop as the elevator started going down. "He seems to think I'm good with people. And Priscilla, I do love it. I really feel for those people. Some have been in state hospitals for years. This Halfway House helps them re-enter society. I'd love to quit, too. If I could afford it, I would, Priscilla. Now that I see how much else there is to do. But listen, it's going to be a long haul. You really can't get any kind of job without a Masters, and that's expensive and takes a long time."

"So what?" Priscilla said as the elevator hit the first floor. "The point is, you found something else you could do and were good at. Christ, I could have told you you were good with people. Why didn't you ask me, for God's sake."

Letty embraced Priscilla and watched her dash down the street, almost knocking a man over. She bent down to pick up his newspaper which she had dislodged from under his arm, and disappeared into the crowd.

Letty walked in the opposite direction. Feeling good. She was feeling very good.

42

Priscilla was setting the table in David's apartment. He certainly was casual about things, she thought. She was determined to straighten up the chaos of his kitchen and to brighten up the place. She had bought four plants that morning, a beautiful Saturday, cold but exquisitely clear, the way she loved Saturdays to be. She had treated the window in the living room with the plants, thrown away the newspapers and journals David had piled up almost to the ceiling in front of his fireplace, and had bought bags full of fresh vegetables she intended to sauté in the wok. It was all too domestic. She couldn't believe how domestic it was, but what was more difficult for her to understand was how she was enjoying it all.

It was dumb, she thought, just loving the fact that David was reading the New York *Times* near the front window, feet up, and that she was here in the kitchen chopping up Chinese vegetables, and the whole thing made her want to cry. It wasn't the onions. It was something else. It had to do with trust, she had known that from the minute she started talking to him. She had known she could trust him. That he would never hurt her.

Pouring some oil into the wok, Priscilla heard a heavy knock on the door.

"Door, David."

The sounds of *The Magic Flute* drowned out her words and the knock.

"David, the door," she shouted, then heard him grunt and shuffle over to it. She heard it slam hard behind him, and then the sound of men's voices.

"Who is it?" she said, and when no one answered her walked into the living room.

"Let's see your I.D., fellows. You know you can't just barge in," David was saying.

"Just calm down, sonny, and tell us where Frank Jones is. Just tell us and you won't get in any trouble."

"Why the fuck should I get into any trouble? You guys have come barking up the wrong tree. Now as I said, let's see your I.D."

"Who are those men, David?" Priscilla looked at the two men with suits and ties who were edging David up against the wall. "David, what is it?" she was frightened.

"It's nothing, Priscilla, stay in the kitchen. Just some old friends of mine who seem to think I know where an old friend of theirs is."

"O.K., Stryker, let's have it. We don't have all day. We know you know where Jones is, just tell us and you can get on with your dinner." The tall blond one shoved David hard against the corner of the bookcase. Priscilla winced as his shoulder cut the edge of the wood.

"Keep your fucking hands off me. I don't know where Jones is. Show me your I.D., and then get the hell out."

"Listen, Stryker, we need the likes of you like a hole in the head. We want out of here as much as you want us out," the shorter man had a little button in his lapel, Priscilla noticed. She wanted to jump on his back and smash him, but she was paralyzed. David just didn't seem to be afraid of them.

"You know, you FBI guys slay me," he said, as the

tall one started to shove him over to the other one, as though he was a basketball, as though he was an old hat. "This is a hell of a way to make a living, it seems to me. What a fucking way to make points in this world."

This last remark infuriated the tall one and he pushed David hard, almost across the room so that he fell to the floor with a thud. Priscilla didn't move as she looked at David screaming at them from the floor. "Get the hell out of here, you creeps. Don't you dare touch me. Who the fuck do you think you are?" He was screaming at them and rubbing the back of his head. There was blood on his hand Priscilla saw and she rushed toward him.

The FBI men could tell they weren't going to learn what they wanted to know. They shrugged at each other and headed for the door.

"I'm telling you, Stryker," the shorter one said, his hand on the knob, "next time your chick won't be here. Next time, we really work you over, but by next time we will have flushed out Jones anyway. Just watch your step, lawyer boy. Just watch it."

They slammed the door shut.

As Priscilla rushed to put ice into a washcloth in the kitchen, she couldn't stop shaking.

A man, she thought, I've got myself hooked up with a man for once. He's not afraid of anything. She kissed the ice before wrapping it in the cloth.

43

Becky hadn't been home in three nights. She knew her mother would be worried about her, but the Krauses knew that it was a losing battle, trying to contain their daughter.

She couldn't remember where she had slept the night before, but tonight she was sure she would sleep here on this white couch in this Soho loft. She was so tired. Her face was drawn, and the purples and plum colors with which she had made up her eyes did not enhance the haunted look she had acquired in the months since she had left Arnold. The world in this room seemed three-dimensional to her. The sound of glasses touching the glass tables echoed and reverberated like the inside of a cymbal cave. Candles were burning in parts of the room, and the only direct light came from the Pullman kitchen somewhere far off.

Becky was wearing a tie-dyed wisp of gauze fabric which revealed her thin arms and tight jeans encased the reed-slim flanks.

"Light, babe?"

A thin man, almost as short as she, lit a joint for her, lighting the match with a grand flourish on his custom-made jeans.

"You look like Nefertiti," Becky whispered to the tall black model who stood beside her friend with the joint. The model ignored Becky, and running her fingers up and down Bobby's arm, retrieved a joint out of his hand.

Becky's old friends had welcomed her back with open arms, especially Bobby de Milo, Becky's forty-year-old friend, father, lover, what have you. She had been so grateful before to say good-bye to him, to say good-bye to the stuff, to everything, but it wasn't easy out there on the streets. Visions of Arnold and the water from the mums making dancing puddles on the mahogany dining room table haunted her. It all came and went too fast. She had gone back to oblivion. It was all she could deal with now.

As she followed Bobby's snapping fingers out the door, down the filthy stairs into the night, she bent down into the white Eldorado that rested at the curb. The black chauffeur body guard opened the door for her, and she slid in beside Bobby.

Her world was a blurred world. A world of the body guard's curling kinky hair on the back of his head, the fog in the night, the sound of Bobby's voice, "Back to the place." Becky, feeling dizzy and forgetful, watched, fascinated, as Bobby pushed a button that cut the car in two. A large sheet of black glass separated the driver from the back seat. Bobby flicked on the overhead light and clicked on the stereo as he pulled out an envelope of cocaine. He took out a tiny gold spoon from his shirt, hanging on a diamond chain. He touched the coke to his tongue.

Before long, the car pulled up to the curb, in front of the club that Bobby owned and ran. "Want a snort, sweetheart? You seem cold."

"I'm O.K., Bobby," Becky said. She heard the music blaring out from the windows and saw the garbage in the streets, the empty lofts on either side of Bobby's club. It was one of the most successful clubs in Soho, and Bobby was the kingpin of the area.

Inside, Becky was assaulted by sound, and strobe

lights, bodies gyrating like giant shadows. She watched Bobby nod to the waitresses and bartenders as he made his way to a table set apart from the crush of people.

"Still cold, honey? Hey, get the kid something hot," he bellowed to no one in particular. "Look, babe. Go dance or something. I got business."

Becky nodded dumbly. He was good to her. She took a tiny vial of coke in her palm and tore off a match box cover. Using the corner to snort with, she blew into each nostril.

"Hey, baby," Bobby said, catching a glimpse of her out of the corner of his eye, "go a little easy, kid. It ain't that bad." Bobby patted her on the shoulder and began to walk off to the back of the room.

Without looking at him, Becky grasped his hand. "Keep me company a little," she said in a little girl voice.

"Can't, babe. Be back soon."

A buxom blond waitress in black leather shorts brought Becky a mug of steaming coffee and a brandy.

"So how's the boss's old lady tonight?" she said, assuming a sweetness. "Or are you only for the week, kid. I must say, you've outlasted most. What is it, baby? A month now?"

Becky nodded vaguely, staring at the bony hands that were holding the mug. The nails under the thin coat of pink polish seemed dirty, and it was as though they were growing roots before her eyes.

"Want to sit with me and eat?" she said.

But the waitress had already gone to another table.

Becky tried to pick Bobby's back out of the crowd, but could not find him. She felt as though her hands were on fire from the coffee, but she was not able to move them away. She tried to gesture to someone passing that her hands were stuck to her cup and couldn't someone please help her, but everyone ignored her. She spilled some of the steaming coffee over her legs and wasn't able to get her hands to wipe the sticky hot stuff away. Finally, she was able to drop the cup to the floor, but no one seemed to notice or hear it splash. She would have to clean the spot on her dress. She would have to do something about the nausea.

She watched her hands turn the knob to the bathroom. Inside it was dirty. Tampax was on the floor. What was she doing in this dirty place? She was Becky. She saw her hand embrace the porcelain of the toilet bowl before she was sick.

Struggling up, Becky went to the basin and poured water on her face. Her purple eyes looked like sockets. "It's worse than before," she said out loud to the purple girl in the mirror. "What's going to happen now? It's worse than before."

44

The next three years passed with the predictability of the seasons. And yet, even though it seemed that a sameness permeated Letty's life, it was not actually so. They were, indeed, the happiest three years of her life.

Yet still, on the eve of her fortieth birthday, she celebrated the "life begins" year alone. She could have gone to a lecture by Dr. Albert Ellis on "changing sexual mores" or she could have gone to Wilma's for home-made gingerbread. Wilma was getting married in two months. Wilma had decided that the peace and the humor, the sex and the joy Howie brought into her life, was a blessing. She had learned, forced herself over the years, to overlook what he didn't know.

Will had to go to his son's graduation, then preside at a family party on her birthday. So she spent the evening ruefully reading *Feminine Psychology* by Karen Horney. At two in the morning, Will called. He had left Kathy's bed and had gone to a booth on the corner to present his own private singing telegram to her. She knew it was a rotten way to spend a birthday, especially the fortieth, which she had been dreading for so long. "I'll make it up to you Thursday, baby. I'll prove it to you over and over how your life is going to do nothing but begin from now on," he said.

He stayed over that Thursday and he brought a cake from Cake Masters in his neighborhood and they ate it in bed, washing it down with domestic champagne. It took the edge off a little, not celebrating on the exact day, but then, of course, they never celebrated Christmas Day or Labor Day or Memorial Day together either. Letty never got used to it.

And Kathy never got used to knowing about Letty, either. But she never said a thing. Somehow, somewhere, she had decided that she didn't know. That somehow, somewhere she still had her husband and her family intact, and that is what mattered. When Will came home late, or stayed out all night, she would go on a shopping spree to punish him.

His boys were getting older, they were people now, and Will spent hours deep into the night explaining Marx and *Das Capital* to the three of them. Even the youngest, although he wasn't studying it, would listen, all of them amazed at the abundance of information their father had amassed. There were sprinkles of gray in Will's hair now and even the blond hairs on his chest were turning white, one by one.

Kathy had lost a good deal of weight, had discovered Loehmann's uptown and dressed with more care, but it was too late. There was no more sheen. She and Will never made love anymore, but it didn't matter. In the long run, she was the one who was triumphant, she was the one he couldn't leave. It was enough. She had completed her practical nurse training, and for a few weekends had stayed with a newborn. She registered with an agency and hoped she would get more jobs. Kathy operated on denial; she was determined to forget that Will and his other woman and his other life existed. Period.

Letty continued at Robertson Stellar but only gave lip service to the job, devoting most of her energies to school. She was vitalized by her teachers, the interchange with the students. She traveled uptown often to be with her mother who fared remarkably well under the circumstances. Since Letty left, Fran had been forced to do more on her own and had taken to lunching with "the girls" twice a week and even went once a month to a matinee with a Golden Age Club she joined at the neighborhood temple. Occasionally, Mrs. Birnbaum, who lived in the building, slept over. Fran was going to be seventy-eight and seemed to function as well as she had several years before.

Letty created a home-away-from-home for Will downtown, and it became a haven for them both.

At first, the East Village had scared Letty. She was used to the more benign Upper East Side, a place punctuated by only an occasional violent eruption. Downtown, there always seemed to be rumblings. Yet the drug scene seemed to wane a bit, the ranks of the junkies appeared to be thinning, and Letty made friends quickly with the remaining vestiges of what had formerly been a solid Ukrainian family neighborhood. She was always on her guard, however, and never walked alone on the streets after ten, did her shopping in the mornings and on weekends. She brought some things from her room uptown, but after it seemed to upset Fran so to see so much of Letty leave, she picked up bits and pieces at antique and thrift shops in the new neighborhood. She covered the furniture in gaily colored patterns and picked up a tape machine on sale to listen to music. She left her stereo uptown for Fran who adored listening to the opera. She couldn't bear to take it from her.

She was spending more money than she could afford, and Will had little to spare, but weeks, months, and then, slowly, imperceptibly, somehow the next years went by.

Only once in the past three years did they part, when Will came to the New School cafeteria to surprise Letty after class one night and she was having coffee with two male students from her class. Will had come up to her, stood by her chair, glared, and dropped two quarters down on the table. Letty had run after him, but he brushed her off. Sometimes she was unbearably tired of his jealousy, a pathology she did not know how to cope with, no matter how she understood it. Sometimes she felt mother, sister, confessor, anything but mate to him, and then, sometimes, in the little bedroom off Tompkins Square, a Mozart quintet on the tape, they would lie in bed, with Will reading to her, and it would all be all right. For a moment. She was beginning to understand that now. That life was made up of these peak moments, moments of joy, just moments, surrounded by struggle. She knew that now.

The office had changed. MacKail still blustered and Letty was sure he was drinking too much. She began covering up for him more and more. Will had always said he had sold out for the mortgage and the boat, but whatever it was that was eating him, he wasn't dealing with it well.

Every time she passed Agnes' desk, she remembered that terrible day. The day Agnes lost herself. Little by little, a few years ago, after their Christmas vacations, Agnes had begun to act strangely. She began coming to work in jeans and polo shirts, in the dead of winter. Then she stopped wearing make-up and didn't wash her hair. It just hung. MacKail had told Letty to do something about it, he was worried about her, and she wasn't doing any work to speak of —in fact, was beginning to make work.

"She used to be such a neat kid. What the hell happened to her?" MacKail had said to Letty the day it happened.

It had been a particularly freezing day, and Agnes, who had been so careful, who had always been so meticulous, had left her apartment that morning wearing sandals, despite a warning by the radio announcer that snow was promised for late that afternoon. She had poured all her precious things into a shopping bag. She would become a shopping bag lady, she told Letty later that day. She took her favorite perfume, Youth Dew by Estée Lauder, and after sprinkling some drops between her breasts, flung it into the bag along with three brightly colored scarves, a peanut butter sandwich and a copy of *How To Be Your Own Best Friend*.

"It's not enough," she muttered, wrapping her voluminous cape around her, and "being your own best friend isn't enough, no matter what they say," were the first words she had said to Letty that morning.

Letty noticed that Agnes' ankles were swollen and scaly, like the woman who surfaced every winter in Grand Central Station, wrapped in a torn fake Persian lamb coat, her black skin white with scales and dryness from the cold. She would stand there huddled in a corner, and once the station began closing at 1 A.M., Letty wondered where she went to sleep.

"You know that, don't you, Letty, that being your own best friend is not enough?" Agnes had said when she got to her desk that morning. She then walked over to Priscilla and, reaching into her shopping bag, pulled out the book and gave it to her.

"Hey, Ag, what gives? You sure look pale this morning. What happened to all the eyeliner and rouge?" she said, not unkindly. "Are you feeling O.K., kid?"

"I am feeling fine. A little funny, but fine," Agnes said haughtily. "I just didn't get much sleep last night. They were trying to get in again."

"Who, Agnes, dear?" Letty said, joining them, helping Agnes off with her cape.

"Whoever is at my window at night. They try to get in, but I had the super put bars on the windows. But they're there, I know they are."

"Well, did you call the police?" Priscilla said, concerned.

"They won't talk to me anymore. But it's all right. Don't worry, I've got it all under control. Everything's under control."

Janet walked over to the group, "Anybody got a light? I filled this damn lighter just the other day and it's out of fluid already. Agnes, are you crazy? You are really going crazy, look at your feet. They're almost blue. What the hell is the matter with you. God, is she crazy."

"Janet, shut up, for Christ's sake," Priscilla shouted as she watched Agnes slowly begin to slip away from them. "I think you better sit down, Agnes, and tell us about it. About who's at the window. Look, there's a pantyhose machine in the john on the third floor. Why don't I just dash on over and buy a pair for you. No sweat."

"Yes, Agnes," Letty said, "let Priscilla do that for you. It's really cold outside and it's not too warm in here, either."

Stan MacKail and Bob McKern were approaching the area when Will Robbins intercepted them, waving a batch of papers. "Let's go, girls. Simon Legree passing through," MacKail said a bit too heartily. No one moved. They were all watching Agnes who had slowly begun to unbuckle the belt on her slacks.

"Well, all right, Priscilla, if you think so. If you think I should wear some pantyhose, I will. My mother always said you should always carry a clean pair of underwear, an extra pair, that is, wherever you go, but I didn't get around to it. I just haven't been able to get around to a lot of things lately. These men have been at my windows and then they call up late at night, too. And they haven't picked up the garbage from my apartment in two weeks and the super is really angry at me. He said he was going to make me move unless I put the garbage out, that the other tenants on the floor were complaining about the smell, but how could there be a smell in my apartment? I'm the neatest, cleanest person I know. My mother, Mrs. Friedman, always trained me to be meticulous, to be very clean about my person and I am, so how on earth could Mr. Mosley think that I was not putting out my garbage? I told him it must be somebody else on the floor, that it couldn't possibly be coming from my apartment."

Everyone stared wide-eyed at Agnes during this monologue which was delivered in monotonous nonstop fashion. She was stepping out of one leg of her slacks when Letty finally stopped her. She was wearing cotton pants, the kind little girls wear in fifth grade, the kind you get in the 5-and-10-cent store with an elastic band at the waist. And they were wet. She had urinated in them.

She had started to scream then; it started with little moans and then the screams began. Sobs and cries like an animal in captivity.

"God, Christ," Janet said, "the kid is out of her fucking mind. She's gone looney on us," she continued backing away.

"Call an ambulance," Letty commanded as Bob McKern ran for the phone.

"Mrs. Friedman, somebody call Boston," Priscilla said, tears in her eyes. "Good God, this poor kid," she said over the wails.

"It's all right, Ag, it's all right," Letty soothed. "Let me zip up your slacks, babe, that's it, here, let me help you. You're going to be all right. You're going to be just fine."

Agnes just stood there screaming, shoulders down, feet bare, her face so contorted she was barely recognizable. Letty put her arms around her and held her as though she were two years old, as though she had just learned to walk and had fallen down, as though it was what she needed more than anything in the whole world.

Before they took her away, she pulled Letty down to her, lying there on the stretcher, just before the orderly gave her a shot.

"You're only supposed to sleep with men you love, you know," she whispered hoarsely. "You know that, don't you?" and then she had begun screaming again.

They took her to Bellevue and when her parents came, she was released in their care. Letty heard from Mrs. Friedman every year when she got a Hanukah card. Agnes was still in the Framingham Hospital, and the prognosis was not good.

There was a new girl at Agnes' desk now, but Letty thought of her every time she passed. Her desk always triggered the thought of Agnes the day of the Christmas party a few years ago, face flushed, showing off all the clothes she had bought for her week at the Lord Windsor.

The office still heard Herbie whistling through the halls. He was back on booze now, he told Bob McKern, since coke and hash were harder to get now and really not worth the hassle with the cops. He and McKern had come to a tacit truce these days, Letty thought, the generation gap closing a bit due to Bob's lack of tension and relief now that the doctors promised that Eleanor was definitely going to be all right. Her last operation was indeed a success and, by living a moderately active life, she could look forward to living a ripe and loving old age.

It was God's gift to him and McKern wouldn't forget it. He had his Eleanor back and nothing could touch him now. Nothing.

Priscilla wasn't there anymore, either. She had left almost a year ago after falling in love with the lawyer. Her desk had another stranger sitting there. Letty really missed Priscilla. The girl had been a presence. A force. She had married her lawyer finally and was pregnant with her first child. Letty really missed her.

And Becky was gone, too.

The last time Letty had seen her they met as arranged in the lobby of the Museum of Modern Art. She had not seen Becky in a year, and hearing her voice over the phone Letty had been jolted into the time of the wedding when Wilma and she had drunk together and wished her happiness. She had heard that Arnold and she had parted and wondered what had happened to her.

Letty checked her watch. Becky was only a few minutes late. Letty's eyes traveled to a bench and the spectacle of a Hari Krishna's shaved head and white clothes and a heavy black braid in the back of a pristine white skull. The person she could not identify is man or woman turned, and she saw the soft black eyes of Becky.

Becky saw her immediately and gently embraced Letty. Even in the close embrace Letty could see her shaved head, and she felt her bone-thin body beneath the light fabric. Her body felt cold. Letty wondered if she had a coat.

"Oh, Letty, I'm so happy to see you. So happy," said Becky.

Becky watched her, sensing her surprise. "I'm fine, Letty. I'm wonderful."

"Let's get something to eat in the cafeteria," said Letty. "I'm starving."

People stared at Becky. One didn't see Hari Krishnas inside the Modern very often. Letty and Becky made their way into the cafeteria.

"Is this all right?"

"Yes," Becky answered. "I almost never take food outside the temple, but if I have some fruit and milk, it will be all right. I have fruit and milk every morning with cereal." Becky spoke slowly and very distinctly. Letty tried not to be rude but couldn't help staring at her.

Seated at a table next to the window, Letty watched Becky demolish her apple. She seemed famished.

"Tell me, Letty. Tell me all about you now. I'm so happy to see you. Are you still going to school?"

"Yes. I'll get my degree and then hopefully become a therapist. But I'm fine, really fine. Office news is sparse, I must say, since you left. Agnes, as you know I think, had that terrible breakdown. Pris got married to a guy she absolutely adores, and is having a baby."

"A baby," Becky said with wonder.

"Yes. She's settled down and quite respectable. She turned out to be more respectable than any of us."

Becky laughed.

"How are you, Beck?"

Becky started coughing. "Do you have a tissue, Letty? I never have one." Letty found a small package of Kleenex which Becky used, one after another.

"We slept outside in front of the Pierre last night. It was awfully cold. I tried not to concentrate on the cold, to pray, but I guess I haven't reached that spiritual plane yet."

Letty couldn't eat her salad. "Why did you sleep outside, Becky?"

"It's part of my spiritual training," Becky explained. "I couldn't make enough money to get back to the temple. I didn't raise any money."

"Are you really all right, Becky? You seem so thin."

"Oh, I'm so well, Letty. I've never been better. I've given up all material relationships. I've devoted my life to Krishna and to spiritual cultivation. And the wonderful thing about the spiritual life is its simplicity. I even sold my ring. You remember the diamond Arnie gave me. And all the money went to the temple. Every bit."

"What do they use it for?"

Becky looked confused. "I'm not really sure," she said vaguely. "The religious figures have so many beautiful outfits. I suppose it goes for that."

Becky began to peel an orange, talking with a zeal not unlike her conversation about silver patterns and Bonniers before her wedding.

"What do you do?" Letty asked. "I mean during the day."

"Oh, Letty, it's so lovely. We arise early, usually before four o'clock, and shower. And then there's an Amatrika ceremony, and we chant and worship the Lord. Then we have class, and then breakfast. Then we chant on our beads. We chant for each bead, Hare Krishna. There are a hundred and eighty beads on a strand."

Becky wiped her mouth with her napkin. Letty no

376

ced that her hands were dirty, and that her nails had
een cut very short.

"We worship the tulase, a plant that's dear to
rishna. Then in the evening we have a class on the
ectar of Devotion, and then we have individual
udy before we take our rest."

"It sounds like a full day. Have you made friends?
o you have any close friends?"

"I've never been so peaceful. I don't really have
iends in the old way. I don't need them I guess.
y relationship is with Krishna. I'm really happy.
have everything I need, Letty. Really, I do."

"How are your parents?" asked Letty. "Do you see
em?"

"I don't see them too much. They are less philo-
ophically oriented than I hoped. But it's all right."

"You miss them, don't you, Becky? Do you need
ything?"

"They think I'm trying to convert them," said
ecky. "They hate me. But it's O.K."

Becky finished her food quickly and then stood to
, frightened by the confrontation. "I have to get
ck to the temple, Letty. I loved seeing you. Don't
orry about me. You have such pain in your eyes. I
ly hope my life will be an example for others and
at in ten years I will be as happy and devoted to
rishna as I am, even more devoted than I am today.
ll pray for you, Letty."

When was that lunch? Letty thought about when
ilma and Letty had been talking about the inequities
their upbringing. We didn't have all the options and
l the freedoms, Letty thought ruefully. And now we
egrudged ourselves that. How we envied the endless
ternatives of Becky's age. All the old values were
one, but where were the new ones? They were yet to
e created.

Letty stood up. "Can I drop you anywhere, Becky?"

Becky, as though not hearing, made her way out of the cafeteria, past the long line. People stared. Letty watched the braid disappearing down the hall. She looked at the plate, empty except for an apple core and orange peel.

She sat like a stone. She wasn't able to move. A man with a white apron pushing a large cart took Becky's tray. He looked inquiringly at Letty, and getting no response, went off to the next table, leaving Letty alone.

She stared out the window at the huge sculpted maiden washing her stone hair in the water fed by the fountain. The garden was filled with squares and circles, alabaster and bronze.

As she walked out to the lobby, Letty became dizzy. Perhaps I got up too fast, she thought. No. She knew what it was. Life has a way of tripping up your expectations, Letty thought. Who would ever have thought that Priscilla, of all people, would become the most respectable of them all? Or that Agnes, the most fastidious, the most circumspect, would wind up having to be dragged out of Robertson Stellar peeing on the office floor? Or that Wilma was now going to be married to a garage mechanic so far beneath her often-stated standards and yet perhaps happier than any of them, at fifty-three? Or that Becky, the most promising, the most attractive, the girl who had made, would wind up with her head shaved, sleeping on the sidewalk in front of the Pierre Hotel?

And me, she thought. What about me? What's next? She found herself smiling as the light changed and she began crossing the street. No surprises, please.

45

Will planned it carefully.

The money his uncle from Staten Island had left him had slowly been gathering interest in an uptown bank. He hadn't told anyone about it when the lawyer contacted him two and a half years ago. He simply went up to 105th Street and Broadway and deposited it. The interest accrued was not phenomenal, but it was enough. It was enough to take Letty away for a while.

Somebody had advertised in the *New York Review of Books,* somebody who lived in Virginia Beach. Will had carried the ad around in his breast pocket for months before he decided to write. "Charming small villa in exotic Haiti. Petionville. $100 weekly," it read. The reply he received was crisp and businesslike.

He planned laboriously. Kathy had a two-week job with a terminally ill old man up in the Bronx. The money was too good to ignore, so she accepted it. Will would get the Bryant girl from upstairs to come in and cook and clean for the boys. They were old enough to stay alone. He would stay for two days after Kathy left, and then would leave, explaining to the boys he had to get away. They knew he hadn't been feeling well lately, strangely short of breath, unfamiliar pains in his arms. He felt like a character in a Simenon novel, paying meticulous attention to every minute detail. He didn't tell Letty until he was sure. Until he was sure every aspect had been covered. At this point, he did not even feel it was a betrayal of Kathy. But he did not want to hurt her. There was no point in that.

"Pack your bags, we're going away next week. Tell MacKail you've got to take the week off." He had organized the trip when he knew Letty would be off from school. MacKail would just have to get along without her, that's all there was to it.

Letty was delighted. She bought a bathing suit and slinky white velour shift to cover it. She ruefully discovered that she was now relegated to one-piece suits since her stomach muscles, no matter how flat, lacked the resilience of her youth. She couldn't imagine where Will got the money to afford this unexpected trip, but he had showed her the ad and a Mr. Lamoureux' response, describing this very private, very beautiful villa he owned and had rented out for years. He said it was in an exquisite section of Petionville, which was just outside of Port au Prince. A maid would come in every evening to clean up and make dinner, he said, for just a few dollars more. He said life in Haiti was once again back to normal; after the dictatorship "died down."

Will put his desk in order. He organized his accounts neatly in the left-hand corner of his desk drawer, and alphabetized an entire year's file, something he had been meaning to do for a long time. Letty made sure Mrs. Birnbaum in her mother's building was on call, assuring the two old women that she would be gone only a week.

"You write me every day and maybe call once. Check up on me, Letty. What's he doing about his children?"

Fran still refused to address Will by name and could never resist her acerbic remarks about him. But

Letty had learned to ignore it, even though it hurt. It always hurt. Fran had never met Will. Refused to meet Will. And, no matter how grown-up Letty felt, no matter how emancipated, it still hurt.

Haiti turned out to be a magic place for Will and Letty. They were alternately fascinated and appalled by the beauty and poverty that greeted them on their drive from the airport to their villa. Magnificent looking women, teeth shining, smiling out of heads swathed in red kerchiefs moved rhythmically up the roadways with large baskets of fruit on their heads, buttocks swaying for balance. After viewing a particularly picturesque scene, the car passed through a section of a shantytown where slats of wood, pieces of tin, old pieces of cloth pasted together were the fabric for houses. The people there were wearing rags.

Passing through Port au Prince, she had felt as though she were in another era, and even though there were anachronistic flashes of white suits and ties, dresses and white high heels, reminders of this century, still the old French style architecture of the buildings conjured mysterious images of The Emperor Jones, Toussaint, voodoo.

"Promise me we'll go to the fort," Letty said, "the one on top of a mountain, The Citadelle. I read about that story when I was a child. Will, do you think we can?"

"C'est loin," the driver said, explaining it was necessary to go to Cap Hatien two hundred miles away on the north coast to the town of Milot, and then travel two hours more by horse or mule up the mountain. The fort was built by Henri Christophe on a three-thousand-foot peak, he said, in a tone that intimated he had said it just this way to thousands of tourists before them.

"Next time, Letty, do you mind? Somehow, it seems a bit strenuous for me."

"Of course." Letty was silent for the next fifteen minutes of the ride. She had felt a coldness in her throat when Will said it would be too strenuous. Why? He was strong. Why would a two-hour mule ride be too strenuous? Looking over at him, she saw the gray tint to his skin she had been trying to avoid noticing these last months. He didn't look well.

She took his hand and pressed it to her breast.

"Feel how my heart is beating. This is so wonderful, Will." She took his hand and kissed it.

The higher up the winding road they went, the paler Will was getting.

"Will, are you all right? Are you okay, darling?"

"Yes, Lett, I'm just a little out of breath. Who knew the altitude was going to be so high. What's it like since Poppa Doc is gone here?" he shouted, leaning over to the cab driver. "Things are much better? *Beaucoup mieux?*"

Letty saw the man frown and wrinkle his forehead into deep waves.

"The New York *Times* had a piece on Haitian tourism," Letty poked Will, "and they said it's not a good idea to get into political discussions."

"That's a political discussion?" Will said, bending forward to hear what the man had to say.

Letty fished in her bag and came out with a dog-eared piece from the Sunday travel section. "Will, listen," she whispered. "It says here 'and although calm prevails, the tourist is well advised to avoid getting involved in heated political arguments.'"

"Letty, I asked the man a simple question. That's not a heated political argument."

"*Voilá, votre villa. Lamoureux,*" the relieved cab driver said, stopping short.

The villa turned out to be tiny but clean, situated on a sedate bluff that looked out on the valley below.

382

"It's beautiful, Will. It's so beautiful."

The maid attached to the house was there to welcome them with two rum punches, the large bed in the one-bedroom house turned down.

Every morning that week, Will and Letty rose early to watch the sunrise, and sat on a rocky bluff not far from the house.

Will insisted on taking Letty everywhere, and when he tired easily so often, finally, after she insisted, he explained:

"All right. I didn't want to worry you. It's nothing. I swear. I had a checkup recently, and the doctor said I just have to cut down a little. That's all, hon. I just have to take it easy. And I'm trying. This trip is an antidote to all the crap of New York and that office and, and everything. Letty, now promise me you won't say anything anymore. I'm fine, I really am. Come on. We're late. I want to get to that gallery in Petionville before it closes."

As they walked to the rented car sitting in the carport, Will thought, God, let her believe me. Let her not worry. I will not think about the worst. The tests weren't conclusive. The doctor said that. And he made that appointment with the big guy at Sinai for when I get back. And there is always the operation. He did hold that out as a possible hope. O.K., so it's dangerous. So's living dangerous. So's driving down these winding roads dangerous. So what? All I know is that now is now.

"Will, do you want me to drive?" Letty asked, quietly.

"No. I love driving down these crazy roads."

They arrived at the Petite Galerie, 14 Rue Pan Americaine, which a handsome Haitian lawyer they had met at a bar at the Hotel Oloffson the night before had recommended. Letty was enchanted by the exquisite colors in the primitives.

"I wish I could find something I could afford," Letty whispered. "Some of these are so marvelous. There's something so mysterious about them, something sort of mysterious about the whole place, isn't there, Will?"

"God, can you imagine what it must have been like under the dictatorship with the Ton Ton Macoute or whatever it was called swaggering in the streets arresting people, stealing them away, torturing them."

"How much is this little one?" Letty asked one of the two women proprietors.

"Fifty dollars, madame," the woman answered.

The small oil was different from many of the others. It was not pastoral or sweet. It did not pander to the tourists' taste. It was done with little color, except in the sky. It was simply the picture of a woman standing half in shadow behind a battered door. Her face was of indeterminate age. She, like all the women here, get old so quickly, she might be thirty, she might be fifty. She was nursing a tiny infant. She caught for Letty the life that she had not experienced. Yet she could feel an enormous oneness with this woman standing in shadow, carrying on life feeding her child.

"We'll take it," Will said.

"Oh, Will, that's too much. I can live without it."

"It's yours." He paid the woman the money.

That night they went, skeptically but curiously, to a voodoo exposition at Le Peristyel de Mariani. It may not have been the real thing, but whatever it was, it was impressive.

Letty watched one participant after another. She saw a man walk on fire, another chew and swallow glass. A third man bent an iron crowbar under the influence of the spirits. An old woman who couldn't have weighed more than ninety pounds picked up a full-size man of about 180 pounds and carried him effortlessly around the room.

After the performance, they downed their drinks and listened to the Boston educated chemical engineer and voodoo "high priest" who ran the exhibition explain how, to him, there was no contradiction between the occult and science.

Lying next to Letty that night in the large oversize bed, Will said, "Tomorrow's our last day, and we're getting up early to go to Jacmel. I hear the beach is breathtaking."

They did not make love. Like an old married couple, Letty thought, like we have all the nights in the world in bed with each other. Like normal everyday people, Letty thought, who can make love, or not make love, just as they please.

The next morning, the drive to Jacmel took ninety minutes on a road winding over the mountains to the coast. It turned out to be an exquisite beach, and they were able to find a totally deserted area. They had brought a lunch basket, with a carafe of wine, and settled down on the lonely wide expanse of sand.

Without a word, they took off their bathing suits and lay flat. Although he was fair and had to be careful, Will had developed a resilience to the rays of the sun, and finally some color was rushing to his face.

Letty felt the sand, hot, playing on her back. She felt the grains between her buttocks, under her calves. The heat from above and below nurtured, beguiled her. Will, supporting himself on his elbows, looked at her without speaking. Sensing his eyes, she opened hers and looked into his face.

"What?"

"I'm away from everything. All that shit. All that crap. I feel as though somebody took the straitjacket off, just untied the buckles off me and let my limbs go free. I think, Letty, this is the first time I have ever felt free in my life." He took his index finger and wrote his name on her belly, lightly stroking her breasts, making eights and fours over her thighs.

"What would happen if we just stayed, Letty? What would happen if we just never went back, and lived in this little villa, and caught our own fish? Lived simply, lots of books. I'd import all the books I've ever wanted to read and never was able to. I'd build outdoor bookcases. I'd stretch them up and down the beach." He bent down and softly kissed her nipple, watching it harden as his mouth came close to it.

Aroused by the tiny dots of water between her breasts, the mounds of her hips rounding into the sand, he put his hand gently on her cheek. The tenderness in his touch was like cotton, like air. She felt the love, she felt everything he was feeling in that touch. In that look. Will bent down and kissed her. Their lips tasted of salt, but it was so soft, so quiet, the passion so distilled into the sweetness of the moment, that Letty became dizzy from it. The sun, giving its blessing, the surf lapping the sand was witness.

"I will never be as happy as this," Will whispered into her ear. "Nobody should ever be this happy. I don't deserve this. I will have to pay for this moment. I've lived in a box all my life. Four sides. Always four sides surrounding me. For now. For this time, the roof has been taken off, Lett. There is air. You have given me air. The only air in a long life."

Will sighed and put his hands on her head, pulling the hair back tight. He moved himself softly on top of her, never letting go of her face. "I never want to forget your face, looking just the way you do now. Sweet, beautiful Letty."

He put himself gently inside her, feeling the sweat of her under him. He moved in her slowly, their tongues caressing while they touched.

"You will come out the other side," Letty whispered.

"Safe, safe in here," Will murmured into her mouth

46

Three days after returning from Haiti, sitting in the bus on the way to work, Letty passed her stop. She hadn't done that in years, but she had been lost in thought.

For the past six months she had been working once again at Hillcroft with retarded children. There had been something about the children that drew her back.

She had gone to see Dr. Proteau and pleaded with him to let her continue.

"First you have to learn to care for something," said Dr. Proteau. "Something it isn't easy to care for in the kind of world we live in. Life. Life itself. Because it's not what you can do for these children. It's what they can do for you."

Before he would take her back, Dr. Proteau insisted that she work for a while in another part of the institution. The children there ranged from ten to the early teens. They were the most severely retarded. Children who would never leave their cribs.

Letty followed Dr. Proteau. He stopped at the crib of a boy whose tag read "Daniel Perkinson." His legs were literally bones. His face was without expression.

Dr. Proteau turned to the food tray and took a cup of purée from it. He dipped the spoon into the purée and brought it to his mouth. Daniel did not open his mouth. Dr. Proteau forced the food into it.

Dr. Proteau walked on. Letty followed.

One of the children had a cold, and Dr. Proteau went to her crib to attend to it. As he passed from crib to crib he talked to the children. "Hello, Leo." He took the boy's hand and walked on. "Hello, Beatrice." Beatrice, a girl of about twelve, looked up at him and said the only word she could say, "Mama."

"You're full of baloney, you know that Beatrice? You're full of baloney." He mussed her hair. She giggled a little.

Letty worked in this section of the institution on her Sundays off, and at the times she couldn't see Will, still wishing she were back with the normal children.

Then something happened. It happened to a boy named Alvin. He was a hydrocephalic, a boy whose head was almost larger than his body. He lay inert, without expression. There were debates among the case-hardened volunteers whether or not death for Alvin was not the most merciful thing of all.

Letty was looking at Alvin one day, and she noticed something. She noticed his eyes were following the sun. She watched him for a while.

The next time Dr. Proteau came around she said, "Dr. Proteau, look at this boy. Look at the way his eyes follow the sun."

Dr. Proteau looked at her a moment with an unresponsive look as though to ask what significance it had.

"Do you think he'd feel better if we moved his bed closer to the window?" asked Letty.

Dr. Proteau asked an attendant to help them move Alvin's crib to the window.

The next day, Sunday, after dealing with the other children, Mrs. Henderson, a white-haired woman who had worked as a volunteer for many years in the

ard, turned to Letty. "Look at Alvin," she said. "He's
miling. It's the first time I've ever seen him smile."
Letty looked at the boy's face, the large head was
miling. The gratification she felt was enormous. She
ouldn't wait to tell Will.

Letty could tell something was wrong the minute
ne walked into the office. Great globs of mascara were
l over Florence's eyes. That was the first thing she
w, Florence's smudged eyes. A fight with her boy-
iend, Letty thought, a failed exam in law school.
ne was going to have to convince Will to go back to
w school. Maybe he could make it this time. She
lt filled with strength and power this morning.

"Florence, what is it? Why are you crying?"

"You're rude to a guy, you trade jabs with him, and
en all of a sudden one day you wake up and he's
t going to walk into your life anymore. No more.
nito." Florence waved her magnificent hands at her.
e went for the switchboard like a robin for her
ung before Letty could get an explanation.

Walking to her desk, Letty saw clumps of people,
nches of threes and fours spread over the main of-
e. Bob McKern was sitting at Letty's desk, his head
his hands. Stan MacKail had his hand on his shoul-
r. Wilma and Janet were huddled in conversation.

"Bob, what is it, what is it?" Letty cried out when
e saw his tear-stained face. "Is it Eleanor, is she all
ht? The last operation was a success, you said."

"Will's gone," McKern sobbed. "The son-of-a-
ch went and died on us before anybody could find
t how much he meant to them."

Letty stood there, her coat on her back, her brief-
se in her hand, her bag on her shoulder. She was
are of perspiring, of great mountains of water pour-
g out from under her arms. How could the body
ard such reservoirs of liquid?

"He was a turd," Letty heard Janet say, her words

cutting through the air like chalk on a blackboard "He fussed and he fumed and nothing was ever good enough for him. Anyway, who else could stand being an underwriter for so many goddamn years?"

An underwriter, Letty thought, is that what he was? My Will? Is that what he did for a living? Checking up on people's claims? She had forgotten. Will was an underwriter.

"Christ, I really liked the guy," MacKail said, patting McKern on the back. "I know he never liked me, never approved of me really, but I liked him. Respected him. He was his own man, I'll tell you that. Not many of those around."

"What happened?" Letty could barely recognize her own voice.

"Dropped dead," Wilma said, moving over to Letty noticing immediately the absence of color in her face, the shaking hands she was unable to stop.

"Letty, nobody's sure, one of his sons called in this morning and he was crying so hard, Florence could barely understand him. Something about the brain, something about his father's headaches, something about tests and a tumor, something about the kid just going into his father's bedroom to wake him up and his not moving."

"Oh." Letty let out a scream. Will moves. My Will moves, she felt like crying out to them all. My Will moves his legs and his arms and his whole body moves when he is inside me. What do you mean he doesn't move.

"Are you all right, Letty? God, are you all right your whole body is shaking."

Letty had no control over it. She felt herself twitching. Eyebrows, and hands, thighs did not belong her. There was an earthquake inside her making all those parts move.

"He took me home to dinner once," Herbie offered

_ate one Friday, he just invited me home because I
_s just sort of hanging around, really had nowhere to
_, for Christ's sake, and somehow he knew. You
_ow, in that gruff, I-don't-give-a-damn-if-you-listen-
_-me-or-not, attitude he had. So I went home. Three
_oovy boys. Deadhead of a wife, but she made sen-
_tional veal piccata. The youngest and me got to be
_ds. Just like that, out of the blue he invites me for
_nner. Just like that."

Letty had a lot to do. Her desk was piled high with
_rk; she had to prepare for class tomorrow night.
_ll would be coming to dinner tonight and she hadn't
_ne any shopping yet.

Letty started to walk away but her legs were like
_ur. She held onto the row of desks as she made her
_y to the bathroom. Got to be alone, she thought.
_st things first. Got to be by myself. Air, he had
_d. First time he had air. Got to think about him.
_t to make his face appear in front of my eyes.

Wilma made a move to help her as she watched
_tty walk like a drunken person, but she stopped.
_ddenly, she knew. Suddenly, Wilma understood the
_ssing link of her friend. She watched her make her
_y to the ladies room. She knew she would have to
_ alone.

Letty went into the toilet booth. Sitting on the seat,
_ felt the open circle embrace her buttocks. I will
_ through my dress, I will stay here forever. For-
_er. Will wanted to stay on the beach forever. Why
_ln't we? He knew, she thought, he knew. He knew
_ was going to die. Such a little bit of happiness he
_d in his life. So little joy.

Letty stood up and took some toilet paper and
_ped her eyes, then blew her nose. Will was gone.
_iesdays and Thursdays were gone, back to being
_dinary days of the week.

Letty saw herself in these next few days. She would

391

not be able to go to the funeral. Kathy would be there and Will's sons; but she would not be able to be there

Images, pictures flashed in front of her eyes. The painting with the oranges and the yellows, the red and the greens in Haiti. The look on Alvin's face when he smiled. That's what she wanted. Not working for Robertson and Stellar. Not doing the things that people told her were worthwhile but defeated you in the end, made you nothing in the end, that destroyed you like Will.

Letty splashed cold water on her face. Her cheeks were burning. She put her hands on her face and pulled her hair back tight. This was the view of her Will liked.

There is a forty-one-year-old woman in that mirror, Letty thought.

"Sweet, beautiful," Will had said. And so I am. And so I am beautiful, Letty thought. You only have one time around. I'm going to be all right. I swear.

She unclenched her fists and went back into the office.

Bestselling Novels from POCKET BOOKS

_____ 81785 A BOOK OF COMMON PRAYER Joan Didion $1.95
_____ 81685 CATCH A FALLING SPY Len Deighton $1.95
_____ 82352 THE CRASH OF '79 Paul E. Erdman $2.75
_____ 80720 CURTAIN Agatha Christie $1.95
_____ 81806 THE INVESTIGATION Dorothy Uhnak $2.50
_____ 81207 JOURNEY Marta Randall $1.95
_____ 82340 THE LONELY LADY Harold Robbins $2.75
_____ 81881 LOOKING FOR MR. GOODBAR Judith Rossner $2.50
_____ 82446 LOVERS AND TYRANTS Francine Du Plessix Gray
             $2.25
_____ 80986 THE NAVIGATOR Morris West $2.50
_____ 81378 OVERBOARD Hank Searls $1.95
_____ 80938 PLAGUE SHIP Frank G. Slaughter $1.95
_____ 81036 PURITY'S PASSION Janette Seymour $1.95
_____ 81644 THE STARMAKER Henry Denker $2.50
_____ 81135 THE TARTAR Franklin Proud $2.50

POCKET BOOKS
Department FB 6-78
1230 Avenue of the Americas
New York, N.Y. 10020

Please send me the books I have checked above. I am enclosing
$_____ (please add 50¢ to cover postage and handling for each
order; N.Y.S. and N.Y.C. residents please add appropriate sales tax). Send
check or money order—no cash, stamps, or C.O.D.'s please. Allow up to
six weeks for delivery.

NAME_____

ADDRESS_____

CITY_____ STATE/ZIP_____
                                        FB 6-78